The Starlight Motel

by

Amy Craig

The Wild Rose Press, Inc.
PO Box 708
Adams Basin, NY 14410-0708
Visit us at www.thewildrosepress.com

Publishing History
First Edition, 2024
Trade Paperback ISBN 978-1-5092-5607-5
Digital ISBN 978-1-5092-5634-1

Published in the United States of America

Praise for Amy Craig

"In *The Starlight Motel*, Amy Craig tells a fresh story of love, family, and conflicting ideals between Kada, the strong and independent motel manager, and the commercial farmer, Dane. Intense sparks fly in this contemporary love story that is filled with a delightful cast of characters to keep you entertained."

~P. L. Jonas, author

~*~

"Set against the evocative background of Palm Springs, Amy Craig has created a page-turning, slow-burning romance with Kada and Dane, who both have depth and personality. With her wry humor and attention to detail, Amy's fresh voice is a pleasure to read."

~ Robin Palmer Blanche, author

Chapter One

Two Days Before The New Year

Kada considered the turquoise *casita* at the Starlight Motel. Standing beneath the late afternoon sun, she endured sweat dripping down her neck and dry wind picking up the loose hairs around her face. She kept her gaze trained on the *casita's* southern wall. Something about the mural-in-progress felt off, but identifying her concern felt like a deep dive into self-doubt. She tapped her chin and considered her brushstrokes.

"Cannonball!" a child yelled before splashing into the heated pool.

She smiled. Kids had no need for self-doubt. Behind her, spotless lounge chairs circled a deep concrete pool, lush date palms lined stone walkways, and cushions ringed a pale-pink firepit. The Starlight Motel sat on State Route 111, and for seventy years and four generations, its botanical oasis provided a haven for weary travelers. Her great-grandfather chose the site to catch tourists before they arrived in Palm Springs, and his ploy worked, but mortality required succession.

When her grandfather, Hall, passed, she reluctantly took on managing the motel so her mother could grieve her loss. The old man was a force of a nature, and Kada missed him, but he left this world without regrets. She hoped she could do the same, and Los Angeles beckoned with a heady mix of need and opportunity. If everything went according to plan, she would relinquish her responsibility for the motel and resume her artistic pursuits at the start of the New Year.

In the meantime, she retained full control of the motel's retro, adobe buildings and glowing, neon sign. The gig wasn't bad, but it required an attitude adjustment. She glanced at the tinsel wreath adorning a palm tree. At this rate, the motel's mid-century Christmas decorations might stay up until Twelfth Night or the Fourth of July. Being the boss had its perks, but she wondered where she would find the energy to take down the tinsel kitsch. No matter how much she loved sleigh bells and spiked punch, running twenty *casitas*, studios, and standard rooms left her exhausted.

She checked her reflection in the *casita's* window. Paint splatters marked her serviceable jeans and button-up shirt, but shiny, metallic sneakers gave her step a little pop. The desert wind whipped her long, black hair across her face, and she pulled the strands from her eyes. She could be cynical about her circumstances, or she could look back on this year as a gift to her family. Mom deserved time to process her grief, and Kada's work was flexible. The stack of toilet paper rolls waiting at her feet was not. She filled her arms with the cottony rolls and turned her back on the mural.

After stocking the toiletries in the supply shed, she turned toward the cantina and the reception desk. Paperwork beckoned. She swung her arms.

An insect buzzed her face.

She paused and swiped the sensation from her skin.

Glancing at the turquoise *casita's* exterior wall one more time, she cocked her head. Late afternoon light cast shadows, but her work depicted a native ocotillo plant swaying in the wind. Painting native fauna at a desert motel felt like hocking postcards to tourists, but she needed ways to maintain her skills. One day, she would return to the students who inspired her work and who drove her to finish graduate school. They would catch her mistake in an instant. The ocotillo plant needed a shadow. She shook her head. "Rookie mistake. Maybe I can pay off my student loans by selling paintings to tourists."

Behind her, a child splashed in the pool and yipped like a coyote.

"Okay, I'll stick with Plan A." After she left the Coachella Valley, she hoped guests would appreciate the desert landscape. They probably wouldn't recognize her signature in the bottom right corner, but she had to finish a work before she could sign it.

Plan A depended on a looming New Year's Eve deadline forcing her to define her future. She could run the family business and give Mom additional time to grieve, or she could accept a multi-year grant and return to printmaking and public art installations. She craved artistic expression, but she couldn't walk away from her family. If she left the motel in her mother's hands, she had to trust her mother's capabilities. Failure on Mom's part meant the family would have to hire a manager or sell the motel, and the half-finished mural would be the least of Kada's worries. Perhaps she should stay.

A man cleared his throat.

She turned away from the mural and found a pair of thirty-year-old men clutching guidebooks and cross-referencing mobile phone apps. Their bright, desert-themed shirts and chino shorts sported store creases. Sunglasses shaded their eyes, and leather loafers encased their feet.

"Can you recommend a good restaurant?" the shorter man asked.

His ears were red from exposure to the winter sunshine. She adopted her guest-service smile and searched for their names. "What kind of food do you like?"

"Organic, fresh, and local." The taller guest kept his gaze locked on his phone screen. "Nothing too fancy."

She pegged them as first-time motel guests, but if she could make a good impression, she might convert them into regulars. Scrolling through her mental inventory of restaurants, she tapped her foot to signal her thoughts.

"But not too crowded." The shorter, sunburnt guest loosened his collar and glanced at his partner. "We hate to wait."

Did he hurry out the door and forget to put sunscreen on his ears, or did his companion heckle him? Unasked questions kept life amusing. "I hear you. Waiting's the worst."

The shorter man dropped his shoulders and exhaled. "So I've heard."

She pursed her lips and considered their options. The quirky desert town from her childhood visits was in the midst of a hipster renaissance. Downtown restaurants offered caviar service and fifty-dollar martinis. Japanese small plates competed with street tacos and chili cook-offs. Highly curated selections of local arts, crafts, and dry goods filled local boutiques. Yet, despite the last decade's lodging boom, the Starlight Motel thrived. Would mentioning the motel cantina be too obvious? The Desert Empire Café was a local favorite, and its eclectic delicacies could soothe most travel-strained nerves.

"Have you eaten at The Desert Empire Café?" The taller guest scrolled down his phone's screen. "It has excellent reviews."

Grabbing her hair to keep it from the wind, she popped her lips and pointed toward him. "I was just about to mention that place. You'll love their options, and the location is excellent for window browsing and shopping."

"We love to shop!" The taller guest pocketed his cell phone and turned with military precision. "Let's go!"

Rubbing together her fingers near her thigh, she itched to extoll the valley's charms and hidden boutiques, but she kept quiet.

His partner clutched his guidebook to his chest and wiped the sweat from his forehead. "Thank you." He turned tail and hurried after his companion.

She watched the pair depart and hoped their relationship had lighthearted moments. Given her current level of stress, she couldn't imagine time for romance, but she remembered its charms. Candlelight and bubble baths. A poem read aloud wouldn't be amiss.

Like her ideals, the pair disappeared down an alley of palm trees sporting hot-pink wreaths. As she had hammered a nail into each tree's rough, brown trunk, she had winced, but desert plants and weary travelers were tougher than they looked. She hoped the pair enjoyed their meal.

Leaving the unfinished mural for another day, she walked toward the main two-story building housing the lobby, office, and cantina. Toiletries weren't her only administrative concerns. If she didn't approve the menus for the coming week, she would have to face Chef Benito's overheated emotions. He preferred to hold court in his steam-filled kitchen, and she was one of the few employees brave enough to enter his domain. He looked like a teddy bear, but he glowered at bussers and barked commands at servers. When she intervened on behalf of new hires, she ended up covering her ears while he threatened to send her back to Los Angeles where she belonged.

Sometimes, she wished he would.

Stepping inside the building, she admired the chic lobby's pink-and-turquoise decorating scheme. Her family filled the space with warmth and vintage treasures, but she added modern touches. The bright neon sign spelling *Starlight Motel* was all her.

Beyond the initial "wow" factor, color-blocked prints popped off gray-and-white striped wallpaper. On a brass entry table, bubblegum-pink glass ornaments rested in an opaque glass bowl, and a white ceramic pineapple welcomed guests. In a place of honor by the roaring fireplace, a tinsel Christmas tree twinkled, and two pink nutcrackers held court on the white mantle. Christmas memories might be fading, but anyone who entered the building knew she was serious about holiday cheer.

If guests preferred to linger, they could relax in the peacock chair and while away the hours with a newspaper, but they had to cope with the gold, disco ball pillow. Brass flamingos peeking from potted plants were relatively easy to ignore.

Randi, the motel's best and least predictable employee, stepped out of the cantina and planted her hands on her hips. A twenty-five-year-old, statuesque woman with coiled braids, she obsessed over microgreen placement, recited jazz album track lists, and wore killer heels. She also knew about every party in town. Her knowledge base made her an invaluable resource, and she humored Chef Benito, but she only showed up for half her cantina shifts.

Kada covered a yawn and regretted skipping her afternoon coffee. "What's up?"

"We're out of dates," Randi said.

"Excuse me?"

"Dates." Randi raised her eyebrows. "The sweet, little gems you stuff into local treats like brownies, energy bars, and smoothies? You know, the chewy, caramel fruits with the sugary skin?"

She held up a hand. "Wait. I know about dates, but how did we run out?"

Randi shrugged. "The supplier doubled our avocado count, but he left out the dates."

Rubbing a hand over her face, she hoped she didn't smear the remnants of her mascara. Dates were one of the motel's signature products. California grew ninety percent of the country's dates, and most of the fruit came from the Coachella Valley. Starting in October, farmers sent their best fruit to packing facilities and sold extra produce at weekend markets, but December dates might be an oddity. "That's okay. We have plenty of other appetizers and treats to offer our guests."

"Nope." Pointing toward a man taking a call from a patio table, Randi shook her head. "He's a travel writer, and he wants date bread. Goat cheese stuffed dates. Fudgy date brownies. Peanut butter buckeye balls…"

"I got it." How on earth had they run out of dates, and how many dates did she need? She tugged down Randi's pointing hand and counted the guests in the cantina. Two couples sipped drinks, a family devoured nachos, and a dog snoozed on the patio at the travel writer's feet. When the sun went down, guests would return from outdoor adventures and fill the building with laughter and the sound of rumbling stomachs. Toilet paper was the least of her problems, and she needed more than a pint of dates from her mini fridge.

If she had known about the travel writer's reservation, she would have scanned his social media account and looked for little quirks and preferences the motel staff could anticipate. If he liked long hikes, then she would leave trail maps near the coffee station. Giggle yoga? She knew a yogi. "How long is he staying?"

"Two more days." Randi yawned behind her manicured hand.

"Okay, we have time." She exhaled. The valley specialized in the caramel, sweet superfood. Picked fresh from a date palm, the fruits were sweet and full of fiber. As natural sugars rose to the skin, the fruit took on a light, white crust. They lasted one to two months stored at room temperature, six months in the refrigerator, and about a year frozen.

Pops' old, metal filing cabinet probably contained a list of backup date suppliers. Her grandfather left her and Mom the motel, but he brushed off her logistical questions and passed on his terms. Judging by his medical bills, he knew about his cancer, and she was glad she savored their last days together instead of burdening him with mundane questions. "I'll take care of it."

Randi turned away and paused. "And another thing."

She held her breath.

Facing her, Randi squared her statuesque shoulders. "I want to take off New Year's Eve."

Of course, Randi wanted to take off the holiday. She did, too. Given a stretch of vacation days, she would hop a plane and zoom up to Wyoming to visit her hometown and see old friends.

Instead, her parents were coming south, and their visit amplified her stress. In little more than a day, Mom and Dad would arrive on-site, and she wanted the motel and her emotions to be ready. Her future as an artist depended on Mom accepting her past and embracing the motel's future. She couldn't afford to run off Randi or the loyal staff, but she couldn't run the place by herself. "Like, next year?"

"This year," Randi said. "Like, the day after tomorrow."

"And if I tell you we're really busy and I need your help?"

Randi flicked a spec of dirt from beneath her long nails. "At will employment."

She didn't know why she wasted her breath on logic. Instead of screaming, she closed her eyes and made a tight fist. Windmill tour vans, bachelorette pool parties, and bangle-wearing festival-goers booked out the motel, but she had advance notice and staffed accordingly. New Year's Eve might be relatively tame, but tending to the motel guests was more than a one-woman job. "I really need your help."

"Fine." Randi rolled her eyes.

She blinked and released the tension in her hand. "Fine?"

"I'll stay." Randi glanced at the exposed beam ceiling. "I don't know what you'd do without me."

"Neither do I!" Wrapping Randi in an impromptu hug, she squeezed tight and considered squeezing tighter. Randi's *bravata* pulled her out of so many funky afternoons, she wanted to give the woman a raise or a talk show, but she had a motel to run. "Also, you're the worst."

Randi patted her back. "You mean the best."

She cleared her throat. "Actually, I mean the worst." Her voice wobbled. "Sorry."

Randi pulled back. "Are you gonna crack?"

Stepping back, she smoothed her shirt and tossed her hair over her shoulder. Four generations of her family kept this motel afloat, and she would make sure it thrived under her watch. "Absolutely not."

Randi raised an eyebrow.

Who was she kidding? She dropped her shoulders.

"Uh-huh." Randi pursed her lips. "Here it comes!"

"Not here it comes!" She exhaled. "When Pops passed, I wasn't prepared for the onslaught of decisions. I figured since I worked with kids, I could take care of guests, but I didn't think about the emotional toll of running this place. The move out here was just"—she frowned and searched for the right word—"a lot. Maybe I'll grow into the role, but I'm hanging on by a thread, and you know it. I need your help. You're an excellent server."

"Okay, you're not the worst, either." Randi scratched the side of her nose with a bent knuckle. "But, we still need dates."

"I know." She exhaled and rolled down her sleeves. She needed dates more than she needed a pity party. If Randi was strong enough to carry the world on her shoulders, then she could, too. "I'll find the little nuggets. Stall him with free liquor."

Randi grinned. "Now, you're cooking!"

She needed more than an ounce of Randi's self-confidence. "The holidays were fun, but seeing the ins and outs of this place took away some of the magic I remember. Keeping this place going wasn't always this hard, was it?"

Crossing her arms, Randi tilted her head. "And we're back to the pity party."

She swallowed. "I mean, growing up, I'd visit Pops and Grandma Nana, and running the motel all seemed so...effortless. Who wouldn't want to escape to the desert for beautiful memories? Now, everything depends on me, and reality bites. I want to slink off to the candy table and open a bottle of champs. Instead, I'll probably have to canvas grocery stores." She shook out her hands and drew a deep breath. "But no, don't worry. I won't crumble. Crack. Whatever. Go pour shots."

Randi laughed. "Welcome to adulthood, sister."

She rolled her eyes.

Shaking her head, Randi turned and walked back toward the prep area. "You'll get the hang of it," she called over her shoulder. "We all do."

"I hope so!" The click of Randi's sky-high heels on

Saltillo tiles drowned out her response, but she appreciated the moment to gather her wits and fortify her resolve.

Speed walking back to the reception desk, she flipped through Pops' files. The motel used local vendors whenever possible, but after ten phone calls, she set down the motel's phone and dropped her head in her hands. The valley was sold out. Drumming her nails on the counter, she eyed the fading holiday decorations and wondered if the travel writer enjoyed pomegranates.

Chapter Two

Reservations trickled into the motel management system while Kada reconciled invoices. Accountancy was a weak spot, but if Pops could do it, she could, too. When happy hour began in the cantina, the late afternoon lull that let her consider her mural would come to a sudden halt. She had twenty minutes.

A truck horn sounded.

She rolled her shoulders and set aside the paperwork for the delivery driver whose announcement gave her a moment to collect her thoughts.

He walked into the reception area carrying a clipboard. "Where do you want the crate?"

Rounding the motel desk, she rubbed together her hands and peered past his shoulder. She had tracked the package for the last week and worried it wouldn't arrive in time for New Year's Eve. Even if the crate did arrive, she questioned how she would fulfill the ignition team's contract terms. Thinking about housing volatile explosives made the hair on her arms stand on end, and she rubbed away the chill seeping past the forced heat. "Can you stage the fireworks supplies inside the building?"

He scratched his head, turned in place, and hip-checked the foyer tables. Glass ornaments rattled. "Um, lady, the crate weighs a couple of hundred pounds. I have a lift. I can stage it anywhere, but it won't match your décor."

"Right." She wanted to pry open the box and examine the ridiculously expensive pyrotechnics she ordered, but the driver was right. She also had too much work to do and zero dates to spend the next hour checking invoices. "Bring the crate around back to the service entrance and leave it by the loading door."

"You're the boss." He offered the clipboard and pulled it back at the last minute. "Just so you know, this delivery is box one of two. The other part of the shipment is delayed."

"Oh." She dropped her shoulders. What would she do with half as many fireworks? "Does it say what's missing?"

"Bases. Punks." He scratched his head and looked around the lobby. "Maybe your crew will bring them the day of the event?"

She frowned. "So the crate has zero fireworks?"

He lowered the clipboard to his thigh. "Who ships explosives in commercial freight?"

Hiding her confusion, she extended a hand for the manifesto, signed her name, and wondered how late the vendor took phone calls. On the bright side, motel guests wouldn't get their hands on anything more dangerous than a sparkler, but she wanted to see the festive explosives up close. Downplaying her disappointment, she focused on the driver and offered him a bottle of water. "Thanks for the help."

He took the bottle, saluted, and returned to his truck.

She wondered if she could barter firework supplies for dates. Local ordinances permitted "safe and sane" fireworks, but she wanted to go out with a bang. By hiring an operator with a California Pyrotechnics License, she would get a professional show and a lasting memory.

The company representative had waxed poetic about candles like comets, screamers, and shells.

She envisioned bright lights and doodled on a notepad.

The rep described mines, comets, and waterfalls.

Suddenly able to visualize the show, she interrupted his pitch with her credit card number, confirmed the company representative would arrive on New Year's Eve, and directed supplies to the motel. Naively, she had thought the juiced sparklers would arrive ahead of time. She still had so much to learn.

The door opened.

A man wearing a yellow-and-white patterned shirt, a blue fedora, and a long, white beard stepped into the entryway. He held two metallic, hard-sided suitcases. Setting down a suitcase, he pulled off a pair of black sunglasses and hooked them on his shirt. "Am I too late for check-in?"

Smiling, she woke the laptop. "Of course not! What's your name?"

"Chris," he said.

"Last name?"

"Chris. Chris Nicholson." He winked. "I know it's a mouthful."

She struggled not to laugh. The name conjured up tall tales and snowy nights. His parents might have had a sense of humor, but if he had received the name "Fred," she doubted he would have grown a long, white beard. "I love your name. It's a great name."

"Of course, it is!" He puffed out his chest. "I come

from a long line of great men."

Keeping her smile and paging through the reservation system, she found him booked for the next day and looked up. "You're a day early, but we have plenty of *casitas* available."

He rubbed together his hands. "Excellent. This year, I found good help, and I started my vacation with gusto. The younger generation"—he laughed, and his belly shook—"is so eager to take on challenges."

"Mmm hmm." She double-checked her system. "Have you stayed with us before?"

"I come for every New Year. I served with Hall himself."

At the mention of her grandfather's name, she looked up. Chris might be a decade younger than Pops, but she treasured anyone who could share memories of him. Pops served in three military branches and had daring stories from the Merchant Marines, the Marines, and the Navy. Along the way, he made a thousand eclectic friends like Chris Nicholas.

Wanting to offer Chris a cigar and listen to his stories, she blinked back the tears welling in her eyes. She missed Pops like crazy. He taught her so much about the desert, but she thought she would have more time with him. She cleared her throat. "Hall was one of a kind."

"You look just like him." He tapped his temple. "You're a little crazy around the eyes. I like it."

She processed the compliment and offered him a wide, surprised smile.

"That old man was as stubborn as a goat. Well, given the locale, we'll say a ram."

She grinned and leaned an elbow on the counter. "I

believe you."

To beat back the desert sun, Pops had proudly rotated his veteran hats.

One time, she asked him why he spent so long in the services.

He took off his hat and scratched his full head of white hair. "Just stubborn, I guess. Your great-grandfather was a tough old man. I thought I could be tougher."

She had believed him. She also thought Pops would live forever, and she bit her lip to keep from ending up an emotional mess at Chris' feet.

Chris ran a hand over his jaw. "I'll sure miss that old fart. And which descendant are you?"

Clearing her throat, she straightened. "His granddaughter."

"Ahh, the muralist." Taking off his fedora, he bowed. "It's a pleasure to meet you."

Her cheeks warmed. She had the credentials and the experience to create great works of art, but most guests treated her like anonymous staff. Hearing someone describe her as a muralist validated the tiny flame she kept alight on dark nights. "You, as well."

Randi delivered a cup of coffee and set it on the desk.

Looking up, Kada smiled. "Thanks."

Dates. Randi silently mouthed the word and backed away.

"Right." Kada returned her attention back to Chris, walked around the peninsula, and jerked her head toward the door. "Let's get you situated in the turquoise *casita*, sir. It's close to the lobby."

He picked up a suitcase. "If I'm lucky, the ladies

will clear out of the pool so I can dip my old bones in the water and cool off."

Laughing, she picked up his second suitcase. "I'll declare a happy hour special and clear the pool."

"Just save me a dance at midnight." He dropped his voice like a weary soldier hoping for respite. "Does that tradition still stand?"

"Of course, the tradition stands." Every year, guests ushered in the New Year by the pool. Wind pushed peppermint-shaped floats along the pool's surface, mist fans softened the dry air, and patio lights swung in the breeze. The guest counts and the musical accompaniment varied, but at the stroke of midnight, someone sang "Auld Lang Syne," and the motel served a champagne toast. Pops and his caterwauling peers always stole the show by leading the finale. "If I dropped the ball on that tradition, I know Hall would haunt me."

"Probably." Chris peered through the window. "You said the turquoise *casita*?"

She opened the front door and led him into the fading sunlight. Each building sported a vibrantly painted door and a palm frond wreath. If guests grew up in the area, they appreciated the balance between sustainability and sun-kissed luxury. If they grew up elsewhere, they wanted to feel like Marilyn Monroe, and vibrant doors gave them a sense of celebrity panache. She grabbed the luggage cart, loaded the suitcase, and gestured for Chris to do the same.

He braced his back and stretched. "I carried two inside the motel. I can carry out one."

"True, but if you wear out your arms, you can't dance with me." She pushed the cart toward him.

Grumbling about impudent young women, he dropped the suitcase in place and followed.

The sky shifted toward pink, and the sunset cast the San Jacinto Mountains into silhouette, but remnants of daylight remained. She pushed the cart along the path and admired the patio lights shining over the garden and the landscape spots illuminating the plants. Pool lights shimmered beneath the turquoise pool waters. "How did it get so late?"

"I ask myself that every day," Chris said.

Honoring the weariness in his tone, she led him to the turquoise *casita*, handed him the brass key on a red plastic tag, and stepped back. The early evening wind blew her hair in her face, and she gathered the strands into a loose ponytail and tucked it inside her shirt. "You have plenty of time to get settled. If you need anything, pick up the phone and let me know, okay? The night is young."

"Sure thing." He unlocked the door and lifted down the first suitcase from the luggage cart. His arms shook, but measured footsteps helped him accomplish his goal.

She would dig through the record collection and send a few of the best LPs to his room.

A moment later, he returned for the second suitcase. "All good."

Smiling, she left him and pushed the cart back toward the main building. Before she could take ten steps, a flash of light on the hillside caught her gaze, and she turned toward the aerial show.

Heat lightning happened during the summer months, but December's cooler temperatures usually kept the natural wonder at bay. The fall had been unusually rainy, and the December rain gauge had recorded three inches of rain, but desert weather could be fickle. Given warming trends, she wouldn't be surprised to see another storm roll into the valley, but the cloudless sky suggested a dry night.

Shaking off the flash, she considered the half-completed mural on the turquoise *casita*. The ocotillo plant's twenty-foot tall, spiny stems looked too regal for an incomplete stucco canvas. A fat lizard sat at the edge of the design. Deep breaths moved its chest in and out with the lazy, contented sigh of a full meal, but the work was incomplete.

After prepping the wall, she used the grid method to split her design into proportional squares that fit the wall's dimensions. Strings let her mark squares on the *casita's* wall, and she created a low-tech canvas that allowed her to scale up her design. What if her original design had an error? What if locals spotted a mistake?

A deep, steadying breath calmed her uncertainty. She would have to finish the design without disturbing Chris Nicholson. Maybe she should have given him a different room.

A long shadow crept up the wall.

Turning, she found two men on horseback, picking their way through the desert toward motel property. Both men wore cowboy hats. The shorter man rode a Palomino. Its lighter coat, white mane, and long tail nearly glowed in the low light. The second man rode a taller, chestnut horse with a black mane and a black tail. Both animals were the most handsome horses she had ever seen.

She straightened her shoulders. Instead of admiring the horses' gaits, she should order the pair back to their Hollywood lot and return to the mountain of waiting paperwork. In Wyoming, she saw plenty of cowboys, and she could do without the riders' souped-up swagger…or the mess two tethered horses would make.

Determined to send the cowboys packing, she noticed a horseshoe nailed to a *casita* header for good luck and thought of Pops. For years, he worked with a local barn to provide trail rides for motel guests. The concession worked throughout the early 2000s, but when modern cowboys on dune buggies spooked a horse and endangered a guest, he tabled the outings. Maybe she should welcome the visitors.

She thought of the complications. *Sorry, no shirts, no shoes, no horses.* Except, she always kept the vacancy sign lit. Her family and her grandfather's legacy depended on her. She prepped a smile.

The first man on horseback kicked his boots, and the horse quickened his pace. Drawing up, he pulled off his hat and draped it over his thigh. "Miss Kada Ritchie?"

Tucking her chin, she checked her button-up shirt for a nametag before looking around. Nobody else could answer to that name, but if she needed help, she didn't want to rely on an eighty-year-old veteran who had missed World War II. "Who's asking?"

The men exchanged glances.

"I'm Dane Palmer," the man on the chestnut horse said. "My family owns the land next door."

"Oh, thank goodness." She shaded her gaze. "I've heard about you." For as long as her family owned the motel, the Palmer family owned the surrounding farmland. Once or twice, the Palmer patriarch offered to buy the Starlight Motel, but Pops resisted and counted the family as friends. They produced the area's top

21

vegetable crops, cultivated table grapes, and managed fields of fruit trees. Every once in a while, Dane's mother, Mariah, came by the motel to visit and give her business advice, but Dane and his younger brother remained enigmas. She exhaled. "I've met your mother."

"I'm sure," Dane said. "She gets around."

The second man laughed like a rusted pail swinging in the wind.

Dane glanced at the seated cowboy. "This is Walter. He's the farm's crew manager."

Tipping his hat, Walter nodded.

She tented her gaze. "Could you two get down? Between the horses and the low sun, I can't see you to save my life."

Hanging his hat on the saddle horn, Dane handed his horse's reins to Walter. He threw his leg over the horse's saddle and slid down its side with an easy, athletic grace.

Standing, he was six feet tall, long, rangy, and reserved. He wore boots, jeans, a dark shirt, and a fleece-lined leather jacket that beat back the wind. A hat had smashed his sun-kissed brown hair against his forehead, but he wiped away the mess, cocked his head, and held out his hand.

"Pleasure to meet you," he said.

Maybe the local cowboys had a leg up on the Wyoming variety. Dark lashes framed his tawny, golden eyes, and full, chapped lips softened his square jaw. If she needed help cleaning gutters or rounding up stray guests, she would know which local heartthrob to call to her side. She took his hand, shook it quickly, dismissed a small jolt of static electricity, and nodded her thanks. "Likewise. That's much better. What brings you to the motel?"

Opening a saddlebag, he withdrew a package wrapped in brown paper and tied with red-and-white cotton twine. He turned and offered it. "Mom said she had the feeling she should send over a bit of warmth and love."

Kada eyed the package and wiped her hands on her jeans. After her afternoon, she needed more than a nailbrush to remove the paint and dust from beneath her nails, but curiosity compelled her to reach for the package. Taking the brown paper, she avoided brushing her fingers against his fingers and stepped back. "Thanks. Most people would drive."

He shrugged and crossed his arms. "I'm not most people."

Walter dismounted and cleared his throat. "Don't mind him. He's been on the trail all day."

At eye level, she could see he was also a remarkably handsome man with weathered, dark skin and a bright, Hollywood smile. She could line up the pair for a photo shoot and redo the motel's branding. "Why are you riding horses?"

Walter adjusted his mount's bit. "Less impact on the crops. If you'd prefer, we can go back for the tractor. Farming rarely requires speed."

The last year of her life felt like a race to the finish. She shifted her weight and hefted the package from the Palmer family. "What is this thing? A brick of butter?"

"Date cake," Dane said.

She groaned. The homemade delicacy would be a treat, but every bite would remind her of her quest. "Awesome."

23

Walter choked on a laugh and slapped his chest. "It's an acquired taste."

"No." She held up a hand to apologize. "Mariah's gift is generous, and thank you both for bringing it over. It's just, I'm fresh out of dates, and we have a travel writer staying at the motel. If I could find a pound of local fruit, I'd pay twice the price." She tilted her head and eyed the package she held. "Maybe the writer likes date cake."

Dane turned and removed a large plastic bag from his horse's saddlebag. He thrust the bag into her arms. "Here."

Taken aback, she gripped the bag and balanced both loads. "What's this?"

He frowned. "Dates."

"You carry dates?" She wanted to throw her arms around his neck, but running a business required propriety. She retained a shred, but throwing herself at a handsome cowboy might be a fine way to go out. Instead of indulging her impulse, she cleared her throat.

"I'm a date farmer." He plucked at his black cotton shirt and pulled it away from his chest. Flexing his arms, he worked his hands, a smile ticked up the side of his mouth. "Among other things."

She wet her lips, but her reaction had nothing to do with the dates. Mariah had been holding out. "Good to know."

He scratched his chin. "Maybe we can make a deal to get you out of this pickle. A lifetime supply of dates in exchange for the motel deed."

"Huh." She tilted her head. "What a generous offer. How could a woman refuse?"

He barked out a laugh, pulled his hat from the

saddle horn, and tipped it on his head. "Worth a try."

She had tried many things, but bartering for her family's future would be a new low. Dane's rusty laugh intrigued her, and she imagined painting his broad back beneath the desert sun, but obligations kept her from exploring her interest. They didn't keep her from being practical. Looking past his shoulder, she tilted her head and considered the horse's smooth, oiled saddlebag. "What else do you have in those bags?"

"Hungry?" he asked.

"Opportunistic."

He laughed. "Not much."

The heartfelt sound dampened her impulses. She would write Mariah a thank-you note for the date cake, but she refused to annex acreage for emergency supplies. "Too bad, but I appreciate the cake."

"My pleasure." He turned and lifted one foot to a hanging stirrup. His thigh muscles bunched and strained his jeans.

Her interest in his saddlebag flared into a steady warmth in her core. "Wait!" She gripped the dates. "I mean, hold up."

Both men stared.

Her throat went dry. "Can I offer you a drink?"

Dane shook his head. "We have to get back to the farm. Walter's family is in town for the holidays, and I promised my mother I would be home before sunset."

She looked at the shadows creeping down the mountains. The idea of a grown man obeying his mother and running errands on horseback amused her, but holidays were the perfect time for whimsy and cheer. If this pair visited the motel more frequently, then she could incorporate the two handsome, rangy cowboys into her next mural. The possibilities sparked her creativity, but she doubted she would be on-site long enough to captures their subtleties. "You'd better hurry home."

Lifting into the saddle, Dane placed his hat on his head. He accepted his horse's reins from Walter.

Walter swung up to the Palomino's back and tipped his hat. "Ma'am."

She grinned. "Evening."

The pair of horses and riders set off at an easy walk.

She watched their dignified retreat. *What a mighty good lookin' pair of...*

Lightning cracked overhead. A brilliant display arced across the sky. She covered her ears and inhaled the ozone remnants.

Dane's chestnut horse reared and came down hard on a rock. The animal's whinny ricocheted between the *casitas* and turned the heads of motel guests.

Horses reared in movies, but watching the muscled animal paw the air amazed and scared her more than any celluloid scene. If twelve hundred pounds of horseflesh decided to careen through the motel's grounds, she would need more than a happy hour to soothe startled nerves. Then again, if the horse came out fine, her motel guests might enjoy the show. She held her breath.

Leaning over the horse's shoulder, Dane patted its heaving chest and spoke softly.

The horse stepped and shifted.

He urged him forward a few steps.

Even to Kada's untrained eye, she saw the horse's gait looked off. Lowering her hands from her ears, she waited for Dane to lead the animal home.

Dismounting, Dane ran a hand along the horse's leg and then picked up the hoof.

She exhaled and empathized with the startled animal. "Hurt?"

Dane nodded. "He's tender and warming." He looked at Walter. "Same foot. He's lame again."

"Too bad." Walter shook his head.

Looking back and forth between the pair, she wanted to comfort the horse, but she felt clueless. After running the motel for a year, the feeling should be familiar.

"I'll stay with Smoky until you get the trailer." Walter looked over his shoulder toward where she stood. "Could you get Dane a ride back to the farmhouse?"

She adjusted the bag of dates and the wrapped bread she held. "Sure. Let me deliver these gifts to the kitchen, and I'll find someone to give Dane a lift home."

"No." Dane stood and soothed Smoky's sidestepping jitters. "I'll stay. Walter, take your horse back to the house and send one of the guys to come get Smoky and me. We'll be fine for a few hours. Your family's waiting."

Walter ran his tongue over his teeth and used a thumb to scratch out a spec of food. "You're hiding from your mama."

"I'm no good in the kitchen." Dane ran a comforting hand along the horse's neck. "The holidays upend my routine, and I never finish my work enough to relax. Who needs a dozen types of cookies anyway?"

Mariah's cookies could win awards. She raised a

hand.

Neither man acknowledged the gesture.

"All right," Walter said. "I'll tell Mariah to expect you in an hour or two, but I'm eating your cookies."

Dane winked. "Make it three hours."

Walter laughed and rode off toward the farm.

Gripping Smoky's bridle, Dane turned the animal and oriented him toward the motel. "I guess you're stuck with us."

"Is he okay?" Watching the horse move, she looked for signs of distress. She didn't have a barn, but she was sure she could find a few carrots and an apple to ease the animal's discomfort. "That was quite the bolt of energy. I might have jumped, too."

"He'll be okay. An old injury crops up sometimes. We think we have a handle on it, but it flares up when we least expect it."

Shifting her bounty to her left hand, she held out her right hand and hoped the gelding was friendly toward out-of-work muralists running quirky, desert motels.

Dane loosened his grip on the bridle.

Smoky swung his great head, sniffed her fingers, and left a friendly nose wipe along her white shirt.

She appreciated the affection, but after scratching the horse's sleek coat, she pulled back a hand and rubbed the gelding's hair off her fingers. "Yep, now I definitely need a shower."

Dane and the horse snorted.

The horse's shallow huff reminded her of lazy afternoons watching Pops prep for a trail ride. She ached to return to Los Angeles, and she simultaneously feared she hadn't done enough during her year in the desert. "The dates…"

"Don't mention it." Dane pulled lower his hat.

Smoky pawed the ground.

He looked around. "Do you have any outbuildings?"

She rubbed her arms against the cooling wind and considered the motel from a stranger's point of view. She had twenty *casitas*, studios, and standard rooms. A listing, aluminum recreational vehicle occupied the parking lot's RV camping spot, and desperate motorists could always sleep in their cars. Lounge chairs surrounded the pool and the desert gardens, but she had zero barn facilities. "We have a maintenance shed, but I doubt Smoky would fit inside the building and be comfortable."

"Let's find an out-of-the-way place to tie up his reins. Somewhere nobody will bother him, and he can keep weight off his leg." Dane shook the edge of his leather jacket. "You cold?"

She made a half-hearted sound.

He shrugged. "Suit yourself."

"I don't know what would suit him." She considered her options. Palm Springs was never part of the Wild West. Indigenous people inhabited the desert before citrus and date farmers arrived and staked claims. Even though Southern Californians loved the desert's beauty, shot westerns in aged outbuildings, and posed for Christmas cards with towering cacti, working barns never graced the site that would become the Starlight Motel.

She couldn't imagine what kind of person would play out a West Texas fantasy in Palm Springs but make zero provisions for stock. If the motel resembled a small village, it should have a barn. Any cowboy from the high plains of Wyoming to the Sonoran Desert would look after his or her animals before they looked after themselves. *Maybe the rented studio ponies all went back to the stockyard.* Dismissing the maintenance shed and the parking lot, she considered each *casita* and assessed its potential.

None of the occupied *casitas* would work. The unoccupied buildings left Smoky too much room for mischief. She looked at her tiny abode.

A short fence kept staff and visitors from infringing on the small, private oasis. Set back from the paths, the little house matched its stucco neighbors, but she worked hard to make it her own. Red clay tiles kept back the sun, wooden beams made interesting shadows, and a small porch created shade. Unlike the other buildings, thorny roses growing in planters stood sentry by the front door. "I know the place." Leading Dane and Smoky toward her home, she opened the gate and spread wide her arms. "*Mi casa es su casa.*"

Smoky bit the head off her favorite rose bush.

Cringing, she blinked and hoped Dane missed her response.

"Are you sure?" he asked. "The horse will drop enough waste to ruin your yard. I'll help you clean up the mess, but you won't win any landscaping awards."

"He'll be comfortable here. I can find him a bucket of water, and nobody will bother him in my space. You can camp out at the cantina and surf the web or monitor the weather. Do whatever farmers do when they have an hour off from work."

He grunted.

She looked away from the roses. "You do take

breaks, don't you?"

Smoky huffed.

"I do." Stripping off Smoky's saddle, bags, and blanket, Dane set the gear by the front door and laid his leather jacket over the pile. After removing the gelding's bit, he pulled a halter from the saddlebags and applied the nylon gear. Looping the lead rope around a fence rail, he left enough slack to contain Smoky and keep him from vaulting the fence.

She admired his capability. How did a person make such practical skills look so effortless?

Slapping dust from the animal's flank, he shut the gate, tested the latch, and brushed clean his hands. "Thanks. He'll be fine, and I'll be zero trouble. Get back to running your motel, and don't worry about us. You'll barely know we're here."

I doubt that fact. Clutching the date cake and the dates, she shifted her weight. "Great."

"Great." He raised his eyebrows.

Lightning flashed in the distance.

She frowned. "I'd better get these dates to the kitchen. You can hang out by the firepit or join the rest of us in the main building. Night will fall soon, and the temperature will drop."

"I'm aware. You're the one who needs a jacket."

"Right. Of course." Turning her back on his wry smile, she fled before she said something stupid. She had a million things to do, and reprioritizing her task list to make s'mores with a handsome cowboy shouldn't be at the top of the list.

Chapter Three

Slowing his pace, Dane followed Kada toward the main building and kept his mind off her backside, her honey-brown eyes, and the way her hands moved like they never stilled. If he stopped his life for every pretty woman in Palm Springs, he would never get a seed in the ground or a crop to market.

Given his workload and his family expectations, he fell into bed after sunset, tackled problems like a rodeo cowboy, and shouldered the weight of every decision he or his staff made on his behalf. He had no business admiring a woman or the way she moved.

Then again, her lush hips swayed like an off-balance metronome, and the quirk intrigued him. If she had an old injury, then he knew a dozen ways to soothe it. Shaking off the thought, he scanned the guests for a familiar face, found none, and assumed his momentary weakness would stay confined to the motel's shadowed, verdant walkway.

Clutching her caramel bounty, Kada walked through a lobby and waved toward the cantina. "Have a drink on me."

"I will." He could drink a gallon of water, but instead of following her into the cantina, he lingered in the lobby and removed his hat. Candy-colored Christmas decorations peppered the room. The eclectic, cheerful mix had no place amid the desert's shifting sands and sunbaked shadows. Nearly a week after the holiday, he found them garish.

Picking up a bubblegum glass ornament resting in a ridiculous bowl, he hefted the glass's weight. The piece was decidedly heavy, but it was as fragile as new fruit. Given a squeeze, the ornament would shatter in his hand, and he'd be another loafing farmhand with a mess to clean up. Putting down the ornament, he remembered his place as a guest came with little tolerance for ineptitude.

He walked right past a tinsel tree, pink nutcrackers, and a disco-themed peacock chair. He questioned why women spent so much time decorating buildings. His mother was worse than Kada. Mom erected seasonal displays worthy of the local school's bulletin boards, and she had a craft closet worthy of its own zip code. This year, she put away the flickering tinsel and fake snow as soon as possible. He'd hauled her boxes to the attic and wondered at the change of pace. Had she mentioned Kada came via Los Angeles?

The woman's providence and Mom's quirks were anecdotal to his workload. He and Dad kept the farms neat as a pin. Spotless storage buildings and barns looked like advertisements for tool catalogs.

Walter kept the office organized, and he ensured the equipment ran with quiet efficiency. In a modern, resource-constrained world, nothing less than exacting attention to detail would do.

A brass flamingo peeked from a large, potted plant in the room's corner.

He stared at the ornament. "Maybe I will get a drink."

Striding past a neon sign and a check-in counter, he

stepped into the cantina. Dim lights created intimacy, but a fire roared in the hearth, and two servers moved between occupied tables. One server looked like she moonlighted as a choir director. The other server looked like a goddess. Judging by her nails, she knew it.

Leaning against the cantina wall, he tracked Kada walking toward the kitchen. Without a doubt, he knew her cheerful efficiency ran the motel. Her name popped up over dinner conversation so often that when Mom asked him to run over a date cake, he knew he had two choices: complete the tasks or renounce his inheritance.

He chose a joyride on Smoky and brought Walter for company, but his favorite horse spooked easily. Given the gelding currently occupied Kada's front yard, he was glad he'd given her the dates. If Smoky's rosebud snacks were any indication, the stubborn, old beast planned to make himself at home.

Kada acted like she adapted to running her grandfather's motel, but she wouldn't be the first person to dip their toes in a Palm Springs pool and flee before summer set in. Her shiny black hair and lush backside would catch a man's eye, but she hailed from Wyoming, a state that recorded subzero temperatures. Given a few more blistering months in the desert, she would sell the motel to investors, turn tail, and leave him the lush crops, skittering roadrunners, and fat-cheeked kangaroo rats. He placed his hat on a table. A man couldn't ask for better company.

The perky server walked up. "Can I get you anything?"

Running a hand along his hat's brim, he treated her with the same courtesy any person deserved.

"Lemonade, please."

"Coming right up!"

"Thank you."

She approached the sidebar where pitchers of *agua fresca* and a tea dispenser sat atop a cooler holding bottled beverages.

Agua frescas were refreshing fruit drinks made from fruit, water, lime juice, and a hint of sweetener. He preferred lemonade's kick.

The server turned from the bar, walked clear across the room, and presented him with a tall glass of lemonade.

A lemon wedge anchored a jaunty umbrella and bobbed next to a bamboo straw. Beneath the glass, a white cocktail napkin kept the glass's bottom dry.

"Would you like anything else? A table? We have excellent appetizers."

He took the glass and inclined his head. Was she being polite, or was she flirting? He hated to think he'd given her the wrong impression. Spending most of his time with pickers, he had little experience with women, and the one who caught his eye was currently having an intense debate with the chef. A pass-through let him see the pair engaged in intense conversation and the orange flames from a neglected grill. "I'm good. I won't be here long."

"Okay!"

She bounced away like a wind-up toy. Taking out the frilly garnishes, he rolled them in the napkin, raised the glass to his parched lips, and drained the sweet contents. The lemonade deserved a trophy. It possessed the perfect balance of sweetness and tart delight that hit all the right spots. If Mom had hauled over a case of lemons, then he would attribute the drink to Palmer Farms produce. More likely, someone in the kitchen knew how to work a juice press and make magic from commercial produce.

Flames flared in the kitchen.

A man wearing a chef's hat swore in a mix of Spanish and English that warmed Dane's cheeks. "I doubt the chef goes in for sweets."

Assuming a brisk walk, Kada left the kitchen and approached a patio table where a man and a dog sat outside with a menu and a notepad. She looked back and forth between the kitchen flames and the guest.

The dog's compact, brown, muscular body looked familiar, but its angular head caught Dane off guard, and a trick of the light made the animal appear hairless. The combination of strength and delicate skin intrigued him, but he had better things to do than sweet-talk mutts.

Ceramic shattered in the kitchen.

Hurrying across the cantina, the two servers entered the kitchen ready to fight fires.

But Kada retained her cool.

The flames intensified. A woman screamed, and the dining room's occupants went eerily quiet.

Eyes wide and cheeks red, Kada retreated to the kitchen.

Dane grinned.

Left stranded in her wake, the man with the dog on the patio glared at her retreating form.

"You know, I might need a table, after all." He knew how to isolate a threat and make sure it caused limited harm. Peeling himself off the wall, he walked past the fireplace, opened the patio door, and sat next to the man and his chocolate-colored dog. Picking an adjoining table, he set his hat on an opposite chair and placed his glass square in the table's center. Stretching out his long legs, he crossed his hands over his midsection. "Nice night."

"Lousy service," the man said.

The guy's face looked too smooth, and his hair glistened with too much oil for rural life. Dane would peg him as a Los Angeles writer sentenced to local interest stories to pay the rent. "Where you from?"

"Orange County."

"Hmm." He stretched out a hand toward the dog. "Nice place."

Raising its head, the animal sniffed his fingers and nudged him for more affection.

He complied. Scratching the dog behind the ears, he resolved to keep the conversation light and distract the OC honcho from whatever gripe left him upset with Kada. As long as she ran the motel, she was nearly a local, and desert people had to stick together. "You staying long?"

"I thought I'd be staying longer." The man shifted in his seat. "They're out of everything I want to eat. What good is a write-up on Palm Springs dates when the motel doesn't have dates?"

"You're out of season," he said. "If you want the best dates, show up in October when we pick them from the trees."

The man frowned. "I thought the crop lasted all winter."

Dane smiled and straightened his frame in the smooth, wooden chair. "Not when they're good."

The man laughed.

Even the surliest city dweller could catch on to a joke. Dane stuck out a hand. "I'm Dane Palmer. I farm a bit of land next door to the motel."

"Gustavo Dyson," the man said. "I write for the *Los Angeles Times*. You've probably seen my column on local hot spots in the Los Angeles area."

Dane shook the ice in his glass. "Can't say that I have."

Gustavo frowned. "The tortilla wars? The *cotija* rodeo?"

Cocking his head, he stared.

"Right." Gustavo closed his laptop and drummed his fingers on the case. "I forget how isolated some people end up."

Dane grinned. If he was isolated, he chose the condition. Like every member of his family, he left the valley to attend Cal Poly San Luis Obispo, but he returned to the farms he stewarded and quietly loved. "So, what brings you to the Starlight Motel?"

"My dad raves about this place. He and his new girlfriend took a cruise for the holiday, so I traveled the highway to check out his favorite haunt." He scanned the cantina and shook his head. "So far, it's a huge disappointment."

"Huh." He figured the man's disappointment had more to do with his paternal relationship than his experience at the motel, but not every son could grow up with a father as awesome as Dad. "Which *casita* do you have?"

"The green one."

"Oh, that might be the problem. I prefer the orange one. It's closer to the pool."

Gustavo stared.

He should stop lying to the writer before the man packed up his vegan leather travel bags and demanded a new room. As far as he knew, the *casitas* stood equal distance from the pool, had vibrating beds, lava lamps, and scented soaps. "Have you tried the southwestern eggrolls?"

"They weren't on the menu." Gustavo scratched his head. "Maybe I missed them."

"Oh, they're good. These aren't your ordinary eggrolls. The kitchen takes crispy flour tortillas and wraps them around chicken, black beans, corn, jalapeño Jack cheese, red peppers, and spinach. After deep frying the rolls, the chef serves them with avocado-ranch."

Gustavo cocked his head. "I feel like I've had those before…"

He bit back a laugh. The rolls anchored a chain restaurant's appetizer menu, but if Gustavo found them intriguing, he deserved them. "It's a popular dish."

Gustavo frowned and wrinkled his brow. "Wait a minute!"

Kada made eye contact across the room, spared him a smile, and walked toward Gustavo's side carrying a cheerful, red ceramic plate. On top of the plate, goat-cheese-stuffed dates glistened with a fine drizzle of honey. "I have the best news," she said. "We sourced the fruit from a local provider…"

Dane coughed.

"…and the chef whipped up these morsels. The dates have the perfect balance of sweet and savory flavors, a satisfying creamy texture, and a little pecan crunch." Setting down the plate, she linked her hands and waited.

Gustavo picked up a date and took a bite.

The man worked his jaw like a wine steward with a flight waiting on his opinion. Dane rolled his eyes and leaned back his head to watch the stars emerge.

"Kind of bland." Gustavo set down the half-eaten date. "Maybe you should wrap the dates in bacon or blend a little chili oil into the cheese. You know, give it a little kick."

Straightening in the chair, Dane crossed his arms and considered how to respond to the writer's suggestions. If he wanted a little kick, he could go to a Mexican restaurant, or he could stand behind Smoky.

People deserved opinions on the food they ate, but business owners deserved respect. He would gladly pony up to the salsa bar for salsa *picante* and discuss the merits of homegrown peppers, but Kada's goat-cheese dates weren't trying to set a style trend. A staple in the valley for seventy years, the dish's sweetness and hearty bite made it a perfect seasonal appetizer. He cleared his throat. *So he heard.*

"Bacon." Kada blinked. "What a great idea."

"Everybody loves bacon," Gustavo said.

She wet her lips and smiled.

He recognized that smile. Mom taught at Coachella Valley High School and managed an agricultural-based curriculum. The minute one of the students went on a tear about hydroponics and zero-impact agriculture, she unleashed the same indulgent smile. Neither woman could keep their exasperation out of their expressions.

If Mom's smile didn't quell the student's dissidence, she reminded the student he or she grew up eating the valley's produce, and to improve the system, he or she should dirty their hands and start from the ground up.

Her approach usually worked. Beyond the students, the Coachella Valley hosted music festivals, tennis tournaments, and wealthy snowbirds with a fondness for pool parties. Nestled two hours outside of Los Angeles, the valley's sunny winters made it an ideal location for chic resort towns and productive farming communities.

Where manicured houses, restrained condominiums, and boutique hotels ended, the desert thrived. Honey mesquite and indigo bush leaned toward the surrounding mountains, and bighorn sheep hopped along the ragged cliffs. Beyond the towns, farms mixed with the landscape and lined the highway with stately groves. The Starlight Motel stood alone on the highway, but farms surrounded it like acres of inaccessible land. He often wondered whether the *casitas* should stand down and let his agricultural pursuits reign. Given the chance, he could ensure Kada never ran out of dates again.

Guests could go into Palms Spring proper. The reporter might prefer the artsy town. A welcoming sign portrayed jolly old St. Nick lounging poolside. The city's residents decorated the town with candy-colored accents and glittering tinsel. They strung lights on cacti, painted vintage convertibles on shop windows, and erected a twenty-two-foot Christmas tree in Frances Stevens Park. Ornaments hung from streetlights, reindeer peeked from rock gardens, and manufactured snow filled the aviation museum's parking lot. Days after Christmas, the decorations still stood, but nobody elected him Chief Sentimental Sot or ordered him to take down the festivities. Perhaps Gustavo could gift the town an opinion piece.

Kada cleared her throat. "You know, if you like bacon, we have an amazing breakfast planned for tomorrow morning." She straightened the salt and pepper shakers. "I'll save you a few select pieces. Chewy or crisp?"

"Oh, chewy," Gustavo said. "I like a little give in my pig."

Pulling out her phone, she opened a text app. "Noted."

Dane stood. The man was hopeless. "Kada, could you point me toward the facilities?"

She looked up from the phone. "Excuse me?"

"The bathrooms?"

Coughing, she covered her mouth and slid her phone in her jeans' back pocket. "Sorry, I assumed you knew your way around the motel. You've probably spent more time here than I have."

"I've hardly set foot on the land." He crossed his arms over his chest.

"Smart move," Gustavo said.

Dane considered carrying the writer to the pool and giving him a first-class bath. As far as he could tell, Kada and her staff provided everything they advertised. She went out of her way to bring the writer his requested dish, and she looked as pretty as a picture doing it. He could imagine her in a dress with red lipstick—he cleared his throat—he didn't have time for those thoughts.

"Well, let me show you the way," Kada said. "Follow me." Turning, she walked toward the cantina where a growing crowd occupied tables and kept the two servers busy. Flames subsided, and the kitchen bustled with activity.

Dane uncrossed his arms, but he lingered at the table.

Gustavo opened his laptop and typed into a blank document.

Dane risked a glance.

The backwoods, without the trees, are as bland as the... Gustavo typed.

He shifted his weight and stepped on the man's canvas sneaker.

"Man, you're on my foot!" Gustavo cried.

Relocating his boot, Dane picked up a date from the shiny, red plate and bit into the cheese-filled fruit. The appetizer was as sweet and tangy as he expected. It recalled childhood memories with his brother, long-winded stories from his grandparents, and deep-seated pride. "My bad. I grew those dates, and they're the best you'll ever eat."

Shaking out his foot, Gustavo nodded. "I get it. Go chase down your girlfriend."

"She's not my girlfriend." He watched her move through the crowd and picked up his hat. "But a man could get lucky in this town."

Gustavo shook his head and pecked out another line of text.

At this rate, he'll finish his column for New Year's Eve. Don't they teach touch typing in the basin? Then again, if he has any sense, he's writing about strip mining and not the Starlight Motel. The impulse to do more than step on Gustavo's foot grew stronger, but he couldn't blame the man for his bad taste. Plenty of people grew to love the rich complexity of a ripe date, but expectations mattered as much as experiences.

Squaring his shoulders, he left the patio and followed Kada into the cantina.

Turning in the crowd, she stopped and made eye contact.

He raised a hand and paused a respectful foot away from the woman.

She leveled a finger. "I don't need your help scaring off customers."

Scratching his throat, he nodded, but the desert could brutalize unprepared visitors.

"And that man's a travel writer! If he puts out a favorable review, reservations will jump. Who wouldn't want to idle away a few days in Palm Springs?"

He scanned the cantina. Each table held a small, white ceramic vase stuffed with pink and red carnations and a candy cane. "Someone who doesn't like pink?"

She put her hands on her hips. "It's a festive color!"

"So's red. Royal blue. Orange."

Crossing her arms over her chest, she glared. "Do you actually need to use the facilities?"

"No, Miss Kada. I'm fine on my own." He rocked back on his heels. "Thanks for the hospitality."

"Good!" She blew out her breath.

The loose hair surrounding her face danced. He wanted to tuck one strand behind her ear, but he shoved his hands in his jean pockets.

"I'll let you know when Walter returns." She turned and headed toward the kitchen.

He watched her hips sway. She ran the motel, but he could see her in a cocktail dress at the steak house Frank Sinatra had favored. Tucked into a corner booth at the swanky restaurant, she would sip a dirty martini and smile indulgently while a server prepared steak Diane. Would she enjoy the show or call it kitsch?

The valley offered delights, but she had seen more of this world than the people who never left the valley. That group almost included him. While steak house patrons paused their meals to watch servers flambé a sauce made of cognac, garlic, and mushrooms, he hoped she would smile with red-lipped indulgence and savor the experience. He wanted to be in the booth with her and share her joy. "Kada?"

She stopped and looked over her shoulder.

Despite the stakes and the staff hovering for her attention, she made eye contact and tilted her head. He could lose himself in her caramel-brown eyes. "For a holiday weekend, the motel has quite a crowd. Don't worry too much about the travel writer's review. You must be doing a lot of things right. Word travels faster than newspaper columns."

She scanned the cantina and exhaled. "My grandfather left behind a solid property with a good reputation, but thanks for the feedback. I appreciate it."

He nodded. Based on his observations, the motel had been busier in the last six months than when Hall lived. If she thought she owed her grandfather for her success, she should review last year's tax returns and check her profit margins. Watching her depart, he released a smile. "My pleasure."

Chapter Four

Kada checked on the kitchen, settled a dispute between Randi and the new server, Stephanie, and confirmed the reservation system's guest count. With twenty people staying overnight, and one handsome farmer lounging in the cantina, she had her hands full.

After Pops' death, she knowingly and lovingly embraced managing the motel, but sometimes, she wondered what in the world she had gotten herself into. None of the anecdotes and shiny pictures on the walls prepared her for life behind the check-in counter.

Guests threw fits, broke lamps, and made impossible demands.

She had to manage the quarrelsome toddler-like miscreants, focus on their redeeming qualities, and remind herself every profession came with difficulties. On the other hand, her paintbrushes never talked back, and she sorely missed the feel of their balanced weight.

"Um, Ka-a-da," Stephanie said.

She looked up.

The server twisted her hands in front of her. "Um, one of the guests said there's a horse in the pool."

"What?" She widened her gaze, peered through the windows, and spotted a large equine silhouette drinking pool water beneath glowing patio lights. Thank goodness, darkness had fallen, and none of the motel guests had used the pool for an early evening dip.

Rubbing her face, she nodded. "Thanks, Stephanie. I'll take care of it."

Hoping she could lure Smoky back to the garden before Dane noticed his gelding's escape, she snuck out the side door and walked up to the animal. The horse wasn't precisely in the pool, but he looked like he was about to make a cameo as a trick pony. "I'm sorry, handsome," she said. "I forgot your water."

Smoky plunged his face into the water and raised his head. Water ran over his lips and dripped to the pool decking.

Holding out her hand, she let Smoky sniff it and hoped she could lure him back to the gated *casita* without too much fuss. Gripping the horse's halter, she tugged.

The animal backed up, shook her off, and lowered his head for another drink.

Stubborn male.

Smoky's horseshoes *clipped* and *clopped* on the pool decking. Over the years, a few patches needed replacing, but the original 1950s cement had withstood the desert sun. Beneath the artificial lighting, the material glowed a soft white and surrounded the rippling turquoise water like a wind-softened mesa. But after hosting Smoky, the decking might need more than a power washer to regain its shine.

"Right." Water ran down her arm and stained her shirt. Well, she hoped the moisture was water. Based on Smoky's drool, the wetness could be a combination of pool water and rose-flecked spit. "I guess I'll go find that handsome cowboy you brought me."

"So, you think I'm handsome," Dane said.

Turning, she ran straight into the man's chest.

Based on her limited experience, he had an exquisite chest, and she had no business inhaling his deep, masculine scent. He smelled like lime, warm spices, and a hint of honey. Backing up, she lost her balance and stumbled toward the pool.

He stepped forward and caught her elbow. "Hey now."

His slow entreaty reminded her of the way he soothed Smoky. Embarrassment and frustration stole the easy camaraderie she found with most people, but she couldn't blame him for her near miss. He brought her dates and a belated Christmas loaf. So far, she brought him trouble and a chlorine-tinged horse. Pulling free, she made two fists at her sides and chose her words. "I forgot to bring Smoky a bucket of water."

"That's my job." He reached for the horse's halter and tugged. "Come on, old man."

Smoky blew out his lips and shook off Dane's grip.

Watching horse spit spray Dane's chest, she felt a little better about the situation. The patio lights glowed above the oasis, the stars twinkled in the darkening night sky, and the stubborn horse would soon go home. She could handle a little amusement before the motel's New Year's Eve shenanigans. *Also, I'll add more chlorine to the pool.*

He gripped each side of the horse's halter. "I'll let Mariah braid your mane."

Smoky laid back his ears.

"And put a bow in it." Dane released the halter and raised his eyebrows.

Shaking his great head, Smoky backed away from the pool. Water dripped from his mouth. Actually, it was more than water. Long, drooly strands hung from his pink lips.

Dane frowned. He shifted forward, pried open the horse's mouth, and looked at his back teeth. "What have you gotten into?" He ran a hand over the animal's side, stopped to feel his heartbeat, and checked his eyes. "Did you find a bad batch of clover?" He turned. "What plants are you growing in your little garden? Please don't tell me you have a fondness for butterflies and a three-gallon tub of milkweed."

"No, I have…" She recalled what she planted. Most of the time, she picked up whatever haggard plants the nursery put on discount. With a little tender loving care and a lot of water, the plants regained their strength, and she enjoyed their beauty. "…some roses, marigolds, a jade plant, and a little grass."

"You're growing grass in the desert?" he asked.

She put her hands on her hips. "You're growing dates!"

"Look who's talking." He pointed. "You have a pool."

"And your horse is drinking from it!"

Smoky shoved his mouth back in the pool and took great gulps.

"Stop that. You'll make yourself sick off the pool chemicals." Shaking his head, Dane tugged on Smoky's halter until the horse relented and followed him back to the *casita*. "Good call, old man."

Kada fell into step with the man and his steed. "The grass is a putting green."

Her admission felt less like a betrayal and more like a glimpse into Pops' depths. He worked so hard to care for the motel and the guests who visited. He deserved a few feet of green grass and putting practice.

Then again, she hadn't taken care of the patch or weeded out whatever sickened Smoky, so maybe she had betrayed her grandfather, after all. "I'm sorry if the grass sickened your horse."

"Slaframine is a fungus that afflicts clovers. It produces a toxin that stimulates a horse's salivary glands and causes the horse to drool," he said. "Horses grazing on red and white clover can get the slobbers from the mold. In these temps, I'm surprised it's still active."

Judging by Smoky's wet grin, the horse had the slobbers all right. She hoped the condition wasn't permanent. An ooey-gooey horse was the last thing she needed to augment the motel's online description. "What's the cure?"

"Water."

"Well, take him back to the pool!" Stopping beside a palm, she clasped a hand over her mouth. The demand came out so loud she wondered if the cantina guests heard her outburst. "I don't want him to suffer on my behalf."

"He'll be okay. I'll find a hose and give him fresh water."

Exhaling, she wondered whether she could nab a five-gallon pot from the kitchen. If worse came to worse, she would open her *casita's* bathroom windows, fill the tub, and let Smoky have his fill. "Are you sure you don't want to call a vet?"

"Trust me. He'll be fine." Dane shifted his hat to his left hand, led the horse back to the *casita*, filled a bucket, and shut the gate hard.

At the clang, she wondered if it would ever open.

Smoky plunged his head into the bucket.

Wrinkling her nose, she considered Dane's mix of easy charm and steady control. His mother, Mariah, came to the motel like a breath of cinnamon-scented fresh air, coached her grant-writing skills, and reminded her to give the desert time to sink into her skin.

The day Kada received the announcement email confirming she won the grant, she called Mariah, but walking away from the Starlight Motel would be harder than she thought.

Mariah said what felt difficult on one day could turn into joy the next day. Most of her challenging stories revolved around Dane and his brother's childhoods, but the stories always had a happy ending. Now, a handsome cowboy stood on her property, and he was too ruggedly handsome to ride a stick pony.

Walter liked his boss, and Pops had mentioned Dane once or twice. If three people could get along with Dane Palmer, she could, too.

"How long are you staying out here?" Dane asked.

She checked the time on her phone. "The dinner rush usually ends around nine."

"That's not what I meant." He cleared his throat and shifted his stance.

Looking past his shoulder, she considered her response. Before Pops died, she came to the motel frustrated and confused. She had finished an artist-in-residence gig at the Los Angeles County Museum of Art, but her next steps hadn't gone as planned.

When she started the residency, the position enabled her to organize a multipart community mural project at the Technical Vocational High School, and it allowed her to feel like she made a difference in the world. Working with the kids, she designed the mural, sketched it on the school's exterior, and brought the work to life. Every day, she bounded out of bed and felt like she had a noble calling. Deflecting praise back to the students, she was a woman who could empower the next generation.

At night in her tiny, rented apartment, she replayed her exchanges with the students. They influenced her in ways she would never have expected. They broadened her understanding of nature's power in urban environments. She grew up with Wyoming's charms. They grew up with equal parts concrete, glass, and grass, but they made it work.

Teaching her about local creeks flowing through underground culverts, the students showed her the places where the creeks pooled at the surface, pointed out hidden pockets of nature, and offered her produce from a community garden.

She felt humbled.

When bolder students spoke about freeing the water, they bubbled with the same excitement she expected from a spring downpour. The rush of feelings inspired the final mural's conception and execution. Titled "Life Finds A Way," the mural showed water falling from one side of the wall to the other side. Along the way, neighborhood symbols rose to the surface in punchy, rainbow-hued graphics, and local silhouettes bathed in the downfall. When she and the students finished the project, she thought the work represented nature's undiluted power and the students' vibrancy.

Wanting to repeat the experience, she used a crowd-funding platform to fundraise for a follow-up project and give another artist the experience she had.

Reporters covered the project and wrote nice pieces in local papers. On the day the campaign ended, she had a quarter of what she needed, the students left dejected, and she felt like a one-hit-wonder. So much for good press.

Before she could spend the afternoon drowning her sorrows, Kada received a call from Mom asking her to check Pops. Kada fled her disappointment, took a commercial bus to Palm Springs, and hired a car to take her to the Starlight Motel. A week later, Pops passed, and she remained. He left her everything she needed, but she struggled to find her balance. "I don't know," she said. "I'm not sure what I'm supposed to be doing with my life."

"Who is?"

She laughed and met his gaze. In the floodlit botanical gardens, he looked as relaxed as a tawny mountain lion, but she didn't want to start something she couldn't finish. If she had the man's measure, then he knew exactly what he wanted to do each day, and the crates of produce from Palmer Farms proved his efficiency. "Pops had a way about him."

"Well, that's true. Once or twice, I took Smoky for a walk, and he shooed me off his lands. I offered to buy them, but he didn't take me seriously. It must be a family trait."

Smiling, she looked away and scanned the mountains. Whenever she felt like she had big problems, she looked up and let the looming ranges put her life into perspective.

After Pops' funeral, her parents came to the valley, but Mom spent half the visit in tears. Every day, Kada picked up more and more responsibility. By the time she watched her parents depart, she had assumed management of the motel and convinced the staff to humor her presence in honor of Pops.

The transition still hurt. While she struggled to paint and complete daily tasks, she lost weight and spend several nights wide-eyed and overwhelmed. Her feelings paled in comparison to her mom's tearful phone calls. Once a week, Kada worked up the nerve to call and ask for help. Mom's tear-soaked memories overshadowed her daily struggles. As Kada listened, the remembrances made her grateful for her family's love, but Mom's grief stole her thunder. In comparison to losing a parent, what kind of problems did Kada have?

A light flashed halfway up the mountain.

She frowned. The Starlight Motel occupied five acres of land off the highway. Past the motel, the acreage rose toward the mountains. Half the remaining landscape belonged to Dane's family, and the Bureau of Land Management administered the rest. If she had her bearings, the flash came from the Bureau's land, and she doubted rangers were out patrolling this late at night. "I just saw a flash in the foothills."

Dane turned and cocked his head. "Probably more lightning."

"No." She craned her neck for another glimpse. "More like headlights coming around a curve. Do roads run up there?"

"Maybe a few off-road tracks."

She frowned. The local monuments offered a diverse range of landscapes, plants, and wildlife. She explored the area, but most of the time, she followed the gravel paths winding among the *casitas*.

Along most of its length, the valley stretched

fifteen miles wide. To the northeast, the San Bernardino and Little San Bernardino Mountains capped the valley, and to the southwest, the San Jacinto and Santa Rosa Mountains formed a towering horizon. Wind turbines captured down currents, solar panels absorbed the sunlight, and the valley's population rolled with the punches, but she couldn't depend on urban neighbors to investigate everything that went bump in the night.

The lights flashed again.

"I'll, uh, get you some water for Smoky." She started toward the main building, but she kept her gaze fixed on the mountains.

"Oh, no you won't." He moved alongside her. "He's fine."

Startled, she turned. "Excuse me?"

"You look like a jackrabbit ready to bolt."

"Do we even have jackrabbits?" she asked.

He ran a hand through his hair. "If you're running up the mountain on a whim, then I'll go with you, or I'll never hear the end of it from my mother."

She chewed her bottom lip, glanced at the shadowed range, and considered her options. "Your horse is...uh...sick."

Smiling, he slapped his palm against the fence.

Smoky raised his cocked his head and drooled.

"He'll be fine." Dane raised an eyebrow. "Unless you want to go for a ride?"

"As if." She wanted to investigate the flashes, but she couldn't ride double with Dane Palmer. Pursing her lips, she debated how to escape his helpful presence.

"And how were you planning to scale the mountain?" he asked.

She crossed her arms. "Pops' truck."

He donned his hat. "Well, I'll bet that trusty old truck has room for two."

Opening her mouth to argue, she pulled back and considered her options. Whatever light flashed halfway up the mountain signaled a need. Maybe the flash came from a pair of teenagers setting off fireworks who needed a chat about wildfires. She obtained a permit from the local fire authority for the New Year's Eve show, but she doubted the kids did the same. Maybe a backcountry driver broke down and needed a tow. If she found out someone spent the night in distress when she could help them, she would never forgive herself for ignoring their signal. "Fine."

"Fine?" He rubbed his jaw.

"You can come." She could summon courage, but well-muscled reinforcement would soothe her nerves. "You'd probably just follow me, anyway."

"Well, aren't you generous?" He glanced over his shoulder. "Let's get Smoky an all-you-can-drink water bowl and find out who's sending smoke signals from the backcountry."

"Smoke signals?" She peered up the mountains. Night left thick shadows, and she struggled to identify the outcrop where she saw the last flash. Without Dane's help and familiarity with the landscape, she might never figure out what she saw.

"It's a figure of speech," he said.

"Right." She walked past Smoky, opened her front door, and rooted through her *casita* closet until she found a tarp and an old, galvanized tin beverage bucket. On hot days, Pops set the bucket by the registration desk and filled it with glass-bottle sodas. Fresh out of sodas fit for a horse, she threw the tarp over the clover-infested grass, dropped the bucket in the middle of the lawn, and filled it with clear, cold water.

Turning, she found Chris and Dane in deep conversation. Chris stood ramrod straight in the middle of the path. He could give lessons in posture. Dane leaned against a palm. If he shifted to the left, he would come face-to-face with one of the hot-pink wreaths she made. Maybe a neon halo would do him good.

"Nah, he's been a workhorse all his life, but I'm glad you think he's handsome. Chestnut horses have red bodies, manes, and tails. Sometimes, you'll hear a chestnut horse called a 'sorrel' out west, but Smoky doesn't qualify. The black gives away his pedigree. That old man's soot-stained and handsome."

Smoky swished his regal, black tail and pawed the ground.

She swallowed. Given a chance, she would have called the gelding a chestnut, too. *So much for my familiarity with the local fauna.*

"Smoky's a bay horse. They also have reddish coats, but they have a black mane, tail, and other true black points." Dane scratched his jaw. "You can pet him if you like, but you might get a bit wet."

Chris shook Dane's grip with a nod, walked through the white gate, and with slow steps, he approached the horse. "I don't care what they call you. You're the most handsome thing I've seen all day."

She swallowed a laugh. Why should she advertise handsome cowboys when she had charming old men on-site?

Chris extended a hand. "My riding days might be behind me, but we could have had great adventures. The New Year will be here soon. I should have known

I'd see something inspiring."

Raising his slobbery mouth from the galvanized tin bucket of water, Smoky peeled back his lips and grinned. Dropping his head, he nosed Chris's hand, offered his neck, and sidestepped for more attention.

"Well, I can see I've been replaced," Dane said.

Chris leaned against the horse and stroked his muscled neck. "Aren't you the best?"

Kada tilted her head and watched the pair. For all his mobility and strength, Chris approached the beautiful old horse with the respect of a man who knew how to stop, smell the flowers, and savor life's memories.

Unfortunately, Smoky ate most of the flowers, but if the pair wanted to pass the evening on her *casita's* front porch, she couldn't think of a lovelier sight. "Why don't you take the rocking chair? I'll see if I can find some apples and carrots for Smoky." She looked toward Dane and raised her eyebrows.

He nodded. "We'll wait for you to return."

Looking over her shoulder, she imagined painting the three males in a moment of intimacy. Dane, with his capable, handsome strength, Chris, with his jolly, stooped nostalgia, and Smoky with his proud, workhouse drama made quite a trio.

Doubt tugged at her, and she wondered if her art would ever make an impact.

In a famous mural, *The School of Athens,* a muralist showed philosophers, inventors, and polymaths with different belief systems and different histories, but the brilliant minds stood in a pillared school. No longer framed in isolated portraits or posed in static busts, the historical figures clustered in groups and debated life.

The first time she saw the mural on paper in a textbook, she thought the figures were smart, cultured, and elite. Maybe she would mature into an artist who could do them justice. The first time she saw the mural in person at the Vatican, she had a decade of art experience under her belt, a taste for inequality's impact, and looming life decisions.

The figures in the painting wanted to solve problems and answer questions. She didn't care if she painted the next work of art, but she wanted more people to see themselves in the painting and know they could contribute to improving the world.

Smoky and his two admirers might not revolutionize the world, but they could shape the Coachella Valley, and she wanted to capture the moment. First, she had to figure out what in the world had flashed on the mountainside, and if Dane volunteered to accompany her, she would feel a lot better about her investigation.

Chapter Five

Leaving the trio outside her home, Kada set out on a brisk walk through the motel gardens and opened the kitchen's back door. Clattering, stainless steel pots and wafting steam hovered above the electric range. Randi and Stephanie passed tickets like a well-oiled machine, and Chef Benito churned out dishes in short order. He could handle twenty guests with ease, but the rushed date order almost sent him over the edge.

Opening the refrigerator door, she pulled out a bag of long carrots and a few apples. "Do you need these things tonight?"

Benito shook his head, jiggled onion sizzling in a frying pan, and slapped Stephanie's hand away from a plate of fresh French fries. "That's my dinner!"

She wrinkled her nose. "I only wanted one!"

He presented his cheek.

Kada wondered whether Stephanie would slap his cheek or kiss it.

Leaning in, she pressed her lips against his clean-shaven cheek. "I'll pay you back later."

Benito returned the affection with a hip-check and laughed. "I know you will."

"Huh." Kada took an apple bite. The tangy-sweet juice coated her tongue. *When did I miss that development?* Shrugging off her employee's good fortune, she turned toward the door, thought about her expedition, and turned back to the familiar faces. "Benito, I'm taking Pops' truck to check the back roads. I thought I saw a flare or someone flashing their headlights in distress. Dane Palmer's coming with me."

Benito emptied the onions into a prep bowl and nodded. "Good man."

She looked up from the apple. "You know him?"

He sliced jalapenos without looking at his knife. "I was his confirmation sponsor."

Four hundred thousand permanent residents lived in the Coachella Valley. The odds of Dane and Benito bonding over catechism lessons seemed as unlikely as the odds of her becoming a billionaire. She could suspend belief, but when life came too easily, she had suspicions. "Really?"

Pausing the knife, he made eye contact. "Really. I wouldn't let you wander off with anyone. Hall would haunt me." He crossed himself, stuck two fingers in his mouth, and whistled. "Order's up!"

She turned away.

"His family's been part of this valley for generations," Benito said. "You can trust him."

She looked over a shoulder. "Or I can trust he wants this land."

Benito wiped his sweaty forehead on his white sleeve. "If he wanted to buy this motel, he would make you an honest offer. He doesn't have time to play games."

She understood rationing time and weighed her choices.

Benito had been with Pops for nearly a decade. He made corn tortillas from masa and an old Mexican process. Nixtamalization unlocked nutrition and made the corn lighter and sweeter. When guests pressed him for his secrets, he shifted the praise to the landrace corn his brother grew. The grain had a tangy bite, and his brother maintained an online store. Would the guest like a card?

When exhaustion hit her, she craved a strange and wonderful mushroom *barbacoa* he made but refused to divulge the recipe. With a little more time in the desert, she might figure out why the dish captivated her, but tonight, she feared she had little time to dawdle. If Benito trusted Dane, then she would, too. She gave a brief nod. "I'll be back in an hour or so."

"No problem."

From the main floor, Stephanie dropped a plate on the Saltillo tiles.

Ceramic shards flew. Chairs scraped back, and the mother from the aluminum recreational vehicle swooped her young son into her arms.

Benito winked. "Like I said, no problem."

Gaze wide, she left through the back door before someone handed her a broom. Most nights, she would happily clean up the mess, but she had a feeling someone in the hills needed more than a quick cleanup on aisle two. Stepping outside, she waved to Dane and brought him the snacks for Smoky.

He took them from her hands and handed them to Chris. "He's all yours."

She jerked her head over her shoulder and urged Dane to come to the parking lot.

"I'm right behind you," he said.

She nearly skipped down the path. The Starlight Motel filled her days with joy, but she yearned for a bigger impact, and she missed the teens she worked with in Los Angeles. If she could help whoever signaled from the hills, the holiday season would be off to a grand start.

Pops' old blue truck sat in the lot's sole covered spot. Over the years, the glacier-blue 1955 all-American pickup truck earned new paint and fresh wood bed-lining. Pops reupholstered the front seat in blue, perforated vinyl to match the truck's blue dash, but the vehicle's chrome bumpers, grille, trim, and badging were all original.

She opened the driver's side door, pulled the keys from behind the sunshade, and started the engine. The engine's steady rumble soothed her. Despite its age, the truck's interior paint, kick panels, gauges, switches, and headliner looked brand new, and the upholstery smelled like Pops' spicy aftershave.

Dane opened the passenger door and climbed inside the cab.

She turned and smiled. "You're sure you're up for this ride?"

"Chris is sitting on your front porch, and Smoky is nearly lying at his feet." He buckled his seat belt. "They're good."

Doing the same, she pulled the truck out of the covered spot, stopped at the highway, and checked for cars.

The empty highway stretched for miles in either direction. Nautical Twilight came around six o'clock. This darker, heavy sky belonged to pure night. The deep-blue sky and bright, visible planets reminded her to breathe, because the Earth spun with or without her help.

Going right, she aimed for a limited-access road a

mile past the Starlight Motel. If she had gone left, she would have ended up in Dane Palmer's backyard. "I guess I could drop you off at your house. Smoky will be okay until you or Walter bring back the trailer."

"I expect he'll beat me back to the motel," he said. "I don't mind riding along. It's a beautiful night."

She slowed for the access road. "It is lovely."

A gate impeded her progress.

He moved to jump out.

"What if it's locked?" she asked.

Shaking his head, he climbed out of the cab. "This is the Coachella Valley. Nothing's ever locked."

Sure enough, the moment he pushed on the gate, it swung open.

She looked up toward the hills. If she couldn't find the flash's source in thirty minutes, she would admit defeat and retreat to the Starlight Motel.

He reclaimed his seat, rolled down the window, and rested his elbow on the jamb. "The weather's just right for being outdoors. When summer days want to break me, I think of nights like this one."

Air-conditioning buffered her summer days, but he and Smoky worked the land. Rubbing her arm to ward off the chill, she wondered why he left his jacket over the saddle. Surely, he knew better. She cranked up the truck's heater. "The stars are so pretty out here."

"And where you're from?" he asked.

Bumping along the dirt road, she considered how to answer him. When Mom and Dad met in the 1970s, he was a seasonal caddy at a Palm Springs golf course, and she was a cocktail waitress, saving tips for college. They eloped and settled near his family in Laramie. For a decade, they occupied a space in the community and deeply loved each other. Then she came along.

All of a sudden, three was a magic number, and she never felt more loved, but as she grew up, she realized she had a rollicking case of Only Child Syndrome. In art school, she did a lot of self-reflecting on the role OCS played in her personality. Of course, she liked to believe she had all of the good parts of the condition like fierce independence, ingrained studiousness, and extreme loyalty, but she hoped none of the selfish, bratty bad parts stuck around. Who was she kidding? Her parents spoiled her and loved her. She had to actively fight the self-assured battiness they cultivated and remember how much she owed them.

College was the great equalizer. By the time she graduated from the University of Wyoming and received her B.F.A. in Studio Art, she knew she needed space to start her life on her terms. If she stayed in Laramie, she would always be Bobby and Larissa's little girl.

"I grew up in Laramie, Wyoming, but I bounced around. Before Pops passed, I lived in Los Angeles. I'm a muralist." She glanced over. "By training, I mean." She had never described herself as a muralist before finishing her degree. What would her peers and their families say about her rambling drawings, art classes, and doodle-filled notebooks? Could she defend her career choice? More importantly, could she pay her bills? Something told her that success came easily to Dane, and she didn't want to preach about the power of art to transform lives.

She navigated around a scrubby tree and glanced over. Despite her jerky driving, he loosely drummed his fingers on the door. The prospect of discussing her work with someone so removed from the art world filled her with an odd sense of anticipation. She wanted to see his reaction and measure his words against his handsome facial expressions. Her selfish desire for approval smacked of the self-absorbed approach influencers took toward co-opting artistic works for social media posts, pouting their lips, and raking in thousands of likes. Where were the likes when she needed them to fund her last venture?

She swallowed her frustration and adjusted her grip on the steering wheel. Bitterness stifled creativity. As a lovingly-raised, well-educated woman, she had a leg up in the world, but she also had questions. She made friends wherever she went, but she also sought peers who appreciated her passion. Would Dane ask what drove her creativity or yawn through her descriptions? She smiled. Mariah probably drilled enough manners into him to ward off a yawn.

"I know you're a muralist. Everyone who visits the motel sees your work." Dane shifted.

The seat's vintage springs creaked.

"Your murals are beautiful," Dane said.

Her cheeks warmed. Most of the praise she received came from the press or students associated with her work. This time, the compliment came from within arm's reach. "Thanks."

"Why do you paint at night?"

Drawing back, she wondered how he knew her habits. "The air's cooler at night. Fewer interruptions. I have time to think."

He wiped a thumb along the dusty dash. Brushing the dust onto the jeans covering his thigh, he nodded. "From the house, I can see you working by floodlight.

Sometimes, you're up until three in the morning. Most people know when to call it a day."

"I'm not most people." Throwing his line back should amuse her, but she appreciated his patience, and she looked for a way to soften her retort. "Also, most people are asleep at three in the morning."

He worked his jaw. "Fair enough. We're all a little odd."

"Yes, we are." She tore away her gaze and wet her lips. Her high school suspension record proved she had a flair for truancy. Mom and Dad hated those years. Once she learned to funnel her questions into her art, the relationships improved, but lying dormant inside herself was the teenager who enjoyed colorful Holi festivals with her academic father, smashed clay pots with her artisanal mother, and ran through art supplies without considering the cost. She hoped Dane had an outlet, too.

"If you don't slow down, you'll blow a tire, and we'll have all night to get to know each other."

She slammed on the brakes.

The truck lurched.

He braced a palm against the dash. "Easy does it."

Exhaling, she scanned the landscape. Tall bushes cast shadows, but the white sand shone beneath a field of stars. "I'm not sure I'm in the right place."

"Well, I can think of worse ways to pass an evening."

"Such as?" she asked.

"Singing Christmas carols."

She turned. Even the over-scheduled, suburban moms staying at the motel sported a post-holiday glow. Nearly thigh-to-thigh in the old truck, she wanted to know more about Dane and his broad shoulders, but his attitude toward the holidays might be a deal breaker. "You don't like Christmas?"

"It's a fine idea, but it's a lot of hoopla."

Shaking her head, she eased off the brakes and chose a slower speed. "Like pink."

He laughed. "Like pink. I'm not opposed to the holiday or the color. I think people behave badly most of the year, but they pull out their fake-friendly smiles for Christmas. The minute the trees come down and the hangovers wear off, they're back to business. Trust me, I know when someone's putting on a show."

She glanced over and noted his tight jaw. "Who's been mean to you?"

Shifting in the passenger seat, he looked out the window. "Nobody in particular, but I wonder if the valley would be better off without local agriculture. Sometimes, I feel like Sisyphus pushing his damn rock up the hill."

"It's a lot?" She turned on the wipers to clear dust from the windshield.

He sighed. "Yes, but the people we support would suffer without us. Farming is a balance. From time to time, I encounter people who don't understand the trade-offs. They want my family to disappear. They also want bell peppers in December."

"Trust me, I'm happy with the dates," she said.

He cleared his throat. "Good."

She slowed for a fork in the road.

"Go right," he said. "The left branch ends at a cliff."

Nodding, she put on the blinker and turned right.

He laughed. "I'm glad you're signaling to the

kangaroo rats."

Rolling her eyes, she kept the truck to a moderate pace and looked for a repeat flash.

For thousands of years, sand from the surrounding mountains washed into the Coachella Valley and formed a dune system. Behind the dunes, the rift mountains rose. Her painting buddy, the fat, fringe-toed lizard, belonged among the shifting plains.

Along the highway into town, placards marked other unique species like the Coachella round-tailed ground squirrel, the giant red velvet mite, the flat-tailed horned lizard, and the giant palm-boring beetle. She didn't want to arbitrate between the lizard and the beetle, but she appreciated the local ecosystem and its diverse flora.

The road winding along the dune would take her into the foothills, but once the grade rose, the road would probably dead-end at a sheer cliff face. Whoever flashed the lights found themselves in over their head or took too big of a risk.

Dane knew the landscape, and despite his daily burden, she doubted he needed assistance in this type of terrain. If the person they sought lived locally, she would give them a tow back to town, wish them a happy New Year, and give everyone at the motel a free dessert.

The road curved around a palm oasis. The San Andreas Fault lines allowed water flowing underground to rise to the surface. In some places in the valley, endangered desert pupfish dwelled in year-round pools. Creosote bush, burrobush, smoke tree, and desert lavender made an alluring backdrop for tourists and performers documenting their stay in the valley. "Does this road connect to your land?"

"No. It cuts through a pass and connects with Sky Valley."

Sure enough, she spied a canyon break in the mountains. The cliffs would shield anyone's signal from the Starlight Motel, so if a person needed help, they had to be close or recovered and on their way.

Following the road, she wondered if it paralleled an old creek bed. The pathway twisted and turned beneath the stars. In five minutes, she would put the truck in Reverse and shake off her sillies.

Dane gripped her arm. "Stop!"

She slammed the brakes and followed his gaze.

A white car sat on the roadside. All four doors stood open.

Frowning, she scanned the vehicle and found it empty. Relief mixed with frustration, and she sighed. Whoever sent up the flare changed their mind, but she spent her evening riding to the rescue. If Dane hadn't come along to pique her senses, she might have considered the outing a waste. "Someone will have to tow the car out of here. I'll call the sheriff and ask what happens next."

Dane reached for the door release. "Maybe their tires got stuck."

"Maybe." She put the truck in Park and opened the driver's side door.

"Where are you going?" he asked.

She lowered one foot to the rocky sand. "Investigating."

He exhaled and rubbed his temples. "Stay in the truck. I'll do it."

"Look, I didn't ask you to come along. I didn't ask

for the date bread or the dates or"—she chose her words carefully—"the pleasant company, but I don't need a chaperone. If you want to stay in the truck, stay in the truck!" The last bit came out too forcefully, and she swallowed. "Although I do appreciate your concern."

"I'm sure." He opened the passenger door.

If he pulled a revolver from his waistband and turned this outing into a horror show, then she would run for the hills. Instead, he followed her through the sparse vegetation and kept the night wind from ruining her vibe.

The white car looked abandoned. A few fast-food wrappers littered the dash, and if she peered into the footwells, she suspected she would find more trash. "Maybe they got lost."

He kicked a tire. "Maybe they got spooked."

Looking up, she considered the star-filled sky. "By what?"

"Searchlights? Immigration control? Drug Enforcement Administration?"

She scanned the mountainside. One hundred miles away, the Mexican border waited, but migrants made their way to the Coachella Valley. Agricultural jobs and tourism suggested cash-only jobs, but some migrants found themselves dumped onto downtown streets with little guidance on how to secure food, transportation, and shelter. She brushed her hair out of her eyes. Global issues deserved more than a rocky, backcountry road and two Good Samaritans who wanted to help. "Right. I'll call for a tow in the morning."

He cupped her elbow.

She felt the pull toward the truck and acquiesced. Tilting her head, she listened to the wind shift the sand

and whistle through the mountains. Below the soft symphony, she heard a growl. "Wait!"

Stopping in his tracks, he tightened his grip.

The low, protective growl came again from the car.

Pulling free, she walked toward the car and peered past the driver's seat. A tan-and-white dog lay on the backseat. Her distended abdomen filled the bench. She barred her teeth, but her glossy coat marked her as a treasured pet. "What the…"

The pregnant dog growled once more and closed her eyes like the long day had been more than she expected.

A bowl of water sat on the floorboard. The dingy, white plastic bore gnaw marks and looked like it saw better days, but it held water. Someone left the vessel next to their pet and hoped for a positive outcome. Kada leaned forward. "It's okay, sweetie. We're going to help."

The dog sighed.

Dane gripped her elbow. "Be careful."

She drew a deep breath, pulled free, and stepped back from the car. Walking circles beneath the starlit sky, she considered her options. Animals tugged at her heartstrings, and when she imagined herself in the dog's place, she felt fear. If she dwelled too long on the dog owner's painful choice, she would definitely cry. She looked over her shoulder and saw Dane bracing an arm against the doorframe. "Dane! Why aren't you being careful?"

He jerked his head toward the dog. "I'm making sure she doesn't bolt."

"I'm sure you could catch a heavily pregnant dog." She mirrored his stance on the other side of the door and wondered if the dog would trust them.

The wind shifted.

It lifted her hair and amplified Dane's warm, leathery smell. Spending time with him interested her in ways she didn't fully understand, but her attraction did nothing for the tan-and-white mutt. Lifting her chin, she crossed to his side and gave the animal an escape route.

The dog opened her eyes and halfway bared her teeth.

"Right." She spotted black fur ringing the animal's doe-brown eyes. She had seen more fearsome expressions from festival goers confronted with a *No Vacancy* sign. Knowing the effort might earn her a rabies shot and a stern reprimand from everyone who loved her, she ran a hand along the car's backseat and stopped near the dog's head. "Hey, sweet girl. It's okay."

Lifting her head, the dog scented the air.

If Smoky's scent gave her a stamp of approval, she would find the gelding a bucket of apples and hand-feed him every tangy morsel. Taking a deep breath, she skimmed her fingers down the seat's back support, stopped short of the dog's face, and waited. "I have a nice, soft bed waiting. Does that sound good?"

A second sniff.

Closing her eyes, she lowered the hand a few inches and waited. A heartbeat later, she felt the dog's soft whiskers, and she froze. A hesitant nuzzle. Releasing her breath, she opened her eyes and grinned. "You're going to be okay."

The dog lowered her head and huffed.

She visually checked for a collar. *What do I call her?*

Feeling brave, she edged her weight onto the backseat, shifted closer, and scratched the dog's ear. She had the smoothest, silkiest fur. If fine desert dust made it soft, she might need to go into the skincare business. "I'm guessing you feel lost. I've felt that way, too. I'll take care of you."

The dog nudged against her palm.

"What's your name?"

Closing her eyes, the animal breathed deeply.

"All right," Dane said. "Let me get her."

"I can pick up her." She scratched the dog's chin. She might have a nose for Dane's warm cologne, but the dog needed help. In the confined space, the dog's soft, musky scent reminded her of a neighbor's dog she had almost forgotten. "Plus, what if she doesn't like you?"

"All animals like me," he said.

Looking up, she wished the moon shone brighter and she could make out his shadowed expression. "Is that so?"

He crossed his arms. "No, but if the mutt's going to bite someone, it might as well bite me."

Part of her wanted to sit outside on a beautiful night, exchange stories, and let the animal relax, but she had too much to do to indulge in late-night confessions. "I keep beef jerky in the truck."

The dog lifted her head.

"It's in the glove box," she said. "I'll go get it. Maybe I can lure her out of the car."

He nodded.

Sliding out of the car and leaving the pair to get acquainted, she walked toward the truck and popped open the box. The half-eaten bag sat right where she left it. Feeling good about her instincts, she turned and peered through the car's front seats.

Wedging his large body into the car's backseat, Dane slid an arm under the dog and pulled her weight toward his frame. Bent at the waist, he eased the animal out of the backseat, straightened his legs, and lifted her against his chest.

Apparently, I didn't need the jerky. She wanted to be annoyed he ignored her plan, but sometimes, the most thoughtful plans backfired. If her slow approach had warmed up the dog's demeanor, she and the dog agreed on one thing; Dane Palmer was a good man. Pocketing the jerky, she opened the truck's tailgate and stepped aside.

Dane lowered the animal to the wooden bed.

The dog whimpered and laid down her head.

"Shh." Climbing onto the tailgate, she settled beside the animal and offered reassuring comfort. Looking up, she found Dane staring. "We're helping her, right?"

"Helping her have a litter of puppies?" He worked his jaw and closed the tailgate. "Yeah, she'll be fine. We'll be fine. Puppies are a dime a dozen." Shaking his head, he walked toward the driver's seat, paused with a hand on the door handle, and looked back. "I can drive, right?"

She nodded and wondered if displaced muralists were a dime a dozen, too.

"Hold on tight."

Repeating the phrase, she settled a hand on the dog's smooth back and a hand on the truck's cold wall. She wondered what kind of American Pit Bull Terrier Mix she and Dane had rescued. Really, the dog's breed didn't matter. The animal needed a safe, warm home, and an abandoned car would never do. Plus, whoever flashed the car's headlights and made sure the sweet animal had the help she needed had surely loved her. She would make some family a great pet. "Don't worry, you'll be fine. It's a beautiful night. What else could go wrong?"

The dog nudged her pocket.

Pulling out the jerky, she broke off a piece and offered it. "Good call."

The dog took the piece and delicately chewed it. Lowering her head, she closed her eyes like she knew exactly how she landed in this mess, but she questioned how it ended.

Dane started the engine.

Meeting his gaze in the rearview mirror, she smiled encouragingly.

He frowned, shook his head, opened the driver's door, and climbed out of the cab. Leaning on the truck's side, he rubbed his face and dropped a hand with a sigh. "I can't have such pretty ladies bouncing around the truck bed. On these rocky roads, it's not safe. Do you think she'll sit between us?"

Ignoring the pretty lady jibe and comparisons with her silky, canine friend, she peered into the cab. If Pops lived, he might object to tan-and-white dog fur littering the perforated vinyl, but she possessed the title and half ownership in the Starlight Motel. She stood, hopped over the bed wall, and opened the tailgate. "Just go slow, okay?"

"It'll feel like crawling."

She laughed and hefted the dog into her arms. The animal looked smaller than it felt, but she could do this.

How had Dane carried her so easily? Taking small steps, she reminded herself asking for help might be the smart course of action. Making eye contact with Dane, she adjusted her hold, but the dog must weigh seventy pounds. "So, I have no clue what I'm doing"—she swallowed the whispered confession—"but I'm doing my best."

The dog licked her cheek.

The wind slipped past the wet spot and left a cooling sensation. Rubbing her chin against the dog's fur, she staggered toward the truck. "Hang on, sweetie. We have you. You're lucky we found you."

"Kada…" Dane stepped forward.

She shook her head and thought of an ex-boyfriend's tattoo. *Not all those who wander are lost.* In the desert, the dude's tech-bro credentials were useless, but Dane was a different breed. No matter how much she appreciated his capabilities, the grant deadline loomed. She wasn't lost, and his graceful strength couldn't be more than a late-night anecdote. She shifted her hold on the dog. "Don't worry. I've got her."

Chapter Six

Dane appreciated quality construction, but if he had to drive a woman and a pregnant dog over cross-country terrain, he would prefer modern controls and quality shocks. Setting an easy pace in the old truck, he turned the vehicle and followed the road back to the highway.

A small mammal ran across the road.

He slowed. "What will you name her?"

"I'm not keeping her," Kada said.

Risking a glance, he found her staring out the window and looking as stoic and disciplined as his mother leading weekend detention. "You'll take her to Animal Control?"

Her lip quivered, and she nodded.

Backtracking fast, he cleared his throat and focused on the road. "Kada's a pretty name. Unusual. How'd you come by it?"

"My parents," she said. "They liked cicadas."

Every few years, periodic cicada broods made the news, but the East Coast musicians usually skipped Palm Springs. Hall had mentioned his daughter moved to Wyoming and started a family, but Dane had no idea whether cicadas made their home there. He worked through a childhood named after a bug and figured Kada's parents might have spent too much time in the sun. "Did your mom spend a lot of time on the East

Coast?"

"No, but we took a lot of day trips to Horsetooth Reservoir. It's near Fort Collins, Colorado. My parents love that place."

Nodding, he replayed his trip to the Four Corners region in the southwest. As majestic as he found the area, he had plenty of rocks in his fields back home. If the reservoir she mentioned hosted vacationing Wyomingites, it probably had crystal-clear water, sandy shores, and a few rental cabins. He could see the appeal.

"When Mom was pregnant with me, she said the first day she felt me kick, the cicadas chirped at Horsetooth Reservoir. When she returned home, she said I kept my kicks to myself, and the silence bugged her. The day the obstetrician confirmed everything was fine, she heard a cicada buzzing outside her bedroom window."

"I can't imagine carrying a kid. That kind of vulnerability amazes me." Settling into an easy downhill section of the road, he risked a glance at her expression. The truck's gauges illuminated her face, and the soft light gave her hair an inky depth he wanted to explore, but he kept his hands to himself.

She stroked the dog's head. "I know. My mom and dad poured so much love into me. Sometimes, I feel like I can't repay them. How can you ever be ready for that kind of commitment?"

The dog huffed.

Out of his venue, he focused on the road.

She cleared her throat. "Hearing the cicadas is one thing, but actually seeing them in Laramie is a challenge. As soon as you get close, the little bugs hush up. They move around and make themselves indistinguishable from foliage. I don't know why Mom thought she could find one. What would she do? Pin it in my baby book?"

He laughed and gripped the wheel with both hands. "I don't think cicadas bite or sting, so there's no harm in trying. Although if you found yourself surrounded by a million of the little critters, the constant buzzing might annoy a person."

"You like your solitude?" she asked.

He nodded.

"Don't tell my mom, but on my tenth birthday, I found one sitting in the sagebrush. I let it go."

"Good call." Most bugs had a mission, and occupying a collection jar didn't make the cut. The talk of bugs and puppies worried him. He barely had time to eat, much less take on a pet, but he spent ninety minutes rambling through the valley to satisfy a pretty woman's whim. How quickly would she let him go?

In a short mile, he would return to his obligations. His mother's New Year's Eve itinerary started with calisthenics and ended with a headache. Kada had a motel to run. He tapped his fingers on the steering wheel. "You shouldn't mess with your namesake."

"Is that why you carry dates in your saddlebags?"

Kada's little quips made life interesting, and he wanted to spend more time with her. "Maybe I like the way dates taste." Turning onto the highway, he cruised the short distance back to the Starlight Motel and turned into the parking lot, where a dusty collection of cars waited beneath the stars and a retro sign advertising the motel. Insects fluttered in the yellow haze, but the sign's bare bulbs made it shine like an invitation to a pink-themed casino. Instead of fast-paced gaming tables, the motel's guests would find a welcoming haven, a cool pool, and a talented proprietor he had no business mooning over.

She pointed toward the covered spot where the truck sat parked earlier in the evening. Past the spot, a silver recreational vehicle with Midwestern plates occupied a small campsite. "Just park the truck in the same place."

He slowed for pedestrians and glanced at both passengers.

The dog raised her head.

He braked, put the truck in Park, and shifted on the seat. "Can she walk?"

"I guess we'll find out." She slipped the animal another piece of jerky. "I think she'll be okay. I'm not the one who carried her like the queen of the desert."

"You're right. You almost threw out your back stumbling to the cab."

She snorted. "See if you get any jerky."

Laughing, he unbuckled the seat belt, gripped the keys, and stepped out of the cab's quiet intimacy. Turned his face to the stars, he inhaled. The wind slipped across his face and reminded him how much he loved the desert and all his occupants. He might have complained about Kada's floodlights, but while he struggled to sleep late at night, he appreciated her unintentional company.

No matter how late he went to bed, he awoke around one in the morning. Wide awake, his mind raced with new ideas and unending tasks. Instead of sitting in bed for hours, he often moved to the front porch and let the night sky's slowly moving stars focus his thoughts.

Watching Kada's shadow move between the far-off *casitas*, he knew her name by reputation, but he wondered, if like him, she needed a strong cup of coffee to start her day. *I doubt she wants to know how much I think about her or her property.* His family had been trying to buy the motel for seventy years. Fighting a grin and putting that option out of his mind, he faced the intriguing woman.

"I owe you one." Standing by the truck, she rested her weight against the metal frame.

Reaching inside the cab, he pulled his hat from the dash. "Don't mention it."

She eased the dog to the cement.

He waited to see if the animal could walk.

Wrinkling her nose, the dog ambled toward the motel.

She feigned a dramatic, Hollywood gasp and clasped her hands to her cheeks. "She *can* walk! It's a miracle."

He laughed. "I think you have a few more days before the puppies arrive. If the cantina smells don't keep her close to the motel, nothing will."

Silently clapping her hands, she turned. "Do you want a drink? Dinner? Naming rights?"

He wanted a kiss and her telephone number. "I have a better idea…"

Scratching her scalp, she tilted her head and waited.

With her back to the road, and the sign shining overhead, she almost had a halo. If rescuing the stray had softened her abrupt efficiency, then he would buy the dog a truckload of bones. Kada wasn't exactly an ice queen, but she was so damn confident he wondered if her life had room for a rough-and-tumble romance. Given her success with the motel, her smooth complexion, and her lustrous hair, she deserved more than a spot as some man's tittering eye candy. He reconsidered his normal approach. Kicking the dirt, he mumbled a pleasantry.

"Come again?"

The dog had waited patiently at the edge of the parking lot.

He scratched his hair. "Kada, you did good with the dog. She probably would have eaten me for lunch. You have a way." He cleared his throat. "Animals can tell when someone cares."

She wrapped an arm around his middle, squeezed, and smiled.

The beautiful sight tripped his heartbeat. Keeping his hands to himself, he slipped out of her embrace before he embarrassed himself. "Nice night."

She bit her bottom lip. "Are we seriously talking about the weather?"

He grinned at the temptation and crossed his arms over his chest. He would be happy to talk about her beauty or her alluring ass, but he didn't want to spoil the moment. Something had changed between them, and she wasn't bristling or rushing off to appease a guest. He reached toward her hair drifting in the wind.

She brushed away his hand and raised an eyebrow. "I can't get a read on you."

"Moth." He wet his lips. The small hairs at the back of his neck stood on end. "What do you want to talk about?" His voice deepened. He was a man of a few words, and he imagined flipping her around, pressing her against the hot car, and gorging himself on her smooth skin and fevered moans. If she could read the direction of his filthy thoughts, she would leave him speechless in the parking lot.

"Talking wasn't high on my list." Her pupils dilated, and she chewed her bottom lip.

He knew she wasn't immune to him, but he wasn't exactly the type of man who specialized in fancy poetry or slow seductions. He researched the things he wanted, and he made them happen. Having stumbled into her life, he doubted he had the time to put together the pieces and find out what made her tick, but he wanted her hot and restless in his arms. He looked toward a shadowed corner and considered throwing her over his shoulder, but he suspected her outrage would wake the entire motel.

A semi raced past the motel, and the driver laid on the truck's horn.

Blinking off his frustrated daze, he watched the trailer's red taillights recede.

"Thank you for coming with me," she said. "I could have done it alone, but I felt a lot better having you along for the ride."

People usually reduced his brother to a muscled meathead. Frowning, he wondered how to assert his interest without throwing her over his shoulder and taking her back up the mountain. For the first time in a long time, the possibility intrigued him. He knew he was in deep, but he didn't know what to do about the notion. "Um, no problem."

At that moment, Walter pulled the truck and the horse trailer into the parking lot.

The truck's adaptive headlights flooded the parking lot and blinded him. Working his jaw, he hoped his best friend realized how much improvement his timing needed. Dropping a hand from his eyes, he raised it in greeting. "Company's here."

Parking the truck, Walter cut the big diesel engine and hopped out. "Dane, your mom is fit to be tied! She thought you'd be back an hour ago."

"Well"—he jerked a thumb toward the motel—"she's responsible for this fool's errand."

Kada waved to Walter and turned back. "I'll take care of the dog. Thanks again for the help. Good luck with Smoky." She backed up. "Really, thanks again, guys. Tell Mariah thanks for the bread. Happy New Year!"

He gave her space to retreat. In the blue truck's quiet intimacy, he thought he and she had something going. At least, he thought they might be friends. Under the motel's pink, neon sign and Walter's chaperoning smile, he felt like an unwanted neighbor. He shoved his hands into his pockets. Women, like horses, could be fickle. "Sure, any time."

The mother and father from the silver trailer approached her in the parking lot.

The pair looked like Midwestern adventurers, but their arms moved with the agitated frequency of peeved guests. If Kada saw them coming, he could understand why she beat a hasty retreat. *Maybe it wasn't me*. He grinned.

Unbolting the horse trailer's rear door, Walter lowered the ramp. "Where is that feisty old horse?"

He watched the trio.

The man stood back, but the woman invaded Kada's personal space.

Lumbering to her feet, the dog waddled back

toward Kada, sat, and tilted her head.

"I'll get Smoky in a minute." He crouched and rubbed at a mark on the trailer tire, but he kept his gaze on Kada.

"I thought you and Kada Ritchie had something going," Walter said. "I made myself scarce for a reason, you dense idiot."

"Hmm." Ignoring the good-natured ribbing, he scanned the horse trailer and looked for a way to help prep the space and remain nearby. Walter would probably shoo him out of the way and insist on doing the work himself. Walter loved the horses as much as he loved running the farm. He excelled at both, too, but Dane had a stake in the outcomes.

Given an excuse to ride out with his friend and skip his family's shenanigans, he would have ridden clear across the local range to catch a falling star and would have enjoyed the fool's errand. Instead, he had landed in Kada's backyard, and now he was about to miss his chance to make something of his first impression. Shaking his head, he banged a boot against a tire and knocked off the dust. "So did I."

"So, why aren't you going after her?"

Looking up, he exhaled. "I don't know what I want, and she doesn't seem that interested." The lie rolled off his tongue. He caught her curious glances, but she looked like a woman with a lot going on, and he didn't want to add to her stress.

"What are the choices?"

"Dinner." He picked up an errant piece of hay and rubbed it between his fingers. He knew a few grumpy, reclusive locals who had refused to fall for the friend next door. The thought of who had fallen summed a smile. But Kada wasn't a childhood friend, and he wasn't in denial. "If dinner doesn't work out, I'll settle for three kids and a vacation house."

He made the joke because friends expected it, but he had no idea how to make room in his life for more responsibility. Of all people, Walter knew him best, but the stubborn man hadn't settled down, either.

Laughing, Walter slapped the trailer's metal frame. "Well, unless you do something to narrow the outcomes, you're about to find yourself with holiday cookies and nothing else."

"Great."

The dog barked.

Looking up, he found the dog standing between Kada and the Midwestern couple.

The strange woman moved to pet the animal, but the dog bared her teeth.

He grinned. *Well, at least the dog has a protective streak.*

Kada gripped the dog's scruff, said something to the motel guests, and walked toward the *casitas*.

He could give her space, or he could go after her. Making up his mind, he squared his shoulders. "I'll get Smoky."

"Yes, you will," Walter said. "Idiot."

Having already dropped his weight onto the travel writer's foot, he shook his head and jogged after Kada. Her wants mattered as much as his interest, but she had a head start, and he needed to catch her. "Hold up."

She turned.

Slowing, he looked over his shoulder. "The dog doesn't like motel guests?"

"Um." She lowered her voice. "Not those in

particular."

Dismissing the couple, he fell into the step. "Why's that?"

"Their trailer isn't pumping water. They think the motel is the problem. Maybe we lost water pressure." She sighed. "After I get the dog settled, I'll check the taps."

"She needs a name," he said.

"Lucky."

In step, neither of them needed clarification.

Lucky waddled between them.

"I think you should keep her for a few days," he said.

She nodded.

"Give her time to recover."

"Sure." Her voice wavered.

He cupped her arm. "Hey, are you okay with all this?"

"Sure." She swallowed. "I'll adjust to the pressure."

He didn't think they were talking about water pressure anymore, and he recognized a person who might buckle. Running a customer-focused business could drive a person insane, but she handled the motel's whirlwinds with grace and warmth. If the hot-pink palm wreaths, candy cane pool floats, and festive lobby decorations said anything about her efforts, she excelled at the job, too. Even he could see the guests and the grounds looked festive. "I haven't had a dog in a while, but they're pretty self-sufficient. Let nature take its course."

"Yeah. Come to the Starlight Motel, leave with a puppy." She exhaled. "What will I do with all the puppies?"

If she collapsed in his arms, he wouldn't mind two bits. Instead, he toed the line between friendly neighbor and helpful peer. He would like to skip the friend zone and jump straight to dinner, but her vulnerability gave him pause. "Lucky is a good-looking dog, and I'm sure the puppies will be cute. You have enough staff with connections in town. You'll find the puppies homes."

She tilted her head. "Are you taking one?"

Lucky sat and mimicked Kada's gesture.

Faced with two inquiring females, he raised his palms and backed up. "I don't have enough spare time to raise a puppy. They need love and"—he thought hard—"puppy pads."

"That's what I thought." Shaking her head, she walked along the path. "Everyone will have an excuse. I'm about to have a pack of dogs, aren't I?"

Lucky stretched and waddled into step. Her belly swayed.

"I have a lot of staff, too." He raised his voice. Standing in the parking lot, he wanted to start with steak and a good-night kiss, but the path was about to detour, and he didn't have his bearings. "Take pictures. I'll help you circulate them around town. Call the pups late Christmas presents."

She shook her head and continued walking.

His offer felt as shallow and spontaneous as an online dating profile. *Good call. Giving someone an unexpected puppy is a terrible idea.* Loosening his collar, he hurried to catch up and cleared his throat. "Kada, I want to help."

"Find some old tennis balls. I have a feeling I'll need them."

He cleared his throat and tried again. "I meant I want to spend time with you. If I'd met you in town, I would have asked you to dinner, and I would have spent the evening listening to your stories. Doesn't that interest count?"

Stopping, she turned and brushed her hair out of her eyes. "Maybe. That's a thoughtful approach to a date."

His life lacked glitz and glamor, but he could work with *thoughtful*. He cocked his head. "Another time?"

She nodded.

Relief pushed the air from his chest, and he covered his response with a cough. "Okay. Anywhere in town, my treat."

Lucky yawned.

Frowning, Kada stared and turned back to the path. "I don't need you to pick up the tab for dinner. I need you to take a puppy home to Mariah and tie a big red bow around its neck!"

His progress toward a date eroded like a shifting dune. If he wasn't careful, he would land on his battered backside and have a prickly cactus for a dinner companion. "Fine, you pay for your meal."

His joke diminished her worries for a brief second, and he felt like he got something right.

Laughing, she opened the white gate. "Fifty-fifty."

"Deal!"

The old man slept in the rocking chair on Kada's porch.

Smoky scratched his neck against a post. Turning, he approached the gate and head-butted Dane.

He checked his teeth for suspicious plants. "Your favorite human's here."

Walter's ear-splitting whistle cut through the quiet night.

Walking out the gate, Smoky headed for the parking lot.

"Shouldn't you lead him?" Kada asked.

He scratched his head. "He seems to have the right idea."

Chris wrinkled his nose and sat. "Where's the pretty bay horse?"

"Headed home." Kada opened the *casita's* front door. "But I brought you a new friend."

Sniffing the porch, Lucky raised her head.

"I don't do dogs," Chris said.

Lucky walked past him and headed for the warmth of Kada's living room.

Dane envied the dog, but he stood outside the gate where he belonged.

Leaving open the front door, Kada settled Lucky in the *casita*.

He smiled at Chris. "Nice evening."

"You might have to wait for them, but they're worth the trouble."

Rocking back on his heels, he wondered if the man spoke of quiet evenings or strong women.

Walking out of the *casita*, Kada checked the water bucket and offered Chris her arm. "Well, if you don't do dogs, let's make sure you get dinner. You've earned it."

"What's on the menu?" Chris asked. "Hall made a mean steak."

"Is that how you lived to a ripe old age?" She closed the gate and smiled. "Steak?"

Keeping to the side, Dane watched her fall into

management mode like a pro leading a horse to water, letting it drink, and convincing the beast it was his idea all along. Admiring her skills, he hated to interrupt, but she left him behind like her new pet. "Do you mind if I grab my gear?"

She waved a hand over her head and kept walking.

"Chocolate and steak. Where could you go wrong?" Chris asked.

Laughing, she led Chris toward the main building.

Arms full of tack, Dane let himself out of the gate and navigated the path through the palms. He had worried about her in the parking lot, but seeing her in her element confirmed his interest. Who wouldn't be worried about rehoming puppies? Who wouldn't want an easy night before the holidays? Who... Looking up, he found himself standing in a weathered field of asphalt beneath a bright sign, and he questioned how he arrived there.

Two children clustered around Smoky. They stroked his sides, played with his mane, and pumped Walter for information.

"How old is he?" the taller kid asked. Two red braids swung down her back.

"What does she eat?" the shorter kid asked.

The boy looked suspiciously like a child who spent too little time outdoors. Glasses rested on his nose, and his arms looked strong enough to carry only books.

Dane wore glasses for reading, but his childhood started with toy tractors and ended with real ones. Despite the kid's arms, anyone brave enough to approach a towering horse stood a chance in life. He dropped the saddle, blanket, and bags onto a trailer rack. The temperature had dropped, and he kept his jacket over his arm.

Smoky kept his hooves clear of the ramp.

"Grass," Walter said. "Horses love grass. It's their natural food, and it's great for their digestive system."

Dane kept his mouth shut. Walter would have checked the *casita*'s grass for clover before setting Smoky loose in the enclosure. Every year, he walked the beds surrounding the horse barn, and he annihilated everything except Mariah's decorative, pre-approved planting.

"But this is the desert," the boy said.

"They like hay, too." Walter ran a hand along Smoky's back. "Hay keeps a horse full and keeps them regular."

"He means it makes them poop," the girl said.

The younger boy stuck out his tongue. "I know what he means."

Making eye contact with Walter, Dane jerked his head toward the ranch. "We should load up Smoky and get going."

Walter nodded, but he refocused on the kids. "Over at Palmer Farms, we make sure the horses have the right mix of foods. You and your family could come visit after the holidays."

The girl shook her head. "My dad has an i-tin-er-ary."

The boy widened his gaze and nodded.

Dane kept his laughter to himself.

"Okay," Walter said. "The next time you guys come through the Coachella Valley, we'll be here. Come on by and say hello to sweet Smoky."

"Neat!" The boy fist-pumped the air. "We'll do it!"

Sneaking in a last pet against Smoky's warm neck,

the girl turned back to the silver trailer.

The boy followed and hung his head.

Left with two familiar admirers, Smoky walked up the ramp and politely waited for Walter to close the door.

Easing it closed, Walter checked the locks, turned, and dusted his hands. "You ask out Kada Ritchie on a date?"

"Kinda." Shrugging into his jacket, he counted two burned-out bulbs on the motel sign. Kada probably didn't have a ladder tall enough to reach the sign, but he had a fruit picker or an extension ladder and two steady arms.

The hydraulic picker was probably overkill. For the pleasure of watching her climb the rungs, he would come by next week and hold the ladder. Once she started climbing, and he had a chance to admire the view, he would offer to change the bulbs himself.

"Kinda?" Walter asked. "When's the last time you kinda did anything?"

He exhaled. "Can you let me do this my way?"

"Only if I want to see you single for the next decade or two." Walter hitched up his jeans. "Always have been too stubborn for your own good."

He considered channeling the younger kid and sticking out his tongue. Instead, he rounded the trailer and opened the passenger seat. Invoices waited.

"Wait!" Kada said.

Turning, he spotted her weaving between cars to get from the main building to where he stood. In her hand, she held a slip of paper.

"You forgot my number."

His cheeks warmed against the wind.

Walter slapped his thigh. "I'll be…"

Taking the slip of paper, he cleared his throat. "Thanks. I figured Mom had it."

"Probably." She smiled and shrugged. "Better safe than sorry."

He grinned.

Walter clicked on the truck's flashers and walked up. "With all the commotion, I missed dinner."

The man took an hour longer than necessary to return with the trailer. If Dane were a betting man, he'd guess Walter sat to a plate of ribs and shot the breeze with his parents and anyone else who listened to his stories. "Is that so?"

"Starving," Walter said.

He narrowed his gaze. "Liar."

Walter shrugged. "I can eat."

"But Smoky?" Kada asked.

"She'll be fine." Walking toward the main building, Walter looked over his shoulder. "Are you two coming?"

Dane offered her his arm. "Do you have room?"

She smiled and took his arm. "We always have room at the Starlight Motel."

Strolling through the parking lot with her at his side, he understood why guests returned to the motel year after year. Light glowed from the windows, palms swayed in the breeze, and the Ritchie family made everyone on-site feel like guests in a well-run home.

Chapter Seven

Dane slowed his pace, but Kada relished the chance to take a deep breath and enjoy his steady rhythm. He was easy on the eyes and easy to like, but she sensed intensity beneath his smiles. Given the circumstances, she second-guessed writing down her phone number and carrying it through the parking lot like a schoolgirl with a crush, but he had mentioned a date. She wouldn't give him an excuse to back out.

Walter stopped at the front door and knocked his boots against a potted plant.

Pulling free before someone in the motel got the wrong idea about her special guests, she opened the main building's front door.

A woman screamed.

A man shouted. "What on earth do you think you're doing?"

Plates shattered.

Gaze wide, she blew past her two new friends and rushed inside the lobby.

Stephanie pranced and jabbed in front of Gustavo. She patted a wet cloth against his embroidered shirt and pulled back. Each jerky swipe left a wet spot on the white shirt, and the movements made zero impact on the large, red stain.

"Enough!" Gustavo held up his hands and warded off her attack.

Benito stood outside the cantina's kitchen. Broken plates lay at his feet.

Kada rushed toward Stephanie and Gustavo, pulled back the server, and shifted her back toward Benito. "I'm so sorry!" she said to Gustavo. "What happened?"

"Your waitress spilled a bowl of salsa all over my new shirt. My mother made this shirt." Gustavo swiped at the red stain. "My mother!"

"It's beautiful." She exhaled. Of all the things that could have happened and led to big drama, she could deal with a salsa stain on a beautiful, homemade shirt. Hopefully, Gustavo could deal with it, too. "We have a washing machine on-site. Let's get out the stain before it sets. Can you change and bring back the shirt? I'll take care of it. It'll be as good as new."

Shaking his head, Gustavo walked to the front door and stopped in front of Dane and Walter. "What are you two looking at?"

The men stepped aside.

She tried not to laugh. *I don't think menacing cowboys will make the revamped promotional materials.* Shaking her head, she checked on Stephanie and Benito. The pair walked toward the kitchen. Benito's arm kept Stephanie close to his side. The kitchen might slow down for a few minutes, but the dinner rush could linger over appetizers.

Counting guests, she found Chris sitting by the fire in deep conversation with a famed vocalist named Inés. In front of the flames, their cheerful silhouettes cast long shadows. They laughed and swapped stories like old friends. Families made plans for the next day and reviewed outings. A couple stared into each other's gazes like honeymooning lovebirds. She wouldn't disturb any of them.

Picking a table close to the patio where Dane and Walter could listen for Smoky, she pulled out a chair and gestured toward the seat. "Come on. I hear you're hungry."

Dane remained standing.

"Walter?" she asked.

He took the offered chair.

She pulled out a second chair and dipped her head toward the seat.

Shaking his head, Dane crossed his arms. "You sit."

"I'm working," she said. "I'll join you in a minute."

"When does your day end?"

She pondered the question. "When I turn off the lights?"

Shaking his head, he sat and drummed his fingers on the table. "If I were you, I would throw that ridiculous man's shirt in the washer, peek in on Lucky, check on your staff, and gulp a glass of water when nobody's looking. Walter and I might as well go back to the farm."

"If you had my job, you'd tear down the motel and plant five acres of crops."

He tried not to smile, but he failed miserably.

Randi walked up and set a bowl of hot chips in front of the men. "Well, if it is not Uncle Walter and his grumpy boss, Dane Palmer."

Kada stared. "You know these two?"

Setting down a salsa bowl, Randi toyed with a hoop earring. "More or less."

Walter stabbed a chip into the salsa bowl. "You

know, when I was a kid, I had chores. I had responsibilities. I had…"

Randi shook her head. "Save it, old man."

"I'm forty-three! You're…" He jabbed the chip toward her, paused, and ate the chip. "Spoiled. Look at those nails. How do you get anything done?"

Laughing, Randi leaned down and kissed his cheek. "Forty-three is young in Palm Springs."

Walter laughed. "I know it."

Kada had hired Randi after a quick interview, but she should have asked more pointed questions. Like, when Randi wasn't decamping to parties on North Indian Canyon Drive, was she decamping to Palmer Farms? Was she spying on the Starlight Motel? She narrowed her gaze, looked at Dane, and wondered if his flirtations had less to do with her and more to do with buying the motel. She raised her eyebrows.

Looking between Walter and Randi, he shrugged.

The man couldn't look more innocent. His family wanted to buy the motel and turn it into acres of cropland, but their intentions didn't mean he arrived on horseback to undermine her operations and look good doing it. Maybe it did. She shook off the thought. "Right, well, you three enjoy a little chat. I'll scrub salsa out of Gustavo's shirt."

"Use a toothbrush," Randi said.

"Give him the toothbrush." Dane pushed back from the table, and his chair scraped along the tiles. "Better yet, give him the toothbrush and a mop. What an…"

She held up her hand and wondered when she started accepting applications for assistant managers. Randi spoke her mind, but she also rolled silverware. So far, Dane was more eye candy than institutional asset. "That's not how we treat our guests at the Starlight Motel."

He leaned back in his chair. "That's how my mother treated me."

She tilted her head. "And look how you turned out."

He worked his jaw.

Walter laughed.

Leaving Randi with the guests, she kept her gaze on the floor and looked for spilled salsa. The last thing she needed was a guest slipping on wet tile. She caught her reflection in the window and straightened. She could handle these little hiccups. At least, she would have stories to tell her friends about her first holiday season running the Starlight Motel.

The woman from the aluminum recreational vehicle poked her head into the lobby. Her name was Sue, and her husband's name was Mack. Kada had a hard time separating the pair. Mack and Sue. Mack and Sue. Where one went, the other followed, and two rambunctious kids trailed their parents.

"Did you check the water pressure?" Sue asked. "My kids can't shower without water."

She cleared her throat and smiled. "Just a sec."

Gustavo returned, wearing a yellow T-shirt. He nodded toward Sue, thrust the stained shirt into Kada's arms, and cocked his head. "I'm getting my dog from the patio, and then I'm going to bed. I'll look for the shirt in the morning. Happy New Year."

His curt nod said everything, and she gripped the shirt. "I'll check on Lucky."

He frowned. "My dog's name is Esmeralda. She's a Xolo. My ancestors believed her line possesses healing powers, and like Chihuahuas, they guide the dead through the afterlife. She's attentive, courageous, and the perfect family dog." He sighed. "Alas, she has only me."

Tilting her head, she heard the yearning in his voice and wondered if travel writing and exotic vacations deprived him of the thing we wanted most from life—a vibrant family and unconditional love. She loosened her grip on the stained laundry. "I've always wanted a pet, but I've never felt ready for the responsibility. Tonight, I found a sweet dog who needs a home."

Cupping his elbow and his chin, he considered his words. "Rescues make the best pets."

She leaned forward. He was right. He could trash the Starlight Motel in his review, but she would remember this moment and her realization Lucky had a new home. "My dog's name is Lucky."

"Good for you." He stared.

She felt like he weighed her life in his hands. Blinking, she processed her statement and felt the ramifications of letting Lucky stay. A pet would keep her company at night while she painted, but seven pets might be a bit too much. Maybe she could start one of those cat cafes...with dogs. She struggled to imagine Lucky padding around the motel with a litter of puppies. What would the health board say?

"Well, animals are wonderful companions." Gustavo dropped his chin. Still gripping his elbow, he circled his palm to encompass the lobby. "You should have dog treats on the cantina menu. All the great boutique hotels play up their pet services."

Shaking off her thoughts, she refocused. The

Starlight Motel catered to people on their way to somewhere else or in need of space. If the motel guests wanted a boutique hotel, they should drive to Palm Springs. "I'm sorry the motel has disappointed you so far, but we're trying our best. Until recently, my grandfather ran the motel." She swallowed past the lump rising in her throat. "He died."

He shuffled his feet. "How long have you been in charge?"

"Almost a year." She forced a smile. "Pops was the best."

"I'm so sorry." He held out a hand. "Family is the most wonderful blessing."

She gripped his hand and squeezed. "It is, is it not?" Smiling, she released his hand. "Don't worry, I'll get the salsa stain out of your shirt. You can wear the garment for our holiday breakfast."

"I have a few more." He blushed. "No rush."

She laughed. "Okay." Thinking through her task list, she froze and turned back. "Can I ask a favor?"

He narrowed his gaze.

"Can I borrow some dog food? I'll replace it, I promise."

Rolling his eyes, he released an exaggerated sigh. "I guess."

Fearing she overstepped, she raised her hand. "If it's too much to ask..."

"It's nothing," he said. "I have an extra bag in my car. I'll bring it to the reception area. Take what you need."

She nodded her thanks and wondered where she heard the phrase.

"Excuse me?" Sue asked. "Water pressure?"

"Right! On it!" Walking past the pair, she left the main building, turned the corner, and opened the door to the room reserved for laundry, extra supplies, and tool storage. A deep enamel sink, a metal chair, and concrete floors attested to the building's age, but the facilities held up.

A commercial washer and drier let her do laundry, but the cleaning crew also used the relatively modern appliances to clean rags and mops heads without waking guests or setting off local seismographs.

In the morning, the ladies from the Palm Springs Cleaning Company would descend on the motel and replace linens, vacuum floors, and replenish toiletries. The soiled linens went to a local service that provided fresh sheets, pressed napkins, and starched uniforms. She wondered how the motel would operate without the infrastructure. Pops had certainly never washed twenty sets of sheets and hung them out to dry.

Spraying Gustavo's embroidered shirt with a light, homemade detergent, she opened the washer's lid and started a delicate cycle. The machine bumped and rattled, but the tub remained dry. Bracing her hands on the cold, white metal, she exhaled. *Maybe the drain line's blocked. Maybe Sue's right, and we're going dry.*

Checking the drain line and the filter for blockages, she found them clear and wondered what else could be wrong with the machine. If it had a faulty internal component, such as the motor or the control board, she would need a professional with a multimeter and a wealth of experience. Gustavo would downgrade the motel to one star. She might as well burn his shirt.

Shaking off her spiraling thoughts, she replayed Mac and Sue's complaints. They struggled with water pressure, and the washing machine wouldn't fill with water. If she had a site problem, she could call the water company. If she had a blocked line, she could check the hoses. Gripping both sides of the machine, she pulled it forward.

The door opened, but she had better things to do than shoo off a curious guest.

"You want some help?" Dane asked.

"Not really." Relaxed enough to leave the farmer with a view of her backside, she grunted and levied her weight. "I can't always rely on handsome strangers showing up to help me."

"I don't know why you insist on doing everything yourself."

"Because"—she inhaled and shifted her stance—"I'm in charge around here."

The washing machine slid forward on the smooth concrete.

Exhaling, she released her grip and hung her head. "Before I took over this motel, my biggest problems were hormonal teenagers and sidewalk hecklers."

"I can stand in the doorway and run commentary," he said.

She smiled. From his viewpoint, he had a good sightline on two industrial machines, a shelf full of cleaning products, and her backside. She could imagine his commentary, but she doubted she could fix the washing machine and listen at the same time. "Good to know."

Turning the machine, she checked the water hoses. Pops had mentioned the hoses sometimes kinked from frequent use or accumulated blockages. All she had to do was to check the lines and to reposition them for free-flowing water. "Right."

She ran her hands along the lines, made a tight fist, and wanted to scream when she found them smooth and free of bulges. Instead, she counted to ten. "The lines feel fine. What on earth is wrong with this machine?"

"Beats me," he said.

"Well, aren't you helpful?"

"I grow food."

Turning, she opened her mouth to sass him, but he came to find her in the workroom, and his presence counted for something. "Thanks for checking on me."

He rubbed his jaw. "I should have come sooner."

The heat in his voice captivated her, but her livelihood and inheritance demanded her attention. Facing the machine, she pulled open drawers, peered into compartments, and hoped the manufacturer included a friendly QR code for remote diagnosis. No such luck. Wiping the back of a hand across her forehead, she popped open the side panel.

Wires and control boards leered.

"Great. I need an electrical engineering degree to fix this heap."

"Maybe there's a reset button," he said. "Where's the manual?"

"The what?" She popped up and hit her head on a low-lying shelf. Rubbing away the pain, she reached for a basket stacked with manuals from every appliance on the property. "If Pops saved the booklet, it's probably in this basket."

Dane pulled out a pair of glasses from his jacket pocket and slid them on his nose.

She stared. He wore boots, jeans, and a leather coat, but the glasses caught her by surprise. They brightened his sun-kissed hair, shadowed his golden eyes, and balanced his square jaw. When he rode down the hill on a majestic bay horse, she thought him handsome, but the glasses undid her. "You wear glasses."

"Farsighted." He thumbed through a white, paper manual. "It's a pain."

"It's hot."

He looked up and furrowed his brow.

She fanned herself. "Sorry, the room's so small."

"You want me to go back to the cantina and give you some space?"

"No!" She cleared her throat. She needed a lot of things from the man, but she doubted space should be at the top of the list. If he lived a hundred miles farther from the motel, then she would be a hundred percent happier about his interest. Watching him plow under the motel for a field of dates was the last thing she would do. "I mean, I appreciate the help, but let's keep things simple. Does the manual say anything about a reset button?"

He checked the index.

She rubbed her brow. Of all the nights to meet Dane Palmer, he had to arrive two days before her grant deadline when everything she managed felt ready to implode. His apathy toward Christmas bothered her, but his helpful, solicitous presence unnerved her. Half the time, she relied on instincts and training to complete her murals. The other half of the time, she studied photographs and searched for inconsistencies. She had a hunch Dane could see them, too, and she needed to hold on to the magic that fueled her.

"No mention of reset switches." He flipped through

the manual. "Try unplugging it. Most new washing machines come with a reset feature to restart the machine after it experiences an error code or a fault. This behemoth might be a few years short of that feature, but unplugging it and plugging it back in could serve the same function."

She chewed her lip. He looked so handsome in his glasses and leather jacket that she had a hard time focusing on her problems. *I don't have time for this kind of indulgence.* She shook her head. "That trick only works with computers."

He laughed and tossed the manual back in the basket. "You won't know unless you try."

Tilting her head, she examined the machine's circuitry. She could unplug the washer, call a repair technician, or tell Gustavo to eat his shirt. Despite the travel writer's quirks, she respected his trade and his pet ownership. Plus, if she refused to unplug the washer, and the technician did it for her, she might never hear the end of the story from Dane. "Fine."

"Good call."

Shaking her head, she reached behind the machine, gripped the plug, and tugged. Closing her eyes, she plugged the prongs back into the outlet and exhaled.

The motor spun, and the dial lit.

Releasing the power cord, she pressed the wash button and waited.

The machine filled with water.

"Wouldn't you know?" So pleased she could cry, she dropped Gustavo's shirt into the drum, closed the lid, turned, and grinned.

Dane stared.

The intensity of his wide-eyed gaze made her

mouth go dry. She backed into the cold, vibrating machine. On second thought, he looked handsome without the glasses. If the room felt smaller, she blamed his shoulders. They blocked far too much light for easy breathing. "We should go back to the cantina."

Gripping her hips, he raised her atop the washing machine lid. "Are you sure about that?"

The cold, metal machine contrasted with the heat radiating from his large, warm hands. She was sure she could push him away, but instead of pointing out the indignity of being lifted off her feet, she swallowed. "I can't think of anything else I have to do out here."

"You don't *have* to do anything." He dragged his hands down her thighs and jerked his head toward the main building. "You have your hands full. Take a break."

She gripped his bicep and steadied herself. The muscles felt as solid as she imagined, but they flexed beneath her touch. "I can't take a break. This place depends on me."

He smiled. "I know the feeling."

Her skin warmed from the heat of his palms. "I can't afford to sit around the laundry room and gossip with the guests."

"Trust me, Kada, I'm not here to gossip."

"You're ready to pitch in on odd jobs? You're being a good neighbor." She swallowed past the dryness in her throat. She had a three-date rule, but if she never started the first date, did the rule apply? "Thanks for helping with Lucky."

"Any time." He tipped up her chin. "Are you sure that's where you want to stop? You brought me your number and rode out into the desert with me, but now you're skittish?"

Her throat felt parched, but she wanted to lean forward and test his intent. Instead, she kicked her feet against the machine's vibrating drum. "I'm not skittish, but I'm not into quick romps on a washing machine."

He raised his eyebrows. "I wasn't suggesting a quick romp."

She wanted to test the innuendo behind his offer, but the sequence felt out of order. Before she considered kissing the handsome farmer, she needed dinner, candlelight, and time to breathe.

Her body offered a different opinion. Clearing her throat, she hopped off the washing machine, ducked under his arm, and ran her tongue along her teeth. In the tiny room, his skin smelled like fresh lime, warm spices, and a hint of honey, but his shirt held the leathery undertones from a hard day's work. He looked handsome, and she wanted to taste his kiss, but she needed a different setup. "Or long romps."

Nodding, he stepped back and gave her space.

She stretched wide her arms. "Plus, I smell like dirty horses, dusty dogs, and stale laundry."

He narrowed his gaze and rubbed his lip. "That's not necessarily a bad thing. You put in a hard day's work."

"Imagine the online reviews."

He dropped his hand. "Travel blogs were the last thing on my mind. How about you let me kiss you and I write a glowing review of your equine facilities?"

"I think paid reviews are illegal."

He chewed his bottom lip. "I'll take the risk."

"Noted." Suppressing a smile, she turned and rooted through a closet for a drying rack. Setting aside the metal frame, she then climbed a stepladder to retrieve an iron. In the morning, she would have a steady head to greet her parents, time to implement her exit strategy, and a better handle on her attraction to Dane. If she walked out on him, she doubted she would get a wink of sleep, but at least she would know where she stood.

Chapter Eight

Scratching an itch behind his ear, Dane watched Kada reach for cleaning supplies and avoided looking at the box of toiletries higher on the shelf. The label inventoried safety razors, feminine hygiene products, and condoms. To be sure, his view of her ass held his interest, but her response threw up a no-go signal so pronounced that even a dunce like him knew to back off. Yet, here he stood, admiring a pretty woman, eying a box of condoms on the top shelf, and wanting more than a flirtatious smile.

Piecing together what he knew about her life, he searched for another angle to hold her interest. She came to the valley to check on Hall and stayed past his funeral, but running the motel didn't match her training. The half-finished *casita* murals seemed like an ode to desert life, but he suspected she was capable of more creativity. "Did you design the murals you're painting?"

"Yep."

Her single-word affirmative stalled his progress faster than a dry well. He cleared his throat. "Why did you pick plants? Most people would have gone with the sunset."

She handed him the iron. "A solid choice."

"But not yours." He set the heavy, metal tool on the floor and leaned against the wall. "Why?"

"Pouring my free time into the murals gives me an outlet. When the guests act bonkers, the staff goes on the fritz, or the facilities need professional intervention"—she glanced at the washing machine—"I can take a deep breath and think about the plants. I can think about what I'll paint next and how I'll approach the design."

"Have you heard of crossword puzzles?"

She laughed and moved items on the shelf. "Plus, most visitors don't get to see the plants bloom. Pops showed me the hidden pockets of vegetation. He had a sixth sense for when they would reveal their glory."

"Probably hard-earned experience." He peeled his gaze off her backside and looked at his boots. "People who live their life in nature learn to appreciate it."

"That's the problem," she said. "Not everyone has that luxury. Did you order dinner?"

He looked up and wondered why she was so taciturn about her art. "A salad."

She shifted her weight and looked over her shoulder. "You ordered a salad?"

"With meat and cheese. The lettuce is more like a garnish. Maybe cilantro." He rubbed his stomach. "Also, *elote* garlic bread."

She climbed down the ladder. "Is that on the menu? Do we make *elote* garlic bread?"

"You do now." He loved the charred, mayo-slathered corn too much to reserve it for grill night. Benito mentioned ancho chili powder and seared corn as if he could make the dish in his sleep. Dane felt his stomach rumble. A second later, he remembered how much he wanted to share the meal with Kada. "Benito brought me a taste, and I decided to propose."

"To Benito? Maybe he'll give you the recipe." She grinned and set the iron on top of the washing machine. "Don't count out Stephanie. She can get fierce over splitting tips. Imagine what she would do if you moved on her man."

"Funny." He wanted to pull Kada close. Instead, he checked a row of keys hanging on a piece of pegboard. Hall's precise handwriting marked the color-coded labels. The blue ink, faded with time, looked like the speckled aluminum cups he used while camping. Had Kada ever been camping?

First, he wanted a dinner date, and now, he wanted the intimacy of a shared campfire. He shook off the thought and focused on her needs. *Keeping track of her Palm Springs crew must keep life interesting. She's as invested in the motel as I am in the farm. She might not know it yet, but she doesn't want to leave this place. I want to give her a reason to stay.*

She unfolded the drying rack. "Well, the *elote* garlic bread might break your keto salad, but it's probably ready now. We can head back."

He reached for the door handle.

"Unless you want to stay a minute."

Her voice dropped to a slow, hesitant whisper, and he replayed the comment ten times before he turned.

She cleared her throat. "Unless you changed your mind. I know what I'm getting into."

"Getting into?" Women usually came to him. This time, he stepped forward. "You sound like you're going into battle."

She rubbed together her fingers.

If she couldn't tell whether she had silk or snakeskin within her grasp, then he would give her silk.

113

Frankly, he would give her anything she wanted for a simple kiss. Afraid of scaring her, he stopped within arm's reach, but she had room to bolt. He hoped she had other intentions.

"You ride into town like an old west cowboy."

He stepped closer. "Kada, I rode into a motel courtyard on a horse."

"And you're handsome, and handy, and attentive"—she frowned—"and the glasses."

"Do you want me to put them back on?" He kept his hands pinned to his sides.

She wet her lips. "No, but I've seen plenty of cowboys in Wyoming. I didn't have to move here for a glimpse of what I've seen and let go."

"Just a cowboy, huh?" He cupped her elbow and pulled her closer.

"And your family keeps trying to buy the motel."

He tilted his head. Her lips looked sweeter than anything he'd seen on-site. "Ambitious fools."

"Don't you run that farm?"

He smiled and wet his lips. "I run a lot of things, but the stress keeps me up late at night. Sometimes, I see you moving around the motel like a ghost, and I can't quite get a grip on what you're doing down here at all hours of the night."

"Painting. When you're wide awake up there," she whispered, "at all hours of the night."

"Exactly." Pulling her close, he lowered his head, brushed his lips across hers, and waited for a hint of enthusiasm before he truly kissed her. She thought him handsome, but did she want more than laughter? He hoped he knew the answer.

Sharing the same breath, she tasted like sweet

nectar and hard-earned sweat. He swore he would never forget the taste, but he gave her space to flee.

She closed the distance, draped her hands over his shoulders, and shifted her weight.

Her confidence kindled his senses. Forgetting the drab storeroom and the impatient dinner crowd, he smiled against her lips. "The next time I'm awake, I'll remember this kiss."

"Well, let's make sure you have something to remember."

He deepened the kiss and forgot about the tangle of weather, water, and weevils threatening his crops. A moment later, he forgot his name. The feisty, capable woman in his arms kissed away his worries, and she was certainly kissing him back.

Then she stopped.

He struggled to form a coherent thought.

"Wait!" She pushed against his chest. "I can't do this. I have a motel to run."

He could do this all night. Instead, he cleared his throat. "I'll rent a room."

"No vacancy."

"Liar." He held her gaze and challenged her to accept his proposition.

She blushed. "Where would you put Smoky?"

Responsibility nagged at his consciousness. He wanted to squash it like a bug, but he and Kada had one thing in common; they knew how to get a job done. Also, they knew how to kiss. Good grief, the woman had passion. If it flowed from her artistic training, then he would open a gallery and worship her work.

"Dane, I can't…"

Hearing her hesitation, he reconsidered the merits

of subtlety and respect. "Let Walter take her home. Tell Mariah your water pump failed, and I need to fix it."

"Is that a euphemism?"

He smiled and pulled back. "Maybe."

She slapped his chest.

He caught her hand and held it flush over his beating heart. His balance felt off-kilter, and indulging his need for her might be the only way to regain his equilibrium. "Kada, don't hide behind the motel. Admit you want to spend time with me. Naked. In a bed."

Leaning close, she pressed a kiss beneath his ear. "I want to spend time with you."

He could feel the warmth of her breath against his neck. Instinctively, he tightened his grip.

She shifted her head.

Without missing a beat, he claimed her lips, and let the kiss unfold in slow motion. No longer content with the soft prize of her lips, he sank into her warmth and unleashed the hungry, lingering kiss he wanted. She met him, and his head swam. Someone tapped on the door, but he moaned and obscured the noise. They could find a bar of soap themselves. The woman in his arms was the only person who deserved his attention. As he deepened the kiss, he cupped her butt in both hands.

She leaned in, gave a little hop, and wrapped her legs around his waist.

"Closer," he whispered against her lips.

Winding both arms around his neck, she complied.

Clasped close, he hardly noticed her weight. He needed to feel her body, but a man could only do so much standing in the middle of a laundry room. Telling himself he did it to keep her safe, he hitched her against him. The moment he felt her heat press against him, he nearly dropped her flat on her ass and took her on the concrete floor. Backing up two steps, he leaned against the washing machine and pulled away from the kiss. "Tell me to stop." His voice came out ragged. "We can stop."

She tugged the hair teasing his shirt collar. "I don't want you to stop."

He grinned. She didn't sound very put together herself. Turning, he settled her on top of the machine, braced his arms on either side, and dropped his head to her chest. She had a beautiful ass, but he wanted to spend the evening savoring her breasts. He looked up. "How many appliances do you have on the property? I can fix all of them."

"Is that so?" Leaning forward, she pushed him back, unbuttoned his shirt, splayed her fingers on his chest, and ran her thumb's edge between his pecs and toward his waistband. "Let's see what you can do with this machine."

Her exploration stopped short of giving him what he wanted, but watching her investigate his body was almost as much fun as kissing her. If she wanted to use all her senses, he would find the patience to indulge her.

A car raced down the highway. Its meaty, throaty rumble echoed in the valley.

He doubted they had all night to play games. "Or we could drop the pretenses."

Looking up, she faltered and dropped her hands.

The sweet hint of vulnerability unnerved him. He grabbed her hips. "Ignore me. I'll fix everything."

She smiled. "I tried to ignore you, but I don't need you to fix me."

Before he said anything else stupid, he slipped his hands under her pretty shirt, massaged her back, and kissed her. Every inch of her skin felt like an erotic prize. Unsnapping her bra, he lifted her shirt over her head, pulled off the bra, and set the clothes beside her. "Working for you?" He rolled a beautiful, peaked nipple between his fingers. "Feel good?"

She leaned close and pressed a kiss to his shoulder. "Should I turn on the spin cycle?"

"Maybe? This isn't my normal venue."

Laughing, she scooted to the edge of the machine and reached toward him. "Good."

He shrugged out of his shirt and tossed it on the floor. She pressed her beautiful, naked beasts against his overheated skin and kissed him like a woman who found messing around in a laundry room perfectly exciting. He straight-up moaned. If she wanted to get her kicks living on the edge, then he would help her fall.

She pulled back and chewed her bottom lip. "You're wearing too many clothes."

He slowly kicked off his boots, unbuckled his belt, slid down the zipper of his jeans, and pushed the denim to the floor. Left wearing his underwear, he crossed his arms, raised an eyebrow, and nodded toward her attire. "So are you."

Lifting her hips, she slid off her jeans, scrambled to her knees, and matched his stance.

A man didn't need an engraved invitation. He hooked a forefinger in her panties, pulled them from her hips, raised his head, and waited for her kiss. Balanced on the machine, she had the advantage of height, and her hair flowed over her shoulders in a silken wave.

She dropped her head and kissed him.

He let himself go wild. His hands went everywhere he could reach, touching her skin, as his mouth tasted her lips. The combination of her soft skin, clever lips, and growing heat stoked his desire. He wondered if he would explode before they even got close to having sex. "Kada…"

She slipped a hand beneath his briefs and stroked his erection.

"That, um"—he cleared his throat—"touch will get you in trouble."

"I only have time for trouble." She gripped him harder and made eye contact.

He closed his eyes and struggled to form words. Giving up subtleties, he took a deep breath and enjoyed every minute of her touch. If life wanted to test his resolve with a beautiful woman, he would weather the storm. The moment she released him, he stepped back.

"Dane?" She frowned.

Two could play this game. Pulling her hips forward, he spread her legs and dropped his mouth to her heat. She tasted better than anything his fields could produce. As he licked and sucked, he felt her hands gripping his shoulders. Her quick breaths urged him to continue. He might just try the spin cycle…

Gripping his hair, she pulled him back.

He looked at her glistening folds like a kid yanked from a candy store.

"You planning to tease me all night?"

Looking up, he met her gaze and savored her warm, easy smile. She could play it cool, but a flush stained her cheeks, she held her lips slightly open, and the pulse he felt in her thigh beat much faster than a woman tolerating his attention. "Maybe."

She narrowed her gaze.

"Maybe not." He would bend her over the washing machine and make love until the entire valley heard her release, but he retained some restraint. Barely. Turning, he found the box of condoms he saw stashed in the supply closet and tossed them next to her.

"Ambitious."

He laughed and hoped the latex wasn't so expired it cracked in his hands. Tearing open a packet, he then sheathed himself, pulled her off the washing machine, and dropped his ass into the cold, metal chair sitting by the laundry sink. The slap stung, but not as much as losing his momentum would. "You're my only ambition."

She cocked a hip. "Is that so?"

Crooking a finger, he beckoned her.

She eased toward him.

Watching her move, he said a quick prayer that she could accommodate his girth in such rough conditions. He had nothing else to offer, and she was as skittish as woman torn between two desires. If he pulled off this feat, then she would only think of him.

She straddled him, wrapped her arms around his neck, and inched forward.

The wet smack of skin beckoned, but he had to do more than claim her. He nudged the head of his cock in first.

She perched over him, her muscles shaking as her heartbeat pulsed along her neck.

Leaning forward, he kissed the soft skin. "Second thoughts?" His harsh tone betrayed his straining control.

"No." Adjusting her seat, she made eye contact and sank down on his girth without breaking the connection.

He inhaled and watched her expressions. Every inch of acceptance claimed his loyalty, and every soft, amazed sigh left an imprint on his body. Seating himself deep in her heat, he groaned and gripped her waist. "Oh yeah, Kada. Damn, you feel good."

Arching sharply, her hair spilling down her back, she rode his thrusts.

Skimming his palms up her back, he crushed her down, pinned her hips before he blew his load, and kissed her wildly. Holding her close, he rocked her forward as their bodies slid in sync, and his muscles tensed. Gasping for breath and endurance, he loosened his hold and drew a deep, ragged breath.

She shimmied up the girth of his cock with slow undulations of her hips. Making eye contact, she slammed back down and bit her bottom lip.

"Damn me." Holding tight to her ass, he pumped up and down faster. Her heat and wetness eased his concerns, and he pistoned into her as shouts shredded his throat. "Kada…" Her groans urged him toward satisfaction, but opening his eyes, he found her back bowed and her hand spread flat against his chest. Worrying he'd taken too many liberties, he stilled her hips and buried his face in her neck. "Tell me what feels good, Kada. Tell me how fast. Tell me how slow." The effort about killed him, but he wanted more than a fair ride. Whether she stayed in the valley or returned to LA, this moment mattered, and he doubted he would ever forget her honeyed taste.

"This feels good." She guided him inside her and

rocked forward. "Make it feel better."

He didn't need to be told twice. Gripping her hips, he pulled her against him, set a heady rhythm, and lost himself in her heat, her sweat-slicked breasts, and the wild tangle of hair curtaining her moans. Her hands braced against his shoulders, and she let him set the pace.

Frantic to find his release, he felt it building, but he didn't want the encounter to end. How often did Kada let herself go like this? Her moans, and the slick slap of skin, were a moment in time. He envied her ability to capture memories and recreate them on paper. Given a thousand years, he could try to describe this moment, and nothing he could say would describe the feel of being with her.

"Now." She gasped and raised her head. "Don't stop now."

"I know." His mouth covered hers, and she shuddered in his arms. They could have been in a five-star hotel or a king-sized bed. His release had nothing to do with location and everything to do with her, but he couldn't hold back any longer. He groaned at the same time she tore away from his lips and bit his shoulder.

Pulling her arms to her chest, she dropped her head where her teeth left a mark and leaned against him.

Maybe he would get the love bite tattooed. He smiled. His body had no bones, but he held it together while his breath came in measured exhalations and his muscles knitted themselves back together. Had he lost his mind making love to a woman in a laundry room? Dropping back his head, he stared at the ceiling tiles and grinned. He would gladly lose it again in her arms.

She braced a hand against his shoulder, stood, and slipped off him.

Seeing her turn, he caught her hand and tugged. "Kada?"

She paused and looked over her shoulder.

"This isn't my normal thing."

"Oh yeah?"

Nearly sprawled in a metal chair, spent, and smelling worse for wear, he didn't have a lot to recommend him, but she had ponied up for the ride. He released her hand and smiled. "Thanks for being extraordinary."

"You're…"

"Ridiculous?" His ego could stand a few letdowns. "An asshole?"

She smiled. "Cute."

He lunged forward and tugged her back onto his lap. She landed with a soft, satisfying smack. He pressed a kiss to her shoulder. "I can work with cute. Give me ten minutes."

"Absolutely not." She danced out of his arms and gathered her clothes. "I was about ready to skip town and do great things, but you showed up looking like a muscled muse. Where have you been for the last several months?"

He ran a hand through his hair, stood, and put himself back together. Two could play at this game. "Where have you been?"

"Managing laundry services, paying taxes, and settling staff disputes!" She planted her hands on her hips. "I run a business!"

He laughed, but he had a feeling the conversation would have been a lot easier if he could forget what she felt like when she came apart in his arms. He kept his hands pinned to his sides to avoid reaching toward her. She probably wanted to scratch an itch. "Trust me, I know the feeling."

The washing machine lurched across the floor and started a spin cycle.

A car horn honked.

Laughter floated on the wind.

She looked out the window and frowned. "Who else laughs like Mom?"

A stolen moment of pleasure held the world at bay, but reality rushed in. He ran a hand through his hair. "More guests? I should probably go."

"The reservation system said all guests had checked in." She turned an ear toward the laughter and shook her head. "Dad's too predictable. Maybe someone drove by and needed a place to stay."

"Right after the holidays? Also, I did a number on your hair." The next time he stole a kiss, he would have a multipart plan and a better setup. Doing his best to pat down her hair, he realized his efforts were making things worse and hoped the new guests spent more time admiring the décor than her hair.

She batted away his hands. "I run a motor motel."

He shoved them in his pockets. "This is not the 1950s. People have cell phones and GPS systems."

"You're right. They should have called." Scooting past him, she shoved the condoms back into the box and tossed it into the toiletry bin. "Geez I hope I'm wrong."

"Wrong? You don't like guests?" he asked.

She spun away from the window and blinked. "Of course, I like guests. They need a place to lay their heads, and I need to make a profit. During the holidays, nobody's a stranger."

Fixing his shirt, he cleared his throat. "Right. And the innkeeper never sleeps."

She stilled his hand.

He doubted he was about to get another kiss.

"Love, goodwill, and brotherhood are the true meaning of the holidays. Without them, we're all lost. And if you ever want to see me naked again, you'll stop dumping on the holidays."

He barked out a laugh. "Not even a little..."

She zipped her lips. "I know you don't like the holidays, but give the season another chance. Humans aren't meant to weather darkness alone. We paint. We sing songs. We..."

"Erect things." He raised an eyebrow.

She glared. "Don't fall back on sex to avoid intimacy."

Pissing off a beautiful woman was the last thing he wanted to do. He nabbed her hand. "I face life head-on. You can't run this place without recognizing the mechanics behind the curtains. You want intimacy? Let me take you out for a real date."

She opened her mouth and stared.

"In the meantime, I'm holding my ground. The holidays are nothing but commercial ruses to shake people out of their winter doldrums, empty their wallets, and round up every family's black sheep."

She gathered her hair into a messy bun and shoved a branded pencil through the tresses. "Is that how they captured you?"

He rolled his eyes. "I mean, look, I still think people behave badly during most of the year, but they try to behave for Christmas. They're good people. I get it. But your motel guests?"

"Are lovely." She crossed her arms and raised her chin.

He jerked his head toward the brightly lit buildings. "They bring you all their complaints. The food's too bland, the laundry doesn't work, and the family squatting in the parking lot wants to delouse their traveling caravan."

"Wait, Mack and Sue's kids have lice?" She widened her gaze.

"I was speaking metaphorically!" He rubbed a hand over his face. "The kids look fine. Not a scratching finger in sight."

"Whew." She shivered. "It happens, but at this stage in the game, I don't need that level of deep cleaning."

"I know. You need fewer problems, not more of them." Looking past her shoulder, he focused on the bare bulbs surrounding the pink neon sign. If every driver for twenty miles could see the signs, why couldn't he? He turned. "Can we go back to the kissing and the fondling?"

"Hilarious!" She ran a hand over her face. "Just"—she exhaled—"ha."

"Ha?" He mimicked her empty, breathy exhalation, but the gesture sounded as empty as the metal chair scraping along the concrete floor. Tonight wasn't the night to get to know Kada Ritchie. Sure, he whetted his thirst with her stellar kiss, but if he hung around too long, he would turn into a nuisance...or an unwanted guest. Shaking off the possibilities, he looked away from the window and inclined his head toward the beautiful, competent woman who had a job to do. "You'd better go and attend to your guests."

"Yeah," she said. "The motel won't run itself."

He stole a quick kiss, turned her, and tapped her butt into gear. "Scat so I can go home and tell my mother how much I love the smell of stewed cabbage."

Laughing and letting her hips swing, she sauntered out the door.

The washer rattled.

Scooting it back into position, he glared at it and closed the storeroom door. Sleep would evade him for weeks while he thought of Kada, and he had nobody to blame but himself. Delivering a date cake was one thing. If Smoky hadn't gone lame…

"Mom! You weren't due until tomorrow!"

Kada's cry of delight bounced off the *casita* walls. Looking up from the desert pavers, he watched her launch herself into an older woman's arms. The pair grinned, and their smiles shone brighter than the swaying patio lights. Staying back, he leaned against an adobe wall and watched Kada and Mrs. Ritchie greet each other. The pair did the hug-shake mother-daughter thing he never understood. In twenty years, Kada would be just as beautiful as her mother. She soaked up her mother's presence like a drought-stricken plant. He envied their connection. His mother gripped him hard, examined him, and spun him back into the world to do good work.

"Just look at you, runnin' around the desert like Pops." Ms. Ritchie gripped Kada's long, black hair and rubbed it between her fingers. "If I hadn't seen you for myself, I wouldn't have believed it. I thought you would stay in Los Angeles, but here you are, the queen of the desert!"

He cocked his head and imagined Kada tearing into a sourdough loaf over drip coffee. She would look at home on the winding streets wearing a wrap-tie dress, but he preferred her stained jeans.

"I thought I would stay in Los Angeles, too, but you needed me." Reaching to the side, Kada shifted into her father's arms.

Lean by most standards, he sported the small belly that developed from a desk-bound lifestyle.

"Hi, Daddy."

He kissed her forehead. "Princess. Good to see you."

Easing off the wall, Dane figured he could slip back into the cantina, take his salad to go, and sink into one of Walter's tales. The old cowboy had plenty of stories about what went wrong when a man took his gaze off the land.

"Mom, meet my friend, Dane Palmer," Kada said.

He looked up and blinked away his surprise. Unless his father had ambled down the hill and presented himself on cue, he was the only Dane Palmer within a quarter mile of the Starlight Motel. *Her friend, huh? What other rights do I have?* Straightening his shoulders, he forced a smile, walked forward, and extended a hand toward Kada's parents. "Pleasure to meet you. Dane Palmer."

Mr. Ritchie took his hand. "Are you a guest?"

Swatting her husband's chest, Mrs. Ritchie shook her head. "No, Bobby, that's Mariah's oldest boy."

Dane nodded. "I live next door. My family runs Palmer Farms." Business taglines bubbled to his lips, but he suppressed the urge. "Mom seems to have adopted Kada. She sent me down here with a belated Christmas present"—he smiled—"and a few Medjool dates."

"Bobby Ritchie," he said. "Pleasure to meet you."

"Larissa." Kada's mother nudged her husband out of the way and gripped Dane's hand with both of her hands. "How sweet of you to stick around."

He met Kada's gaze and worked his jaw. He had no idea how much information she wanted to share. As far as Larissa and Bobby Ritchie were concerned, life at the Starlight Motel was going swimmingly. As long as nobody mentioned Smoky drinking from the pool, Lucky's impending delivery, or the bevy of guests with issues only Kada could resolve, life at the motel looked perfect. Understanding a person's desire to impress their parents, he grinned. "I do what I can."

"Oh, Dane's being modest. He"—Kada covered a yawn—"what *are* you still doing here?"

If she wanted to give him an out, she couldn't look cuter. He laughed at how wildly their interactions swung. He could act like a friendly neighbor, but he wanted her to remember their kiss. "I'm picking up my dinner and heading home with Walter." He glanced at her lips. "Kiss me good-bye?"

She blushed.

If a few knowing looks from Mom kept him in Kada's mind, then he would take the risk. Instead of forcing her hand, he dropped his head, skimmed his rough cheek along her jawline, and pressed a sweet kiss to her cheek. "I'll call you."

She gripped his shirt and released it within a heartbeat.

He wondered if he imagined the impulse.

"Not so fast," Bobby said.

He turned and raised an eyebrow.

"We haven't eaten yet, either. Why don't you join us?" Bobby gestured toward the main building. "I'd love to hear about life in the Coachella Valley. After Hall's funeral, I wanted to stay, but Larissa couldn't wait to get away."

"When have you liked the desert?" Larissa asked.

Bobby scrunched his nose. "It has its charms."

"Apparently, it does." Larissa glanced at Dane, elbowed her husband, and linked arms with Kada. "Let's find a table."

Left standing next to Bobby, he cocked his head and watched the pair depart. They had the same gait and skirted lush shrubs like they knew every rock and planter by heart. He wondered whether the palm trees overheard the details of his laundry room tryst.

"You dating my daughter?" Bobby asked.

"Not technically." He cleared his throat. "I met her earlier this evening."

"Yeah. I met Larissa at a gas station, and we eloped the next day."

Bobby's comment landed like a gut punch. He pivoted and held up his hand. "Whoa, not so fast."

Bobby laughed and slapped his shoulder. "Don't worry, Kada has more sense than her mother. Also, I'm much more handsome. Larissa said I looked like Sylvester Stallone, but that was decades ago. My students barely know the name. Larissa promises I'm quite the silver fox." He winked. "And I don't think she's talking about an endangered species."

"Wait, they say that to your face?"

"God, no!" Bobby rolled his eyes. "You have to

read the class reviews to know if you're staying relevant. If hip shoes help the kids feel more confident in my classroom, I'm fine with geezer chic." He jerked his head toward the cantina. "You want to stand here all night?"

He walked a step behind Bobby and picked out the strong features Kada inherited from her father. She had his nose. A strong widow's peak shaped both their foreheads, but Kada's long, dark hair came straight from Larissa and Hall's lineage. "Did Kada know you were arriving tonight?"

"Oh, no way. We thought we would surprise her. Ever since Los Angeles, she's been tight-lipped and reclusive. 'Everything's fine. The motel's fine. I'm fine.' " He looked over his shoulder and pantomimed Kada's bright smile. "She inherits her stubbornness from her mother."

Larissa stopped in her tracks. "We can hear you!"

Bobby walked straight into her, shook off the collision, and kissed her cheek. "Yes, *mi amor*."

Larissa gently pushed him away. "How is your Spanish accent still so terrible?"

Laughing, Bobby linked hands with his wife. "I'm open to more lessons."

She smiled. "You're impossible."

Dane glanced at Kada. She watched her parents with the indulgent smile that children reserved for well-behaved parents. Her ease might fool him, but Bobby's offhand comment made him wonder what happened in Los Angeles. Without an explanation for her tight-lipped restraint, he was liable to ruin his future dinner plans by putting his foot in his mouth or saying the wrong thing at the wrong time. She wouldn't let his mistakes slide, either. She faced conflict head-on, and her fearlessness fascinated him.

She caught him staring and raised her eyebrows.

Before he claimed her time, he needed intelligence. Smoky had food and water in the trailer, and he was old enough to have a bit of patience. Before he left the motel, he would do his best to find out what happened in Los Angeles and left Kada so tight-lipped about her art. "Dinner sounds good. I seem to have worked up an appetite."

She blushed.

Walking past Bobby and Larissa, he dropped his head. "Admittedly, you did most of the work, but your secret's safe with me."

She touched her cheek where he kissed her. "Is it?"

Dropping every pretense, he nodded. "Yes."

Chapter Nine

The deep, rumbling intensity of Dane's affirmation sent heat straight to Kada's core. She thought washing Gustavo's shirt might earn goodwill, but the pleasure reaped from her encounter with Dane more than made up for the gallons of wash water. She could trust Dane and the way he made her feel, but she needed more time to process his unexpected arrival. "I should check on Lucky."

"Who's this lucky?" Dad asked. "Do I need to scare off someone else?"

Mom swatted his arm. "Come on, you old fool. You need food, and I haven't been here since Pops died. Let me soak up my childhood."

"And sangria," Dad said.

Tugging him into motion, Mom blazed a trail toward the main building.

Dane hung back. "I can come with you." He rubbed the back of his neck. "I can stay, or I can head home. Your call."

"No, stay." She appreciated his moment of indecision and hoped he had more going on upstairs than rugged masculinity and high-yield crop plans. *Where did that come from?* If he weren't such a handsome package, his behavior would speak for itself. Shaking off her unfair assessment, she placed a hand on his arm to anchor him. "I mean, stay as long as you like. I know you have responsibilities, but if you don't want to celebrate the holiday season at home, celebrate it with my family. We won't bite. Hard."

He laughed and dipped his head. "Okay, then."

The laughter deepened the lines near his eyes, and she considered handing him a book and asking him to wear his glasses again. She never knew she had a thing for spectacles. Maybe the kiss distorted her memory. She hadn't planned on expanding their new friendship, but she felt like two lives had collided, and she needed her bearings before she made her next move. Shaking off her uncertainty, she turned to her *casita*, walked through the gate, and looked for the sweet, tan-and-white dog.

From the duvet covering her bed, the animal snored.

Well, if Lucky can hop on the bed, she's probably okay for a solo evening. Backing out to keep from waking her new pet, she collided with Dane's chest. "Ompf."

He wrapped an arm around her waist and tightened his grip. "Caught your balance?"

Blinking, she untangled her thoughts. She could lean into his weight, turn her head for a kiss, or forget her responsibilities and spend all night exploring him. Knowing she should skip each indulgence, she pulled free and brushed off her shirt, but the warmth of his touch lingered. She might have misread the entire situation. "Can you hang out here a minute? I want to change my shirt."

"Need any help?"

Chewing her bottom lip, she enjoyed his heated gaze. "With my shirt?"

"Life can be challenging." He stepped closer. "I know a few tricks."

She doubted he bantered with the farm workers, and his teasing comments left her feeling closer than she felt when they were skin-to-skin in the laundry room. "Do you, now?"

He reached toward her.

She moved to meet him halfway.

A motel guest walked past and whistled.

The guest's gesture hit her like a cold bucket of water. Straightening, she remembered her priorities. Responsibility and creativity were two halves of her personality. She wanted to make room for Dane, but she was maxed-out. Turning, she offered the guest a friendly wave, but instead of exploring Dane's lips, she met his gaze. "Thanks for the offer, but I can handle it."

He stepped onto the porch. "Any time."

The look he gave her said he would much rather be inside the *casita*, but complications required time, and she had none to spare. Heartbeat pounding, she walked past Lucky, stroked the dog's back, and headed for the closet. *Priorities.* Inside the small space, she had stacked jeans, serviceable work shirts, and a few cocktail dresses she refused to donate. The rest of her work clothes went to a Pacific charity. Who needed black dress pants and interview attire in the desert or in front of a half-finished mural? Fingering a fringed, white dress, she knew it would be too much, but she pondered Dane's reaction. *How would he look dressed for a date?*

She poured her heart into the grant application. Winning thrilled her, but the grant meant she might have to sacrifice the taste of Dane's lips. Pulling a sequined tank from the hanging rod, she slipped on a black cashmere sweater, swapped out her jeans for a clean pair, and told herself she wasn't the kind of woman who sought out intimacy in a truck's front seat. The washing machine was a fluke. Maybe she could be that woman. Pulling off her boots, she slipped on a pair of banded slides and hoped her parents accepted her attire as rustic chic. Whether Dane liked the outfit intrigued her, but wearing it made her feel good. Leaving on the lights, she walked out the open front door and scanned the porch.

Dane sat in the rocking chair Chris had occupied. The tarp lay folded at his feet, and the beverage bucket sat stowed in a corner. The sight unnerved her as much as his alluring, sweat-tinged scent. She crossed her arms. "Why do you always take care of things?"

He stood and stepped forward. "Why do you always look good enough to eat?"

The man looked hungry, all right. Before he could pull her into a kiss, she laughed, walked to the gate, and rested a hand on a white, painted post. His compliment affirmed his interest and eased her nerves. She tilted her head. "Are you coming to dinner?"

He ambled toward her. "I wouldn't miss it for the world."

Pool lights cast flickering shadows on the palms. Content to linger in comfortable silence, she set an easy pace and considered stopping for a second kiss. Maybe she had her wires crossed.

He liked what he saw, but he also wanted to buy the motel and plant acres of vegetables in the space where her family's legacy took root. "I think you'll like my parents. My dad is a professor. My mom's an artist."

"The apple doesn't fall far from the tree."

"No." She stopped. "I replicate what I see. She builds amazing vases and bowls from scratch. The vessels lean and swell with a beautiful, hand-built symmetry. You like coffee? Try drinking from her coffee cups. Nobody builds a better mug."

"It's coffee."

"Trust me, the mugs are works of art." Quickening her pace, and uncomfortable with the idea of being on par with her mom, she steered toward the main building and the cantina where her parents waited. Drawing up at the front door, she looked at Dane. "Do you need to check on Smoky?"

"I'll check with Walter first."

She tilted her head. "You two are more than coworkers."

He nodded. "If I'm the analytical worrier, then Walter's the crushed earth intuit. He smells the weather, hears a pin drop, and can find a pest amid an acre of crops."

"Why doesn't he run his own farm?" she asked.

"He doesn't want the stress. Once in a while, I push him too hard. Instead of talking back, he threatens to leave me stranded, throws his hat in the dirt, and peels out in a cloud of dust."

"And if you defer too much?"

Rubbing his jaw, he shrugged. "Walter runs roughshod over me and plants varietals I never approved."

"Is that so bad?" She admired his profile against the botanical lights. When he swiped his hair out of his eyes, he looked like a Hollywood heartthrob with too much on his mind.

"If Walter wants a community garden, he can buy a lot in town, rent a backhoe, and scrape off a few inches of topsoil. If he wants to make money, he needs to trust my analytics."

She laughed. The glasses made a lot more sense. She ran the motel like a rambling country house. He ran his family farms like a well-oiled machine. No wonder he struggled to sleep at night. Opening the main door, she scanned the reception area and the cantina. The dining room's rustic wooden beams and hanging chandeliers looked intact. Guests occupied wooden chairs, Randi and Stephanie ferried dishes, and candles flickered between patrons enjoying dinner conversations.

Mom and Dad sat at the table next to Walter.

Counting chairs, she debated table arrangements and the impact on the cantina staff. "Let's push these tables together and share a meal." She pulled back the nearest chairs. "That fine with you guys?"

Walter nodded. "I could use a bit of company."

Dad shrugged.

Mom looked so lost in her memories she would have agreed to an alien invasion. Kada wondered what changes she noticed. Instead of worrying, she adopted a bright smile. "All right, let's have a meal."

Dane slid the second table toward Walter's table, rounded the far corner, and took a seat next to his friend.

Stuck between her parents and her guests, she wanted to spend time with both parties, but she had no clue how long either intended to stay. Mom and Dad might try to make a quick holiday exit. Kada couldn't hold hostage their car keys, but she could block their vehicle until she said her piece. The thought of a parking lot standoff made her fuss with the centerpiece to camouflage her smile.

Leaning toward Walter, Dane spoke softly.

She gave the men their privacy and focused on her parents. "I wish I'd known you were coming a day early. I would have prepped."

"The motel looks great, Kada." Mom smiled. "I can't believe how good it feels to be home."

"Home's in Wyoming." Dad cleared his throat. "This is a vacation."

Mom patted his hand. "I know."

Tenure was such a lure. Dad fell in love in the desert, but his livelihood depended on publications and research. The fact that Mom followed him always comforted her. A woman who gave up the things she loved found someone she loved more than her comfort.

Randi walked up, set out glasses, and poured water from a pitcher. "I know you two."

Dad slung an arm around Kada's shoulder. "I'm her father. Give me the best steak in the house. Medium-rare."

"Oh, you're a year too late." Randi winked. "Hall took it to his grave."

Laughing, Dad dropped his arm and picked up a menu. "Fine. I'll have a hamburger."

Her stomach rumbled, and she wondered how much time she could spend with her parents before the motel's guests called her back to action.

Stephanie set down Walter's and Dane's meals.

True to his word, Dane ordered a salad topped with the three B's: blackened steak, black beans, and blue

139

cheese. Spiced garlic bread sat on the side of his plate. Walter ordered a hamburger and a side of fries. She wondered what the pair would think of Benito's more creative menu offerings.

"You guys need anything else?"

Both men shook their heads, but their hands remained in their laps.

"Oh, go on and eat." Mom waved them on.

The men exchanged glances. Nodding, they dug into their food.

The clock chimed eight o'clock.

Kada caught Stephanie's eye. "Does Benito have any more mushroom *barbacoa*?"

"He made you a fresh batch."

Her stomach went into overdrive. "Thanks. I would love a bowl and a side salad."

"Make that three and cancel the burger," Dad said. "I've had enough patties in my life."

Her father lived on a diet of meat and French fries. If he wanted a comforting soup, he ordered French onion soup. Narrowing her gaze, she wondered if her parents' visit had a new urgency. If Dad had cancer, then she needed to know the details, and she needed to find him the best doctor on the West Coast. Her leg jumped. She chewed her thumbnail. *When had he ever turned down a hamburger?*

Dane laid a hand on her thigh and leaned close. "What's wrong? You itching to dance?"

"Hardly." She stilled her leg and glanced at his hand. "You're handling things."

He removed his hand, but he leaned closer. "I'm good at it."

Rolling her eyes, she reached for her water glass

and downed the liquid. Adjusting her seat, she acknowledged her professional career had signaled the end of her dad's helpful calls and friendly cash donations, but she valued their relationship. *What really brought Mom and Dad down here?* The question lodged in her throat. She glanced at Dane and wondered if he and his parents danced around issues. Given Mariah's decades in the schools, she probably taught Dane to speak his mind.

Dane replaced the hand on Kada's thigh and squeezed.

She appreciated his steady heat.

Randi bent to retrieve an errant napkin, caught her gaze, and raised her eyebrows.

She met the woman's appraising stare, but she looked away and checked the guests. Inés and Chris still sat by the fire. Families used dessert to lure their children into finishing their dinner, and the lovestruck couple held hands. She exhaled and squeezed Dane's hand on her thigh. "I'm starving."

He moved his chair closer and lifted a forkful to his mouth.

"So, Dane" Dad said. "You run Palmer Farms. Seems to me I've heard that name. Didn't you try to buy out Pops?"

Choking on a sip of water, she waved her hand. "Not tonight, Dad."

He shrugged. "Why not talk shop? He runs the largest-scale farming operation in the valley. He has zero room for mistakes."

She scanned the cantina, caught Stephanie's gaze, and pantomimed something stronger than water. "He's here to relax. If you want to talk about farming practices, then I'm sure he would give you a tour." She dropped her chin. "Tomorrow."

Dane rubbed his thumb along her thigh.

The rhythmic pressure distracted her from her anxiety.

"Why talk about tomorrow when you have today?" Dad tapped the table. "Successful agriculture takes luck and strategy. I cannot imagine a better scenario for a lifecycle analysis. Let's talk shop."

She groaned.

Laughing, Dane retrieved his hand, lifted his fork, and paused. "I'm all ears. What do you want to know?"

His warm, seasoned voice soothed her as much as his kiss excited her. If he wanted to go head to head with her father, then she would sit back and watch the show.

Stephanie returned with a cup of hot coffee.

Well, the server had her charms. Lifting the warm mug to her lips, she sipped the strong, dark coffee and hoped caffeine carried her through the night. She wanted to paint, but she had to make it through dinner first.

Randi set down three dishes of vegetarian *barbacoa* stew.

Kada wet her lips in anticipation. Benito browned mushrooms in a skillet with chipotle and spices to create a smoky, meaty sauce. He layered the stew over rice and pinto beans, added fresh herbs, and drizzled *crema* over the beautiful, hearty dish. Every time she took a bite, her shoulder muscles loosened.

"How can you justify your crops in the desert?" Dad asked.

She squeezed shut her eyes and suppressed another

groan. Maybe her dinner companions would attribute her reaction to hunger.

"Valley farmland is one of the largest crop-growing regions in California." Dane put down his fork and rolled his shoulders. He sipped his water and met Dad's gaze. "The location baffles some people, but think of the nearby population centers. Most of the valley's irrigation water comes from the Colorado River and the Coachella Canal."

"So, you're stealing it." Dad took a bite.

"Dad!" Kada let her utensil clatter to her plate. The Coachella Valley Water District relied on groundwater, recycled water, imported water, and the Coachella Canal. Unpacking two hundred years of water policy could unleash a torrent of politics and inequities. "You might as well ask him to defend Westward Expansion, too!"

"Is that an option?" Dad stroked his chin.

She glared. "Not over dinner!"

Dane laughed. "I can handle the water rights. Every year, the Coachella Valley Water District delivers three-hundred-thousand acre-feet of imported water. The irrigation system is an engineering marvel. I guarantee you I pay for every drop of canal water I use."

"The canal's an artifact of poor decision making." Dad shook his head. "The All-American Canal should never have been built."

Cocking his head, Dane adjusted the salt and pepper shakers in the center of the table.

She imagined him arranging the pieces of an argument in his mind. He needed her protectiveness like she needed him to run the motel. Having made her initial protest, she waited to see where he would take the debate and wondered if he would continue it after-hours, naked, over a bottle of wine.

He looked up from the condiments.

Caught staring, she felt her cheeks warm.

He winked and turned toward Dad. "More than sixty percent of area farms use drip or other micro-irrigation. Palmer Farms is no different. The delivery system reduces water use, allows me to add pesticides and herbicides directly into irrigation lines, and contributes to increased crop yields."

Looking toward Walter, she made eye contact and waited for him to chime in and support Dane.

He chewed a bite, set down his hamburger, and sighed like a man who wanted to enjoy his meal.

She knew the feeling.

"Palmer Farms is one of the most efficient agricultural water users in the state." Walter picked up his burger and raised his eyebrows.

Dad pursed his lips and squared off against Dane. "Tell me how irrigating the desert is efficient."

Dane worked his jaw.

She understood their discussion, but she wanted to stir a leftover candy cane into her coffee, take pictures in front of the tinsel tree, and peruse the box of worn picture books celebrating the holidays. Having her family in town meant the world, but having Dad badger her future date could turn any woman into a recluse.

Couldn't he camp out on the casita porch and clean his shotgun like a normal dad? The thought brought a grin to her face. Dad knew more about computers than shotguns, but he never shied away from an opportunity to learn.

Dane sipped his water. "More than a century ago, farmers came to the valley for cheap land, a warm climate that facilitated winter production, and a seemingly endless abundance of water. Artesian wells brought water to the surface, but agricultural growth led to a dramatic drop in the groundwater tables."

"Should have been a sign to go home." Dad mixed his rice, beans, and *barbacoa*. "You're depleting the aquifer."

"Me?" Dane held his hand to his chest. "I get water from the canal."

Didn't Dad know keeping the flavors separated highlighted the best bites? If he hadn't whisked Mom away to Wyoming, then the three of them might have grown up in the valley, Pops could have retired and handed over the reins to Mom, and she wouldn't be debating politics two days before her grant deadline.

Then again, maybe she would. If her alternate reality played out, she might have missed Wyoming's hard, beautiful winters, attended a different university, and planted roots so deep in the Coachella Valley that leaving would feel like a betrayal.

Letting go of the implications, she focused on the future and wondered if she could free Smoky and send the gelding stampeding through the cantina. The motel's books could deal with the lost revenue, and she could close down the main building and regroup. If the people at her table wanted to debate agricultural practices, they could sip cocktails by the pink firepit like civilized guests.

"Fine, your industry," Dad said.

Dane pushed his half-eaten salad toward the middle of the table. "You're right, Mr. Ritchie. If the CVWD hadn't imported Colorado River water to the valley, the farmers would have overdrawn the local aquifer and stalled the valley's residential growth. But where would Southern Californians get their bell peppers in December? If you study lifecycle analysis, you know the alternative means shipping produce over long distances."

"Transportation is going electric." Dad jammed his pointer into the table. "Wait for it!"

"When?" Dane scratched his chin. "In the meantime, transportation means diesel emissions. Did you know gravity sends water down the canal? The irrigation system requires none of the electricity costs normally associated with pumping."

"Humph." Dad took a bite and chewed. "Agrarian civilizations have perished because of inadequate farmland drainage and accumulated salt in the soil. The problem will solve itself."

Dane leaned back in his chair. "We have an underground tile drainage system that carries used irrigation water to the Salton Sea. We're meeting market demands."

Staring at him, Kada marveled that she asked him to help her fix her washing machine. "I didn't appreciate the system's complexity."

Exhaling, Dane nodded. "After World War II, large grocery chain stores appeared in big cities. My great-grandfather was one of the first people to realize the growth in chain stores would eliminate wholesale terminal markets. If he could grow and package the food, he could cut out the middleman and sell directly to large stores."

Mom sipped her tea. Her jaw twitched.

Kada doubted Mom worked a piece of ice. She followed the conversation but kept her opinions to herself. Letting people talk out their differences was a skill she taught Kada from an early age. Sometimes, Kada had to count to ten to keep from smoothing over a conversation's rough edges.

"At the same time, the distribution system for Colorado River water supplied gravity-fed water to Coachella Valley farms. My great-grandfather bought as much land as he could afford, and he helped turn the valley into a hotspot for winter vegetable production."

She heard the pride in his voice, but their families had shared a fence line for four generations. Despite their ancestry, they had to look forward. "He offered to buy this land, too."

Dane worked his jaw. "Your great-grandfather beat him to the punch."

"Maybe we should have purchased more land." She scanned the cantina. Biting off more than she could chew seemed to be her *modus operandi*, but humor could diffuse the tension building between Dane and Dad. She swept a palm to take in the dining room. "I could preside over a resort."

He grinned. "You'd be good at it."

Mom laughed. "Granddaddy didn't have the cash."

Having eaten half his stew, Dad shook his head and pushed away the dish. "It all comes down to cash."

She loved her father, but he lived in a land of orderly spreadsheets and scientific debates. As far as she knew, he'd never risked his savings for a commercial venture or put his self-worth on the line and sold a work of art.

"The desert's still sinking," Walter said.

Every person at the table turned and stared.

Walter dabbed his napkin to his mouth. "As residential growth exploded, golf courses and homeowner associations used the Colorado River water for landscape irrigation. Palmer Farms grows peppers, but those fools grow grass."

She thought of Pop's putting green lawn and felt her cheeks warm, but she kept her mouth shut.

Walter pushed back from the table. His wooden chair clattered over the glazed tile. "Folks say the canal water helps conserve the valley's potable groundwater, but the ground's sinking. Anybody who spends time outdoors can see the signs. It's gotten so bad they're pumping canal water into two groundwater replenishment facilities. If you flush a toilet in Wyoming, the treated water might make its way into our aquifer. If the farms have to go, the suburbs have to go, too."

Dishes wobbled.

Eavesdropping guests shook their heads.

Shutting down the conversation might be akin to censorship. Trusting the audience, she covered her mouth and waited.

Dane raised his eyebrows. "Walter makes a good point."

Dad burst into laughter. "I like him. Do you give speeches?"

Walter winked. "Only during happy hour."

Exhaling, Kada scanned the room. She appreciated Dad's scientific mind, but she preferred to keep his debates confined to his lecture rooms or office hours. "Dessert?"

All three men shook their heads.

"Cocktails?"

Dane squeezed her thigh and laughed.

She covered his hand and squeezed back. Knowing he could defend himself made exposing him to her family's eccentricities much easier. He kissed her cheek in front of her parents. If anything, he opened himself to the challenge.

Mom leaned close. "Don't pay Dad any mind. He's testing Dane because he loves you. When I first met Bobby, I knew I'd found a man with passion. Maybe he and Dane share different interests, but they're passionate about what they do. We're the artists, Kada, my love. We create. They analyze. Without each other, we're all lost."

She recognized her mother's intent, but a year of suppressed frustration bubbled in her throat and stole her words. Her family loved her so much they poured their hearts into their work and her life, but after failing in her career, she wondered if she deserved their love.

"What about you, Cicada? Where do you stand on water rights?" Dad angled his chair.

Swallowing, she looked around the dining room. Without fresh water, life in the desert valley couldn't exist, but she could take a cue from Palmer Farms and modernize Pops' operations. Infrastructure from the 1950s served her family, but she could find ways to modernize the arrangement. Caught off guard, she settled on an observation. "I can't criticize too many people, Dad. The Starlight Motel has a pool, and I keep it full."

Dad nodded.

"Well, Smoky certainly appreciates the feature," Dane said.

"Stubborn horse." Walter crossed his arms over his chest. "Gets it from Dane."

Raising his water glass, Dane saluted Walter and sipped.

Walking up to the table, Sue frowned and shuffled her feet.

Her lipstick looked fresh, and Kada wondered if she and her family planned to drive into town for dinner. She stood and smiled. "Can I help you?"

"We need more linens. The shower's trickling, and we're using washcloths. I burnt dinner." She hiccupped and squared her shoulders. "That last bit doesn't matter. Just, can I have a few more washcloths?"

Hearing the desperation in the guest's voice, Kada rounded the table and wrapped an arm around Sue's shoulders. "No problem. Tell me what you need."

"Kada?" Dane asked.

She turned.

"I can get the linens, and you stay with your family." He set his napkin on the table. "Where do I find them?"

Shaking her head, she led Sue toward the lobby, but she looked over her shoulder and met his gaze. She had taken on responsibility for the motel, and she would stick with her commitment, but she appreciated his offer. *Thanks*, she mouthed. Amid the cantina's bustling dinner service, he wouldn't hear a word she said, but she hoped he understood her appreciative smile.

When she returned to the table, if she found Dad and Dane on speaking terms, she would take their camaraderie as a sign for the coming year. The thought lightened her step.

Chapter Ten

"What's going on?" Kada asked.

Drawing a deep breath, Sue picked up a glass ornament and held it. "These balls are so pretty. They look artistic, but they're strong, right? They're supposed to last." Her hand shook. "How do they last?"

Lifting the ornament from Sue's hand, Kada set it back in the bowl, gripped both of the guest's hands, and dropped her chin. She recognized stress, but she didn't know the cause. "What's going on?"

Lip quivering, Sue looked at the red tile floor. "Choosing a classic, American trailer seemed like the right choice for my family. After all, the vehicles are iconic, and they must have something going for them, *right?*"

"Of course, they do." Kada loosened her grip. Vacation woes were a lot easier to manage than interpersonal conflicts. "But they might have a few downsides, too."

Sue looked up. "A few? You try driving halfway across the country in an aluminum bullet with two small children! First of all, that traveling hot dog cost me seventy-five thousand dollars!"

She swallowed. *I thought they were vintage chic and cheap.* Sue looked like the kind of woman who monitored her IRA on a monthly basis. Laying out that kind of investment must have hurt. No wonder she resented a few hiccups.

"That aluminum exterior that looks so cool? Corrosion! Dents! Have you ever polished a trailer?" Sue asked.

She led Sue toward the peacock chair. "I can't say I have."

Sue resisted the gesture. Widening her stance, she brushed her bangs out her eyes and picked up another glass ornament. "I thought the bunk beds would help with the narrow aisle. You know what helps? Keeping Mack occupied with discrete tasks. And where does that leave me? Parenting two kids who can't remember song lyrics they learned ten minutes ago." Her voice wavered, and then it cracked. "We've watched the same movie fifteen times! And there's no storage. None!"

"Okay." Prying the second ornament from Sue's grasp, she chose action over empathy. "Let's get you a fresh set of towels. Are you going somewhere tonight?"

"We're releasing floating lanterns." Sue hiccupped. "My childhood neighbors released them every month for the full moon. It's a tradition."

She considered espousing the magic of hanging lanterns, but after Sue's description of life in a recreational vehicle, Sue needed wide, open space, not a dangling fire hazard. In Buddhist culture, releasing a floating lantern into the sky represented optimism and new beginnings, but Kada had no idea what the motel guests chose to reveal. No matter who influenced Sue's childhood, the symbolism stuck with her, and Kada would honor it. "You still have time to release the lanterns."

"The water…"

"I haven't had other water complaints, but you can

shower in an empty *casita*."

"Really?" Sue wiped her dripping mascara.

"Really." She opened a wooden door and pulled out spare linens staged next to miniature toiletries, light bulbs, and bug spray. After she took over the motel, she added USB chargers, feminine hygiene products, and crayon boxes, but every guest had his or her needs. "Here are the towels. I'll get you a room key, take away the old towels, and check on your family in about half an hour. Okay?"

Sue clutched the towels. "Amazing. Thank you."

Inventorying what else she had to offer, she tilted her head. Sue's hands no longer shook. Kada wondered whether the towels, the shower, or the sympathetic ear mattered most. "It's the least I can do. Let's get the old linens out of your way."

"Okay."

"So, what do you miss most about"—she wracked her brain for Sue's registration information—"Oklahoma?"

Sue widened her gaze. "The food! Chicken fried steak. Fried okra." She wet her lips. "Cornbread."

If cornbread could soothe Sue's anxiety, she bet Benito could whip up a batch in an hour. She might have to bribe him to exclude the candied peppers or ancho chili oil, but comfort food went a long way toward soothing nerves.

Sue walked toward the aluminum vehicle like a prisoner entering a cell.

Trailing, Kada gave Sue and Mack's recreational vehicle a second glance. The vehicle had seen better days. Corroded panels suggested the family drove on snowy roads. Municipalities often used magnesium to treat roads because the salt melted ice and snow. If a savvy person looked under any Wyoming vehicle, they would find clear coating or telltale corrosion.

"Sorry about the dust." Sue waved toward the vehicle. "We try to keep it up."

She stopped a respectful distance from the mobile home. It looked large enough to have separate black water and gray water tanks. Since the family struggled with water pressure, she would suggest checking the tanks, but rivets and leaks exceeded her responsibility as innkeeper. "It looks great."

Two children clambered down the aluminum steps.

The older child wore two red braids, a ruffle nightgown, and pink, fuzzy bunny slippers. "I don't want to go driving around in the cold!"

"Me, neither!" The younger boy stuck out his tongue. Navy cords trimmed his white pajamas, and he clutched a teddy bear. "And you can't make me."

"Kids!" Mack walked to the doorway, braced his hands above his head, and sighed. "Come on. Listen to your mother. We need to get ready!"

Sue held up the clean towels. "We're showering in one of the little houses!"

The kids exchanged looks.

"No," the girl said. "We're staying here."

"Resolutions." The boy nodded. "We're writing plans for the New Year. I'll grow three inches and have a pet iguana."

The girl planted her hands on her hips and turned to her brother. "Will not!"

"Mary Elizabeth and Robert Ross!" Sue wagged a finger. "You two get over here right now."

Robert grabbed Mary Elizabeth's arm and lifted his

chin. "Three inches."

"Not happening, Sue." Mack sighed. "Let's call it a night. We'll release the lanterns tomorrow evening."

"No!" Sue stamped a foot. "Tonight's the full moon."

Scratching her head, Kada looked away and wondered if Sue could open her heart to new traditions. She missed her childhood activities, too. Volunteers in Laramie transformed the University of Wyoming Art Museum into a holiday wonderland, complete with trees and fake snow. The Mayor's Tree Lighting promised old-fashioned hijinks, and the candlelight collegiate choral concert sold out weeks ahead of time. Lying in bed after the spurt of holiday magic at the Starlight Motel, she thought of her family and how much she missed them.

Her childhood wonder couldn't transform the Coachella Valley, but she felt tomorrow's promise as keenly as she felt it back home. Admittedly, the valley floor was a lot warmer than a freezing, wind-scoured Wyoming plain.

"Sweetheart…" Mack took a deep breath.

"Sue, why don't you shower first?" Kada asked. "Mack and the kids can come inside and sing a few songs, read books, and make hot chocolate in the kitchen."

Mary Elizabeth leaned forward. "You have hot chocolate?"

She smiled. "I sure do, if that's all right with your parents."

The pair of kids looked at each other and clasped their hands beneath their chins.

Mack waited in the trailer's doorway.

Looking between Mack and her kids, Sue furrowed her brow. "Fine!" She drew a deep breath. "Yes, please. I won't turn down a hot, quiet shower."

Kada wondered which adjective meant more to Sue. Beckoning the kids, she led them and Mack back to the main building. "Why don't you grab a table? I'll check with the chef and see if now's a good time to invade his space." She hoped Benito would let them use the microwave. "Do you want marshmallows?"

"Yes!" Robert pumped a fist into the air. "I love marshmallows!"

Mary Elizabeth fingered the tinsel tree. "This tree is fake!"

She absorbed the waves of energy emanating from the kids and took a deep breath. "I have a real one in my office. Pops picked it up at the grocery store when it was a crooked sapling. Over the years, it has almost taken over the workspace. Don't tell anyone we're keeping a dwarf fir tree in the business office. If you return next year, it will be seven inches taller."

Robert solemnly nodded.

Inés walked out of the cantina. Seeing the children, her lined face broke into a soft smile. "Did you come to hear me sing?"

Mary Elizabeth hid behind her father.

Robert ran to the vocalist, gripped her skirt, and looked up. "Do you know any songs from cartoons?"

Laughing, Inés put a hand on the boy's shoulder. "I know many songs. Come on, buddy, I know a table by the piano that's perfect for assembling puzzles. After you've had a sip of hot chocolate to warm your voices, you can join me for a few songs."

Mack took a knee and wagged a finger between the

children. "Behave?"

They nodded.

He returned the gesture, stood, and faced Inés. "Thank you."

"My pleasure." She offered her hands.

The pair took her hands and pulled her toward the cantina.

Watching the kids leave with Inés, Kada turned to Mack. "Do you also want a drink?"

He sat in the peacock chair and closed his eyes. "I want to rest. Kids are precious and precocious, but they take over your life. I thought I could reclaim a little adventure with the trailer, but I should have known taking those rascals to a playground was adventure enough."

"I always wanted a sibling," she said. "The kids will help you remember the best parts of the trip."

He smiled like a man recalling his childhood scrapes. "I hope so. I'll be there in a minute."

Leaving Mack to his well-deserved break, she checked the computer behind the reception desk.

The piano started, and Inés sang a cheerful ballad.

The song's lyrics brought back childhood memories, and she thought about how much Mom and Dad loved her. Their appearance in the valley shouldn't be a surprise, but asking them to visit left her queasy. Mom demurred and said the holidays would be too stressful. They negotiated for New Year's Eve, but Kada worried. If being on-site pained Mom, she handled her grief like a champion. Why couldn't she run the motel?

The ballad ended.

"Are you coming back to dinner?" Dane asked.

Blinking, she looked up and found him standing to the counter's side and holding his hat. In a minute, music would fill the cantina, and talk of water rights, politics, or religion could wait for a quieter venue. She smiled and logged off the computer. "I'm coming back."

He nodded. "I think your food's probably cold."

She checked the time. Twenty minutes had elapsed since she had left him and subjected him to a paternal inquisition. Most people would excuse themselves or change the topic, but he met Dad's questions straight on. She wondered if his approach stemmed from his work or his romantic interests. If a kiss gave him indigestion, then she might never see him again. She scanned him. He looked no worse for wear. "I thought I was quick."

"Beautiful, but not quick."

She laughed off the compliment. "Hardly. The Midwest family needed a break, but now, they're squared away for the time being." She tilted her head. "I guess I could lock the doors and keep anyone else from barging into the motel and ruining our meal."

He straightened a brochure rack. "Isn't that against the hotelier code of ethics?"

She gasped. "Wait, how do you know about the code?"

Smiling, he picked up a brass peacock figurine. It wore a faded red Santa hat. "If there's a code, I'm sure you know it by heart. You're obviously capable of making this motel a success."

"Thanks." She toyed with the computer mouse. "Being a smaller venue has its quirks."

The hotelier code of ethics didn't exist, but Palm

Springs had an association of small hotels that allowed smaller venues to pool their resources. The association hosted an annual walking tour where guests donated a toy and viewed member properties decorated for the holidays. She couldn't ask tour-goers to drive to the Starlight Motel for a holiday tour, but she hoped the New Year's Eve fireworks display captured their attention. She arranged a stack of brochures. "I hope I'm making Pops proud. I want people to be happy."

He set aside the figure. "I can tell. How about you come back to the table and let yourself be happy for a spell? Your mom and dad are nice people, but they didn't come all this way to listen to Walter and me debate the weather."

Walking around the reception desk, she hesitated. With so many problems on her hands, he represented an indulgence, and she feared she hadn't earned it. Watching him handle himself in front of her parents eliminated a worry, but she rejected the idea he worried about her. "You're so helpful, but I don't need you to manage me."

"It's a hard habit to break." He worked his jaw. "On my land, everyone chips in."

"I can do it." She lifted her chin. "I can take care of the motel and the guests."

"Nobody said you couldn't run this place." He cleared his throat. "You're doing a good job."

His second compliment nearly floored her. She had admired his long, rangy muscles on horseback, but as she spent time with him, she suspected he cultivated patience like he cultivated crops. Without the all-hands-on-deck attitude, his farm and his staff would suffer. She didn't want to add to his burden or feel like one of his workers.

Yet, after kissing him in the laundry room, she embraced their mutual attraction. If he had room for another complication, she could make room, too. *Who am I kidding? I barely have time to shower or paint.* The thought of sending him away hurt as much as the thought of falling short, but she stepped back. "Thanks for looking out for me."

He exhaled. "I guess this is good-bye. Smoky won't wait forever."

His send-off came too soon. She swallowed. "I hope he feels better soon."

He scratched his neck. "And that date?"

The uncertain gesture kindled her interest. After the holiday, she could make time for romantic nonsense and rangy cowboys, but she didn't know how long she would remain at the Starlight Motel. A few weeks could feel like an eternity, and the distance between her and Dane loomed. She doubted he would kiss her in the lobby, but she wanted him to try. Admiring his perseverance, she smiled. "The fruit?"

He shifted his weight. "Um…"

If she had stayed behind the reception counter, she could brace her weight on the desk and keep her cool, but she would miss the pleasure of his fading scent. She clasped her hands behind her back and took pity on him. "When life calms down, I'd love to go out with you."

He exhaled and smiled.

She wet her lips and prepared to repeat her caveats.

Picking up the flamingo a second time, he rubbed a thumb along the hat. "You made this?"

She nodded and opened her mouth.

He set down the piece and made eye contact. "It's cute. I appreciate the touches of whimsy you scattered around the motel. I couldn't put together cheerful, seasonal decorations to save my life, but I recognize the effort you put into them." He smiled. "You're killin' it, Kada."

Maybe she would kiss him.

He cleared his throat. "I'm looking forward to seeing the finished murals."

"Are you sure you don't care for the holidays? You're awfully cheerful now."

He shook his head. "Not my cup of tea, but if the festivities makes you smile, I can learn to love them."

She laughed.

"Also, my birthday is January first. Nobody wants to celebrate it, so like a toad, I've just written off the whole season. I'm selfish." He smiled. "You should know who's in your bed."

Leaning on the counter, she folded her arms. "Where is this bed of which you speak? So far, my ass and your ass haven't had the comfort of a fitted sheet."

He crossed his arms over his chest. "I have an excellent bed."

"At your parents' house?" She raised her eyebrows.

Scanning the lobby, he cocked his head. "Good point, let's try the chair."

Laughing, she accepted his easy affection but refused to let him bury his frustration. "Don't apologize for feeling left out. January first is a crap birthday. Did your birth make the local papers? Were you a New Year's baby?"

He turned and swallowed. "Gift basket and all."

"You poor thing." She tapped her fingers on the counter. "Here, I am, worrying about student debt, social engagement, and family dynamics. You want"—she worked her jaw—"cake and balloons on your birthday."

Blushing, he offered a smile. "Busted."

His merriment stopped short of his gaze, and she held her breath. She understood wanting moments of carefree joy, but the difference between finding those moments of happiness and waiting for them to appear kept people from enjoying their lives. Every time she painted, she found freedom in her artistic release. He was a generous lover, but could he identify what he needed?

"Kada?" he asked.

She smiled and tried to keep the banter light. "Yes, birthday boy?"

"What happened in Los Angeles? I don't want to put my foot in my mouth and ruin our date, but your father said you fled to the motel. What chased you out of the basin?"

In a heartbeat, the spotlight turned. Her cheeks warmed. The flamingo's jaunty red hat mocked her, and she stared. The decoration required a hot glue gun and little skill. *Why do I think art can solve every problem?* Henri Matisse said, "Creativity takes courage," but few people mentioned the downside of an artist's life. At the Starlight Motel, she worked late, fought dejection, and bolstered her confidence for the coming day. Would her efforts be enough?

Exhaling, she gave herself a familiar pep talk. Her parents bolstered her creativity, and her professors encouraged her work. When she stepped into the world, she fell flat on her face, but she could own her mistakes. Failure was okay. She had a therapist. The sting remained, but every smooth brush stroke helped her move on. The choice between the motel *and* an artistic career remained.

Looking up, she made eye contact and swallowed. "I attempted something big, and I failed. That's okay. Art is subjective, but fundraising is clear. When I proposed a big project, I couldn't find enough backers, and that project floundered. The failure stings, but I'm getting over it."

He settled a hand over her hand. "Kada…"

She flinched and made a fist.

"Okay." He raised his eyebrows and withdrew his hand. "Not my place."

Holding his gaze, she swallowed. "We just met."

He cleared his throat.

Her excuse sounded as lame as she felt. Sex and intimacy were two different things. He could hang with her family, but making her come and taking on a year of indecision were different levels of commitment. Breaking eye contact, she wondered how long the cheerful lobby would seem fresh. One day, she would run out of new ideas, and the shine would wear off the brass. Her attraction to Dane had potential, but he should understand how messy and complicated her life could be. She squared her shoulders and faced him. "Dane, I don't need you to fix my mistake. I wanted to make a big contribution, and I failed. People fail every day. It's okay, right?"

He nodded. "Yep, it's okay."

She wondered if he had ever failed. Taking a deep breath, she opened her mouth to explain herself.

Walter walked into the lobby. "You about ready?"

Dane hesitated.

"It's fine. Head out." She waved a hand toward the cantina and absolved him of responsibility. "My family's here. I couldn't ask for a better reason to celebrate."

"Okay." Leaning forward, he kissed her cheek and pulled back. "Enjoy your evening."

Cupping her cheek, she smiled. "Taking liberties?"

"Well, I'll take them where I can." He donned his hat and nodded. "Night, Kada. I'll see you soon."

Missy Roberts flung open the front door.

While the successful realtor renovated her house, she stayed at the motel. She wore a belted robe, curlers in her hair, and black, fuzzy flip-flops. A white facemask let her brown eyes shine through the refined clay, but every other inch of her skin looked prepped for a spa night. Kada gripped Dane's hand. "Wait, don't go yet."

He laughed.

"How am I supposed to get any sleep?" Missy stormed toward the cantina. "If I wanted to sing Broadway tunes, I would have joined a drama club, flown to New York, or rounded up my gay friends for a door-to-door sing-along!"

Dropping his head and letting the hat shield his expression, he rubbed a thumb along her grip, but a wicked expression darkened his smile. "She has friends?"

"Git!" Skirting his warm embrace, she stepped in front of Missy and waved. "Oh! I'm so glad you came over for the evening. How's your renovation? That mask looks intense. Is it organic?"

Missy jerked back her chin. Waving a finger in the air, she opened her mouth.

Inés sang "Seasons of Love" from *Rent* at full tilt.

Frowning as much as her demonological injections would let her, Missy turned her head and stared into the cantina. "I haven't heard this song in ages."

"It's a good one," Walter said.

Missy pivoted. "And you are?"

"Just leaving." Walter tipped his head and walked straight out the door.

Dane followed, looked over his shoulder, and winked.

She made eye contact, felt a little bit easier with the world, and shifted to counter Missy's peering review. "Inés is singing," Kada said. "She's also singing at the venue on Fred Waring Drive. You might have heard her practice in the mornings."

Scratching her nose, Missy nodded. "Once or twice. It's a wonder I get any sleep, but her voice is beautiful. Maybe I could pop into the cantina for a song."

She turned the realtor back toward the front door. "Why don't you go back to the pink *casita* and wash off the mask?"

Hey eyes shooting wide, Missy slapped a hand against her cheek and rushed back out the door.

Exhaling, she checked the time. Her meal might be cold, but her heart felt warm, her family waited in the next room, and life at the Starlight Motel had to calm down soon. At a minimum, the dinner rush usually ended around nine.

Chapter Eleven

After checking on Smoky, Dane climbed into the passenger seat, settled his hat on his lap, and closed his eyes.

"You're taking care of things." Walter started the engine.

"He's a good horse."

"I'm not talking about the horse, you idiot."

He bit back a smile. "I do like her. She never stops, she's beautiful, and she doesn't put up with much of anything."

"Sounds familiar." Walter eased the truck out of the parking lot and turned on the highway. "Then again, I've met easier women."

Opening his eyes, he turned his head and focused on his friend. "Where? Point me toward them."

Walter laughed.

On the drive to the farmhouse, he tabled thoughts of Kada and braced himself for the holiday onslaught. Until he saw her again, he couldn't do much but send her a good-night text, and even that gesture might be too creepy.

People could be funny with text messages. He used them like shorthand radios. His past girlfriends spent so much time picking out emojis that the bouncing dots triggered his headaches. They could have saved themselves the trouble, picked up the phone, and called to get his attention. No matter what he was doing, he would have answered, because people came first.

But Kada wasn't a past girlfriend. Despite his liberties, as she put them, he didn't want to scare her. He also didn't know where his intentions lay. Dinner seemed like a given, but he couldn't commit to three kids and a vacation house. A kiss clarified his interest, but if Los Angeles haunted her, then he refused to leave her saddled with more regrets.

Exhaling, he prepared to face his family. Behind the Starlight Motel, his family farm fanned out in either direction beneath the moonlight. He could draw the layout from memory. The white, remodeled ranch home had a tall roofline and a pretty fountain anchoring a circle drive. To the right of the main house, Walter's house sat atop a small rise. A large pasture, a ten-stall barn, and an arena filled the space reserved for a lawn.

To the left of the main house, farmland and outbuildings began and followed the desert's curves. The family-owned-and-operated date farm and packing facility encompassed thirty-five acres. Nearly fifteen hundred date trees produced four hundred to five hundred thousand pounds of dates each year, and Palmer dates were the best. At other sites in the valley, his family grew a variety of vegetables, and each plot had its own story.

His great-grandfather started with the first thirty-five acres, but as his fruit trees stabilized, he leased additional acreage, plowed profits back into the business, and purchased small plots of land for as little as four hundred dollars per acre. Today, an acre of active farmland went for somewhere between seventy-five and one hundred thousand dollars. No wonder

Dane slept poorly at night.

Walter put the truck in Park. "I'll take care of the horse."

Unloading Smoky was as important as getting him into the trailer in the first place. He was a creature of habit, and teaching him to unload slowly and quietly was the key to success. He preferred to back him out of the trailer because it was safer for both parties, and a slow, easy rubdown would do them both good. "No, let me."

"Mariah gave me explicit instructions," Walter said. "If she sees headlights, and you're not in the house five minutes later, she'll fire me and throw my things onto the highway."

"No wonder the kids fear her." Shaking his head, he opened the passenger door and stepped down. This late in the evening, standing on family land, he could stop worrying about losing his hat, but he might wear it to protect his head. Mom had a healthy arm. "Thanks, Walter."

"No problem."

He faced the main house. Lights shone from every window. Stripped of lights, the tall Christmas tree filled the family room like a shadowed sentinel. Unlit, big-bulb Christmas lights followed the roofline like lurking gargoyles. For a kick, he flipped on the lights, brightened the view, and walked inside the house. Removing his boots to keep mud from the freshly swept floors, he set his hat on a rack.

"Dane Palmer, where have you been?" Mom yelled from the kitchen.

Composing himself, he worked his jaw. No wonder Kada kicked him out. He needed a shower and a good shave. Turning, he smiled. "Delivering packages like you asked."

Mom stood in the foyer, wearing an apron over jeans and a red blouse. Judging by the flour decorating her cheeks and her dyed hair, the annual cookies extravaganza was still in full swing. She delivered the holiday cookies after Christmas, when spirits slipped, and she refused to offer stale sweets to friends and neighbors.

Lifting his nose, he caught traces of cinnamon and ginger. *Maybe I should have fought harder to take care of Smoky. Walter was probably pulling my leg.*

"I asked you to drop off a date cake, not spend half the day sweet-talking Kada Ritchie."

Her level pitch precluded anger. Hearing affection behind her scolding, he walked up, dropped a kiss on her cheek, and brushed flour from her shoulder. "Isn't that exactly why you sent me down to the Starlight Motel?"

"Dane Palmer!"

Maternal indignation never got old. Whistling, he walked through the house. Leather and clean, 1950s furniture reupholstered in performance fabrics occupied large rooms. Abstract art hung on the walls, and bronze sculptures kept books straight on the bookcases. The occupants changed, but much of the house looked like it did seventy years ago. Sometimes, he caught a whiff of cigarettes and wondered where Mom kept her contraband brass ashtray.

Once a guest stepped into the kitchen, hints of the past faded, and modern conveniences abounded. White cabinets, granite countertops, and stainless steel appliances made the room an efficient workspace and the heart of the home. A lavender-scented candle flickered on the countertop.

His younger brother, Jud, sat on a barstool at the kitchen island. A pendant light shone over his jet-black hair. He still had a football star's broad shoulders, but he spent his days selling cars instead of walking vegetable rows. In front of him, a red rolling pin and a bowl of dough waited.

He sat next to his brother. "What are you making?"

"No idea," Jud said.

Mom glared. "Gingersnap stars."

He considered a standoff between Mom's mood and Jud's resignation. Choosing sides always landed him in hot water. Looking over his shoulder, he found Dad reading a newspaper in front of the fire. In recent years, his father had slowed, but his worn, leather chair remained a favorite spot for relaxation. Seeing no sign of a business excuse, Dane turned back to his mom. "Well, that's exciting."

A haphazard push from Jud sent the rolling pin clattering to the floor.

Mom picked up the rolling pin and rinsed it in the sink. The running water seemed to wash the stress from her frame. She exhaled and wrapped a kitchen towel around the tool. "Are you sure you played football?"

"Ha ha," Jud said.

"Boys." Demonstrating, she stretched out the gingersnap dough with long, sure strokes.

The flour dusting her nose lightened the mood, piano music swelled in the background, and Dad's rustling paper made the scene familiar. Dane spent a fair amount of time occupying this barstool, and the tussles and half-hearted arguments he used to stretch the limits of his adolescent freedom summoned a grin. "Would all this have been easier if you had girls?"

Mom paused the rolling. "I hear daughters are as stubborn as sons."

"Possibly." He scratched the back of a hand against his eyebrow and dropped it to the counter. Linking his fingers, he waited for his assignment.

"Maybe I would have heard fewer locker room jokes, but I would have put in the same amount of effort." Using the back of a hand, she pushed wisps of hair off her forehead and rubbed her chin against her shoulder. "Daughters might have hated baking as much as you do."

"I don't hate it." He hated weeds. Baking was inefficient. He happily ate Mom's creations, but the local bakery made a damn good chocolate chip cookie. "It's your thing."

She raised an eyebrow.

Every one of her students feared her and performed for her attention. She was never mean or catty, but she was demanding, and she expected excellence. If she hadn't beaten Dad at the livestock competition in high school and pointed out the flaws in his yearling, they might never have fallen in love and produced such strapping, male offspring.

He looked at his brother.

Jud dug a knuckle into his nose.

Flour hovered in the air. No wonder every one of them wanted to sneeze, but he wasn't about to taste Jud's snot.

Throwing out an elbow, he knocked his brother off balance and hoped a hot oven killed whatever Jud retrieved. Scooting closer to the island, he leaned his head on a hand and looked at Mom's rolling pin. "Why the cookies?" he asked. "Every year, you make them, but you hardly eat them, anyway."

Jud gripped his arm. "Dude."

He gave his little brother a challenging stare.

"It's all on you. Nice knowing you." Jud stood, shook his head, and walked to the seating area. Moving a stack of books, he dropped into the chair across from Dad.

Dad lowered the paper. "Wise man."

Jud snorted.

Abandoned by his potential wingman, Dane faced his mother. After baking the flat cookies, she would stay up all night icing them and double-down on morning coffee. "I'm serious, Mom. If this month is our designated family-feel-good, we could go into town and volunteer, write a check, or watch other people make themselves crazy."

She slipped a cookie onto a prepared baking sheet. "You weren't always this cynical. You used to like making cookies. You used to be my little boy." Her voice cracked. Looking up, she dusted clean her hands. "Now, you're a force of nature, but I remember changing your diaper. I remember your sweet, chocolate-covered face."

He found her sentimentality endearing and inexplicable. Children grew up. He rubbed his rough jawline and tempered his cynicism. She was right. The cookies once rocked his world. "Do I still have chocolate on my face?"

"Ha!" She pointed a finger. "When you were five, you wanted to ride the tractor instead of blowing out your birthday candles. That's fine. You would always be who you were meant to be, but let me have my cookies. You can eat them, or you can shove them up your…"

Dad coughed.

Clamping down her lips, she nodded.

He washed his hands at the kitchen sink, dried them on a dishtowel, and wrapped her in a side-hug. "I wasn't an easy kid?"

"A terror." She laid her head against his chest.

"All right." Would she always smell like sugar, hairspray, and cleaning products? Squeezing her shoulders, he resolved to stay in the kitchen until the sun rose or his fingers went numb from rolling out dough. "You know, I could eat some carrot cake. On my birthday, I mean."

Pulling back, she slapped his chest. "It's not all about you. Some kids at my school don't have a sweet, restful holiday." She dropped her chin. "They appreciate the cookies I make."

"I'm sure they do." He crossed his arms. "They appreciate you."

She raised her eyebrows.

He matched the gesture. "I appreciate you."

She drummed her fingers on the counter. "You want cream cheese icing?"

He grinned.

"Boys." Shaking her head, she braced her hands on the granite. "Do the kids really need the cookies? I can't fix their lives or make their days stress free, but I can give them tools to succeed, and I can show them a little love."

He reclaimed his barstool and waited. She poured so much time into her school and her students, he assumed she found it rewarding. Maybe the rewards came with a heavy burden. "Are problems cropping up at school? Jud and I can scare the shit out of troublemakers."

"No, but all kids need the same basic building blocks." Straightening, she slid the cookie sheet into the oven and leaned against the appliance. "Just because my tiny tyrant turned into a full-grown force of nature doesn't mean he doesn't have a sweet tooth. I know you sneak cookies at midnight. Why can't you sleep through the night? Maybe I should have gone easier on you and your brother."

"Don't bring me into this!" Jud yelled. "Both of you! Ignore me."

Biting back a smile, Dane rolled out the next dough ball and reached for the cookie cutter. Based on his limited experience, pushing the metal cutter all the way against the countertop worked best. He placed the star on an empty cookie sheet. Domesticity wasn't terrible.

"I see thousands of students, but I only have two sons. Just admit you like the cookies."

He looked up. "I didn't ask for an easy life, but I appreciate your perspective. I don't have to be a tyrant. If the holidays put everyone in a good mood, I can participate."

She pursed her lips.

"Cheerfully," he said. "Hell, Mom. You know I like the cookies."

She stepped away from the oven. "Tell me about Kada."

"Mariah Palmer!" Dad said. "Leave the boy alone."

Mom threw up her hands. "What did I say?"

"You lured that boy into a trap is what you did."

Dad shook the paper. "Any fool could have seen it coming."

"Well, we all know Dane's a..."

Dad kicked Jud's shin.

"Aw, come on!"

Laughing, Dane brushed the flour from his hands, wrapped his arm around Mom's shoulders, and squeezed tight. "I loved walking into school and knowing half the kids were scared of you. When the farms give me trouble, you listen like a champion. If you want to make cookies, I'll stay up all night and frost the little monstrosities until we're bleary eyed and surrounded with twinkling stars. Hell, I'll even make your coffee."

She shrugged out of his grip, fixed his shirt's collar, and patted his cheek. "You're a sweet boy, Dane, but you smell atrocious. Go wash up."

Shaking his head, he walked down the hall toward the suite he occupied. One day, he and his parents would switch bedrooms, but for now, he didn't need more space. Stepping out of the shower, he slipped on a pair of drawstring pants and dropped onto his wide bed. He often rose before dawn, and his family expected him to tumble into bed near nine. He doubted they knew how he spent the hours between midnight and two o'clock. Mom's cookie count might expose his secret, but she let him be. At the end of the day, he ran the farm.

Tonight, he closed his eyes and waited for exhaustion, but Kada's sassy, bossy laughter and smiling management style brought a smile to his lips. No wonder she and Mom became friends. The women approached life head-on, but where his mother corralled high school students, Kada managed motel guests. Closing his eyes, he calculated how many lives each woman impacted. He could spout facts about modern agriculture, but a perfect bell pepper had far less impact than a kind heart.

****

Twenty minutes after midnight, Dane stared at the bedroom ceiling. He tried not to think about anything in particular, but crop rotations, personnel management, and impending tasks flooded his brain. Weary of the nightly occurrence, he threw back the covers and padded toward the sliding doors leading to a small porch. Settling into a white rocking chair, he sorted through his thoughts.

Kada's distant shadow moved along the mural wall.

For months, he watched her floodlit motions without knowing what she looked like or why she painted at night. Having met her, he understood midnight provided the sweeping solitude and uninterrupted peace she needed to paint, but he wondered if the cover of night hid her fears, too.

She expressed disappointment with her time in Los Angeles, but he needed to understand her grievances. Grabbing his glasses and powering up his cell phone, he found the mural she painted with a bevy of vocational students. The vivid, wave artwork didn't look like a disappointment. It looked like an ode to a community bursting with pride and ambition. The students clustered around her in press releases looked fascinated by the process and proud of the outcome. He couldn't help but admire her work.

He worked around men and women who valued

hard labor, tight families, and near-perfect produce. They reinforced the farm's commitment to quality, and he paid them a livable wage. The valley's water management issues mattered, but as long as he maintained profitability, he refused to rock the boat. Courting Kada defined rocking the boat. "I don't know what she needs, and I don't know if I have the resources to give her what she needs."

A fat, fringe-toed lizard lunged for a moth.

"I can't walk away after one date." Her unnamed presence lingered in his memories. Having seen and tasted her beauty and passion, he cursed the anonymity of his sleepless nights. "If I go to her, I'll stay. Should I stay?"

The lizard cocked its head.

"You're not helping."

His phone vibrated.

—Are you awake?—

—If I wasn't, you just woke me.—

—Jerk—

He smiled.

—I was awake.—

He wanted to climb back into bed and fall asleep smiling, but the distance between the old farmhouse and the Starlight Motel felt insurmountable. Given another few feet of stretch, the connection might break, and he would wonder if the desert winds haunted him.

—Are you painting? Are you happy with the result?—

—These desert plants burn so brightly, and then they go dormant. It's ephemeral and close to magic. I wish everyone could see them. Maybe with these paintings, they can. Too much, right?—

If she feared peaking and spending her passion, she should look in the mirror and see what everyone else saw. Under the right conditions, she would blossom. If their attraction went to hell, he would be a friend she could trust. In hard times, he was a phone call away. If he couldn't give her love, he could give her friendship. Stability mattered.

In his heart, he knew she wanted more. So did he.

The realization floored him. The acreage and productivity kept him engaged, but Dad and Walter ensured he could run the operations blindfolded. Kada surveyed his achievements and challenged him to find his passion. Head thrown against his pillow, he took measured breaths. Her presence upended his orderly systems, and he didn't need a laundry room liaison to confirm his attraction. Her existence was a risk, but it thrilled and intimidated him. He could invent a thousand excuses to see her over the coming weeks. Like a moth to a flame, he could hover.

He rolled his eyes. Subtly was pointless. She would see right through him. Working his jaw, he exhaled and took a risk.

—*You make my worries seem silly.*—

—*What keeps you up?*—

He rubbed his stubbly jaw. His mind rarely rested. If he somehow trained his brain to take a cat nap and regroup, he could learn to live with nine o'clock bedtimes and quiet, midnight hours. The silence gave him time to think about the things in his life that mattered the most.

—*Tonight, it's you.*—

Response bubbles danced and receded on his phone. He could give her time to digest his honesty.

Raising his head, he looked across the starlit expanse. The sand and plants stood sentinel, but her motionless silhouette captured his gaze. He imagined her looking right back.

—*I don't want to be a problem.*—

He snorted. Local residents clamoring for Community Supported Agriculture were problems. Packing weekly boxes of fresh, seasonal produce for quirky, locavore residents gave his employees a feel-good buzz. It gave him efficiency nightmares. He wondered what Kada would think of his resistance.

You're not a problem. You're an unexpected luxury. You're water in the desert when I forgot how much I thirst. He closed his eyes. Acres of lush productivity, fickle weather, aging parents, and hungry consumers clamored for his attention, but Kada held his interest. If he walked away from Palmer Farms, then someone else would take his place. Let the jackass try. He knew this land and its quirks like the back of his hand. Nobody could farm this brutal, barren, beautiful land better than he could.

If pride was a sin, he learned the trait the same way he learned to sit back and let the land guide him. A person couldn't rush productivity. Staring down a date wouldn't make it ripen. Patience and perseverance would. He could carve out time for a personal life. He could carve out time for his draw to Kada. Whether she became a trusted friend or a romantic partner depended on her desires. He could handle either outcome.

—*I rarely kiss my problems good night.*—
—*Maybe you should. You might sleep better.*—
He laughed.
—*Maybe so. I heard the Starlight Motel has a*

killer breakfast.—

—The best in the valley. Should I save you a table?—

Taking a deep breath, he let cool, clear air fill his lungs and acknowledged his commitment. The holidays weren't his thing, but if his attraction to Kada Ritchie bore fruit, he would treasure the gift. Whether that gift meant another mind-blowing orgasm or a full-fledged relationship remained to be seen. He had only known the woman for one day. Surely, a day couldn't upend his life. He drew a deep breath. It already had.

—Please do.—

—Great, I'll see you at six.—

He stared at his phone. Maybe she went to bed at nine o'clock, too. Maybe he should get down on his knee and propose before she slipped away. Pouring himself a drink might be the saner choice.

—When do you sleep?—

—What's sleep?—

Smiling, he closed his eyes and let his mind drift. Tomorrow was nearly a holiday. He barely tolerated New Year's Eve festivities, but they gave him an excuse to step away from the farm and spend more time with her. He would take the selfish gift, gain a better understanding of his newest neighbor, and find a way to bring a smile to her lips. Based on her unique gifts and talents, flattery probably wouldn't be enough. He scratched his chin. Picking up his phone, he settled for a soft sign-off.

—LOL, I'll see you tomorrow.—

—G'night, Dane.—

—Night, Cicada.—

He stood, stretched his arms over his head, and

listened to the desert. The wind rustled the twisted, shrubby trees surrounding the house. Date branches swayed, pumps hummed, and a hawk screeched.

When the wind lulled, the fat lizard making use of the balcony darted after a tasty treat.

He paused and listened to the inky darkness beyond the drive. Stone amplified acoustics, and somewhere in his acreage, the desert held its breath and waited to bloom. January and February triggered the profusion of color that brought tourists pouring into the valley, but he didn't want to wait until the New Year. Feeling like a clever man, he headed inside and hoped his hunch played out.

Chapter Twelve

Dane's messages should have sent Kada to sleep with a smile, but she struggled to find her footing amid the strong winds and shifting sands. Facing the incomplete mural, she wiped sweat from her brow and examined the half-painted, native ocotillo plant. Once completed, the mural of stunning red flowers and tall, spiny stems would be majestic. In the wild, plants waved in the wind like a fan, but she couldn't mimic that effect. Swiping a bug from her field of vision, she puffed out her cheeks, admired what she could do with static paint, and added orange highlights.

Humming, she realized an hour had passed and set down the paintbrush. Instead of slipping off to bed, she picked up a three-ring binder and cross-referenced it against the gridded wall. After rain fell in January and February, the desert would burst into bloom. Stunning, ephemeral displays would appear throughout the valley, and the desert's lifecycle would begin again. She would be gone.

Movement caught her gaze. Shading her eyes from the floodlight, she found a Coachella Valley fringe-toed lizard inching across the life-size design. The plump lizard skirted the wet paint and crawled across the whitewashed stucco. The animal showed little interest in the motel's rated amenities and storied history, but at least, it respected her art.

Or it had its eyes on a shiny beetle.

The chase might go for hours.

Dropping the hand, she moved her long, dark ponytail between her shoulder blades and flexed her muscles. In a few hours, the winter sun would rise from behind the mountains, and she would start a new day. For the first time in a long while, she wondered if she chased the right lure. Funding guaranteed her stability, but her work would put the sponsor on the map in the art world. Why should she let a looming deadline set her pace?

Dane tempted her as much as the people she met and the music she savored, but he was the only person who heated her blood. Why couldn't he be a caffeine-soaked intellectual with a taste for expensive shoes? The thought of Dane playing boardroom games made her giggle. She would be happy to play with him in the bedroom.

Shaking her head and knowing she had to choose, she decided the rare fringe-toed lizard could have the wall. As the motel's owner, operator, and resident muralist, she had a yawning sleep deficit and plenty of tasks to occupy her time. "Good luck, buddy."

Pulling out a smooth sheet of plastic, she folded a paintbrush into a protective layer that would keep it wet until she could return to her passion.

"When do you usually get snow?"

Dropping the paintbrush, she turned and saw Inés standing near the floodlight. The vocalist's lined face looked as soft and as smooth as a coffee-stained paper filter. She wore a flowing, embroidered dress, a large, wooden necklace, and sensible, black shoes. Kada felt a little underdressed in her presence, and she marveled at the things Inés pulled from her deep pockets.

Tonight, Inés withdrew her phone from a pocket and pivoted the device to reveal pictures posted by Palm Springs' tourism board. "Last year, the snow came December fourteenth. Was that early? Maybe I should ask the people around Indio."

Kada picked up her fallen paintbrush to rewrap it and considered the best course of action. Although she had regularly visited her grandfather, she had never lived in the valley. Inés might need her mother's more extensive knowledge, but doubting the famed vocalist wanted ten caveats, she shrugged. "Snow rarely falls on the valley floor."

Pivoting the phone so she could see the screen, Inés swiped across the glass.

The singer's movements were as quick as a roadrunner sprinting across the sands. Kada waited.

Inés stopped swiping and pointed toward the starlit sky. "I'm not talking about the valley. I'm talking about the tram. When does the snow fall in the mountains?"

Kada laughed. The tram. Passengers on the decisive aerial tramway descended Mount San Jacinto and took in valley views and local frustration. The attraction ran an annual contest awarding free tickets to the contestant who guessed the first substantial snow accumulation in the mountains. If she paid more attention to her guests, and less to her art, she could keep up with their quirks. "Ah." She reached for another brush. "This year's been wet. Maybe early January."

Inés shook her head. "No good. I'll be home by then."

Kada watched a star shoot across the sky. One day

soon, snow would dust the mountain peaks, and desert flowers would bloom in the springtime. Judging by tonight's clear skies, Mother Nature would thwart Inés's desire for holiday snow.

Instead of raining on the vocalist's parade, she wiped her hands on her smock, untied the protective garment's straps, and neatly folded the fabric near her paint supplies. "I have a few passes you can have."

Inés looked up from her phone. "You do?"

"I keep the passes behind the check-in counter." Smiling, she gestured toward the main building. "Let's see how many I have left."

Pocketing her phone, Inés fell into step. "You know it's late?"

She nodded.

Inés rubbed together her hands.

The woman was an accomplished artist, but she looked like a kid set to raid the candy jar.

"What else do you have squirreled away?" Inés asked.

Kada laughed. "Wouldn't you like to know?"

The vocalist had arrived at the motel to stay for a week, visit family, and sing at the venue on Fred Waring Drive. She greeted the sunrise with song and claimed the crisp, morning air strengthened her vocal cords, but her morning songs had also strengthened Kada's work ethic.

Hearing the vocalist's exercises at sunrise would yank her from her bed, but she enjoyed the treat. Sometimes, a second voice joined Inés, but bleary-eyed caffeine deprivation tempered Kada's curiosity, and she had yet to identify the owner. Truly, she liked the motel guests, but she struggled before her first cup of coffee kicked in. Ready to trade her work clothes for cool sheets and a reassuring nuzzle from Lucky, she gestured toward the path meandering through the palms. "I'll trade you two passes for a story."

Inés laughed, walked along the path, and picked a spot reserved for a quiet bench. "How about a song?"

Kada nodded and hoped the vocalist specialized in volume control.

Clearing her throat, Inés sang "Año Nuevo" by Vetusta Morla. She swung her hands with the same rhythmic confidence that lifted her songs, but she kept her voice under complete control.

Kada sat mesmerized. She knew the anthem. Whether the living and the dead toasted together, life moved on. Celebrating life was better than dwelling on the past's pain and difficulties. Why did she let her disappointments define her future? Pops would have read her the riot act.

Inés pushed through the heartfelt refrain.

Guests making their way to their *casitas* stopped and smiled.

With a final hip swish, Inés finished the song.

She joined the clapping, poolside guests. "Majestic. You can have all the tram passes."

Inés laughed and offered her arm. "Let's get moving before you change your mind. I'll only take what I need. That's the secret to life, isn't it?"

Glancing over her shoulder, Kada noted the lizard's inching progress and wondered what she needed. The grant promised to fulfill her career aspirations, but the desert had staked a claim on her heart, and Dane had upended her sensibilities. Pouring her free time into the murals gave her an artistic outlet and honored her university training, but she wondered when she would bloom. Dane's kisses silenced her doubts, but she couldn't factor him into her decision.

By taking care of the motel, she gave Mom time to process her grief, but that time had passed. Did she want it to end? Most days, Kada loved running the place, and she wondered if she should set aside her ego and reject the grant for humble satisfaction. *Maybe the Starlight Motel can be enough. Maybe my art can take second place.*

The lizard stuck out its tongue.

She could never put down her paintbrush. Matching Inés' steady walk, she thought of days she spent arranging her childhood dollhouse and other toys. Her family of dolls led tidy, manicured lives, but as soon as she had the pieces in place, she upset the arranged display, scribbled on the papered walls, and arranged dinosaurs on the dollhouse roof. The coming holiday was a time of reflection. Inés sang an old standard, but Kada felt it in her bones.

The post-holiday letdown felt a lot like growing up. Mom had poured a ton of energy into making holidays perfect, but Kada had outgrown make believe. Now that she wielded the credit cards and the inspiration boards, she understood the effort parents expended, but tidy, manicured lives had never been her thing. Beneath the stars, she had talked herself into running the motel, and it thrived, but she wanted more.

Inés paused beneath an overhead light. "Where are you?"

Missing a step, she slowed their progress toward the main building. "Sorry. I thought you might sing something classical, but I like your choice. It fits the season."

Inés nodded.

Kada wet her lip. "Why did you become a vocalist?"

Patting her hand, Inés smiled. "The lifestyle suited me. I work in the mornings, sing throughout the day, and look for ways to help people. Moments of quiet solitude bring me happiness, but so does music. My life allows me to mix the two approaches in perfect harmony. I'm a lucky woman." She opened her palm to the courtyard. "So are you. Maybe you were meant to be here."

Kada pulled free her arm and reached for the main building's door. Spirituality had never been her bag, but she respected Inés's peaceful tone. "And if you hadn't become a vocalist?"

"*Rancheria* rock star." Inés stroked an imaginary guitar. "What else?"

"Of course." Laughing, she gestured for the vocalist to enter the main building and wondered who else couldn't sleep.

"I'm starving," Inés said.

"Then I'm not doing my job. Can I get you a sandwich? Fruit?"

"Midnight snacks are the worst."

Inés gripped a chair like the furniture might keep her from exploring the complementary snack bar. Kada knew the feeling. She wanted to find her bed, preferably with Dane in it, or sink into the peacock chair and kick up her feet. Instead, she approached the motel's check-in desk and fired up the sleek, gray laptop. After checking her notes, she pulled open a drawer, flipped through Pops' old filing system, found traces of Nana's handwriting, and pulled out two tram tickets. "Here we go!"

Grabbing the tickets, Inés grinned. "Thank you."

She adjusted a brass flamingo dipping its head into a bowl filled with peppermints. "Who will you take?"

The vocalist's weathered face softened into a loving expression. "My niece can't get enough of heights. The minute her mother turns her back, the little hellion's moving chairs, climbing bookcases, or scaling abandoned ladders."

"Oh." She laughed and thought of herself as an indulged only child. She had longed for siblings, but she appreciated how much time and energy her parents had poured into her upbringing. She wanted everything, didn't she? Her cheeks warmed, and she walked from behind the desk. "I'm sure your niece will love the tram."

"Her mother will love the break. Girls need education, but they need adventure, too."

Exchanging a conspiratorial glance, Kada grinned. "With an aunt like you, she'll find it."

Slapping her knee, Inés waved the passes over her head and danced from the room.

Kada turned off the lights and followed.

Chapter Thirteen

New Year's Eve
Lucky's soft snores woke Kada. Stretching her arms above her shoulders, she rubbed Lucky's soft ear, turned her head, and looked at the plants outside the *casita* window. The sun shone above the mountains, the palms looked entirely too crisp, and the guests milling around the pool already wore their swimsuits. Throwing back the blanket, she jumped out of bed, splashed water on her face, and reached for clean clothes.

Past midnight, she saw Dane's light flicker on and knew she wasn't the valley's only occupant taking advantage of cool, evening breezes. Bantering with him soothed the tension in her shoulders. After finishing the ocotillo plant mural, she fell asleep thinking of their next encounter. She expected to see him for breakfast, but judging by the sun's position, she way overslept. Slipping on the first shoes she saw, a pair of all-purpose sandals, she ran toward the front door and skidded to a halt. "Lucky?"

The dog raised her head.

"C'mon, girl. You need outside time."

Lucky dropped her head and closed her eyes.

Pet ownership might be a new responsibility, but she was pretty sure she had to provide more than food, water, and affection. "Come on, let's go to the garden."

Inching forward, Lucky dropped her front paws to

the ground and let her belly slide off the bed. Stomach wagging, she ambled out the front door and squatted in the grass.

"Such a good girl!" Reaching down, she tightened the adjustable straps on her sandals. The dusty shoes felt silly in Los Angeles, but they kept her going in the hot, dry valley. "We'll find you somewhere cool to rest."

Lucky snapped at fluttering, white moth.

She opened the gate and stepped through. "C'mon, girl."

Lucky yawned, turned, and padded back into the *casita*.

"Not an early riser, eh?" Only a bit envious, she refilled the dog's bowls, let the garden gate slam, and considered running toward the main building. Last night, she needed the release painting and flirtation provided. Today, she needed accomplishment.

Sue walked down the path with one arm wrapped around each child's shoulders. Her auburn hair shone, and fresh lipstick graced her lips.

Kada slowed her walk. "Good morning!"

"It's a beautiful day to celebrate New Year's Eve." Sue squeezed her kids' shoulders. "I can't thank you enough for the reprieve last night. Kids, did you have a good time?"

Mary Elizabeth wiggled out of Sue's grasp, rushed forward, and took a hand. "Miss Kada, is Inés a real vocalist?"

She dropped to one knee. "As far as I know. Did you ask her?"

Eyes wide, Mary Elizabeth shook her head.

"She has a niece in Palm Springs about your age. I

think she really likes kids. If you ask her about her life in Mexico, I bet she would tell you."

Scanning the pool area and the gardens, Mary Elizabeth frowned. "She's not here today. Usually, I can hear her singing."

"Me, too!" Standing, she realized how she managed to sleep so late. "I think she took her niece on the tram ride. She'll be back later, and you can ask her anything you like."

"Anything?" Robert asked.

She made an exaggerated, wide-eyed face. "Anything."

Robert pumped a fist into the air.

Facing Sue, she smiled and looked for Mack. "Where's your husband?"

Sue rolled her eyes. "He went into town for parts. A buddy of his thinks he knows what's wrong with the RV's water pressure. It's something about a leaky connection between the pump and the tank. I'm sorry I blamed your motel for the issue. We didn't have time for the lanterns, but we'll do them tonight."

She shrugged. "No harm done. I'm glad you're in good shape. Later tonight, when you release the lanterns, I want to see all the pictures."

Both kids grinned.

"Awesome." She stepped to the side and gestured for the trio to pass. "I'll see you guys later today. Don't forget about the midnight sing-along." She dropped her voice. "Although, you might need to be asleep before the fireworks start."

"Fireworks," Robert whispered.

Mary Elizabeth rolled her eyes.

Watching daughters copy their mothers amused

her. She wondered which of Mom's traits she acquired. Artistic expression and family sentimentality influenced many people, but where did her rugged tenacity originate? Mom and Dad could both claim that trait. Turning away and swallowing her laughter, she walked toward the main house and lifted her nose. Most days, she rose with the sun and expected the smell of bacon to lure guests from their *casitas*. Nine o'clock might be early for some snowbirds, but she expected to see guests leaving the cantina with satisfied smiles. Instead of bacon, she smelled sweet, crisp sunshine and something smokier. *I missed the rush. Maybe Benito tried Chorizo omelets.*

Chris sat in a lounge chair by the pink firepit. He wore a shiny, polyester bomber jacket, black aviators, and a flamingo-patterned shirt so bright she understood why he needed the glasses. A box of donuts rested on his lap, and a steaming coffee cup waited on the edge of the firepit.

She shaded her eyes. "That looks like a treat."

He took a bite from a donut.

"If you want something more substantial, we still make Hall's famous breakfast buffet. Think warm biscuits and rich gravy, crisp bacon, and fresh eggs any way you like them. If you want something sweet, we have blackberry custard French toast."

He shook his head.

"What about a short rib scramble with mozzarella? Chicken and waffles? Avocado toast topped with poached eggs, alfalfa sprouts, and basil pesto? Mr. Nicholson, you have to keep up your strength!"

Picking up a napkin, he wiped his face. "Kada, my friend, your chef's out with a bad back, your servers burned the bacon, and if I wanted an egg, I'd have to make it myself."

Widening her gaze, she took one look at the half-eaten donut, gasped, and ran into the main building. "Randi! Stephanie!"

More donuts sat in boxes by the bubblegum ornaments.

Gustavo had his phone out and snapped a picture. "Nice spread."

"Yeah." If she played this cool, she could turn it into a feature. "We like to keep things simple on New Year's Eve. You know, give the staff a break."

He laughed. "That's not what I heard."

She wanted to give him the full breakfast pitch and promise to make it herself, but if Chris' explanation held water, she had an injured chef and two frustrated servers on her hands. Picking up a donut, she took a bite, smiled around the sweet treat, and calmly walked into the cantina.

Randi and Stephanie sat at a table. Two untouched donuts sat between them on crisp, paper napkins. Discarded sugar packets littered the table, and both women clutched their beverages like weary medical residents.

Kada scanned them for injuries. She listened for complaining guests. A clock ticked in the distance. She released her breath. "So…"

Randi raised an eyebrow.

Stephanie dabbed a tissue near her eye.

Pulling out a chair, Kada straddled the back and laid her donut on the table. "Rough morning?"

The women exchanged looks.

Randi scratched the edge of her mouth with a long

nail.

A tear rolled down Stephanie's cheek.

Nodding, Kada considered her options. Faced with twenty hungry motel guests, her parents, and no chef, the servers made an effort. She wished they woke her and let her pitch in, but she knew them long enough to respect their intentions. Frankly, Randi's presence on-site was a miracle. Wetting her lips, she tried empathy. "How's Benito?"

"Okay," Stephanie said. "But he's laid up in bed, and he can't move his head from side to side. He said it's a pinched nerve, and he needs time for the muscle relaxers to kick in." She chewed a fingernail. "Is that serious?"

"Only if you want to ride him like a cowboy." Randi covered a yawn.

Under the table, Kada nudged her foot.

Randi sipped her coffee. "What? They've been dancing around each other for months."

Stephanie blushed. "He works so hard."

Randi pointed a finger. "He needs to work you hard."

Unsure whether to tackle logistics or interpersonal issues, Kada imagined what Pops would do. She doubted his files contained notes on managing employee love lives. He would have been up before the sun and circumvented the breakfast disaster. She rubbed her hands over her face.

"He should be celebrating or running his kitchen like a boss." A second tear fell. Sniffling, Stephanie dabbed at her eyes. "He misses his family, and it's New Year's Eve. I wish I could help him."

"Did you ask what he needed?" Kada asked. "Is

there anything he wants?"

Stephanie tossed her tissue onto the table and dropped her forehead to her hands. "I don't know! He brushed off my concerns and told me Mexico has more than fifty species of heirloom corn. Life has so many beautiful shades and moments, but he's not tender *elote*." She looked up. "He's *mazorca,* and he's a tough nut.*"*

Randi yawned. "I think you mean kernel."

Stephanie frowned. "Maybe, but don't you see? He thinks he's too old for me."

Randi shrugged.

Pulling a clean napkin from the stack she picked up with her donut, Kada offered the napkin to Stephanie and considered how to respond to her tears.

Mom would hug out the pain.

Pops had a different approach. He was uncomfortable with emotional behavior. To be professional, he thought he needed to ignore his emotions and the emotions of the people who worked for him and stayed at the Starlight Motel.

If she had a rough day or fell and scraped her knee as a kid, then he took her on a long walk and let the exercise purge her feelings. She understood his approach to life and figured it was the norm in most workplaces. Her favorite memories came from the times he cracked, told a joke, or let her wail on his shoulder...before the long walk.

In her experience, people made emotional decisions about what to wear, what to eat, and how to spend their time. Unless they worked on a factory floor, they depended on emotions to guide their days. An occasional tear offered relief, but Stephanie's makeup was long-gone. Pops might leave them to muddle through their emotions. Choosing to engage, she let Stephanie's tears flow without mentioning them. "I appreciate what you two did. Getting the donuts was a brilliant move."

"We didn't get them." Stephanie hiccupped. "Your mom and dad got them. I was too busy putting out the fire."

Randi nodded. "Mmm hmm."

"The fire!" She sprang to her feet and stared into the kitchen. It looked intact, and she took deep, steadying breaths to calm her heart rate.

"It was a grease fire," Stephanie said. "I tried to put it out."

Randi pushed back her chair. It scraped on the tile floors. "With water."

Stephanie dropped her head to the table and wailed.

Rubbing her hands up her cheeks, Kada closed her eyes and took a deep breath. "Nobody's injured?"

"All good," Randi said. "I smothered the flames with a pot lid."

She dropped her arms. Randi's smooth confidence might have saved the day and the Starlight Motel. A fire extinguisher would have made an awful mess. *Thank you*, she mouthed. Choosing public recognition, she added, "Thank you for being here."

Randi stretched her arms over her head. "Where else would I be? I belong in this valley. I was here when everyone still wore 'tribal' print leggings and braided headbands to live shows. I knew the catty indie gossip sites before those bitches had podcasts. The festivals kept me whole through my teenage years, and they thrilled me. As soon as lineups dropped, my friends and I poured over the schedules and schemed. We snuck baggies of weed into our maxi pads, paid cash for bootlegged wristbands, and drank warm beer while the bands played."

"What happened to the weed?" Kada had never been this cool.

"Our stealth pipes fooled absolutely no one, but when security got too close, we smoked ridiculous, pastel-colored cigarettes and blew them kisses."

"I wish I could have been there," Kada said.

Randi waved away an unseen haze. "Why? You don't belong here. You're passing through, and so are all the idiots paying ten thousand dollars for air-conditioned camping tents when they could be staying here. You've got something, but it's as fleeting as the sunset."

Kada rubbed her brow and wondered if she put her foot in her mouth. In the 1960s, developers removed the Black population from Section Fourteen—a one-square mile of downtown Palm Springs—but her understanding of town history stood apart from her responsibilities at the motel. Randi invited her to a town hall to discuss confronting injustices and revisiting modernism, but the event hadn't happened yet. Kada worried she'd missed it and sheepishly checked her phone. "Thanks, I think. I'm trying to add to the valley."

"No problem, but we can do it without you. Just like me, the valley's sweaty, surreal, and a whole lot of fun."

Kada snorted. "Does that pickup line work?"

Randi winked. "Every time. Try it on your cowboy."

She doubted Dane would be her cowboy. He might be the type of man who banked on one-night rodeos. "What if I can't follow through?"

"Well, you'll be good for a laugh, won't you?" Randi rolled her shoulders and picked up her phone. "If we're not serving today, can I have off the rest of the day? Walter's been asking me to come up to the house, and if I don't make an appearance, he and my extended family will come find me."

This morning's excitement gave her mental whiplash. She stood and matched Randi's posture. "Why didn't you tell me you two were related?"

Randi scratched a nail into her braids. "Did you know him before yesterday?"

She shook her head.

"Well, what did it matter?"

"The Palmer family wants to buy the Starlight Motel." She wished she had a cup of coffee to hold.

"Let them," Randi said. "I'd take the money and run."

She stared. After her speech about local roots, why would Randi encourage her to abandon hers? "You would?"

"But I don't love this place like you do. No matter what happens, your family comes back to this motel. I've seen it since I was a kid riding a pony with Uncle Walter. I don't understand it, but I hope I find the same happiness one day."

"You will." She picked up the donut and hesitated. "What do you love?"

Randi finished her coffee. "I'm still figuring out the answer, and that's okay." Smiling, she waved off the intimacy. "Don't worry, Kada, I'll find my place.

Until then, I like this gig. The hours are flexible."

"They're not supposed to be flexible!" She bit into the glazed treat and chewed with purpose. The refined sugar coating had nothing on a date's honeyed complexity.

Laughing, Randi sauntered out of the cantina.

Swallowing the mouthful, she shook her head. The next time she sat with Randi for a performance review, she would give her a raise and a hug. Despite her spotty attendance record, Randi was right. Losing the motel would devastate her, her family, and her employees.

She turned toward Stephanie and the woman's fragile state. Burning bacon to the point of flammability required skill. "Do you want to take off the remainder of the day, too? Do you want to sit with Benito while he recovers?"

Stephanie's lip quivered.

The fire and missing breakfast would fade into a charming story. Why was Stephanie still crying? Kada feared Benito might be in more pain than she let on. She considered a gentle question to discover the underlying issue behind Stephanie's tears. If the question failed, she could recommend a good therapist. "Is there anything else you want to tell me?"

Pulling at her hair, Stephanie stared upward. "I love him. He knows I love him. Why doesn't he love me back? I want a picket fence, a couple of kids, and a dog." Her voice escalated. "Is that too much to ask?"

Her outburst echoed off the cold tile.

Dropping her shoulders and her head, Stephanie made eye contact. "Sorry."

Well, I can help her with the dog. Lucky's about to have a litter of puppies. Wiping the thought from her mind, Kada chose a neutral expression. "Have you told him how you feel?"

"He says he's just a motel cook." Tears fell freely. "Why doesn't he return my feelings?"

Based on Benito's lighthearted swat over stolen French fries, he had feelings for Stephanie, but the hurdles that kept him from returning her affection required more than forced proximity and doe-eyed adoration. "Why don't you make him a sandwich and sit with him? Read him a book. Ask him what he wants to do with the next ten years of his life."

Stephanie tugged an earlobe. "Who knows what the future will bring?"

She had plans, but she didn't know if they would play out. "Maybe nobody does, but asking questions opens up the conversation. If you get to a point where you think he might reciprocate your feelings, ask him out on a date."

"What if I offend him?"

Waving off the notion would get her back to square one. She solemnly nodded. "What if you spend the rest of your life regretting letting him go?"

"He's leaving?" Stephanie gaped. "When did you find out?"

"No, he's not leaving!" She took a deep breath. "I want you to own your feelings. Trust him to respect you and give you an honest answer. Let it all out." She stood. In the last year, she wrapped her head around motel management, but she depended on Pops' staff to know their jobs. He'd hired this lovely, blonde fluff ball. Why wasn't he here to counsel her?

She considered what Pops would have done with a crying server. Well, he wouldn't have overslept, missed the fire, and sat for a heart-to-heart. If he had, Stephanie might balk at his tough-love approach and need a new job. Who put out a grease fire with water?

"My feelings." Stephanie clutched her coffee. "He can't argue with my feelings, can he?"

"Nope. In my experience, your heart skips ahead of your mind. When the two organs find a rhythm, everything falls into place." She omitted the part where her ambition exceeded her abilities, and she found herself unemployed in Los Angeles.

Stephanie nodded.

"Can you return for the dinner rush?" she asked. "I might have to manage the grill, but we should make burgers and stuff for the guests who want them."

"Sure." Stephanie smiled. "I mean, even an idiot can grill things."

She hoped the description applied equally to both of them. Walking away from the table, she considered the kitchen. A few rounds of abrasive cleaner would remove the soot stains. If she could clean up the mess before Benito returned, he could slip into his kitchen without missing a beat. She added the task to her list.

"Kada?" Mom asked from the reception area.

Hearing her mother's voice, she bit back a groan. She wanted to spend time with her family, but she expected to share the morning with Dane, not a scouring pad. Frustration left a bitter taste in her mouth, but she would clean up the mess, find a cup of coffee, and count her blessings.

After unloading details about her blotched fundraising campaign, she understood Dane's need to take a breather. Over the holidays, he must have a ton of obligations, and she didn't want to be another chore on his list.

"Were you up late?" Mom asked.

She turned, found a scrubbing pad, and forced a smile. "No later than usual."

"It's not like you to sleep in."

Spreading her hands and working through the scorched grease, she shrugged. "If I'd known about the excitement, I would have been up early to see the show."

Mom laughed. "Oh, it was a hoot. I haven't seen your dad move so fast in my entire life. As soon as the drama calmed down, we went into Palm Springs and picked up donuts. We're just now getting dressed. Do you still have time to go through Pops' things with me?"

Glancing toward the front door, she nodded. "Of course. Just let me finish cleaning up this mess."

"Great. Your dad's working on an article, but I have all the time in the world."

"Me, too." The lie felt like a lump in her throat. After Pops' death, putting her mother's needs ahead of her own felt like a mature decision. Now, it felt like a burden. Mom knew what needed to happen, but she teetered between being overwhelmed and being adrift amidst her past. Kada needed to take Lucky to the veterinarian, pick up hamburger supplies, and drop in on Benito to understand if he needed more than Stephanie's kisses and candy-colored pink lips. She swallowed. "Where do you want to start?"

Shrugging, Mom looked at the smoke stains on the kitchen ceiling and smiled. "Pops would have torn out his hair to see such a mess. All that time at sea left him as rigid as a flagpole."

She dropped the pad in the sink and opened a drawer for a dishrag. Wetting the rag, she scrambled onto the counter and rubbed at the painted wall. The soot came off easily, and she dropped her shoulders. She could take care of this mess.

"I told him Dad and I decided to elope, and I held my breath. You should have seen his face. I thought he would blow a gasket or take me for another of his forced marches."

"I loved those desert marches." She rubbed at the stain.

"Me, too." Mom picked up an abandoned order ticket and let it flutter to the stainless-steel countertop. "And then I grew out of them. I'm sorry Dad and I stayed away for the last few months. This place holds so many memories, and coming back hurt too much. I appreciate how much you've done. The motel looks amazing."

Stilling a hand, she looked up from the wall. Academic compliments supported her childhood, but dealing with the motel felt like the first time she approached her family as an equal team member. "Thank you. It does."

"Oh, Kada, you're so creative and talented. I must have sent the articles about your mural to a dozen people. Look at my daughter and the things she's doing. In the press photos with the students, you beamed, and they looked as proud as peacocks."

She shook her head and rubbed at the stain. "I was happy working on the mural. I loved spending time with the students and building connections. Once I slipped past their defenses, I found out they were hilarious and witty. I miss them. I wish I could have stayed and made a bigger impact." Her voice hitched. "I tried."

"And I tried to run this motel." Mom traced the writing on the ticket. "I couldn't do it."

She looked up. "What do you mean you tried?"

"Boot camp for wayward daughters." Mom crumpled the ticket and dropped it in a trash can. "Every time things got tough, I let Pops handle the crisis. He said his dad was tough, but the apple didn't fall far from the tree, and he wondered what kind of flighty fruit he produced."

She broke out in a sweat and replayed every maternal heart-to-heart she remembered. Mom's can-do attitude had to spring from a well of strength, not twenty-first century parenting fads. Without Mom at the helm, Kada would struggle to paint. She swallowed. "You could have done it."

Mom shook her head. "I live in the clouds. You?" She smiled. "You're like the best combination of me and Dad. You have your feet planted firmly on the earth, but you're still a dreamer. Your generation has so much flexibility and grace. Nothing exists you can't accomplish with a little patience and elbow grease."

She rubbed at a stain on the wall. *Out, damned spot.* Lady Macbeth's guilt drove her insane, but Kada refused to succumb to her mistakes. She took on the Starlight Motel to honor her family, find her footing, and figure out her next steps, but she worried the desert would swallow whole her ambition. Fearing she would fall flat on her face, she climbed down from the counter. "When you were a kid, did you want to take over managing the motel?"

"Oh, absolutely not." Mom backed out of the

kitchen. "It's so intense."

Laughing, she set down the rag. "I still want to paint. It soothes me and gives me a way to examine the world. Maybe you and Dad could run the motel from time to time and give me a break? One day, I would like to do more than paint *casita* walls." Holding her breath, she wondered if asking for a partnership would be enough.

"But the murals are beautiful!" Mom waved both hands. "I don't want to ruin your groove. Let me sort through Pops' record collection, wipe my tears, and go back to Wyoming where I belong. I'm glad we came down, but you have this covered."

"But...b-but..." She struggled to find a rebuttal. Without Mom, she had to fall back on Plan B. The family would have to hire a manager or sell the motel. If she stayed, the half-finished mural might be the last thing she painted. She wiped her palms on her jeans.

"The desert is beautiful this time of year." Mom stretched her arms behind her back. "Motion is lotion, as my yoga teacher says. Being outside does a body good."

"I couldn't agree more," Dane said.

Kada gasped and turned toward the sound of his voice. He wore neat jeans and a crisp white work shirt. His hair, damp and dark against his forehead, looked recently combed. He looked like the kind of unencumbered problem she could tackle in a heartbeat. Memories of their tryst on the washing machine promised he could make her forget the quagmire of family remembrances and uncertain loyalties threatening to pull her under. "You're here."

He inclined his head. "I meant to be here earlier,

but a hand drove a tractor over an irrigation line, severed it, and flooded the pump shaft." He lifted his nose. "Did I miss breakfast? I can usually smell the *chorizo* a mile away."

She and Mom laughed.

Raising a donut, he eyed the sugary, sweet confection and took a bite. "No matter. I'm here." He frowned. "Who ordered bear claws?"

Tossing the rag into the sink, she walked out of the kitchen. "I can't do much about breakfast, but I have cold cut sandwiches for lunch. Stick around for a while. If you mean to escape your relatives, you couldn't pick a better place than the Starlight Motel."

"Oh, did you cancel the New Year's Eve shenanigans?" He bumped her shoulder. "They come every year."

The warm flush of contact steadied her, and she looked over the cantina. Each table still held a small, white ceramic vase stuffed with pink and red carnations and a candy cane. Guests still sunned themselves by the pool, and children still played hide and seek between the palm trees. The motel would endure, and she had to find a way to thrive. "No, but we're rolling with the punches. If you hang out long enough, you'll pick up on the magic."

"Maybe I already have." He rubbed his thumb along his fingers.

"Oh?" She walked out of the kitchen, grabbed a carnation, and tucked the flower behind her ear. "Are you ready to lead the sing-along? We have story time scheduled from two to four."

He braced his legs and crossed his arms. "Absolutely not."

She laughed. "Fair enough, but if I see you floating in the pool with a drink, I'll charge you a day use fee."

"And if I see you doing the same?"

She exhaled and considered the possibility. In the mid-morning light, he was as handsome and charming as the cowboy who rode in near twilight and stole her breath. She hoped the daylight might dull his charm, but he fixed an irrigation leak and honored his commitment. If she checked her phone, she would probably find a few text messages telling her about his delay. She knew in her heart he was too good to be true, but as long as he stuck around, she would enjoy the gift. "I heard Stephanie and Randi brewed a mean pot of coffee. Care to join me?"

He offered his arm.

Taking it, she savored his sweet citrus smell and enjoyed the moment. Whether or not Mom grinned mattered little. Kada would enjoy his presence and deal with the fallout another day. In the meantime, she had a motel to run.

Chapter Fourteen

"Let me take you to lunch." Dane stopped in the reception area. A fire burned in the fireplace. If he hadn't heard through the grapevine what had happened in the motel's kitchen, he would have attributed the smell of greasy smoke to bad wood.

Kada dropped her arm. "I thought we planned dinner."

"Give me both." He ran a hand through his wet hair and wished he brought his hat in from the jeep. After jumping in the ditch surrounding the pump, he and Walter had emerged as muddy as two schoolboys working out their grievances. The pump hummed to life, and he grinned like he never had more fun. But the day was young, and the sun's height reminded him his interests had recently extended beyond Palmer Farms.

Cupping her elbows, Kada looked at an analog clock. "I have to pick up groceries for a New Year's Eve cookout, take Lucky to the veterinarian, and run a few quick errands."

"What kind of errands? Last-minute birthday presents?"

"Good point. What's your size?" she asked.

He worked his jaw. "Don't mind me. I'm fine with stale, tiny, pink marshmallows." He pulled a decorated ginger cookie from his back pocket. "I forgot. Mariah sends her love."

Snapping off the hook, she took a bite and chewed. "Much better than a donut. Thank her for me."

He nodded. The cookie rode down the hill with him in an old general-purpose vehicle his dad had rescued from a World War II museum. With an eighty-inch wheelbase, quarter-ton capacity, and four-wheel drive, the old battle wagon served Palmer Farms as well as it served the army. If he had his way, instead of sending Kada's thanks to his mom, he'd toss Kada into the front seat and deliver her to the farmhouse for a midday reprieve.

"So, lunch is out of the question. How about that coffee?" she asked.

Whiling away an hour over dark roast held some appeal, but he couldn't squander his reprieve from the farm. "I have bad news."

Her face fell.

He bit back a smile. Teasing her shouldn't amuse him, but her motel management proved her mettle. As soon as she saw fit, she could return to painting the world with vivid murals. Judging by her progress on the *casita* designs, he had six months before she signed the bottom left corner of her mural and packed her bags for greener pastures.

"You can't break up with me," she said. "We're not even dating."

Tipping his finger, he gave her the point. "Noted. However, it's New Year's Eve."

She tilted her head. "Do you have plans?"

He snorted and leaned against the reception desk. "No, but you won't find a walk-in vet on New Year's Eve. Most of the veterinarians have a life, too. I doubt Lucky wants to bump along to the neighboring Imperial

Valley."

She pulled out her phone.

Holding up a finger, he tapped his chin. "I have a solution."

Narrowing her gaze, she set aside the device. "Do tell."

"Dr. Vo is coming to the farm to check on Smoky. If I ask nicely, she might swing down and see Lucky, too." He worked his jaw and left out a few details, like he went to high school with Vo Hạnh.

After graduation, Hạnh went to the University of California, Irvine for a Bachelor of Science degree in Biological Sciences. He figured she would become a veterinary technician or something similar. She was always adopting strays and fundraising for the local clinic.

She might have stuck with those efforts, but after years of accommodating Hạnh's "pets," her parents suggested a degree from the Western University of Health Sciences. Hạnh returned to the valley as Dr. Vo, but he figured she had dyed her hair pink to prove she wouldn't always take her parents' advice. He eyed the tinsel tree and its glittering ornaments. At the Starlight Motel, Vo Hạnh and her hair would fit right in.

Kada tilted her head. "Just how nicely do you need to ask?"

He could work with a little jealousy, but the looming holiday and Lucky's girth left a tight deadline. Swinging one foot along the polished floor, he suppressed a smile. "I don't think she would mind the extra visit." He grinned and looked up. "Honestly, she would probably flay me for recommending anyone else. She has a soft spot for strays."

"Lucky's not a stray." She lifted her chin, poured a cup of coffee, and offered it. "She has a home."

He sipped the coffee. "I'll call the vet on one condition."

"Dane, it's a family motel."

Spewing coffee from his mouth, he cleared his throat and wiped the back of a hand across his wet lips. "That's not what I meant!" A man enjoyed hooking up with a beautiful woman, and his intentions were suspect for the rest of his life. "Kada, I merely want lunch."

Nudging her shoulder against him, she laughed, dropped a handful of napkins over the splattered coffee on the floor, and wiped up the mess with a foot. "I know, but I have a busy day planned. My mom wants to go through Pops' records. Once she gets going, she might unpack every closet on-site. I have no idea what's in those closets."

"Skeletons?"

"Wrong holiday," she said. "I'm more worried about unleashing her grief."

He scooped down an arm and gathered the soiled napkins. The wet paper sagged in his hand. "You can't live off a ginger cookie. Dr. Vo's a great vet. While she's looking at Lucky, come for lunch. I know a little hike you might like. We'll pick up sandwiches and bring them along for a picnic."

Straightening, she tilted her head. "I don't want a vet report by phone. I want to be here with Lucky. Last night while I painted, she stayed with me. She knows we're responsible for each other. Frankly, she slept in my bed all night."

"Lucky dog."

She raised her eyebrows.

He grinned, but he would do almost anything to carve out time with her. Her responsibility toward Lucky made sense, but then again, responsibility toward his family obligations got him into this situation. If he hadn't delivered the date cake on his mother's behalf, he could have met Kada on familiar ground, wooed her like a beautiful woman, and started their relationship on the right foot. Faced with a challenge, he preferred to double down. "Let's do it my way."

She snorted. "You can't have the bed."

He massaged his temples. If he'd known she woke up this playful, he would have rolled into the parking lot a minute after sunrise and waited outside her door. Suppressing a smile, he dropped his hand. "I want to show you something."

"Dane…"

He pointed a finger. "Get your mind out of the gutter."

"Or?" She straightened her head.

"Or get ready to follow through on your insinuations."

Her cheeks blushed.

He dropped his finger. "One veterinary house call for one picnic lunch. I get to choose the spot."

She checked the time. "We can eat cold cut sandwiches by the pool."

"I choose the spot." He enunciated each word. "Or you can call every vet in the valley and test your luck." He crossed his arms. "Your choice."

Stepping forward, she walked her fingers up his chest. "You're lucky I overslept, and Stephanie burned the bacon. If the day started like I planned, I'd be elbow deep in dusty boxes, and you'd have a ham-and-cheese sandwich for lunch."

He captured a hand and pressed it to his lips. "I'll take what I can get."

"Will you?" She raised her eyebrows.

Releasing his grip before things got too serious, he reminded himself to take things easy before his responsibilities returned and he left Kada feeling abandoned. "Check on your motel, and give me a few minutes to call Dr. Vo."

"Do you know her well?"

"She's gorgeous, talented, and generous." He held back mentions of their childhood hijinks and the no-fly zone keeping their choose-your-family boundary perfectly intact. If he wanted a friends-to-lovers story, he would have to look somewhere else.

Kada sighed. "I should have stayed in bed."

Lucky dog. Reaching forward, he wrapped a hand around her waist, pulled her against his chest, and dropped his head. She smelled like almond blossoms, heady coffee, and polished steel. Paint marked her hair, and he wanted to rub the soft strands between his fingers, but he closed his eyes and swallowed. "Thanks for the coffee. I can't wait for lunch."

"Is that so?" Wiggling free, she laughed and strolled out the door.

He watched her hips sway and hoped his plan worked out. If not, he might have seen the end of Kada Ritchie's playfulness.

****

Vo Hạnh approached Kada's *casita* carrying a black backpack. "Where's my patient?"

Dane stopped the rocking chair's motion. After

Kada left him, he camped out on her *casita's* front porch and shot off emails from his phone.

Lucky claimed a sunny spot behind the railing.

Kada darted around the motel grounds like a zigzagging wasp. Her mother might have chosen the wrong insect.

"You almost stepped on her."

Frowning, Hạnh turned and found Lucky's hideout. Dropping to one knee, she offered a hand.

Lucky raised her head and sniffed.

"Aren't you beautiful," Hạnh crooned. "And about ready to pop, aren't you?"

Dropping her head, Lucky huffed.

"She's big, huh?" Kada stepped through the gate and wiped clean her hands. "We couldn't leave her up there on the mountain."

Hạnh made eye contact.

Dane recognized the quick flash of judgment that swept across her face. After hearing about the dog, Hạnh had expressed mild frustration with Lucky's prior owners. He explained the abandoned white car and the flashing headlights. Hạnh gave the owners the benefit of the doubt. He elaborated on Kada's commitment to rescuing the stray. Hạnh had agreed to take the case. "Nope," he said. "We couldn't leave her."

Hạnh stood and offered a hand. "Vo Hạnh, pleased to meet you."

"Likewise. Kada."

Hạnh donned disposable gloves and ran a hand along Lucky's side. She pressed against the swells and whispered to herself. "Canine pregnancies last approximately sixty-two to sixty-four days. Predicting the delivery timing can be difficult because the length of pregnancy varies with breed and litter size."

"What kind of dog is she?" Kada asked.

"A mutt. Some Lab. Some Pitt." Hạnh stilled a hand and looked up. "She'll make a loyal pet."

Kada dropped into the second rocking chair beside him and nodded. "She's already loyal."

"Based on her increased nipple size, swollen belly, and general lethargy, I think you definitely have a pregnant mama. Other conditions can cause weight gain and a swollen abdomen, but let's stay with an optimistic outcome."

"Wait." Kada leaned forward. "Lucky might be sick?"

"Puppies." Hạnh looked up. "Puppies are the best outcome."

Kada nodded.

He tried not to smile. Hạnh was a holistic veterinarian. When California hippies came to her asking about raw pet diets, she worked with the humans to make sure the animals received the protein and vitamins they needed. Holistic veterinarians combined practices like acupuncture and homeopathy with Western medicine, but Hạnh knew when to draw a line and hold her ground on scientific findings.

"We probably don't have time to start deworming," Hạnh said. "It can significantly decrease the amount of roundworm and hookworm in newborn puppies, but I don't want to stress the dam."

Right now, he wouldn't mind taking a walk. Growing up with a brother and acres of vegetables kept him immune from most pregnancy discussions, but he ran a farm. He could man up and talk canine gestation until the sun went down, but his stomach turned at the thought. Walter took care of most of the farm animals. Clearing his throat, he considered the walk and gripped the chair's handrails. "What can we do to help?"

"I don't see any mechanical or anatomical concerns that would prevent Lucky from having a normal whelped litter," Hạnh said. "Put together a whelping box. If you have a kid's plastic swimming pool, it makes a safe, easily cleaned option. Lucky can walk in and out, but the puppies can't escape."

"I can buy a kiddie pool," Kada said.

Shrugging, Hạnh tied up her hair. "Whatever you use, put it in a quiet area with easy access. Let her get used to the space so she avoids your closet."

Kada shifted the rocking chair and peered through the *casita* toward her closet.

The chair rail nearly crushed his toes, but his boots saved him.

"Sorry." She fixed the chair. "My closet?"

"You want her to nest in the whelping box." Gripping the back of Lucky's neck, Hạnh held down the dog's head and took the dog's rectal temperature. "A dam's temperature usually drops about eight to twenty-four hours before delivery. You have time." She peeled off the gloves and dropped them onto the porch decking. "In the meantime, if she ignores her food, don't worry. She'll return to it after the delivery."

Kada nodded.

"I counted six puppies."

"Six?" Kada's gaze widened.

"Don't rush her. A litter of six puppies should normally take about six hours total. As long as she's cleaning the puppies and breathing normally, let her do her thing. If she starts trembling, collapsing, or

217

shivering, please call me." Hạnh extended a business card and a pamphlet. "Otherwise, don't worry. Everything will be fine."

Kada looked between Lucky and Hạnh and repeated the phrase.

He regretted teasing Kada about Hạnh. The pair could be friends, and he didn't want to start a rivalry or give Kada unnecessary concerns.

"Fine doesn't mean easy," Hạnh said. "You and Lucky might suffer a little nervousness, but the right actions, thinking, and mindfulness will pull you through the birthing process. Try to embrace the present moment and live in the now."

She widened her gaze. "The now?"

"Do your best to help her stay calm. If you're too scared about the future or worried about the past, you'll lose sight of what's important."

"Puppies?" she asked.

Hạnh offered a soft, comforting smile and a sheaf of papers.

He remembered that smile from their years running around the playground, and he knew her compassion made her an excellent veterinarian. Walter wouldn't tolerate anyone else.

"After the puppies arrive, I'll take care of the whole crew and get everyone vaccinated," Hạnh said. "Congratulations. Lucky's a beautiful dog."

Kada took the papers, stared at her new pet, and nodded.

He had seen that stunned look on farmhands who plowed through their first day of work, rolled up to a field on day two, and counted the rows. Standing, he offered Hạnh a hand. "Thanks for coming down. Send me the bill, and I'll sort out the charges."

"Oh, you know I can't charge you for this little come-and-see." Hạnh tossed her pink hair over her shoulder. "The Buddhist spirit of giving—*dana*—is about generosity. If I wanted to code every hour of my day and pad my wallet, I would have become a dentist."

Kada looked up from the papers and wrinkled her brow.

Shaking his head, he met Hạnh's gaze with a smile. Her dad was definitely a dentist.

"I'll call this visit a favor, and the next time I need a hand, you'll be the first person I call."

"Does this mean I'm cleaning gutters?" he asked.

"Maybe." She winked.

He crossed his arms. "Maybe you should open a new practice in San Bernardino."

Laughing, Hạnh packed up her tools. "My parents would kill me." With a wave, she stepped onto the path leading back to the parking lot. "Actually, you can carry my bag."

Unfolding his arms, he wondered what game she played. Nodding, he took the bag, fell into step, and followed Hạnh through the palms.

"Your girlfriend looks a little pale," she said.

He looked over his shoulder and found Kada reading the vet's pamphlet.

Lucky snoozed in the sunlight.

Her stomach might have rippled, but he chalked up the effect to a trick of the light. "She has her hands full prepping for the end of the year, running the motel, and worrying about Lucky." Shame warmed his cheeks. He helped out, but if his presence complicated Kada's days, he should retreat and return when she had more free time. Replaying his experiences at the motel, he wondered if she ever had free time.

"My mother might call her a 'hungry ghost.' It's a Buddhist metaphor that describes a person tormented by unfulfillment. Most people reserve the term for extreme cases like a deceased family member who no longer feels venerated. My mother applies it to every angsty-looking individual she meets. Does Kada have the recognition she deserves? Does the motel fulfill her?"

Stopping, he looked over his shoulder and saw the half-finished mural on the *casita*. "She's a muralist by training. This motel gig isn't her end game."

Hạnh nodded at the edge of the parking lot. "Maybe when she picks up a paintbrush, her color will improve."

Tugging Hạnh's ponytail, he handed off her bag. "When will your color improve? What's next orange? Blue?"

Hạnh rolled her eyes. "As if. Who looks good with orange hair?"

He thought of Kada's dark locks catching the sunlight. She would look good in anything.

****

Dane stood in the doorway and considered whether to interrupt Kada as she pored over the veterinarian's papers. Hạnh might be right. Kada looked a little pale, but the shadows this time of day could be funny. He worked his jaw and considered his options.

Kada looked up from the pamphlet. "Where did she go?"

He shrugged. "More patients."

"I need lunch," Kada said. "Now."

"That, I can do." He lifted the pamphlet from her hands, set it on the rocking chair, and led her down the steps. "Everything will be fine."

"That's like what you hear at the beginning of a horror movie. How am I supposed to doula a litter of puppies? Remaking *Ocean's Eleven* a third time might be easier." She walked down the path like a dazed zombie, turned, and pointed toward Lucky. "Don't you dare have those puppies while I'm gone!"

Lucky snored.

Biting his lip, he pulled his keys from his pocket and led her toward the jeep. "Don't worry, I know a spot to take your mind off whatever's bugging you."

"Let me text my mom and tell her I'm heading out." Pulling out her phone, she fired off a message. "I'll ask Mom to check on Lucky every hour."

Instead of a quick reply, Larissa walked out of the motel, headed straight toward them, and shaded her eyes.

He stepped back to give the women privacy and considered whether rescuing Lucky was the right thing to do. Kada would refuse taking the dog to the animal shelter, but she had a mountain on her shoulders. Larissa might catch on to Kada's exhaustion and curtail his outing. He could call Walter and ask for help with Lucky. Kada would give him hell, but at least she would have options. He always had options and the freedom they entailed.

"Where are you going?" Larissa planted her hands on her hips.

Kada looked toward him.

"North," he said. "We'll be back after lunch."

Larissa waved a hand and encompassed the rocky

gardens. "But who will run the motel?"

"You know this place better than I do." Kada cupped Larissa's elbow. "You grew up here, and we still use Pops' systems. The paper towels are still stacked next to the dishrags. The computer password is still *Yucca*. I haven't made any substantive changes. If you want to close your eyes, imagine it's 1992."

"What a year." Larissa shook her head and dropped her raised arm. "I guess I can manage the motel for a few hours. You've picked up so much slack this year."

Kada rubbed Larissa's upper arm. "Mom, we both own this property."

"But it's meant to be yours." Larissa wiped away a tear. "Pops wanted you to have it."

"Oh!" Kada wrapped her mother in a hug. "I'm asking too much, aren't I?"

He shifted. Feeling like an accessory during an intimate moment, he wondered if he should start the jeep or make plans for another day.

"No." Shaking her head, Larissa pulled free and blinked away her tears. "I'm processing my grief. Some people lose their parents and move on with their lives, but I wasn't ready. I lost your grandmother too early, and losing Pops hurts as much as losing my mother. Even though he's gone, I can't walk around incapacitated, pining, and ruminating."

Kada pulled back and snorted. "Ruminating?"

Rubbing a hand over her face, Larissa smiled. "My therapist's words. She said I have to return to previous activities or find new ones. Life goes on. I didn't expect to find so many memories on-site. You're lucky you have this place."

Kaka crossed her hands over her arms. "What if I

want more?"

In the bright sunlight, Larissa's gaze sharpened. "More?"

The two women, standing side by side, looked as similar as siblings, but decades separated their success. He knew the pride and admiration of looking at his old man and seeing his success. Did Larissa recognize herself in the daughter she raised? Did Kada feel the same, and would she take her mother's path? The jeep held a lot of appeal, but he waded into this situation, and he would hold his ground.

"A partnership." Kada leaned her head on Larissa's shoulder. "Even though he was your dad, we both lost someone we loved, and we both love the Starlight Motel."

"You're right." Larissa squeezed Kada's shoulder.

Kada raised her head. "I am?"

Larissa waved a hand toward the parking lot. "Go! Have fun. If you return to sticky notes and carbon paper card swipes, you'll know what happened in your absence. Maybe that will teach you to rethink partnerships."

Kada laughed and hugged her. "You'll do great."

He released his breath and opened the jeep door. For a few hours, at least, he could cultivate Kada's joy and maybe tease her into a dalliance.

Hugging her mother good-bye, Kada turned and stopped short. "What is that?"

"A truck?"

She made eye contact. "Does it have seat belts?"

"Yeah." He had a sedan back at the farm, but he planned to do a little off-roading, and the jeep had higher clearances. "It runs like a charm."

Shaking her head, she slipped her phone into a pocket and jerked her head toward the old, blue farm wagon. "No way. We'll take Pops' truck."

If he had to pick his battles, conveyances wouldn't be one. Pocketing the jeep keys, he grabbed his hat and walked toward the blue truck. "No problem, but I get to drive."

She narrowed her gaze.

"Pretty please?" he asked. "I know the roads like the back of my hand."

"You're insufferable."

Laughing, he pulled his sunglasses from the *V* of his shirt. Most people took him for a pampered son racking up family profits. They missed the log books, fertilizer conferences, and numbing insomnia. Give him a few more years, and he would have an eye tic to go with his reading glasses and high blood pressure, but Kada thought he was cute.

He could fall back on his honed tendencies, but her laughter alleviated the pressure in his chest, and her banter held promise. If she could keep up with him, then he would make room in his life for more than crops and the bottom line.

If she needed space, then he would chock up the day to a good deed. He couldn't fix her life or make her days stress-free, but he could show her something worthy of a smile. Climbing into the cab, he checked the mirrors. "You have no idea how insufferable I am."

She pulled shut the passenger door. "What?"

"Never mind," he said. "Let's roll."

Shaking her head, she buckled her seat belt. "I think I liked you better when you were on a horse."

Backing up the truck, he spread an arm over the

passenger seat, turned his head, and ignored the rearview mirror. "Is that so?"

She scanned the open desert surrounding the motel.

The land near the highway had room for small businesses, but this far out of town, few businesses thrived beside the Starlight Motel. As the land rose toward the mountains, Palmer Farms claimed the desert's bounty. "What do you think of the scenery? It's not L.A."

"Pretty enough. I find all manner of bugs and lizards creeping through the *casitas*. I'm thinking about charging them rent. Your mom said the desert takes time to seep into a person's soul, but the animals aren't as reserved."

Laughing, he put the truck into Drive and pressed the accelerator. "Most animals around here are nocturnal animals. If you didn't stay up so late to paint, you might not see them."

"I like seeing them," she said.

He liked the animals, too. If stubborn rats and bighorn sheep could eke out a living in the desert, he could do the same. "Maybe they're drawn to the motel and its dripping faucets." He glanced at her. "Have you considered selling?"

She ran a hand through her hair. "How much? Ten million?"

Slapping his chest, he refocused on the road. "You think highly of yourself."

"As soon as I finish the murals, every hipster in a five-hundred-mile radius will want a selfie by the pool." Her seat creaked. "Authentic, local interest perseveres, and the Starlight Motel has a lot to offer."

Glancing at her and seeing her reclined in the

sunlight, he believed her, but he wanted to scrap his purchase offer and funnel his inheritance toward a tropical island and a lumbering Internet connection where she could paint to her heart's content, and he could watch her.

Instead, he kept a straight face and reminded himself he needed wide open spaces as much as he needed fresh air. "You're probably right. Palm Springs is having a resurgence. Maybe you should stay, handle the hoards, and keep them off my land."

"You should do agro-tours."

He wrinkled his nose. *I liked it better when we were flirting.* If he wanted to talk shop, he would spend the day listening to Walter's worries, his dad's advice, or the industry newsletters that flooded his inbox. "Why did you come to the motel in the first place? One thing I knew, Hall had passed, and the next thing I knew, you'd taken up residence."

She sighed. "My mom feels things so deeply. The minute Pops passed, she looked around the motel, peered in a drawer or two, and said, 'Gosh, I wish I could do something to help.' She couldn't take the onslaught of emotions. I mean, obviously, she could have done a ton, but she needed time to process her father's death. I thought she would be back in a week or two. Months went by. I was pretty good at picking up the slack."

Family loyalty kept multigenerational businesses profitable. Each contributor stepped in to fill a need. Until she realized how much she did for her family, she would struggle with her participation. "But why you?"

She made a noncommittal sound.

Slowing for a yellow light, he risked a glimpse of

her profile. She looked lost in thought, but she had demonstrated her ability to see the details that escaped most people. When she painted the *casitas*, she brought the plants to life and made their assets shine. If he saw an unexpected plant, he worried about pests.

"I guess grief hits people in different ways. I saw Pops get weaker. I had time to sit with him and listen to his stories. For Mom, he was here one day and gone the next."

Regret dampened her conjecture. She had no more stolen those last hours with Hall than Larissa had stolen Kada's ability to paint. "Maybe she needed more time?"

"Then why didn't she return?" She drummed her fingers on the door. "What did she think would happen to the motel? The books and the taxes would take care of themselves?"

He gripped the wheel and considered the alternative. "Running a business together defines my relationship with my dad. Sometimes, I'm jealous of my brother's role. Jud throws the football with Dad, and their banter never degrades into a cost-benefit analysis or satellite weather reports."

An oncoming vehicle swerved, and he hoped the driver put down his or her phone and focused on the open road. Between driving the old truck and opening up to Kada, he had his hands full. "I guess Jud might resent me, too. Whenever we have a family problem, Mom and Dad come to me first."

"Is that so?"

"Where does that leave him? As a kid, the roles really confused me. Like, why did birth order make me the heir and him the spare?"

"Have you asked him to take up a role in the business?"

He snorted. "Jud hates farming as much as I hate making cold calls."

She laughed. "Noted."

"Huh?" He turned his head.

She smiled. "If you buy the motel, I won't put you in charge of media requests. I bet you'd make a terrible interviewee. When reporters asked you to expound on farming themes, you would probably recite crop yields and market prices."

He laughed. "Who interviews farmers? I'd let someone else handle the media requests."

"Good point." She adjusted the vent. "You'd come off stoic as shit. Bring Smoky. You're looser in your element."

"My element?" He opened his mouth to defend his profession, but her worldview expected glossy produce on demand. He provided it. Shutting his mouth, he adjusted his grip on the wheel. "Well, for what it's worth, I think you're doing a good job at the motel. The guests look happy, and the facility shines. Smoky obviously enjoyed his stay."

Shifting her weight, she put a hand on his thigh. "I forgot to ask. Is he okay?"

The weight of a hand stole the blood from his head and sent it shooting straight south. Her innocent gesture almost caused a one-vehicle accident on a lonely, desert road. Instead of focusing on his desire, he chewed his cheek and thought of the slobbering horse that brought them together. "Smoky's fine. If you tried, you couldn't find a stronger quarter horse."

"I've never tried." She drew back a hand. "On my

first trail ride, the horse bucked, and I refused to ride again."

"Well, I know what we'll do for date number two. You'd give Smoky a chance, wouldn't you?"

"Maybe," she said.

He laughed. "Maybe we'll start with grooming the horse?"

"Riding a horse is an antiquated hobby."

He saw her appreciation for Smoky and Lucky. She might be an urban progressive, but she had a soft spot for cuddly critters. If he were lucky, her soft spot extended to hard-ass farmers with a newfound appreciation for painters. Keeping her engaged would help him break through her preconceptions. More sex would help, but so would more ire. "So is painting. Have you tried computers?"

She laughed and tossed her hair over her shoulder. "Some things don't translate well into the digital age."

Thinking of their stolen kiss and the way his heartbeat accelerated in her presence, he agreed. Some things were timeless. "You might be right."

Chapter Fifteen

Riding with Dane felt easy, but Kada couldn't relax in the moment. She evaluated her reasons for taking in Lucky. Assisting with puppy delivery worried her, but long-term concerns stressed her more than wiggling bundles of fur.

After her residency in Los Angeles, she doubted her motives for grand, empathetic gestures. Failure had a way of burning doubts into a woman's memory. She wanted to give Lucky a home, but would the dog find a better home with a rambunctious family?

Sneaking a peek at the rangy farmer driving the truck, she admired his profile and his kissable lips, but he might be a step too complicated for a woman who ran herself ragged from sunup to sundown. If her attraction to Dane petered out, she had other options. Carrying on with an employee would land her in hot water, but some handsome guest might catch her eye. She suppressed a grin. *Too bad I want Dane.*

Drumming her fingers on her knee, she hoped Lucky's delivery went smoothly, the puppies were cute, and she could look back on this holiday and laugh. Peppermints and tinsel were cheerful decorations, but puppies?

"Are you warm enough?" Dane adjusted the vent.

She glanced at him. Too bad Mariah hadn't produced a school photograph like a good, old-fashioned mama. Kada would have asked for Dane's number and invited him to the Starlight Motel for a drink. Maybe her dating game needed a refresher, and she would have asked him to a local brewery. What if the conversation went flat? She scratched her nails against her denim and flexed her fingers. Instead of thinking about negative outcomes, she reached for the radio knob. A remix filled the cab.

He jerked his chin toward the radio. "What is this? The top forty? When did they let people start saying words like that on the radio?"

"Would you prefer jazz?" She fiddled with the knob and tuned in to a local station. "Public radio? The weather report."

"Anything is fine. I'm usually alone with my thoughts."

"Walter leaves you in peace?"

"Walter and I do companionable solitude like peanut butter and jelly."

She laughed and relaxed her seat. Sliding forward her feet, she settled into the cushioning. "He seems like a good guy."

"He is." Peering through the windshield, he looked up. "The weather looks good."

"The weather always looks good." She adjusted the radio and settled on modern hits. "Earlier this month, I had a guest cry because rain ruined her hike, but everyone is happy with the cool nights."

"We've had a few wet months. I recorded about four inches at the farmhouse."

She scratched her head. "That's a lot."

He smiled. "Relatively."

Adjusting the vent, she directed the soft, warm air

away from her face. "Are you sure Mariah can spare you?"

"She has my younger brother, Jud. They've always been closer. The minute Mom delivered me, Dad claimed me for the farm. Mom took Jud. You would have to ask him whether he enjoys being the spare kid, but he has no interest in the farms."

She knew Mariah as a mentor and an educator. If his parents divided their attentions, then they probably responded to their kids' talents. She always wanted a sibling. Would they have shared interests or been as different as night and day? She turned her head and admired his profile against the scrolling desert landscape. "Did you always enjoy the farms?"

He worked his jaw. "I enjoy the sense of accomplishment. I've always been competitive. If my dad brought me up in another industry, then I probably would have pursued it as aggressively." He slowed the truck for an intersection. "But farming shapes a man, too."

Oh, it shaped him just fine. She shifted on the springy seat and refocused her thoughts. "What does your brother do?"

"Sell cars."

Laughing, she leaned back and closed her eyes. "Mariah said he's a good guy." Peeking, she gauged his reaction for a hint of sibling rivalry.

"Oh yeah?" He glanced over and raised his eyebrows. "Did she dangle both sons and let you choose?"

She expected friendly competition, but he looked genuinely interested in his mother's antics. The thought of Mariah arranging her sons' love lives provoked a smile, but she jerked her chin toward the highway. "Hardly, and I haven't picked one yet. Keep your eyes on the road. Shouldn't you be wearing your glasses?"

"I think you like the glasses," he said.

"I do."

He laughed. "I have a mild case of farsightedness, but I can usually compensate without my glasses. Am I speeding?"

"A little. If you hit a rock, I don't have roadside assistance."

Slowing the truck, he tapped the steering wheel. "Short of hitting a cactus, I doubt we'll encounter any obstacles. I can change a tire."

"Of course you can." She let the truck eat up the highway asphalt while she imagined him shirtless and wielding a wrench. "When did you realize you needed glasses?"

"How's your vision?" he asked.

She wet her lips and tried to focus. "Perfect."

"I'm jealous." He pressed the accelerator and picked up a little speed. "For a while, I didn't know I had a problem. Common vision screenings rarely detect hyperopia. Every time they tested me in grade school, I could identify the letters on an eye chart and pass the test, but I had headaches. I worked my eyes too hard trying to make letters come into focus."

She exhausted herself trying to bring her life into focus. "Your parents made the connection?"

"Well, Mom told me I was an ornery kid, and if I wanted to come home from school every day in a bad mood, I could stay at school."

Covering her mouth, she tried not to laugh.

"One day, I picked up my dad's reading glasses,

and everything came into focus. The eyestrain, headaches, and irritability were all symptoms of my vision problems. Mom held her breath, took me to an optometrist, and cried all the way home. I told you she surrendered me to my dad, but I think she loves me more than Jud."

"My friends say the same thing. Every kid thinks they're the favorite."

He grinned. "I am."

"Poor Jud." She eyed the speedometer.

"You keep away from Jud. Finders keepers." He dodged roadkill and let the truck's tires bounce along the rocky shoulder.

She wanted to laugh, but she questioned the truck's shocks. "Seriously, slow down. Is this how you drive in the fields?"

He eased his foot off the accelerator. "Wide, open spaces have benefits. They're easy driving, and they give a man room to breathe."

A club hit played on the radio.

"Are you planning to stay in the valley?" he asked.

She let the question settle. Her answer, like her artwork, depended on too many variables. She could plan and sketch until her muscles ached, but the outcome depended on skill. As long as the Starlight Motel flourished, she could see herself stewarding the reception desk for a year or two, but she needed to paint more than a *casita* wall. "I'll stay in the short term."

His grin spread into a wide smile. "Lucky bought me a few months?"

Without worries etching lines into his face, he was as handsome as any Hollywood star. His kisses and his smiles could cure her midnight wanderings. He affected her like a calorie-laden desert. Armed with that knowledge, he might become more of a nuisance than an indulgence. She tucked away the memory of his smile and stared out the windshield. "Lucky might prefer the ocean. We have no idea where she lived before landing in the Coachella Valley."

"I have a few guesses," he said.

So did she. She checked the side view mirror. The combination of blue skies, sweeping vistas, and close proximity left her itching to feel the wind. "Do you mind if I roll down the window?"

He shook his head.

Cranking down the window, she let the crisp air soothe her warm cheeks.

At the stoplight, he adjusted his sunglasses.

She opened the glove compartment, withdrew a pair, and settled them on her nose. "Where are we going, anyway?"

"You said you had errands. I assumed you wanted to drive into Palm Springs."

"I don't need a driver. I thought we were getting lunch."

As he settled into the seat, the worn springs creaked. "We are. Do you have any dietary restrictions?"

"Absolutely not. I'm healthy as a horse."

He laughed. "All right then."

She liked how he scanned the intersection for traffic, but she cautioned herself not to read too much into his enthusiasm or his moderated behavior. The laundry room liaison thrilled her, but she refused to be the kind of woman who poured out her problems to a man and hoped he would pick up the slack.

Going into town would be a welcome diversion. People made a town great, and Palms Springs' citizens congregated at local cafes with an ear for gossip and good jokes. Restaurants rolled out new dishes, and the gardening club spruced up the medians. The last time she went into town, barrel cacti with bright-yellow centers, prickly pears with tangy hot-pink fruit, and aloe vera with speckled white flecks overflowed from medians, but the town's residents couldn't conjure snow. She chose her words and kept her gaze averted to miss the judgment in his expression. "I have an appointment with my therapist at three."

"A real therapist or the kind who serves coffee and listens to your woes for a good tip?"

His joke eased her concerns. Turning from the window, she flung out an arm and slapped his thigh. She hit solid muscle. The man would look good in shorts. Taking a deep breath, she waited. "A real therapist. I see her every other week."

He frowned.

She tensed.

"Even on New Year's Eve?" he asked.

She released her breath. "I can cancel the appointment and check on Benito. Stephanie said he pinched a nerve, but she's not the most reliable narrator."

"Do you want to do both?"

"No." She coughed and banged her chest. "The therapist is a precaution. Benito might need help."

"We can swing by after lunch and do both."

"Thanks." Exhaling, she wondered if his family talked about mental health, or he juggled so many problems a quirky muralist with a therapist on speed dial hardly registered. Content to live in the moment, she decided she didn't care. He was a grown man, and if he asked her out to lunch, he could live with the consequences.

He skirted Indian Canyons. The 1960s neighborhood boasted midcentury-modern homes designed by architects like Dan Palmer, William Krisel, and Stan Sackley. Back in the day, the town was a magnet for celebrities like Bob Hope, Sinatra's Rat Pack, and the roommate starlets who wanted to marry rich. Now, the neighborhood hosted aging snowbirds who associated Palm Springs with their misspent youths. They kept a lively scene, but when they passed, she wondered who would take up the sleek, glass-walled homes.

A sandstone cove protected the Indian Canyons houses from the desert winds and the summer sun. Beyond the canyon, the world's largest grove of wild palm trees grew in a lush paradise. Homes sold for top dollar, but she wondered who splashed out the cash. If she stuck around to see who carried the flag at next year's Christmas parade, she might find out. "If you didn't live in the valley, where would you live?"

"I have no idea." He shifted his seat.

He fidgeted like she asked him to choose between a snake bite and a scorpion sting. She turned away from the window and considered his evasive answer. "None? Haven't you been on a vacation and loved the locale?"

He smiled and passed a farm truck with flashing yellow lights. "No. I left the valley to attend Cal Poly San Luis Obispo, but after graduation, I returned to the farm. Maybe you should sell me the motel, and we'll head to Hawaii Island."

"Maybe you should hit a pothole, go off-road, and wander into the desert."

He laughed. "Harsh."

"What would you do with the motel land, anyway? Plant more date palms? You have plenty."

He scratched the side of his lip. "I hear you, but plenty is subjective. As long as I can turn a profit, employ workers, and fulfill community needs, I'll keep farming."

People had to eat, and she couldn't fault his successful profession. If she didn't have resources and a vibrant family business, she couldn't take in Lucky. And despite her relative wealth, she still painted. "What about you and your needs?"

He slowed for the first traffic light, turned his head, and stared. "What about me?"

"Don't you have secret hobbies? Wild Tanzanian safari fantasies? Buried artistic tendencies?"

His brow wrinkled. "I've thought about planting varieties beyond the Medjool family. Date trees can only produce fruit in dry, arid conditions, but to withstand the intense heat, they need water at their roots. Not all dates are created the same."

She wrinkled her nose. Dates had their charms, but if Dane thought a different variety comprised an adventure, she and the man were on two different wavelengths. Then again, she had never shared a kiss with a man in a laundry room.

Thinking about the motel, she wondered what she would do without dates. Stately trees and their finger-like crowns provided a lush backdrop for the motel's publicity photographs, and the fruit charmed tourists. Together, the 1950s *casitas* and the green canopies gave the motel the appearance of a charming oasis. No wonder the National Date Festival chose Arabian Nights as their first theme. She could embrace the fruit, but Dad had a point. Without irrigation, Dane's wealth would shrivel up and leave behind sporadic palms that existed before farmers sunk their wells.

He made a left turn.

"I've seen my life play out a dozen ways," she said. "I could have grown up here."

"We would have already had a date. Maybe even prom."

She laughed. "I've also seen myself in a high-rise tower."

He shuddered. "I've thought about making changes, too, but on a much smaller scope. Palmer Farms has been a family business for four generations. We're committed to growing superior produce, embracing changing technologies, and furthering the farming profession with an emphasis on ecologically friendly techniques, low pesticides application, natural fertilizers, and a solar-generated electrical system."

"Is that your website synopsis?"

"Yes," he said.

She laughed and doubled over until her sides ached. "Come on, Dane. It's good. It's beautiful, but what gets you up in the morning?"

He drew a deep breath. "Family. Responsibility. Pride." Turning, he made eye contact. "Today, it was you. What gets you up, Kada?"

Shying away from the intensity in his gaze, she watched a parade of houses and crisp, green lawns slip past the truck window. "People." She smiled. "I love people. I love the motel guests, the artists I met at university, and the joyous students I worked with in Los Angeles."

"What happened in LA?"

She knew the question was coming, but she had buried it beneath Lucky's needs, the motel's guests, and the magnetic attraction she felt whenever he walked into a room. Taking a deep breath, she gave thanks he drove the old truck and she had the freedom to stretch. If she sat face-to-face with him or held the wheel, she couldn't tell the story without crashing the truck. "I attempted something big."

"Ambition isn't a bad thing."

"It is when you fail." She took a deep breath. "My parents raised me in Laramie, but you know Mom grew up at the Starlight Motel. I mean, she literally grew up tripping around Pops' ankles. After Grandma Nana died, Pops and Mom ran the motel the best way they knew how, but Mom wanted more. Dad rolled into town with long hair and big ideas. She married him and eloped in the course of a day."

He tugged on his shirt collar. "It's a sweet, crazy story."

"Well, we've known each other more than a day. You can't top it."

Putting on the truck's blinker, he checked the side mirror and took the highway exit toward downtown Palm Springs. "Noted."

Their relationship started as a hookup. Now, she was cruising the main drag in broad daylight. Twenty years ago, word would have gotten around. She was glad she had the freedom to find her way. "My parents loved me and told me I could do anything, but I'm not sure they understood how much trouble I could find in the world of printmaking and paints. After I left the University of Wyoming with a B.F.A. in Studio Art, I wanted a bigger stage."

"Why?" he asked. "Laramie is a decent-sized town."

She worked her jaw and thought of the type-casting she encountered in the small town. "I'd already seen plenty of cowboys."

He snuck a gaze. "And here you are."

"I swore you were a farmer."

He laughed.

Their easy camaraderie eased her ability to talk about more than dinner specials and local attractions. "After graduation, I moved to San Francisco, lived in the Tenderloin neighborhood, and worked in advertising. Across the Bay, protestors questioned the roles corporations play, and their rallies prompted me to think about my choices. I worked at a design firm, and the job paid my bills, but I wanted artistic freedom. My boyfriend wanted to settle in the East Bay."

"Is that bad?"

"Only if you're a wandering hipster with a bent toward public art."

He laughed.

"I applied to grad schools and savored my acceptance letters. My boyfriend refused to move. I said good riddance and chose California State University, Long Beach to study printmaking and complete my MFA. My final project was 'Printmaking: Nature's Promises,' and it was good."

"I'm sure," he said. "I pulled up your work on my phone. It's beautiful and powerful."

She let the compliment wash over her, but if she

lingered too long with his praise, she couldn't finish the story. "Thanks. The project was good enough to land me a residency at the Los Angeles County Museum of Art.

"All of a sudden, I had name recognition and financing as an artist-in-residence. I organized a multipart community mural project at the Los Angeles Technical Vocational High School. Engaging student collaborators in the work's conception and art direction broadened my understanding of nature's power in urban environments."

He glanced out the window.

If he could reconsider a familiar landscape, he might be able to understand how much she lost. "Dane, the students were so fierce. They were the same rowdy kids I grew up with, but concrete boxed them into their neighborhood. I wanted to show them they could find freedom."

"You obviously had a connection with them."

She closed her eyes and swallowed the lump in her throat. The mural was good, but whether its power came from her or from the students remained to be seen. If she couldn't give up the desert for her art, did she deserve it? Shifting, she watched the clouds cast shadows on his profile. "The kids taught me about local creeks buried underground for progress. Their grandparents remembered playing in the creeks, but the students saw them bubbling out of catch basins or flooding encroaching neighborhoods. I took so many notes on their discussion and scribbled so many ideas about the mural that a theme emerged. Every generation wants to embrace nature and fight their way to the surface."

He slowed for a tractor. "When people see the natural world, they understand their significance. That's why everyone loves a starlit sky. Serving your peers and fostering connections are some of the best things you can do." He glanced over and smiled. "I mean, short of growing food."

"Yeah." She returned his smile, but she swallowed and wondered if he might be more than the rangy, languid cowboy who rode onto her property at sundown and offered to buy it out from under her. Did he have a poetic streak buried under all that buttoned-down brawn and sun-kissed hair?

She took a deep breath. "After the mural, I fundraised on a crowd-funding platform for a follow-up project. A few reporters carried the story, the students distributed flyers, and the museum posted on social media." She took a deep breath and prepared for condescension. "At the end of the campaign, I had six hundred dollars."

"That's not so bad."

Eyes wide, she stared. "Dane, I needed thousands of dollars. Tens of thousands of dollars. If I want to treat art like a hobby, I have to hold down a day job. If I want to treat art like a calling, I have to eat."

"Oh." He turned onto a small side street. Angling toward a parking spot, he stopped in front of The Desert Empire Café and put the truck in Park. He shifted on the seat. "I'm sorry your campaign came up short. Is that why you don't like to talk about it?"

"I mean, yeah, I failed. The day the campaign ended, Mom called and asked me to check on Pops. I was so disappointed in myself I fled. Pops was slowing and sleeping in, but he took me on the long, cathartic walks I needed. The scenery brought me right back to my childhood and the belief I could do anything. I rallied and decided to try again, but Pops told me to work on logistics."

"And then he died."

She swallowed the lump in her throat. Grief came in waves, but the desert left little margin for sentimentality. "He left me half the motel, but my mother inherited the other half. With my artist-in-residence gig ending, and my crowd-funding campaign flat-lining, I stayed in Palm Springs and took over his gig while I worked on logistics for my art. Maybe I'll stay here forever."

"Maybe." He rested a forearm on the steering wheel and exhaled. "Then again, maybe the valley is a pit stop. I might be a simple farmer, but even I know you have talent. I can see the passion and the technique behind your work. You can stay here and make local people happy, or you can do great things."

"You sound like my therapist," she said.

He smiled and inclined his head. "My advice is probably cheaper."

Laughing, she pulled out her phone to text Stephanie.

—Is now a good time to visit Benito?—

—He's sleeping. Should I wake him?—

—No!—

Kada added a few emojis.

—Let me know when he wakes up? I'll swing by the grocery store. What are his favorite snacks?—

—Those cheddar cheese puff balls. He's right above the boulevard market. I'll text you the address.—

Staring at her phone, Kada wondered if Benito had

a twin brother. The cook she knew preached the merits of small family farms located in community centers. Faced with a choice between price and proximity, he lobbied for the fruits and vegetables grown without the use of synthetic fertilizers, herbicides, or pesticides. Well, except avocados. Sometimes, he cut side deals to secure the green gold, and she avoided asking questions. But cheese puffs? She would enjoy teasing him about his neon-orange indulgence.

Shaking off the incongruity, she rehomed her phone. "Change of plans. Benito's not up for visits right now. Maybe we can do your hike and return for lunch? We just can't stay out all day."

"Are you sure?" he asked. "You said you needed lunch, now."

"I ate."

"A ginger cookie."

She patted her stomach. "Give Mariah my regards. It was delicious."

Shaking his head, he backed out of the spot. "Are you worried about Lucky?"

"Yes and no," she said. "Benito's sleeping, so I legitimately don't want to wake him, but I'm trying not to get too worked up over Lucky's litter. The vet gave me a pamphlet." She picked at her nails and avoided thinking about the familiarity she observed between Dane and the pretty vet. "She was generous to come."

"She's empathetic and astute. I think the animals respond well to her." He slowed and detoured around a group of vultures pecking at carrion below a billboard for a big dollar boutique.

Detouring from downtown Palm Springs brought the desert back into sharp focus, but she kept the conversation grounded and ignored the vet's looks. Mimicking another woman's style never worked. "She's empathetic, but she seems unflappable, too. I can't do all that Buddhist, living-in-the-now stuff she mentioned."

"Why not?"

"After all the global stressors like 9-11, school shootings, and climate change, my friends and I openly talk about mental health, but I can't pretend everything will be okay." She shrugged. "Everybody has their struggles."

"My dad's not the talkative type," he said.

"But your mom?"

He rubbed his thumb along the steering wheel and nodded. "She would listen."

"She is a good listener, but when she comes to visit, I usually focus on the future. I don't know why we talk about mental health so much more than our parents. Awareness has grown, so maybe we recognize the problems." She listened to the truck's tires crunching over gravel. "Maybe the stigma just isn't there."

"Maybe."

Scratching her scalp, she tugged her fingers through her hair. If she couldn't pick up a paintbrush and paint away her worries, talking helped. "I guess I feel like my therapist is a medical professional. If I had hypertension, I wouldn't ignore it."

"Has Mariah been talking?"

"What?" she asked.

"I meant, good." He adjusted the sun visor. "I'm glad you're taking care of yourself."

Humming to herself, she enjoyed the contentment

that came from being heard and tried not to dwell on his limited responses. They shared a mutual appreciation for hot sex, but they were barely friends. "Are we close?"

He nodded.

A worn, brown sign with engraved white letters marked a green metal gate and a dusty gravel road. *Palmer Farms Property*, the sign read.

She looked down the road, but it twisted behind an outcrop. After tourism, agriculture was Greater Palm Springs' second largest industry, but she saw zero signs of the area's iconic, waving palm trees. She craned her neck, but she sat on her hands to avoid ruining the outing. "This is your family's land?"

"Some of it." Putting the idling truck in Park, he opened the door and walked around the hood. He withdrew a set of keys, opened the gate, and swung it wide.

She scooted into the driver's seat to save him from repeating the moves after he secured the gate.

He curled his fingers and beckoned her forward.

Easing into Drive, she stopped past the gate. She still couldn't see a thing except for the scrubby desert plants, the waving brown sand, and the winding gravel road.

Approaching the driver's side window, he tapped the glass. "Will you let me drive?"

She shrugged. "Maybe. I wouldn't mind getting a close-up look at how you plant, cultivate, and harvest your massive, majestic, manly crops, but I have errands. I thought you said this was a hike?"

"Kada, scoot over. If I wanted to take you on the dog and pony show, I could have walked down the hill and met you halfway from the Starlight Motel."

"Okay." She made a show of untangling her legs and slipping back into position. "I cede control of the truck."

"Did you have a hard time saying that phrase?" he asked.

If it took one type-A control freak to recognize another, she would accept the label. Instead of deflecting his question, she stuck out her tongue.

He raised his eyebrows. "Mature."

"Sometimes." Tilting her head, she wondered if she could scrap the sightseeing for a second bout of sweaty sex, but he listened to her drama, and he deserved the same respect. She waved toward the road. "Lead the way, boss."

Following the road, he navigated around the outcrop.

Rows of lush, green vines appeared in a shadowed valley. During midday, the vines would receive full sun, but the outcrop provided intermittent shade. "Grapes!"

"Table grapes." He stopped the truck. "They're too thin-skinned, sweet, and juicy for wine."

She rubbed together her hands. "I love grapes. Have you ever roasted them? Benito makes this kicking dish of fresh chorizo, roasted sweet grapes, and vinegar-tossed onions on a bed of polenta." She reached for the door handle.

"Maybe we can set up Benito with Vo Hạnh."

Pulling back, she turned and grinned. Maybe she would get her second kiss. "I think Benito's already taken with Stephanie."

"Good, but this isn't the stop."

She pulled back a hand.

He accelerated the truck.

As the road circumnavigated piles of brown mulch and black topsoil, she watched the vines disappear in the side mirror. *So much for the grapes. Where is he taking me?* Content to ride, she realized she trusted him enough to go joyriding in the desert, and she looked forward to his plan.

Then her phone pinged.

Opening her email, she stared.

Kada Ritchie, please submit your grand acceptance no later than 11:59 on December, 31. Again, congratulations.

Reading the reminder fifteen times, she forgot the grapes and struggled with the implications of her looming decision. She had poured her heart into the grant application and had devised contingency plans for the motel. Now that her parents were on-site, she was so close to handing control of the motel back to her mother. The mild email reminded her wildest dreams had come true, but the handsome man in the passenger seat tempted her to upend her plans.

Chapter Sixteen

Kada looked so interested in the grapes, so Dane thought about stopping the truck and letting her poke around the vines. The fruit wouldn't be ripe and ready to pick until June, but the vibrant leaves rustled and cast alluring shadows. If his hiking plan crashed and burned, he could take her back to the farmland and regroup.

"How many grapes do you grow? Are they a lot of work? Are they good?" she asked.

He gave her a wide grin. Her curiosity and ability to throw herself into every situation impressed him. She probably didn't want to hear about the rush to harvest before the Central Valley's massive grape harvest undercut prices. The fight to retain workers, the field tastings, and his obsession with weather forecasts made for dry conversation. Clearing his throat, he reached for his hat. "We grow about fifteen hundred acres of grapes spread over multiple sites."

"That's a lot!" She laughed. "Why do you want my land?"

Pausing, he considered the question. He might not own the air's freshness or the water's sparkle, but he could put them to use and feed the multitudes. "Why not?"

She crossed her arms. "It's mine."

Just shy of a pout, her defiance charmed him. Maybe she would stay, after all. Suppressing a smile, he climbed out of the truck and put on his hat and his sunglasses. "Do you have any water?"

"I keep some behind the seats." She pulled out two bottles and handed over one. "Will we need it? I'm not sure I'm dressed for a long hike. And then there's Benito…"

"Enough about Benito."

She laughed.

Turning his back on the grapes, he took a hand and tugged her into motion. The trail gained altitude quickly, but on flat ground, he set a relaxed pace and enjoyed the solitude and the tension of holding hands with a beautiful woman.

"Pops liked to hike."

"Where'd he take you?"

"When I was a kid, we went up the Garstin Trail and followed it up Smoke Tree Mountain. I think Pops wanted to see if I would wimp out on the switchbacks. We usually snacked on the plateau, and he gave me chocolate."

"I'm surprised it survived the heat."

"Ice packs," she said.

He laughed. "Clever."

"The site has breathtaking views of the San Jacinto and the Little San Bernardino Mountains, Palm Canyon, and Palm Springs. When I made it to the top of the trail, I could see the whole valley."

He had a hard time imagining Hall hiking to the top of the Garstin Trail, but Kada knew him twenty years ago. From the top of the trail, the pair could have linked up with the Wild Horse Trail and climbed Murray Hill. "How far did you go?"

"Not much farther," she said. "Pops said the

Murray Hill hike was strenuous, but one day, I should do it." She pulled free a hand and opened the water bottle. Taking a long sip, she wiped a hand across her mouth. "I still haven't done it."

"It's a good hike." He waited for her to finish the sip of water and resumed walking to step into the shadows.

She jogged and caught up. "You've done it?"

He nodded.

"Was it breathtaking?"

"Yeah."

Tugging him to a stop, she stared. "Yeah?"

Exhaling, he debated how much to reveal. "My dad brought a map and pointed out all the family lands. It was like some regal moment from a cartoon. 'Everything the light touches…' "

She laughed.

"Thanks. This is me opening up."

"No, I mean, I can see you up on Murray Hill finding your bearings and figuring out what you're supposed to do with your dad's information. That's intense. Pops let me be. He said time and fresh air would sort out my problems."

"Did they?" He shifted his weight.

She spread wide her arms and inhaled deeply. "Not yet. I'm still here, aren't I?"

"Lucky me." He tried to keep his gaze off her chest, but her inhalation raised more than her shoulders. Admiring her figure was one thing, but he felt compelled to step closer and figure out just what kind of person she might be. In the canyon, she looked as wild as an undisturbed red hot poker. The spectacular flowering plant had a softer name, the torch lily, but when it bloomed, the hot name fit. Insects and hummingbirds flocked to the blooms, and he forbade any farmworkers from disturbing the plants. Walter gave him a hard time, but the blooms attracted the valley's best pollinators, and Palmer Farms depended on pollen. She might be as rare and spectacular as the bloom. People flocked toward her, and he wanted to understand why.

"So, where are we going?" she asked.

"A half mile. I'm not sure this will work out, but I have a hunch." He wanted to hold her hand, but the schoolboy gesture seemed too familiar. Meeting her surprised him, but he'd gone about this relationship ass backward. If he backtracked, he might be able to reorient their connection before she chocked up their liaison to a one-night stand.

"Taking a risk?"

"Something along the lines of that notion."

"As he grew older, Pops couldn't walk as far. We mainly stuck to the land around the Starlight Motel or ambled from his favorite brunch spots to downtown's sunny park benches."

Nodding, he rubbed his fingers against his sweaty palms. Desert wildflowers in December required heavy rains in September and October. He checked the records, but he couldn't be sure if the flowers would agree with the rain measurements. A few days ago, he saw a few blooms in the wash and canyon behind the farmhouse, but he needed more than a spec of white to make an impression on Kada. If the valley bucked his expectations, he would look like a fool.

Keeping his gaze on the climbing trail, he estimated the steps until he and Kada broke free of the canyon and stepped onto the gentle hillside. Patches of mottled greenery coursed along the hillside like prickly, stubborn lichens, but he looked for a low-growing, gray-green annual.

"I think Mom misses Pops more than she lets on. I mean, we came back for holidays, and she sent me down here for school breaks, but she left home. It must be hard, you know?"

He adjusted his hat. "Huh?"

She laughed and waved off his confusion. "Never mind. Family drama."

"I want to hear what you said. I'm sorry, my mind wandered."

Nodding, she walked beside him. "You're a busy man."

"It's not that...it's"—he stopped and grinned at the first sight of a tiny, early-blooming white flower—"I have something to show you."

She shaded her gaze. "That's an interesting line."

Grabbing a hand, he quickened his pace and nearly pulled her toward the patch of small, white flowers. Aptly named popcorn flowers, the blooms resembled popped kernels spilled across the ground by a careless child. In groups, the flowers formed blazing white blankets that shone like snow against the brush. "Look!"

She stumbled.

Catching her elbow, he waited.

"Oh! Look at them! I didn't know *cryptantha* could bloom this early." Dropping to one knee, she lifted a branch. Stiff, erect hairs and finer, flat hairs covered the plant's stems. The clusters of white flowers were smaller than a dime, but they bobbed in a hand like a rich spray of white. "They're beautiful. Is this what you wanted to show me?"

He rocked back on his heels and grinned. "I've seen them bloom up here, and with the fall rain, I thought we might get lucky. I figured we had to act fast before the desert tortoises found them."

Standing, she walked toward him and tilted her head.

Widening his grin, he appreciated her smile and waited. Her gaze was as welcoming as a cold drink after a long, hot day. He dug his hands into his pockets and convinced himself he conjured the snowy magic purely for her benefit. But the hillside air felt as charged as an approaching storm, and he knew Mother Nature put on the display.

She drew close.

He reached for her and wrapped an arm around her waist. "Your murals are beautiful. I hear how much you enjoyed your walks with Hall. I thought you might enjoy the blooms."

She leaned into him. "The Spanish call them *nievitas* or little snow. They're beautiful. Thank you for the gift."

Grinning with pride, he leaned down and kissed her so thoroughly that he prided himself on holding back. Her lips tasted sweet and cool, and he wanted to tighten his grip and find space to explore her body. Instead, he pulled back, straightened, and traced his thumb over her bottom lip. "You're welcome. I'm glad to see you smile."

"What other blooms do you have up your sleeve?"

He preferred not to answer that question surrounded by prickly plants.

She draped her hands over his shoulders. "Bringing me to see these flowers is the sweetest gesture, and I wouldn't have pegged you for a romantic. You rode in on Smoky like a man who could not only ride a horse, but shoe it. I pegged you for the capable leader who makes people feel like everything will be okay."

I'll make it okay. He cupped her hips.

"You're someone who makes sure the world is safe and secure." Walking her fingers up his chest, she stopped and tapped a button. "But inside that strong façade, you might be a softie and a romantic at heart."

"Hardly." His throat constricted. Instead of accepting her praise and its roiling connotations, he peeled back a layer of control and laid bare his motivations for bringing her to see the flowers. "Kada, you're so vibrant, but every time I bring up your art, you go mum. I don't want you to be sad. Your failed fundraising campaign won't define your career. Even I can see your potential. Don't worry about those idiots in Los Angeles. They can't see past the ends of their noses."

"Sad?" She pulled back and frowned.

He forged ahead before he lost his nerve. "Huge, showy impacts make a statement, but the smallest changes matter, too." Nodding, he felt like he was on a roll. "Like the popcorn flowers, abundance lets little moments of beauty shine. Your mural is huge and breathtaking, but it must have taken hours of brushwork. Anyone can see the love you put into the work."

Dropping her hands, she uncapped a water bottle, drained the contents, and screwed on the top. She opened her mouth.

Another kiss would suit him just fine.

Tilting her head, she closed her mouth and stared.

Speechless. He wanted to keep the moment going by telling her how much he enjoyed spending time with her, but he didn't want to come on too strong.

"We should go." Casting a last look at the flowers, she snapped a picture, tucked her phone into her pocket, and set a steady pace down the trail.

Left standing next to the blooms, he scratched his head and wondered where he went wrong. Crops needed soil, sunlight, and water. Based on Kada's reaction, he had absolutely no idea what she needed, but an abundance of sweet, white blooms hadn't done the trick.

Kada leaned against the blue truck. Arms crossed, she looked as friendly as a rattlesnake, but he could stand the bite. He nearly chased her down the trail. The fact that neither party turned an ankle was an absolute miracle. "You didn't like the flowers."

"Loved them." She wet her lips.

"The kiss?"

She worked her jaw. "Better than the first."

He rolled the tension from his shoulders, noticed the crisp scent of the irrigated vines, and felt like he could dig himself out of whatever hole he stumbled into. "Good." Drawing a deep breath, he cocked his head to reiterate his intent, thought better of digging a deeper hole, and opened the door to the driver's side.

"I can drive back to Palm Springs," she said.

Making eye contact through the dusty windows, he left the keys on the seat and switched places.

She executed a three-point turn in the truck, followed the gravel drive, and stopped before the painted gate.

If she wants to ride back in silence, we have a long way to go. Jumping out of the cab, he unlocked the gate, waited for the truck to pass, and locked the gate tight. Reclaiming the passenger seat, he set his hat on his knee and rode for five minutes.

"When I was a kid"—she cleared her throat—"my art teacher carted in a sheet of plywood from the lumber store, laid it flat on the studio table, and invited every kid in the school to paint their palm and lay down a print. After we finished, red, blue, yellow, white, and black handprints covered the plywood. When the paint dried, she added a two-inch border along the perimeter, metal hang tags, and a coat of clear shellac. She hung the art from a chain in the hallway."

"I'm sure it was a colorful piece." Mom had a box of artwork stashed in a hall closet, but he wasn't going head-to-head with a woman as talented as Kada.

"It was more than a colorful piece. Art creates excitement, and when people participate in making the art, they have a sense of belonging and a sense of possibility. Every time I walked by that plywood collage, I touched it. I remember the feel of the paint over rough plywood. The work wasn't flat, organized, or pretty, but it was there, and seeing it, I felt like I was there, too."

She leaned forward over the steering wheel. The speedometer hovered past the speed limit, but the silence was in his best interest.

"Arts education leads to academic achievement, social and emotional development, civic engagement, and equitable opportunity. It does everything we say we want for our kids, and I couldn't deliver it." Her voice hitched.

Taking a risk, he reached across the seat and settled a hand on her thigh. Her muscles contracted beneath his touch, but she let the gesture stand.

"Letting kids muck around in paint, explore textures, and create improves their education. Motivation, confidence, and peer relationships follow. You want to form social bonds and community cohesion? Set out cans of paint and let kids get messy. Parents will take pictures, kids will laugh, and everyone will go home with a load of laundry and a lighter heart."

"Water-soluble paint."

Glancing over, she narrowed her gaze.

He retracted a hand and held it palm out. "I'm in favor of anything that connects people to the world and opens new ways of seeing it."

She eased off the accelerator.

Pulling his shirt collar from his neck, he exhaled. She had so much passion, her knuckles had gone white on the steering wheel, but he wanted the passion directed toward her art, not pointing out his missteps. He had worried he would put his foot in his mouth over dinner, but he should have stuck with plant pollination and let her come to him.

"All those teenagers and young adults making commitments to vocational training deserve applause and scholarship support, but I wanted them to showcase the beautiful, compelling facets that made the neighborhood unique."

The sunlight picked out highlights in her hair. He could imagine her on a stage, or a social media channel, pleading her case for art and raking in donations.

Whatever she wanted to accomplish, he was all in, and he found it hard to believe her fundraising campaign had failed. "What exactly did you propose?"

She stopped the truck at a stoplight. "The wave design worked beautifully and taught me so much, but it filled one wall at the Vocational School. While I packed up my paints, a student came to chat. She said she watched the mural unfold, and she really liked the work. She wanted to paint her grandmother a picture to brighten her room in a nursing home, and I couldn't shove paints into her arms fast enough."

The light turned green.

If he learned one thing from Mom, he learned to let a woman finish her story before asking questions.

"The student said she was too scared to paint and mess up the canvas. I got it. All that stretched linen staring back can feel intimidating, but you have to put paint on your brush and paint. We worked together for a couple of afternoons, and her stories spilled out. I wasn't there to fix her problems, but I was there to listen. I told her that during the times I feel like my life's off course, art keeps me steady."

Family pride kept him steady. Customer expectations, contractual agreements, and weekly payroll kept him awake at night. Instead of imagining his life with a different degree, he imagined his life with entirely different surroundings. "The student finished the painting."

She turned toward the block containing The Desert Empire Café. "She did, but she wasn't the only student who wanted to paint. People need a constructive way to let loose. On my last day at the school, I ran out of supplies, stared at the empty walls, and wondered what else I could do."

A jaywalker wearing four-inch platform boots stepped into traffic.

Exhaling, she waved the individual across the street. "Nice boots."

He snorted.

She grinned, gripped the steering wheel, and eased forward through traffic. "The school administration agreed the facility had plenty of space for public art, but tags and graffiti covered the exterior walls. I couldn't cover the wall with roses, but I could find students who wanted to paint and showcase their technical programs. We sketched designs for chemistry, computer information systems, automotive repair, and registered nurses."

As the size of the campaign grew in his mind, the possibility of making a quick financial contribution faded from view like a disappearing oasis.

"I knew I wasn't alone. I mean, every muralist struggles with technical challenges and community connection, but art can't exist in a vacuum. At most, I showed the students how to execute their creativity on a large scale, and I helped them keep their vision cohesive."

"I doubt that's all you did. You're talented."

She shrugged. "Anyone with experience could do it. I thought if I could leave behind a transition plan, the community would support my replacement, and an up-and-coming muralist would have the kind of one-year appointment that changed my life." She cleared her throat. "I wanted to raise sixty thousand dollars."

His throat went dry. Ten or fifteen thousand dollars might pour in from art admirers and small business owners, but at that level, she needed corporate or institutional sponsorship.

She angled for a parking spot across the street from the café, cut the engine, and turned in the driver's seat. "Fundraising was the wrong approach. I should have written a grant."

Exhaling, he gave thanks he wouldn't have to be the person who laid out that observation. "We all learn from our mistakes. Do you want to talk about it over lunch?"

"Yes, I'm starving," she said.

"Good." At the mention of food, he felt his mouth water. "I want to hear all about the students."

She smiled and pulled the keys from the ignition.

Her smile gave him hope, but given her dedication to the craft and to community involvement, he should have known he wasn't out of the woods...or the desert.

Chapter Seventeen

In front of The Desert Empire Café, polished, chrome-drenched cars cruised a divided street. The whir of traffic, music spilling from open windows, and pedestrian chatter made Kada long for the motel's quiet mornings.

Locking Pops' truck, she gauged the traffic flow and felt like she and Dane crossed a threshold. Her mistake in Los Angeles mattered, but her work drove her passions, and she had a plan. Now, she and the handsome farmer could consider an intriguing future.

A café worker wiped a sold-out special from a black chalkboard, waved, and retreated inside the busy establishment.

She waved back. Restaurants rolled out new dishes for the holiday, and the community's pride shone from festive windows, decorated streetlights, and subtle advertisements for locally made gifts.

Volunteers from the gardening club had spruced up the busy street's median. Looking at it from the far side of the road, she spied a faded red bow adorning a barrel cactus. Prickly pears sprouted hot-pink fruit. Hung with faded ornaments, a stand of cholla cacti looked deceivingly cute. Even the rocks around a patch of aloe vera looked freshly raked. *Mariah was right. This place sinks into your skin.*

A large sign in the median advertised the garden

club's contact information and directed questions, comments, and membership inquiries to a local phone number. Taking care of the desert island couldn't be simple, but the median looked beautiful, and the club deserved recognition. Thinking of the work required to keep up the motel, she cleared her throat and focused on her outing with Dane. "Are you ready?"

"The crosswalk is half a block away," Dane said.

A traffic break left room to run.

"Details." Taking his hand, she sprinted toward the median and the festive plants.

A car honked.

She waved.

Dane lengthened his stride and pulled her onto the median.

Laughing in the bright sunlight, she dodged the prickly plants and gauged the next lanes of traffic. Avoiding municipal workers fixing a water leak, cars changed lanes with sporadic, jerking movements. She had no idea where the cars were headed, but she had her heart set on a salad from the café and sharing a meal with Dane. She shaded her gaze and looked at him. "As long as we don't blink, we'll cross the street without incident."

He placed a hand on her lower back. "I'll follow you. Pick a gap that feels comfortable. I've seen sixth graders run faster."

She snorted. "Is that so? I'm great with still lives, but lousy with objects in motion."

Rubbing a small circle along her lower back, he shifted closer. "You look good out here, Kada. The motel suits you, but so does the city. I'm glad we cleared the air, and I'm happy to see you smile. I don't want you to feel sad."

"Sad?" She spun and faced him. "When have I been sad?"

Pulling in his chin, he stared. "Your art? The failed fundraising campaign?"

Ignoring the buzzing traffic, she replayed the conversation about Los Angeles. She wasn't moping about the desert like the ghost of Christmas past. Couldn't he see her finding her footing and gathering her courage for another shot?

She made fists at her sides, squeezed shut her eyes, and blocked out the traffic whizzing on both sides of the median. "I'm not sad. I'm furious! Why do I have to fundraise for students to express themselves and beautify their community? Pride and quality of life outweigh the cost of art supplies." Dropping her hands, she stared at the shortsighted man standing in front of her. His kisses couldn't make up for his density. She threw up her hands. "Let them paint. Let everyone paint!"

Raising his hands in front of his chest, he stepped back. "You're not sad?"

"Absolutely not! Do I look sad? It might be my internalized frustration. I tamp it down so I don't look like a plotting lunatic."

His lips ticked up. "I get frustration."

She exhaled.

"You made a mistake with the fundraising approach. It's trendy, but without a huge social media following, it's ineffective. You're right. A grant would have been better."

Now, he had advice? Gaze wide, she wondered if she had completely misread his reserved demeanor.

Yes, she should have written a grant, but she didn't need him pointing out her error from his high horse.

Emotion made beautiful art, but arguments killed its potential. Taking a deep breath, she focused on the conversation's core. "I wrote a grant."

He crossed his arms and grinned. "I know a few people who could help you review it before you submit the forms."

Review it? Pursing her lips, she debated playing coy or laying into his arrogance. He rode onto her property with a beautiful horse and a wicked grin, but she didn't need a cynical, rangy cowboy to point out her missteps. He could take his helpful suggestion and shove it where the sun didn't shine. "Is that so?"

He rubbed his chin.

Cars whooshed by in both directions.

"My mother could help you," he said.

"Your mother? Brilliant!" Rolling her eyes, she pivoted and moved to cross the busy street. Before she stepped off the median, she turned and looked over her shoulder. "Your mother and I are friends. What do you think she and I have been doing at the motel?"

He caught her elbow. "I have no idea. Contriving to get me on-site? Coming up with a way to rope me into donating to your cause and falling for your beautiful brown eyes?"

"Donating?" She stared. "I don't want your money!"

"What do you want?"

"Respect. Art. Opportunity! I have the grant, and now you're here, and I don't know what to do with my life." Wrenching free, she saw a break in traffic and pushed off the curb.

A driver made an un-signaled turn and slammed on the car's brakes.

Lunging forward, Dane grabbed her around the waist, pulled her against his chest, and fell backward onto the garden club's prized, spiky specimens.

The fall knocked her breath from her body. Sprawled across his chest, she turned, raised her head, and braced her weight against the bedding rocks. Her breaths came in shallow pants. "Thank you for saving me." She swallowed. "But I still don't want your money."

He groaned.

"I'm not rich, but I know art." She raised a hand and traced the buttons on his shirt. "The neighborhood where I painted isn't one of the world's greatest communities, but the people matter, and they deserve the best art. I have to go back."

He closed his eyes. "I believe you."

Drawing a deep breath, she looked at the cactus sporting a red ribbon and regretted her explosion. The plants growing in the Coachella Valley were drought-tolerant and could withstand temperature extremes, but they weren't robots. Before she reentered the art world, she could use a little more fortitude and a little more patience. Dane wouldn't be the last person to offer helpful suggestions. Rolling her shoulders, she shifted her weight. "Good, I'm glad you believe me."

"I'll do whatever you say."

"Huh?" She pulled back and puzzled over his clenched jaw.

"Kada, darling, get off me before I pass out."

Scrambling to all fours, she pulled back. "Are you hurt?"

"Only my pride." Rolling over, he revealed a flattened cholla cactus.

Locals knew the teddy bear cactus for its needle-like spines that jumped off the cactus and lodged themselves in unsuspecting victims. The plant's fuzzy appearance looked cute, but its defenses were far from cuddly, and Dane must be in a world of pain. Covering her mouth, she stood and offered him a hand.

Grimacing, he took it and stood. "I hate the holiday season."

"What do the holidays have to do with it? I'm the idiot who stepped out into traffic."

Reaching behind his head, he withdrew a flattened Christmas ornament. Blood smeared his hand. "Impaling myself on the cactus is one thing, but slicing open my scalp on broken glass is a whole other type of disaster."

She walked around him and gasped. Blood dripped down his neck from a small cut, cactus spines protruded from his back, and a bevy of helpful onlookers stood in front of the café digging through their purses. They looked ready to charge across the road and render assistance with wadded up tissues and antiseptic wipes, but she feared Dane needed more than a lollipop and an adhesive bandage.

"How bad is it?" he asked.

She walked around him and chewed the inside of her cheek. "You might want to spike your champagne—"

He winced.

"—with gin."

He glanced at her lips. "Only if you'll join me."

She took the compliment and smiled, but she

focused on her choices. Taking him back to the motel would be an excruciating ride. The onlookers across the street might create a fuss, but the locals might also know a few things about removing cactus spines. "Let's get you inside the café and figure out what comes next."

Nodding, he stood, cupped his back, and came back with spines embedded in his fingers. "That was stupid."

She tried not to laugh. "Well, at least they're no longer in your back."

"Aren't you the optimist?"

She smiled. "You have no idea." Waving off the helpful hoards, she waited for a break in traffic and led him across the street. Shame reddened her cheeks, but she would apologize to Dane in private.

"Is he okay?" a customer asked.

A server shook his head. "That car was so close to hitting you."

"What a hero!" An older woman fanned herself.

Kada looked at Dane and expected a grimace. Instead, she found him resolute. If he were mad, then she should amplify her regrets. "I'm sorry. I, just, uh, know you were trying to help. You must be so frustrated. It has to hurt and you're…"

He raised his eyebrows. "You want to see frustrated? Leave me on this blazing sidewalk like an abandoned pincushion. Instead of tripping over an apology, help me get this shit out of my back."

Biting back a laugh, she imagined him giving orders to a green-hand amid a field of wilting bell peppers. Everyone made mistakes. She led him through the front door and settled him in a wooden chair next to a table. When she noticed he didn't lean back, she scanned the café for inspiration.

The building's stucco walls housed a café offering dishes built from local vegetables, fish, chicken, tempeh, and seitan. A large green-and-white kaleidoscope painting stood behind the counter, and white pendant lights hung over a cold case filled with colorful sides. For a desert outpost, the plants inside the café rivaled the Amazon. Scanning the menu board, she debated whether to ask for a sandwich or a pair of tweezers.

"Oh, honey, why don't you take off your shirt so we can see how bad it is?" an older woman said to Dane.

Kada turned from the menu board in time to see his gaze flare.

A second woman hovered near the first.

The pair looked like active Rotary Members with a passion for town gossip, pedal pushers, and weekly salon appointments.

"Oh, yes," the second woman said. "You should definitely strip."

"Not a chance." Dane bit his lip.

The women cackled.

She wouldn't mind seeing him bare-chested, too, but if the cactus needles punctured his skin, she would have a hard time focusing on his pectoral muscles. She jerked her head toward the front door and wordlessly asked if he wanted to leave.

He sighed. "No, but I'm starting to sympathize with the animals at the livestock auction."

She grinned and appreciated his retained sense of humor. Most people would be pitching a fit and holding their cell phone cameras over their shoulders to document the damage. Dane looked like he might dust off his sunglasses. The tightness in his jaw was his only outward sign of distress, but he had to be in pain.

The busybodies returned to their table.

Choosing two sandwiches from the menu, she ordered waters, coffees, and a hearty date shake. "Also, can I borrow a pair of tweezers from your first aid kit?"

The cashier paled. "Is he that bad? The blood looks intense. Maybe you should take him to the emergency room."

Talk about a frustrating experience. She had a hunch Dane would saw off his right leg before he set foot in an emergency room. "Do you have a few butterfly stitches and some gauze in the kit? I'll take him to the bathroom and clean him up before the food arrives. Don't worry. We'll replace everything we use."

Sliding the first aid kid across the counter, the cashier pointed toward a long hallway leading toward the restroom. "Just, um, tell me if you need help."

The poor kid looked like he would faint from a scraped knee. She smiled. "We'll be fine." Swinging the kit from her fingers, she beckoned Dane.

He stood, winced, and followed her to the bathroom.

Opening the bathroom door, she found it empty and set the kit on the vanity. "Okay, now you can strip."

Crossing his arms, he raised an eyebrow.

She smiled. "It was worth a try."

He braced his arms on the vanity and drew a deep breath. "Kada, you want to get naked? Pick a date for dinner, and I'm all yours."

Her cheeks warmed, and she wondered what it

would be like to flirt with him over candlelight and anticipate the pleasure of losing herself in his arms. Instead of fantasying about romance, she focused on the reason for their current predicament. The spines in his back hurt less than a vehicular collision, but she hadn't asked him to take on her pain. He took charge of the situation like he managed everything else that needed his attention. When life calmed down, she would find a way to turn the tables on him and take away some of his responsibility. He needed freedom and pleasure as much as anyone. "Noted, but right now, let me take care of you."

He nodded and dropped his head.

Opening the first aid kit, she inventoried the supplies. Pulling out tweezers, she washed the pair under hot water and located a butterfly strip. Head wounds bled a lot, but as long as the broken glass stayed out of his flesh, he would barely have a scar. She pulled on a pair of latex gloves. The material snapped.

"Be quick, okay?" he asked.

She wiped away as much blood as she could manage and applied the butterfly strip. "I can see how you're not a fan of ornaments."

He grunted.

Picking up the tweezers, she pulled the first needle from his shirt and his skin. The spine wasn't completely buried, and a single straight motion liberated it. When it popped free, she exhaled.

His heavy-duty shirt kept the spikes from lodging too deeply, and she felt like this small favor might repay him for his kindness. After all, he misconstrued her emotions, but he wanted to help. Pulling out spine after spine, she dropped them on a folded paper towel.

A few spines drew drops of blood.

The silence unnerved her. Surrounded by a crowd, she felt at home. "I guess I could order a few shots of tequila, but I need to focus to remove the needles. If you want the stiff drink, I wouldn't judge you. Those needles have to hurt." She was rambling, and she didn't care. Pulling out a deeply embedded spine, she squeezed shut her eyes until she felt the spine release. "Maybe you can save the shot for later when we're sure I don't have to bring you to urgent care. Then again, tequila might get you into the doctor's office." She risked a glance at his face.

He kept his eyes closed and his muscles tensed.

She exhaled. If he could weather this injury without complaint, then she could remove the source of his pain. "I understand why you thought I was sad." She pulled out another spine. "When Pops passed away, I was sad, but sadness comes from losing something that supports self-identity. He was brilliant, rugged, and kind, but he wasn't me."

Dane cleared his throat. "He was kind."

"Sadness hurts because it's like losing a limb. You can feel the absence. I can't feel the absent mural. Maybe the students can. They can be sad. I'm frustrated."

"You and Mom wrote a grant." He exhaled. "Good. She's the queen of educational grants. I'm glad you two found each other. Are you painting murals at the local schools?"

"Think bigger." She pulled out another spine.

"Colleges?"

"It's a multi-year program. I can't manage the motel fulltime and complete the program. I have until

December thirty-first to accept the offer."

"Oh." Looking up, he made eye contact in the mirror.

His lined forehead and flat expression reinforced his pain. She decided not to mention the small dots of blood speckling his back. If he could stand the process, then she could stand removing the reminders of her mistake. Looking away, she pulled out the last spine, laid down the tweezers, and pulled off the gloves. "You're all done."

He turned, rolled his shoulders, and sighed. "I think you got them all."

"No tiny glochids? Pops once recommended using rubber cement or something similar to remove the nasty spines." More specifically, his easy drawl told her to spread on the glue as thick as chili paste, cover the area with gauze, and run her mouth while she yanked off the strip. Running her mouth wouldn't be the problem. The small room felt crowded and thick with relief and tension. She ran her hands along her arms. "You think waxing hurts? Imagine ripping off rubber cement."

He narrowed his gaze. "Is that so?"

"I mean, it must…"

He wrapped a hand around her waist, drew her close, and dropped his lips an inch above hers. "Kada, I'm frustrated, too. There's this woman in town who keeps me on my feet and keeps surprising me. I thought she was a people pleaser, but she's tougher than she looks. You might like her."

"Is that so?" Her voice came out bubbly and light. Spending time with him brought out the best in her. His measured confidence and easy swagger gave her room to make mistakes and know he would catch her, but she couldn't drag him around the country like a security blanket. "Maybe the spines set off an allergic reaction. You might be rambling. Someone might knock on the door at any minute." She glanced at the lock.

"Thank you for not dumping me at urgent care." His teeth grazed her bottom lip.

Turning to meet his kiss, she wanted more than a teasing graze. Pressing up, she claimed his lips and kissed his back. The rush of primal, fulfilling pleasure and the deep, sinking yielding that came from his touch compelled her to shift closer. She could get lost in his arms and still find room to breathe, but she feared losing her directive. Too lost in his kiss to care if it left her limp and aimless, she let life's minor pains and annoyances fade away and gripped his biceps hard.

He bent her back across his arm, took control of the momentum, and kissed her with a fierce possessiveness that made her cling like a carnival rider desperate for a thrill. His insistent mouth parted her lips, sent wild tremors along her sunbaked nerves, and promised cool relief at the end of a long, hot day.

She felt like a lightning flash arching through the sky, but the rumble of thunder settled in her core and demanded release. She would need days with Dane to get the need under control, but she didn't have time for wild, passionate love and sheet-tangled daydreams. Pulling free of the kiss, she reached for the doorknob.

"Why do I feel like you're running away?"

Mouth agape, she stared. "Because I am?"

Taking a hand, he pulled her close and planted another long, lingering kiss on her lips.

She could sink into a hot bath with this man and emerge a new woman, but the café restroom left little leeway for romance.

Settling his hands above her ass, he raised his head. "You're so beautiful and fierce. If I'd known who cast long shadows past midnight, I would have walked down the mountain and come to you the first day. We would have had time." He cupped her face. "If you want to run from me, then I won't stop you, but I wish you would stay."

"I'm here now," she said.

One hand slipped up her back to raise her shirt, and the other went to the nape of her neck and loosened her hair. He kissed his way across her collarbone and removed her clothes one garment at a time. "I'm beginning to like the holidays."

Smiling, she angled for more pressure. She could have fled, asked for better accommodations, or demanded praise, but standing in his arms felt as luxurious as strong sunlight after a cold swim. Shivering, she pressed closer to his warmth.

"I dreamed about you last night," he said.

"And when you were hip-deep in mud this morning fixing the pump?"

His mouth hovered near her nipple, but he glanced up. "I wanted to burn it down."

She stepped out of her shoes and cupped him. "Don't be hasty."

"Like I have a choice." He dropped to his knees and tasted his way from the inside of her calf, past her belly button, and back to her breasts.

He skipped the one thing she wanted most, but she was so ready to feel him she indulged his meandering path. When his kisses skimming her jaw and his fingers running through her hair began to frustrate her more than they pleased her, she grabbed his shoulders and summoned the words she needed.

His lips slid to the soft spot right below her ear. "Going to bite me again?"

Cradled in his arms, she wasn't sure how long the café patrons would let them monopolize the bathroom, but she wanted to push the limits and float in his arms. "Maybe."

He laughed. "I liked it." Turning her toward the vanity, he positioned her arms on the edge of the porcelain and ran a hand along her back.

She looked over her shoulder and saw him fish a condom from his wallet and toss his jeans to the floor. "Came prepared?"

"Hopeful." Parting her folds, he dipped one finger inside her and spread her heat along her lips. "Kada?"

Arching her hips, she met his gaze in the mirror. "Dane." She wanted him so much she gripped the vanity and presented herself for his taking, but she wanted every inch of his possession. He surged inside her with one ravaging thrust, and he was so thick and virile he filled her to bursting before his long, lusty strokes set a heady rhythm.

She dropped her head to the side and exposed her neck.

Kissing the smooth skin, planted deep, he ground against her, and his fingers dug into her hips.

She reveled in the possession and rocked her hips within his grasp.

"You feel so good, Kada." He loosened his grip and pulled back on her right hip.

Unwilling to lose the heady pressure of their connection, she rocked against him until the heat between their bodies and heady arousal of their joined flesh set a punishing pace.

He picked up his pace, and with every thrust, he peppered small swats against her ass.

The swift sting and rushing blood surprised her, but as his hand wrapped around her waist and stroked her sensitized clit, she melted against the onslaught and let him carry her toward satisfaction. Heat liquefied her insides, and every body-jarring impact brought her closer to the edge. When she felt him withdraw, she cried out for more.

Again, he sank his shaft. "I have you."

Her back pressed against his chest, her bottom bouncing off his groin, she closed her eyes and savored his control.

"Tell me you'll come on my dick." He followed his hoarse whisper with a deeper thrust and stroked her clit. "Tell me you'll ache for me."

"I will." She moaned.

He changed the angle.

The pressure building in her core threatened to detonate inside of her. He took her to the edge of her release and pulled back.

At the loss of connection, she groaned and tried to control her heaving chest. She met his gaze in the mirror. "I wasn't expecting to get my kicks in the bathroom."

His nostrils flared. "Neither was I."

Dropping her head to the side, she savored the building tension and her labored breaths. Reaching for him, she grasped his length and stroked him.

His breath came in short gasps. "I wanted to wait, and then I couldn't."

She gripped him. "Don't wait."

Diverting a hand, he dropped it to her clit and stroked her as he slid in and out of her heat.

Slowed down, the flames simmered and built into a raging heat. She no longer felt like a spectator, but a participant in her heady pleasure. A man who could make her feel this good and do it repeatedly was dangerous. He could make every day worthwhile, and she would forget how much she wanted to accomplish.

His pace quickened, she dropped a hand, and she doubted she could utter his name. Gripping the vanity and panting for breath seemed like the only things she could do. Her passion melted into a blinding bliss. As he shuddered behind her, his larger-than-life frame held her, and his arm locked her against his chest. Together, they panted for breath, and he nuzzled his lips against her neck until the ripples of pleasure faded and left nothing but this moment.

"Good?"

His voice, pressed deep against her shoulder, vibrated. She turned her head and looked over her shoulder. "No."

Raising his head, he looked into her eyes.

"Amazing," she whispered the praise.

Keeping eye contact, he intensified the pace.

Locked to him and craving more, she raised her lips for another kiss and shattered in his arms. She barely felt his lips, but his arms gripped her, his cock throbbed deep inside her, and his scent surrounded her. Spent, she tipped her head back to his shoulder and closed her eyes.

Tightening his hold, he held tight.

Her heartbeat slowed. Pleasure left her limbs

tingling, but sex only delayed her concerns. Opening her eyes, she dropped her head and stared at the floor tiled with penny rounds. She anticipated the pain of walking away from the desert and a man she could grow to love, but for a few seconds more, she didn't have to move.

"What's wrong?" he asked.

Looking up, she blinked away her worries and focused on his commanding presence. Her cheek felt the effects of his beard, and her limbs ached to pull him close, but the moment he climbed down from his tall horse, she knew he would come in and out of her life like an unexpected breeze.

"You're not still worried about the cactus? It's a little pain, Kada. I can take it."

Swallowing, she tested the words before she uttered them. The fear of failure tasted as bitter as dandelion greens. "I'm worried if I can take it. This is a big change, and I've already failed once. If I change my mind or fail again, what happens next?"

"You regroup, dust off your ass, and try again."

Before he carried her past her limits, she pulled back and drew a breath. In another minute, the café and the waiting sandwiches would be distant concerns. She inhaled. "They all know we're in here."

"Good." He lowered his head for another kiss. "Maybe they won't interrupt."

"Next week."

Drawing up short, he stared. "Pardon?"

"Take me out to dinner the first week in January." Issuing the command, she looked away from his swollen lips and replayed the kiss. Her decision-making skills might need a little work, or telling him to stop might be the stupidest thing she had ever done. In his arms, life could be easy and pleasurable, and she ached for another pulse-pounding ride. Instead, she squared her shoulders. "I can't confuse how I feel about you with my grant decision. We should go back to the table."

"I don't want a sandwich, but I hear you." He stroked her cheek. "I will take you to dinner, and how far we go will be entirely up to you. None of the university fools you've kissed could steal your breath, could they?"

"Dane…"

"All that frustration? You'll make your art. In the meantime, work out your frustrations on me." He straightened. "I'm strong enough to take it, and when you walk away, you'll still be strong, too."

Pulling out his arms before she took him up on his offer in the tiny bathroom, she hurried into her rumpled clothes, pushed open the bathroom door, and gulped the chilled air. Her heart beat a mile a minute, and her body ached, but she put one foot in front of the other foot. Afraid to meet his gaze, she counted her steps and aimed for the table where two sandwiches sat.

"All good?" the older woman asked with a wink in her eye.

She swallowed and struggled to form words.

"A tiny scratch. You can't sneak up on a farmer any sooner than you can catch a weasel asleep." Dane thrust the first aid kit into the cashier's arms. "Isn't that right, Kada?"

She downed her water and wondered if she had ever seen a weasel in the valley. "Whatever you say, cowboy."

Laughing, he dropped into his chair.

Picking up her sandwich, she paused and made eye contact. He played a tough game, but the cactus spines must have hurt, and everyone in the restaurant saw the blood spotting his shirt. If he couldn't accept a humbling fall, how could he weather life's challenges and reclaim solid ground?

Chapter Eighteen

"Have you ever had a bad crop?" Kada asked.

Dane paused with the sandwich halfway to his mouth. Ten minutes ago, she came apart in his arms, but now she looked as composed as her paintings and wanted to talk business. The woman got his blood running, but she looked at him like she needed to find a flaw. He could bear the inspection. When she found one severe enough, she would bail on their budding intimacy.

In the meantime, he cocked his head. "What do you mean a bad crop? An unprofitable one? Every year, farmers produce the highest quality crops possible, and every year, they face new challenges."

"I know, but have you ever failed? Have you ever tossed the produce into the compost heap, written off the field, and itemized your business expenses?"

"I'd rather talk about sex," he said.

She gripped his free arm and looked around. "Shh! I have a reputation to uphold."

A blue-haired woman on the other side of the café wiggled her fingers.

"Right." He cleared his throat. "My bad."

Kada pulled back a hand and nodded.

He considered her question and took a bite of the flank steak sandwich. At least, he thought the protein came from a cow. Pulling back from the sandwich, he examined the texture and shrugged. The biting horseradish and savory protein fulfilled their roles. "I've come close."

"How close?"

He chewed and considered the question. If an ode to her beauty would get this lunch date back on course, he would cough out a few corny compliments. He doubted poetry would save his backside, and his back was already shot. If she wanted to talk plants, then he was all in.

Plant pathology classes depended on a basic concept called the disease triangle. Given a susceptible host, a virulent pathogen, and a favorable environment, any crop could fail. Pesticide application targeted pathogens and vectors. Fertilizer programs kept crops as healthy as possible. He could finesse those two legs of the triangle, but he couldn't control the environment. Unexpected temperatures, limited rainfall, and biting wind could stress a plant faster than an invasive beetle. Recalling the stressful years, he swallowed.

"Has it been a while?" she asked.

He set down the sandwich. "In any given year, environmental conditions can change and lead to disease development. I might have an easy summer, and the next season, winds carry a swarm of insects across the Salton Sea and drop the little bugs onto my healthy fields."

"But has it happened?" She folded her arms in front of her body and kept her hands off her sandwich.

He nudged her plate. "You eat. I'll talk. Unless you want to get back to the sex talk?"

She picked up her food and took a healthy bite.

"A few years ago, I thought I would lose every bell

pepper I planted. Tomato spotted wilt virus showed up in Palmer peppers in the Mecca area. Thrips carry the virus and could have arrived on transplants. Before a plant goes in the ground, hands have to inspect it for disease." At the memory, he narrowed his gaze and saw the distressed fields in his mind's eye. Shaking off his exasperation, he focused on Kada. "Someone missed something, and it could have been me."

She took a second bite.

She had an agenda or a refined ability to listen. He debated which trait alarmed him more. Taking a reciprocal bite of his sandwich, he replayed the painful year and swallowed. "After the tomato virus, March winds knocked down the remaining bell pepper transplants. The plants recovered, but it was touch-and-go. Then in April, the bell peppers' new growth looked bleached. I blamed nematode damage and nutrient deficiencies."

"Which was it?" She stirred her water with a straw.

"Both," he said. "Samples revealed stubby root nematodes, but the plants also had deficiencies in phosphorus, potassium, and manganese. I adjusted the fertilizer." He exhaled. "Then the aphid-vectored alfalfa mosaic virus rolled into town."

She dropped her chin and stared. "Are your plants cursed?"

He laughed. "I sure felt like it. We've had cucumber mosaic virus, severe nematode damage, beet curly top virus, aphids"—he shook his head—"the list goes on. You want to take pictures in the vineyards? Great. We love the publicity. If you want to understand what goes into farming, pay attention when farmers gripe about managing thrips, aphids, and leafhoppers.

Viruses are the bane of my existence. Farming in the valley isn't all sunshine and sprinkler systems."

"Really?" She rested her chin on a hand.

The pose rendered her as angelic as a wide-eyed librarian. He felt a catch coming on. "Really."

"But you persevered."

He crossed his arms. He came from a multigenerational farming family. He could write a book on perseverance.

She stood and stretched her arms over her head. "You need to fail. Unmitigated failure. Compost-quality crops. Crushing debt."

Writing a book seemed far less interesting than crushing her against his chest and demanding another go in the quaint café bathroom. Standing, he had several inches on her. "You're fired from the Palmer management team. Let's go get a drink."

She laughed, sipped her coffee, and dumped the remains into a potted plant. Setting her cup back on the table, she winked. "I heard the plants like nitrogen."

He rubbed his chin and imagined why she wanted him to fail, but he could only process one quirk at a time. Ten minutes ago, she kissed him senseless, and he still needed his bearings. "Coffee grounds work better."

Shrugging, she shook the keys and walked out the door.

He followed because watching her hips sway mesmerized him more than a ticking metronome. The café might be his new favorite place in town, but nursing his pincushion back and split head over a glass of the *kombucha* wouldn't resurrect his festive spirit. Kada might. Stepping into the sunshine, he blinked and found her halfway to the corner crosswalk. Lengthening his stride, he caught up. "Had enough traffic?"

Her gaze sparkled. "I need to pick up hamburger buns. We probably have meat at the motel, but I'm sure Benito doesn't keep buns in the freezer."

"You have hamburgers on your menu."

She turned down a shady alley sporting a pampered drake elm, and she opened the door to a gourmet market. "But Benito makes the buns from scratch."

Of course, he does. Clearing his throat, he followed her into the upscale market. It smelled like cleaning products and incense mashed into the form of a flickering candle. Tipping his head to the cashier, he walked inside.

Exposed ductwork, colorful art, and arresting light fixtures made shopping at the venue more of an experience than a necessity. Besides groceries, the market offered a deli, craft beer, wine, artisan cheese, nitrate-free meats, pâtés, small-batch condiments, and a robust candy aisle. Customers raved about the market's charcuterie plates. When he shopped here, he preferred the chocolate dipped dates, but if anyone told his mother, he would deny it to his grave.

The produce section beckoned, and he couldn't stop himself from evaluating the quality. Picking up a pretty lemon, he found a Palmer Farms sticker on the fruit and grinned. *At least, management has good taste.* Setting down the lemon, he looked for Kada.

She stood in front of a display rack and loaded buns into a hand basket.

"How many people are you planning to feed?" he asked.

"I don't know. We have twenty guests. Not all of them will eat on-site. My parents. You're probably leaving for your family celebrations."

His smile flattened into a thin line. "Probably."

She turned toward the snack aisle. "Do you know if they have those neon-orange cheese puffs? The ones that come in a big plastic tub and dye your fingers a ghastly color?" She scanned the aisle. "I want the biggest container I can find."

He made a mean brisket and a good chili, but he pulled his sides from the freezer section. If she wanted to serve outlandish junk food at the Starlight Motel, then he had little to offer, and he doubted the market could meet her needs. "Ask the manager."

She shrugged and turned the corner, but her shoulder knocked over a display. Bags fell to the floor like crinkling, cellophane pillows.

Bending, he scooped up the nearest bag and squinted to make out the text. The bags contained popcorn balls baked with organic cheese, natural color derived from paprika, and whole grain heirloom corn. Hurrying to catch up, he found her, slowed his pace, and offered the fallen bag. It weighed as much as a feather and cost as much as a hamburger. "What about these puffs?"

She lifted the bag and grinned. "Perfect! Good call!"

Savoring the accidental win, he worked his jaw. "Why exactly do you want me to fail?"

Stopping in front of a tortilla chip display, she tilted her head. "You've never had a job interview, have you?"

If she moved three steps to the right, she would stand under a sprig of mistletoe, and he felt confident he could master that interview. Batting away the memory of the bathroom liaison, he wondered if their next kiss would come in a utility closet or an industrial kitchen.

"Are you paying attention?"

He blinked. The only thing he'd been paying attention to was his arousal and the memory of her lips.

She tapped her fingers against her chest. "I still talk to my former students. I failed, but I'm trying again with the grant. You need to land flat on your butt, dig yourself out of a hole, and start from scratch."

Since this morning, he had dug himself out of more than a hole. Between his aching muscles and his needled back, he could think of better ways to spend his time than outlining his faults. He cupped her hand and brought it to his lips. The feel of her unbearably soft skin dared him to wet his lips. "Tell me the cactus counts for something."

"Nope."

Deflated, he released his grip. Apparently, a grocery store make-out session was out of scope. He watched her shirt ride up as she grabbed a bag of chips and walked toward the cashier.

"Any artist can talk about their portfolio—"

"Say what?" He hustled to her side.

"—but if they want a stable job, they have to play corporate games. I hated interview prep, but I practiced mock questions until I lost my voice."

Given the success of the Starlight Motel, be believed in her capability to adapt to life's demands. He reached for a package of beef jerky, remembered to watch his salt intake, sighed, and dropped the hand. "Did you go from school to your residency?"

Swinging the shopping basket on her arm, she

looked over her shoulder. "How old do you think I am?"

He scratched his head and realized how little he knew about the woman commanding his attention. "Does it matter?"

She smiled. "Experiencing big city inequality compelled me to think about my life choices. I quit my corporate job and enrolled in graduate school. The residency came next."

"Oh." Counting off her age on his fingers might be cheating, but she looked younger than his experience. Maybe the desert's aging influence had skewed his perceptions.

Stopping in the pet food aisle, she considered several options and toed a high-calorie kibble.

The bag must weigh forty pounds. Bending, he scooped it into his arms and envied Lucky. At least, Kada displayed a commitment to her dog.

"Thanks."

He wondered why he hadn't fallen for a wide-eyed young thing who thought he walked on water. Instead of a cherubic sweetheart, he roped a sassy muralist, and he couldn't be happier... as long as he could figure out how to hold on to her. "Your career is impressive. I work for a family company." He shifted the weight in his arms. "I badger the CEO over dinner."

"You're spoiled." She added salsa to the basket hanging from her arm. "If you can't think of at least three failures in your career, you haven't stretched yourself, or you're too proud to admit your faults."

"I thought we were talking about bell peppers."

She waved a hand, unloaded the groceries in front of the cashier, and beamed. "How are you doing today?"

The cashier scanned each item. "Just fine, and you?"

Dane shifted the dog food bag to reveal the bar code and let Kada and the cashier play out their customer service ritual. If he had to choose between admitting a risk adverse nature and admitting inherent selfishness, he would like to propose a third option.

The cashier handed her a receipt. "Have a good day."

She offered the man a cheerful wave.

How could Dane be jealous of a wave? He fell into step. "What if I'm too good to fail?"

"Right." Shaking her head, she separated the bag of buns and the bag of snacks.

"Do you want to go somewhere else to look for the neon cheese balls?" he asked.

She shrugged and opened the market door to the shady alley. "The ones you found are great. If Benito doesn't like them, he'll have to settle for a salt fix."

Drawing a deep breath, he wondered whether Benito needed a one-way ticket to Las Vegas. He hefted the dog food in his arms. "Does he live close by?"

"Above the market. I'll text Stephanie and see if she wants to run down or have me run up. The last time I checked, she didn't want to leave him." Pulling out her phone, she juggled the grocery bags and sent off a series of messages. Looking up, she smiled. "I'll run up."

Lowering the dog food, he held out a hand for the buns, leaned against the market's stucco exterior, and kicked up a heel. The minute he rested his heel against the wall and transferred his weight, the wounds on his back flared to life. He shifted to lean on only one shoulder. "I'll be here."

She hesitated.

"Kada, you only told me about one failure."

Turning, she grinned. "Oh, trust me, I have more. I could spend a lifetime telling you about them." With a wink, she walked toward the door.

He would hold her to that promise. Watching her go, he considered her challenge. Letting a crop fail never crossed his mind. He had four generations of inherited knowledge, a college degree, and a clever mind. But she made a fair point. Failure might be one of life's great enablers.

Stifling a yawn, he watched seedpods flutter from the drake elm. Between the branches, birdseed ornaments shaped like stars hung from red, satin ribbons. Something sticky held together the black oil sunflower seeds and white proso millet, but the ribbon added a festive touch. He focused on the familiar seeds, but the decorations represented an alluring optimism, ungrounded in practicality, but entirely plausible. He couldn't look away.

A bird landed in the elm's branches and pecked at an ornament.

Good luck, buddy, they're probably as hard as a rock.

The bird flew off holding a sunflower seed.

Rubbing his chin, he considered whether the valley or the farming profession had narrowed his worldview. Having dodged failure, he had never corrected course, thrown out the playbook, or tackled unknown opportunities. What kind of clichés did they use on the East Coast? Scuffing his boot along the pavers, he decided he didn't want to know.

Accounting might suit him, but he passed his liberal arts classes with a *C* average. If failure defined a man's leadership style, he could ward off the accusation by trying new things and broadening his horizons, but he couldn't risk Palmer Farms.

He thought about the tomato virus. Someone put a contaminated transplant into the ground and jeopardized the entire crop. He spent most of his time running inventory lists, making timelines, purchasing chemicals, and putting out fires like the pump house disaster. Maybe he should spend more time rubbing soil between his fingers, inspecting leaves, and talking to staff about plant health. If his leadership style grew too relaxed, Palmer Farms would suffer, and when he failed, he would fail big time.

A second bird landed on the elm and cooed.

What am I doing chasing a woman?

The bird flew off with birdseed.

So much for signs.

Kada stepped out of the stairwell. "He's not as bad as I thought."

Shaking off his introspection, he focused on her glossy hair, warm smile, and relaxed shoulders. She cared about Benito and Stephanie enough to bring the pair snacks, and he doubted she read them a riot act about covering their shifts. Her ability to go with the flow and empathize with people's needs astounded him, but his grand gesture for the day had already backfired. He straightened off the wall. "That's a relief."

She walked toward the street.

"I thought about what you said."

Tilting her head, she waited.

She had the prettiest, almond-shaped eyes. He cleared his throat. "I'm thirty-five years old, and you're right, I might work too hard, and I might take too few risks. If anything, I have a fear of missing out on profits. Fear of dropping the ball. Fear of being a disappointment." He hoped she caught the gist of his confession. Words weren't exactly his thing.

"Cash FOMO."

Working his jaw, he accepted the diagnosis. He might be a little out of touch with the Top Forty, but Jud's tales from the dealership kept him entertained and debriefed on most slang. Fear of missing out had just never applied to his life. "What do you fear?"

She drew a deep breath and looked up at the sky. "I'll never make a difference." Shaking her head, she exhaled and made eye contact. "Doesn't everyone fear they'll waste their life?"

He wanted to reach for her and smooth the worry lines between her brows, but she didn't need his comfort. She'd already proven she could work through her disappointment, enlist help, and gather courage for another attempt. Instead of feeling sad, she challenged him to experience vulnerability, and he would do his best to summon an ounce of humility. "I could brainstorm three failures for your corporate recruiters, but they would be minor transgressions."

She held up a hand. "I get it, you're golden."

He stepped closer. "No, but I inherited a lot of knowledge and a lot of resources. At some point, the unexpected will happen. I should always try to improve operations and leverage new technologies. Maybe your dad's right. I should invest in resources to reclaim and reuse irrigation water. Consumer preferences might change. The river water might dry up. Walter could bail in a heartbeat and leave me stranded."

She dropped the hand. "Would he do that?"

He handed her the buns, picked up the dog food, and stepped out of the alley before he kissed her again and gave Palm Springs something to talk about. "I don't think so, but stagnation is its own kind of failure, and I'm guilty as charged."

"Don't be too harsh on yourself." She pressed the button for the crosswalk signal. "Also, what's a nematode?"

He laughed and wondered how long she held on to that question before asking it.

Her dimples deepened.

Agricultural innovation wasn't exactly a newsworthy headline, but her engagement had given him a much-needed kick in the pants. Silly questions gave him a way out of the conversation, but he would return to the issue. "Nematodes are among the most abundant animals on Earth. They occur as parasites in animals and plants…"

The crosswalk signal changed.

In step, they breezed in front of the stopped traffic.

He scanned the intersection and then looked at her face tilted toward the sun's warmth. Spending the day with her would warm him, too. "Do you need to meet your therapist?"

She glanced over. "I canceled the appointment."

Torn between relief and duty, he tried to maintain a neutral expression and support her needs. "Why?"

"I'm in a good place. I'll see her in two weeks." She smiled. "Even therapists deserve time off."

He exhaled and took in her radiant smile. He

understood Bobby Ritchie's desire to whisk away Mariah. Once a man found what he wanted, he had a hard time letting it go. Losing Kada's smile might be a life-long regret, and he doubted he could recover from the loss.

Chapter Nineteen

Kada regretted buying just one bag of tortilla chips. Turning up the truck's radio, she drove back toward the Starlight Motel. Beautiful, blue skies and temperate weather explained the throngs of tourists pouring into Palm Springs. The town had begun to feel like a home, and she halfway resented the increased traffic. If a few tourists stopped at the Starlight Motel, then she welcomed their reservations, but she had more than enough work to keep her busy.

Sneaking a quick peek as the truck hit a rough patch of asphalt, she saw Dane wince. His fortitude could inspire a country-western song, but his outlook on life needed a spit shine. He was so focused on the bottom line he couldn't make room for the joys surrounding him. When a bell pepper ceased being a sweet, crunchy delight, a man needed to step back and examine his priorities.

No matter his motives, the popcorn flower display gave her hope. Even if he sought out the blooms to relieve her nonexistent sadness, the act meant he could see the beauty around him. She merely had to help him find it.

"You're quiet," he said. "I like your chatter."

She laughed and thought fast. "As a kid, what was your favorite part about the holidays in Palm Springs?"

"The presents," he said. "Kids always like the

presents."

She smiled. "I knew you were spoiled."

He cleared his throat. "The illusion of magic. A massive Christmas tree twinkling to life, sweet treats, and visits from Santa. Even the menorahs and the *diyas* captivated me. When I got older, I remember the resorts passing out flashing, fiber-optic wands to wave while attendants lit up the tree. A big operation hired costumed carolers and hosted a sing-along. I had fun."

"Mariah took you to all those things?"

"She did."

Keeping her gaze focused on the road, she wondered when he lost sight of the holiday magic and saw the production costs. "I guess you outgrew all that fluff."

"Maybe." He cleared his throat. "Maybe my responsibilities left little room for silliness."

She thought about the years she missed Christmas ceremonies. With so many events canceled, scaled back, or made virtual, she threw herself into reinstating old-school holiday joy. "Some motel guests return year after year. Pops left behind a treasure trove of memories, but I have something new planned for tonight's New Year's Eve celebration. I hope it helps our guests celebrate the holidays and creates the sense of hope everyone craves."

"A midnight swim party with neon glow sticks?" he asked.

"Close!" To shape the new tradition, she would have to work hard for the remainder of the day, but the crowd's response would justify her effort. "I wasn't born and raised in this valley, but I like the people here. I like helping the community thrive and grow."

"I wish you'd stay," he said.

"Do you?" Her undefined tenure left her freedom and a sense of feeling adrift. If Mom could help with the Starlight Motel, then she would cheerfully share control. "I might."

"I won't hold my breath. Your talent can take you places."

Did she hear censure in his voice? Turning beneath the motel's pink sign, she parked the truck under the awning, grabbed the buns, and climbed out.

Holding the dog food, he met her in front of the hood.

She hated saying good-bye, but she took the sack from his arms. "Let's have dinner on Saturday night. Just wait until after the New Year. Whatever works best for your schedule."

He scratched his jaw. "Whatever works best for me?"

She nodded. She would leave the Christmas decorations hanging until after Twelfth Night, but taking down the decorations would mark the beginning of a new season. Whether the season with Dane lasted past Lent depended entirely on him.

He stroked her cheek. "Why do I feel like you're saying good-bye?"

"We both have commitments." Arms full, she jerked her head toward the throwback jeep better suited for storming the beaches of Normandy than making a grocery run. "Call me if you need a tow back to the farm."

Dropping his hand, he smiled. "Okay."

"Think about the failure thing? I've spent a lot of time picking myself up after my failed fundraising campaign. Take a few risks, Dane. Plant satsumas."

He scratched his scalp.

She stole a quick kiss. "I'm looking forward to our date."

Nodding, he pulled his keys out of his jeans pocket. "If the holidays mean I get to spend more time with you, I'm starting to like them."

The gesture warmed her heart, but she had her arms full. "Happy New Year's Eve. Now, scoot!"

Laughing, he turned toward the jeep.

A rusty station wagon pulled into the parking lot, parked next to the listing camper, and rattled into place. Mariah and Dane Palmer, Sr. climbed out of the vehicle.

"Apparently, you're tardy," she said.

He rubbed his chin. "Apparently."

Mariah waved like a friendly schoolteacher, but crow's feet fanned from her eyes, and she maintained the set smile of a woman who knew how to accomplish work. Dane Palmer Sr. looked like he had twenty years on Dane. Kada had a hard time ignoring his sun-kissed brown hair and broad shoulders, but he lacked his son's charisma.

"There's my first born," Mariah said. "I thought I lost him in the pump house!" Barreling across the parking lot, she wrapped her arms around Dane's torso and squeezed tight. "Did you forget today's New Year's Eve?"

At the pressure on his wounds, he winced, but he dropped a kiss onto her hair. "Hello, Mama."

Jud stepped out of the vehicle.

The minute Kada saw him, she knew buying extra buns was the right thing to do. The guest count at the

Starlight Motel had increased by three, but Jud looked like he could eat for the team. Lowering her groceries to the truck bed, she brushed her hair out of her face and stepped forward. "I'm so glad you came down to join us. We're playing it by ear, but I think tonight's celebration will be one to remember."

"Wouldn't miss it for the world." Disentangling from her son, Mariah hugged her, but she peered toward the motel. "I haven't seen Larissa in ages."

"She's probably in the main building. When we left, she was hip-deep in record boxes and dusty memories."

Rubbing her hands, Mariah strode across the parking lot.

Kada stared at the three Palmer men. "You guys feeling strong?"

Jud flexed.

Leave it to the younger son to put on a show. She shifted the bag of buns in her arms. "I have a crate behind the main building holding a few surprises. Actually, it's a box full of fireworks supplies."

Choking out a cough, Jud nodded.

Dane and his father exchanged glances.

Nothing about their shared look said "safe and sane," but she tried not to laugh at their assumptions. When she said she had something new planned for the New Year's Eve celebration, she meant the fireworks, but letting community members help with set up fit the holiday spirit. Then again, Dane was more than a community member.

How could anyone dislike fireworks? The company organizing the show promised professionalism, safety, and a spectacular show. If two people could fill the sky with light to celebrate a wedding, she could fill it with light to celebrate the beginning of a new chapter for herself and everyone at the Starlight Motel.

She told herself asking the men to unpack the pyrotechnics was nothing more than a time-saving convenience. As soon as they unpacked the crate, moved plywood sleds into the shrub, and carried out crates of flammable and combustible materials, the New Year would arrive in a shower of sparks. If they bailed? She adjusted the buns. She would cart the supplies to the desert without them.

Dane Sr. nodded. "Point us in the right direction."

Exhaling, she wet her lips. "Are you sure?"

He nodded.

She bounced on her toes and squealed.

Dane picked up the dog food and dropped his head. "You owe me."

"What?" she asked.

"Another kiss."

She felt her cheeks warm. Backing away before she did something familiar and claimed a kiss in front of his family, she jerked a thumb toward the main building. "I'll get you gloves and...things."

"Things?" Jud hooked his thumbs in his belt loops.

"A crowbar." She waited.

His gaze widened.

Laughing, she carried the buns toward the kitchen and set them on the countertop. The cleaning crew had the day off, and the cantina staff extinguished their holiday obligations. She had a secret weapon, her family. With their help, she could handle the next few days.

Inés would be back from the cathedral by sundown. Gustavo Dyson and his dog probably spent the day shooting arrows into archery targets, but he would return with an appetite. She had no idea what Chris Nicholson did with his day, but she had a hunch his activities involved the air museum. If he spent the day regaling the kids with old war stories, then she would probably have to comp him his room. The thought of him bouncing kids on his knee while wearing a fedora made her grin.

Mack, Sue, and the kids might have plans worthy of Midwestern pyromaniacs, but if they wanted to celebrate at the Starlight Motel, she was happy to have them. Missy Roberts? Well, the realtor could be a hot mess, but she was welcomed, too.

Opening the walk-in cooler, she inventories supplies. Benito had enough raw meat to make hamburgers, chilled avocados to make guacamole, and sliced fruit to make *agua frescas*.

The lightly sweetened drinks shined with one hundred percent fresh juice, but they required a lot of work. Benito often mixed the juice ahead of time and kept a pitcher of sweetener set aside to respond to the crowd's mood. More kids? More sugar. Lazing adults? He added things like ginger. Concentrates and store-bought mixes never measured up.

She appreciated his subtlety, but she was a muralist, not a professional chef. As long as she could feed the motel's guests, she would give Benito a raise for stocking the pantry, and she would deflect any compliments to the chef. Actually, as soon as she found Dad, she would inform him he received an upgrade to grill master. Grinning, she headed straight back into the sunshine to check on Lucky. Instead of clean, open air, she bumped into Dane carrying dog food.

"You forgot this bag," he said.

She held out her arms.

"I'll carry it."

Considering her options, she turned toward the *casita*. In all the times Mariah had visited to review her, she had never mentioned knowing Mom. Were the two the same age? Were they high school buddies or frenemies? Given how little she had heard about the Palmer family, she had assumed Mom and Mariah didn't double-date through high school. "Did you tell your mom you sat on a cactus?"

He shifted the weight in his arms. "Not yet."

Despite the oncoming holiday, a light afternoon wind pushed the pool floats into the pool's corner. Mist fans softened the dry air, and patio lights swayed. A few reclusive guests occupied pool chairs and absorbed the sunlight into their bronzing limbs. She could offer Dane a dip in the pool to clean up, but seeing him shirtless would interfere with her work. "Your blood-spotted shirt gives you away."

Craning his neck, he looked over his shoulder and frowned.

She passed two palms, opened the white gate, and leaned a hip against the post. "Make up a heroic story to explain your injuries."

"I saved you, didn't I?" he asked.

For so long, she thought she was the person making grand gestures, but her privilege and her ambitions narrowed her perception of who needed help. Taking the bag from his hands, she swallowed the lump in her throat. He saved her from traffic, and he reminded her successful people still needed art. Said people might be a little nearsighted, but their flaws made them sexier, and in exchange for art class, Dane could offer lessons on kissing. Once she had a handle on him, she might mention how much his attention soothed her anxieties. "Did I say thank you?"

He dragged his heel through the desert dust.

Her hands tingled, and she itched to reach for him, but she held the bag. "Sometimes, I'm too hard on myself. Maybe I was too hard on you, too."

Looking up, he smiled. "You gave me something to think about."

"And in return?"

"I don't know," he said. "My family's crawling over the Starlight Motel, sorting through Hall's treasures, and unpacking tubes stuffed with gunpowder. Despite my shortcomings, you're stuck with me for a few hours. If I come up with a technological innovation or a grand failure, then you'll be the first person to know."

She bumped his hip. "I can think of worse things."

Picking up a strand of her hair, he rubbed it between his fingers and let it drop. "Can you?"

She cleared her throat. "In the meantime, you should lose the button-up and grab a staff shirt. I don't want you to scare the guests. Unless you want to take a dip? I can throw your shirt in the washing machine."

Dropping her hair, he rubbed the back of his head. "I have fond memories of the washing machine..."

"Does it hurt?" she asked.

He grinned. "Only a dull ache."

She understood dull aches and the way they could subside into memories or bloom into unavoidable needs. If kissing Dane Palmer came with consequences, she needed to figure out her stance and fast. "I'll come find you in a few minutes."

He nodded.

Turning from his rangy, laconic smile, she fled inside the *casita* and left the sunshine to those better suited for the breath-stealing altitude. Inside her house, back to the door, she lowered the dog food to the floor and sank to her knees.

From a sunlit patch of flooring, Lucky raised her head.

Checking to make sure Lucky ate and drank, she crawled across the old, worn floorboards, stroked Lucky's ears, and sat with her legs crossed near the window. "How're you feeling?"

Wrinkling her nose, Lucky lowered her head.

With a light touch, she ran a hand along Lucky's side. She could feel the puppies moving. The sensation thrilled her and gave her pause. With lives on the line, she couldn't afford to waver from her priorities. Pulling back a hand, she settled it in her lap. "I ran my mouth about the power of failure, but I don't want to fail you. Would you be happier at the vet's clinic? Dr. Vo seemed nice."

No response.

Taking a deep breath, she lived in the now. Why did the now come fraught with so many dangers? Tomato blight was the least of her concerns. To avoid failing Lucky, she would sponsor an entire field of nightshades, close her eyes, and hope she came through this experience with six wiggling puppies to snuggle.

Remembering the things her therapist recommended, she counted her achievements and focused on the next right thing. She needed to attend to motel operations, supervise the New Year's Eve celebrations, and make sure nobody went to bed hungry.

Instead, she rested a hand on her chin and idly stroked Lucky's ear. The silky texture soothed her. "I'm making a lot of fuss, aren't I? If I could keep to my designated square and stop being such a busybody, I could limit how overextended I feel." Pausing, she thought about how simple life could be.

Lucky raised a paw and scratched at her arm.

She resumed stroking the sweet animal. As long as Lucky took comfort from the gesture, she was happy to continue.

Unless Lucky comforted her? Looking out the window, she replayed the prior year. She had sheltered her mom and kept the motel going, but without Mariah's support, she might have thrown up her hands and returned to corporate advertising. If she needed a pack of dogs to anchor her to the desert's nurturing warmth, she might be the lucky one.

She stilled a hand. "Just so you know, I graduated at the top of my class. I'm an awesome muralist. Also, I haven't bankrupted the motel."

Lucky yawned.

Recalling the price of the artificial tree, she hoped nobody overhead her claims. The centerpiece would make a brilliant social media background, but it would also shine like a beacon and mark her time managing the property. "Okay, I'm not turning much of a profit, but I'm an artist. I thrive on eccentricities."

Lucky farted.

An awful earthy smell filled the *casita*, and she

scrambled to her feet. "Look, Mama, you do you, but warn me next time."

Closing her eyes, Lucky nearly smiled.

She picked up the pamphlet Dr. Vo left behind. The pictures and captions showed happy, healthy puppies. She didn't have a kiddie pool, but she could make Lucky comfortable during labor and the puppies' scramble for milk.

Pulling an old quilt out of the closet, she spread it on the floor beside Lucky's sunlit spot, tugged short bookcases into place, and left an opening wide enough for a baby gate. If everything worked out, tiny claws would scratch up the *casita's* wood floors, and she couldn't think of a cuter sound.

After the puppies weaned, she would find every one of the precious little mutts a home. Taking on new challenges was one thing, but taking on a litter of them would be insane.

Chapter Twenty

Stepping away from the *casita*, Kada eased closed the white gate and checked the time. She should be meeting with her therapist, but she had plenty of time to make patties, fire up the grill, and toast store-bought buns.

Judging by the sound of creaking wood, she assumed Dane and his family found a tool to pry open the fireworks crate. Before she found an apron, she would make sure they put the supplies in the designated spot and knew they had her undying thanks.

Weaving through the palms, she cut through a service corridor and found Dane and his family staring at the open crate. Sheet of cardboard separated rows of pyrotechnics like wine bottles waiting to explode. *Just kidding.* The crate contained a jumble of metal stands and wire racks. "Is this too much to ask?"

Dane turned. "Did I do something wrong?"

She shoved her hands into her jeans and grinned.

He ran a hand through his hair. "What happened to the 'Twelve Days of Christmas?' Seven swans a swimming can't go *boom*."

Raising her eyebrows, she held his gaze. "Really? You think I should send back this stuff?"

"No, but most people start with sparklers. Consider them a gateway drug."

She laughed. "I like to go all in."

"I've noticed." He stepped toward her.

His dad cleared his throat.

Shaking his head, Dane pulled out the first stand, held it up to the sunlight, and glared. "This thing looks like a medieval torture device."

"I think it's meant for explosive candles. I'm not asking you to light it."

He eyed the stand and set it aside. "Good."

His humility intrigued her. Outside his element, he sensed his vulnerability, and she wondered how he would react in an art gallery. She could spot a real art lover from across a sterile, white room. The people who checked a piece's price tag before they experienced art came to be seen. University students came to eat as many appetizers as possible, and gray-haired old women came to chat with one another. She welcomed them all. One in a hundred would fall in love with a piece, and an artist only needed one chance to find their piece a home. Dane would linger.

"Do they come with set-up instructions?" he asked.

"Maybe."

Widening his gaze, he looked up. "Seriously?"

She laughed. "We need to haul them into open space and wait for the professional crew." Mentioning the crate's six hundred pound weight wouldn't make him or the rest of his family members any happier about the job, so she chewed her thumbnail. "Wait a minute, and I'll get a dolly."

He shook his head and hefted the stand over his shoulder.

Turning, she jogged toward the laundry room.

Inés stepped onto the path.

She stopped short.

"Kada! My niece loved the tram ride." Inés pulled a child's handwritten thank-you note from her deep pocket and offered it. "Thank you so much for the tickets."

Taking the note, she read it, and a warm pleasure radiated through her chest. The child's heartfelt gesture reminded her of how much she enjoyed making connections. Looking up, she smiled at Inés. "I'm glad the tickets went to good use. Is your niece coming to one of your concerts?"

"Unfortunately, no." Inés gripped her middle. "She came down with an upset stomach."

"Was it something she ate?" Kada feared an outbreak of gastroenteritis more than she feared a bad review. If Inés might have a stomachache after spending the day with her niece, Kada would be happy to comp her dinner in her *casita*.

"Three churros sounded like a good idea."

Kada released her breath and laughed.

Inés shrugged. "She can watch a rebroadcast. The next time I come to town, she'll be older, and the experience might mean more."

"I'm sure it will." The poster for Inés' concert hung with the other activity guides, but responsibility kept her from purchasing a ticket. If Dane wanted to swap his jeans for a pair of slacks, then she could steal away after the New Year. The future's glimmer left her unsettled, and she slipped the note in her jeans' back pocket. "Is it too late for me to purchase a ticket?"

"I think the concert's sold out. My sister has tickets to the one at St. Francis of Assisi in La Quinta. You could probably have hers."

The adjacent town was a forty-minute drive

through the desert. "La Quinta is a trek."

Inés toyed with her wooden necklace. "She says the building's beamed ceilings and heavy chandeliers remind her of our childhood church. Also, she doesn't feel like a standout in St. Francis' multigenerational, multiethnic congregation."

Kada could slip into the back row, but she hadn't attended church in years. Her parents often went for choir concerts and special performances, but religion hovered near the periphery of her daily experience. Kada found her peace with a paintbrush in her hand. Making the most of each day kept her mind from drifting toward distant futures.

Dropping the necklace, Inés shrugged. "Me, I can perform anywhere. Good acoustics help, but a strong singer can make the most of any venue."

She laughed. "Well, I'm happy to have you back at the motel. I missed your voice this morning, and I overslept."

"I'll remedy that error tomorrow." Inés raised her eyebrows. "Should I start with the 'Hallelujah Chorus' from 'Handel's Messiah'?"

Wanting to flee the suggestion, she decided to advance her proposal before Inés proposed early morning vespers. "Maybe you should stay up late and ring in the New Year. At the Starlight Motel, we traditionally have a homespun celebration, but we definitely have champagne." She gestured toward the pool and circled a hand like a Hollywood set designer staging a scene. "This year, we're firing up the grill, making hamburgers, and setting off enough fireworks for laughter, dancing, and memories. You're more than welcome."

"Everyone is welcome?"

She nodded.

Inés worked her jaw.

"Please don't make me sing 'Auld Lang Syne,' " she said. "I can do many things, but singing sits at the bottom of the list. We need you!"

Inés patted a hand. "You excel at running the motel. You have a good feel for people, a vision you want to create, and the stubbornness to make it happen. You would have made a good nun or teacher."

She clapped a hand over her mouth to keep from laughing. Lately, she'd had very un-nun-like thoughts about a local farmer.

"You're also a good artist. I've spent many quiet hours enjoying your work. I'm not sure how a person paints and runs a motel, but if you're caught between two worlds, you must find your peace and your inspiration. I did."

Dropping a hand, she stared and wondered how many times Inés considered altering her path.

Inés took up her wooden necklace and toyed with the beads. "I hope young people will not be afraid to make hard decisions. Everyone has a calling…"

She stepped back.

Inés dropped the necklace and smiled. "Lucky for you, you are not stuck with the daily interference I bestow on my family members, but I hope you figure out what keeps you up at night. Some vocations have nothing to do with institutions or community service."

Lowering her shoulders, she thought the silence of her late-night painting shielded her from observation, but every guest could see the mural's progress, and Inés saw more than most people. "I want to help people

313

shine."

Inés cupped her elbow. "A heavy heart makes for terrible sleep. Is something bothering you?"

Even without the vocalist's guidance, she gave thanks for the people in the world who listened and mentored. Her mother nurtured her, her professions inspired her, and women like Mariah and Inés supported her. One day, she would be the mentor, but right now, she would take all the help she could get. She drew a deep breath. "Inés, there's a man."

Laughing, Inés squeezed her arm. "Kada, there's always a man."

She planted her feet. "But there's also a motel, a sweet pregnant dog, zero staff, and this unending compulsion to go into the world and *do* something!"

Inés laughed and patted her arm. "Work within your confines or change them."

"Change them?"

"Break the rules, Kada. Ask for what you need. You're the only person who can shake up your world and resettle the pieces as you see fit."

Clamping tight her lips, she held her breath and released it. Staying in the valley would still be doing something, and she had more than most people, but the valley's confines chaffed. Asking for grant flexibility wouldn't change her statement of purpose. If she stretched out the schedule, she could spend time in the desert, accomplish her artistic goals, support her family, and carve out time for herself. Asking for more rankled her, but she considered the implications of choosing her art over her life and knew the decision would burn out her creativity. "I don't know what I need tonight, but I welcome your help."

Taking a hand, Inés patted it. "*Mija*, you have me. Give me something to do before I go stir crazy. Singing soothes me, but productivity keeps me going."

Turning her palm, she squeezed Inés' hand. "How do you feel about making New Year's Eve decorations?"

She threw up her arms. "Love it."

"Good!" She exhaled and wrapped her arms around Inés. "Thank you."

Inés lowered her arms and returned the hug. Pulling back, she cupped her cheek. "Any time."

Kada smiled. "Thank you."

Dane's dad walked past carrying launch sleds.

The reminder of her present needs cooled her desire to pick up the phone and call the grant organization. Easing away from Inés, she offered Mr. Palmer a smile.

He advanced on the gate leading from the pool and whistled like he carted around lumber in his sleep.

An orange flag marked the site for the fireworks launch. Due to the nature of the explosives, the crew came by last week and selected a qualified, safe location to shoot the show. The desert's wide-open field, situated away from buildings and people, fit the bill.

Setting down the sleds amid the scrub brush, Mr. Palmer turned. "Isn't this my land?"

She shrugged. *Who could find property stakes in the desert?*

Shaking his head, he walked back toward the unpacking operation.

The holidays might make people a little crazy, but they roused society's latent energy for good causes.

Looking away from the glimpse of future Dane and the border between their properties, she focused on Inés. "I don't need party hats and selfie backdrops for decorations. Those trappings charm, but we'll let the pool, the lights, and the desert shine."

"Are you sure?" Inés fluffed her hair. "No party hats?"

"We have fireworks planned," she said. "While we wait for the professional crew, I'll ask the guests write out their hopes for the coming year and smile for an instant camera. Their smiles and hopes will be our decorations. We'll create a chain to drape around the pool fence. We're all connected, aren't we?"

Inés squeezed a hand. "Let's do it."

Dane walked toward the pool carrying a box of electrical wire, let himself out of the gate, and marched into the field. Stopping at the launch site, he looked over his shoulder. "Kada, are you sure this is where you want this kiddie dynamite?"

She struggled to form an answer. He wore a staff shirt, and his body stressed the seams. "You know you're carrying setup equipment?"

Eyeing the box, he shifted its weight. "So you say."

"Aren't you a farmer? You probably know more about making explosives from fertilizer than half the people in the valley."

He grinned.

"Yep, let it blow," she said.

Lowering the box onto the sled, he stood from a squat and brushed clean his hands. Shaking his head, he walked back toward the pool, closed the gate, and kissed her cheek. "Ridiculous woman."

She tried not to laugh.

"How many boxes are in the crate?" Inés asked.

She looked at the vocalist. "Lots?"

Inés grinned and fanned herself. "Well, I'm certainly expecting a show. Let me call my sister and tell her I'll be late to her house."

"Sounds good."

Dane returned with two boxes in his arms.

Stepping back, she gave him room and skirted the pool. Beneath desert winds, the clear water rippled. If he fell in, he would make a splash. His track record of catching her said a lot about his reflexes, but if she knocked him off balance, she doubted she could haul out his frame. Smoothing her hands along her jeans, she readied herself to be useful. "Do you think I can carry the smaller pieces?"

Adjusting the boxes, he turned and looked at the shimmering, turquoise water. "Yes, but let me finish bringing out the guns. If too many people move about, someone's bound to land on their backside." He winked. "I've already had my turn."

"This is too much to ask," she said.

"Kada, it's nothing." He lowered the load. "Just don't ask me to light them."

"I wouldn't dream of it." She hated asking for help. "You have a good eye. Once they're airborne, the sequence won't matter."

"This one's called an ass-blaster." He gingerly lowered the box. "Are you sure you hired professionals?"

She nodded.

He lowered the second box. "Okay. Blast away."

"Okay?" She wouldn't have asked the cantina staff to cart out the pyrotechnics. Why did she think her handsome neighbor wanted to spend his evening doing grunt work? Just because he looked capable of surviving a desert siege and bringing her to her knees didn't make him a superhero.

He turned and made eye contact.

Okay, maybe it did. She cleared her throat. "You don't like holidays. Aren't you annoyed you're toting around flammable materials on someone else's property?"

He winked. "If you sold me the motel, it would be my property."

She glared, but she couldn't maintain the expression. A smile cracked her façade.

He leaned close. "I like discrete tasks. Kissing you? Got it. Carting fireworks into the desert?" He pulled back and smiled. "Got it. Keeping my mother from going crazy while she upstages Martha Stewart at the farmhouse?" He shuddered. "You take care of Mariah, and I'll put the sparklers anywhere you want them."

He smelled so good. Pulling back before she had to take herself to confession, she wet her lips and looked for a chaperone. "Where is your mother?"

"Where's yours?"

She scanned the palms, the pool, and the firepit. Something heavy settled in her stomach. The feeling wasn't dread, but the sensation felt like a long-overdue conversation she could no longer put off. "I'll find her and make sure she and Mariah have a plan for the evening. I'll do my best to keep you out of trouble."

"Deal." He tucked his shirt back into his jeans, whistled, and walked toward the pool.

Inés walked up to her side. "Honey, if I had a man

like that in my life, I would have thought twice about becoming a vocalist."

She turned. "But would you have still fulfilled your vocation?"

Inés smiled. "Absolutely."

A caravan of rusty trucks rolled into the parking lot. Men who spent their twenties operating carnival rides, chain smoking, and telling raucous jokes lined up behind a man with a large, black mustache.

"You Kada?"

She offered a hand.

"Sorry we're late. Should have been here this morning, but we got lost in West Texas."

She stared. "You drove here from West Texas?"

The man twirled his mustache. "You have a problem with Texas?"

Stepping back, she gestured toward the gate leading from the pool. "Have at it!"

Half the crew bypassed her. They taped off the firing area, exchanged good-natured insults about the Palmer family's efforts to help, and started assembling the show. The other half unloaded the explosives from their trucks.

She wouldn't ride the highway with a bed full of candy-colored bombs, but she hoped their skill and vocation left the motel intact.

Knowing what she had to do, she turned toward the main building where Mom and Mariah worked through Pops' memorabilia. She had to paint. To do so, Mom had to meet her halfway or choose between her art and her inheritance.

In the year since Pops died, the choice dogged her, but she felt certain about her needs. Two days ago, she could have walked away from the motel and focused on the promise of new students and new art. Then Dane rode into her life. She wanted Mom to meet her halfway. If Mom couldn't make that happen, her decision couldn't change, but leaving the Coachella Valley would be one of the hardest things she ever did.

****

Mom and Mariah sat on the floor in the office beside the tinsel tree.

Half-empty boxes surrounded them, dust mites floated in the air, and Pops' treasures revealed facets of his life. Kada knocked on the door. "Can I come in?"

Beckoning her, Mom held up an old family photograph. "Gosh, I should have done this months ago. I'm sorry I left it so long. If you hadn't volunteered to run the motel, then I don't know what I would have done with it. The place still smells like him. His little touches are everywhere. It's like he's still here."

"Well, tell me if you start seeing spirits." Mariah riffled through hundreds of match boxes. "I don't have the stomach for haunted houses."

Mom laughed and smoothed out an old magazine with a feature on the Starlight Motel.

Judging by the cover photos, the seventies could stay where history left them, but Kada suspected Palm Springs style never aged. She settled down on the floor to join the pair.

Flipping through the magazine pages, Mom stopped on the motel spread. "Pops anchored my childhood, but my grief took an emotional toll. I'm better, but loss never passes quickly. All this stuff is bittersweet." She ran her finger along the text, looked up, and smiled. "I'll read this piece later when I can enjoy it."

"You could stay awhile," Kada said.

Mom shrugged.

So much for an easy transition.

"Larissa, I thought your dad was the best," Mariah said. "He toted you around like you weighed nothing. He was so strong."

"He had to be," Mom said. "He nearly raised me. After Nana died, we were a team, but we had our squabbles. When I met Bobby, I thought he was such a freewheeling alternative to my old man, but the older I get, the more I recognize their stubborn similarities."

Kada pulled a wooden box from the pile, opened it, and revealed stacks of postcards from around the world. The cards thanked Pops for his hospitality and invited him to visit far-flung places. She handed half the stack to her mother and wondered how much her mother remembered. "If you had a sibling, do you think life would have been easier?"

Mom and Mariah exchanged looks, and Mom shrugged. "Sometimes, I was lonely, but I had friends. Maybe Pops couldn't have handled more than one rambunctious kid." Reaching out, she patted Kada's arm. "I had my hands full with you."

Guilt settled on her shoulders. "You poured a lot of energy into my childhood. It was lovely and magical. You worked so hard to set up play dates and to be an activity director. Whenever I had an interest in something, I felt your encouragement."

"You can't have one passion." Mom folded her hands in her lap. "As much as I love you, I also love my art. The minute you went to sleep, I ran to my studio and poured out the ideas I'd saved up while you put on plays about two sheep tied together at the tail."

She widened her gaze and lost her nerve to ask for more. The grant had come through, but Mom had put herself in second place for years. Flipping through postcards, she stared at a picture of the Taj Mahal and wondered if she would see the marble mausoleum in person. Maybe her ambitions were too grand.

"Oh, all kids can be silly." Mariah stretched out her legs.

Shifting, Kada made room.

"Jud keeps Dane's ego in check. He was the sweetest baby. If my first-born fails you, try Jud."

Jerking her gaze away from the postcard, she opened her mouth to respond, but she couldn't switch gears fast enough to stave off the older women's laughter.

"I'm kidding," Mariah said. "Jud's a mess in the best possible way. Stick with Dane."

She chewed her lip.

Holding up an eight-by-ten photograph of Marilyn Monroe and Frank Sinatra, Mom gawked. "When did Pops meet Marilyn?"

Mariah yanked the photograph from a hand. "Forget Marilyn. What about Frank? Frank hated having his picture taken! This picture is worth money!"

Kada leaned back on her hands and watched the two women reclaim their friendship. As far as she could tell, Mom and Mariah took two different approaches to life. Mom sculpted clay and loved life in all its forms. She organized play dates, scavenger hunts, and fairy parties so legendary Kada's friends begged for birthday party invitations.

Mariah followed a playbook so detailed she had the end zone in sight from the ninety-yard line. No wonder Dane kept the goal in sight.

Together, the pair helped her shape her vision for the future, and if she could ignore their emotional involvement, she would explain her conflicted feelings about the motel, her art, and Dane Palmer. Reality forced her to clear her throat. "We can get a large format reprint and hang the picture in the reception area."

Pointing her finger, Mom nodded. "Brilliant. Let's get a statue made, too."

She wrinkled her nose. A twenty-six-foot statue of Marilyn Monroe in her famous, billowing white dress occupied a spot in local lore.

Palm Springs had a love-hate relationship with its illustrious past. Whoever saw the beauty in the desert's striking landscape would claim its future. She already tipped the sand out of her shoes, looked toward the mountains for inspiration, and knew the desert held a portion of her heart, but the desert didn't hold all of it.

Riffling through old scrapbooks, pressed cocktail napkins, and newspaper clippings, she gathered the courage to ask for what she needed. "Who knew Pops was so sentimental?"

Mom ran a hand over a brochure from the 1970s. "It wasn't Pops—it was Nana. She loved him, and she saved everything he touched. He was her hero."

Captivated by the mention of her grandmother, she tilted her head and listened.

"Nana idolized her husband, but she knew his faults, too. When he was frustrated, he couldn't tone down his language. 'Turning off' bothered him more than he cared to admit. When he got too rowdy, she sent him into the desert to wind down."

Realizing how much her sage grandfather changed over time, Kada appreciated his efforts to help her process her feelings.

"So, all these treasures?" Mom asked. "If he wanted to forget the past and focus on the future, then Nana made it her mission to preserve history."

Kada sighed. Her entire life, Nana was a saint gone too soon, but the more she lived, the more she realized Nana couldn't live up to the family myth. "Do you ever think Nana wanted more than living in Pops' shadow? I mean, she was an artist, too. As far as I know, the minute she delivered you, she stopped painting."

Mom stared.

Mariah flipped through an article with the intensity of a high school student cramming for a test.

"She didn't stop painting," Mom said, "but she definitely scaled back."

"Where are the paintings?" Kada asked. "I've never seen her work."

Staring into the closet, Mom frowned. "I don't know. She kept my lopsided sculptures from middle school."

Nana's legacy felt too close to home. Kada could love the Starlight Motel and pour her heart into the property, but where did that effort leave her? In fifty years, another manager would take over the property and obliterate her contributions. As much as she loved her family, she wanted to paint, make connections, and improve the world beyond the motel's adobe walls. If everything was within her reach, she wanted it all.

Mariah looked up. "What did Nana paint?"

Mom worked her jaw.

"Nature," Kada said. "Pops said she painted the world around her, and her work was as beautiful and flawed as life itself." She let the words settle and compared her work to Nana's hallowed art. She might never live up to her ancestors.

As much as she wanted Mom to take over the motel, she wondered if a compromise would be the best solution. Could she keep one foot in the desert and one foot in the art world? The valley could only host so many murals. To thrive and contribute, she had to leave, but could she return?

When she painted, she wondered if her legacy would persevere. Without impact, the paint she laid down would fade, and other artists would claim her canvases, mostly likely with a paint roller.

By devoting her life to a cause, she wanted to help people, and she wanted a record of her presence. The alternative, fading into loved memories, felt like an aspiration and a threat. "When Nana stopped making art, she died."

"That's not true." Mom frowned. "Maybe. I wish we had more of her art."

Picking up a worn, leather jacket, Kada held it up to her nose and inhaled the rich, oiled scent. "I wish I met her. I loved Pops, but he was part of a team."

Mom pulled her into a side hug. "Teams produce the most beautiful art."

Raising her head, Kada wondered if a team always had a leader and a supporter. Dane, as rugged and capable as he was, could no sooner put down his notebook than she could put down her paintbrush. She faced her mother and summoned a compromise that let both women thrive.

Mom tilted her head.

Kada took a deep breath. "Mom, I needed the Starlight Motel to regroup, but I need you, too. I can't spend my life checking in guests and solving their problems. You couldn't do it, either. We both need to create, and I need to paint. Mariah and I worked on a grant. I received it, but I can't run the motel full-time. You have to step up, we have to split the work fifty-fifty, or we have to sell the property."

Drawing a deep breath, Mom held it.

"She'll provide direct, hands-on arts experiences to students, teachers, and community members," Mariah said. "I think her crowd funding failed because it benefited a faceless artist. We solved that problem. The grant funder knows he or she gets Kada's capabilities, and her work speaks for itself."

At the praise, Kada's cheeks warmed, but she stayed focused on Mom. "I love interacting with people. Creating a mural is the final goal, but workshops, classes, and community events feed the process. After the museum residency, I thought I served my role, and I needed to make room for the next artist, but I've only begun to leave my mark. If I'm running this motel, I can't paint."

"And you'll paint beautiful works," Mariah said. "You'll shine. As soon as the corporation receives your application, I'm confident you'll have your funding."

She chewed her cheek. Two consecutive rejections might scar her self-confidence. Pushing away her fear of a life without creativity, she squeezed Mariah's hand. "Thanks."

Mom looked between her and Mariah. Turning, she

stared at the nearest *casita* mural.

"What?" she asked.

"I didn't know. I thought you grew tired of art and decided to become a business owner. This whole time, I thought you were happy in the Coachella Valley." Looking back and forth between her and Mariah, she sighed. "You're so capable. I thought my job was done."

Taking her mom's soft, lined hand, she squeezed it. "I am proud of my work, but I don't feel fulfilled. If I can paint *and* help our family run this motel, I'll do both."

"Both?" Mom bit her bottom lip.

"If you can meet me halfway, then I'll feel like I've won the lottery."

"Both." Mom chewed over the word.

Shaking her mother's hand, she pulled her back into the discussion. "We can run this place together. If the grant application had failed, I would have poured my heart into finishing the *casita* murals, and I would have regrouped, but I would have still wanted to paint in the community." She took a deep breath. "The grant application didn't fail. I have funding."

Mom looked up and squealed. "I'm so proud of you!"

Kada looked toward Mariah and mouthed her thanks.

Pulling free a hand, Mom dropped her chin into it. "We might be similar, but we can't butt heads every day running this place. I know how stubborn you can be, and I know where the gene came from."

"Dad?"

Mom smiled. "Absolutely not."

She wrapped her hands around her knees and realized how much she missed her mother. She didn't need to repay her parents' investment, but adulthood shouldn't mean losing them, either. "I thought I had to take myself out of the process and give someone else a chance to paint, but I'm the only person who paints and thinks just like me."

Mom cupped her cheek and dropped her hand. "My sweet Cicada. You are special."

"Sometimes, I feel like I can do great things, but I need you. If this place means something, can you carve out time for it and let me pursue my art? Can we meet in the middle and find a way to both be artists?"

Standing, Mom brushed the dust from her hands. "Over the years, I've learned tunnel vision is a bad decision. When Pops died, I needed time to process my grief, but I also needed you. That was my mistake. I won't let it happen again."

Coming to her feet, she held her breath.

"I can work remotely half the year. Life has its seasons, and you need time to develop your skills outside the classroom. We can figure out what rotation makes the most sense, but Dad and I have your back. Pops had our backs, too, but leaving something you love never feels like the best answer." She stared out the window. "Maybe I should have stayed."

Interrupting her mother's view, she cupped her shoulders. "Mom, if this motel doesn't work for our family, we can sell it." She glanced at Mariah sitting on the floor. "I know a buyer."

Mariah bit her lip.

"How could we sell this place?" Mom asked. "It matters to us, and I'll learn how to deal with the hiccups. Together, we can keep it going for the next generation."

Finding herself pulled into a hug, Kada blinked back tears and envisioned a cooperative, multigenerational future at the Starlight Motel. As long as her family owned the property, she could return and savor its charms.

Mariah stood and smiled like a benevolent principal watching another student fledge.

Holding her mother tight, Kada swallowed. Solving her professional dilemma took a weight off her shoulders. She could paint and return to the motel, but Dane wouldn't always be here, and the magic of the past two days wouldn't be the same. She drew a deep breath.

Mom released her and wiped away her tears.

Rubbing Kada's back, Mariah smiled. "You come from a long line of strong women. I'm thrilled Larissa is coming back to the valley. Nana sounds like a beautiful woman, and I wish I could have seen her and Hall together."

"Maybe your timing was off," she said.

Picking up an old newspaper clipping, Mariah smiled. "Maybe my timing was just right."

Chapter Twenty-One

As the sunlight faded from the brilliant sky, Kada slipped from the memorabilia enclave, stretched her arms over her head, and yawned. She felt proud of herself for asking Mom for help with the motel, but by five o'clock, guests brought her their problems, and reality set in.

Shaking off the dusty nostalgia, she rushed through the palms, skidded on a patch of gravel, and flung open the kitchen door with a bang. "I have to make hamburgers!"

Stainless steel pots, immaculate work surfaces, and the lingering sooty smell reminded her why she needed to pull out ten pounds of ground meat and heft it onto the counter. *Who makes art out of ground meat? Instead of sorting through memorabilia, I should have distributed gloves and set my family to work making patties.*

Dane stepped through the door. "So, I heard you're leaving town."

Ripping open a package, she managed a smile, dumped the chuck into a large, stainless steel mixing bowl, and plunged her hands into the chilled meat. She felt her stomach clench and suppressed her gag reflex. "Part-time."

He looked so handsome wearing jeans and a staff shirt. The subtle mess his hat made of his hair only added to his charm. No matter what she asked, he delivered, and the people who knew him loved him. If she kept busy, then he wouldn't see the regret seeping from her move back into the art world. "Word travels fast."

"My mother says your grant was as eloquent and alluring as your art."

Her cheeks warmed, but she kept her gaze averted. "That was kind."

"And as soon as you accept the grant, you'll have money to fund years of work at your vocational school. In the second and third years, you'll mentor other artists. If the work pans out, you won't create murals. You'll create a legacy."

She looked up from the meat and swallowed. "You must know what it's like to have a vision and throw your heart into it. I do, but I struck out. This is my second chance. I have to take it. I have to leave the motel. At least part-time."

He rested his hip against the counter. "Art isn't enough."

"College taught me technique, but it didn't teach me the opaque, unspoken rules governing the art world. No wonder I failed."

"You didn't fail, Kada. I've seen pictures of your work. I've seen the plants you're painting on the *casitas*."

Reaching for a wooden spoon, she plunged it into the bowl and flipped the cold meat. Anyone could consider his or her job a work of art. Benito's food nourished her. Hall's service inspired her. The fact she chose paints and large-scale canvases increased her overhead, but she picked a profession, and she would try to succeed. "People say art is all about technique and luck, but my professors said I needed preparation and opportunity."

Shaking her head, she broke the meat into segments. "All those people were wrong. Art is everything, and it's also a business. You have strategic business plans, don't you? So do I. You can't ride into my life and upset my plans."

"So, I guess this is it for us." He exhaled and spun a hanging pot. "We can call off the dinner date."

Dropping her head to hide her disappointment, she replayed his words. No matter what she wanted, she made a part-time commitment to her art and a part-time commitment to the Starlight Motel. She was plumb out of parts.

Guests milled beneath the swaying patio lights and sipped poolside cocktails because she kept open the doors. Admittedly, Dane and his family carted the fireworks into the desert, but she would have found a way to position them. "Some people make long-distance relationships work." Closing her eyes, she waited for him to shoot down the long shot.

"Some people have more than forty-eight hours to fall in love."

Love was a heady term. Eyes wide, she jerked up her head and wondered if she misheard him.

"I want to make sure you know how proud I am of you." He cleared his throat.

Biting back tears, she nodded and dropped the wooden spoon. She could do difficult things like make hamburger patties and say good-bye to Dane.

"You have a good life here. The staff and your guests love you." He cupped her face and quickly dropped his hand. "If you're willing to give up that pleasure to help other people, then I'm humbled."

Her first tear fell. He never admitted a failure or an uncalculated decision, but he laid bare his emotions, and she understood that kind of risk. Even though his family trained him to lead Palmer Farms, his laconic observations and warm grins humanized the operations. How could she demand poetry from a man who faced the environment's arid scorn and found peace amid agriculture's orderly rows? By acknowledging the trade-offs behind her decision, he left an impression as wide as the valley, and his concern threatened to swallow her tears. "Thanks."

He stilled the swaying pot.

She wanted dusky rides through town, long dinners, and sweet kisses, but she had climbed out of bed this morning and accomplished the things she set out to do. Actually, she had overslept and found soot-stained staff, but most days, she rose at the crack of dawn. The fact that he did the same made them kindred spirits, but not every pair of lovers matched and ended happily ever after. For half the year, she would be gone.

He gestured toward the bowl of meat. "You need help with this?"

She barely felt the cold meat in her hands, but she blinked away welling tears. "Why don't you enjoy the evening with your family? I'll have these burger patties made in a jiff, and Dad will throw them on the grill."

He nodded.

For a split second, she thought he would take her advice and settle into a lounge chair by the pool.

He remained smack in the middle of the motel kitchen and frowned. "Why do you look miserable?"

She raised her sticky, cold hands and met his gaze. "I hate hamburgers."

"Then why are you making them?" He frowned.

Swallowing, she furrowed her brow. "Other people like them?"

"Other people?"

She looked up. "I'm a vegetarian."

He widened his gaze.

She gaped. "I'm worrying about life choices to be close to a man who doesn't know I'm a vegetarian?" Closing her mouth, she pressed a hand against it to stop herself from saying something she would regret. When she felt in control, she dropped the hand. "Way too fast."

He worked his jaw. "You didn't know I wore glasses."

"Those are glasses!" She checked her logic. "I don't *sometimes* eat meat."

"Right." He cleared his throat. "I asked if you had any dietary preferences. You could have mentioned you don't eat meat. How was I supposed to know about your restriction?"

"It's not a restriction, it's a choice." She'd had this conversation so many times but never with him. Leisurely getting to know one another was never their fate. "I'm named after an animal, Dane. How could I eat one? Would you eat a dog?"

"Um." He dragged a hand down his face. "Right. If I hadn't spent so much time mooning over your body, I would have put together the pieces. Given a little more time…" Shaking off the possibility, he dropped a hand and leaned on the work surface. "Let's save politics and religion for date number two. In case you're curious, I have hypertension, and I'm allergic to almonds."

She exhaled. Of course, he had high blood pressure. He took ownership of every problem in the Coachella Valley. Saying good-bye would never be easy. Turning her back, she washed her hands and pulled down Benito's all-purpose seasoning. "Noted. I'm sure you have an excellent physician."

He grunted. "I've thought about starting a CSA."

"Cute." Sprinkling the seasoning liberally on the meat, she caught hints of cumin mixed with powdered chili, onion, and garlic. Ground cloves and ground cinnamon added sweet spice. She had no idea if the combination of spices would work in the hamburger, but committing to the decision, she mixed the meat. It felt cold, slimy, and wet, but she trusted the outcome. Still, she wanted to hurl. "You should do it."

"Is that so?"

Biting the inside of her cheek, she nodded. Since the moment Dane rode onto the property, she felt her interest in him and her commitments to herself and to her family warring for her attention. With so little time to get to know him, she viewed her capacity for a relationship as lacking as her credentials for running the motel. Each time she ran her hands down his back or caught him finding ways to smooth her path, she thought their attraction would find a way to overcome their restrictions, but love came too late. Dane belonged in the valley, and she was a mere visitor.

Winning her artistic grant amplified her need to return to her professional training and the honor of amplifying community voices. Without her art, she might lose herself in the desert's shifting sands and her family's legacy. The only thing worse than letting down her mom and her students would be letting down herself. Loving a handsome cowboy wasn't enough reason to extinguish her creativity. She swallowed back tears. "It'll be fine."

"Kada, it won't be fine. I noticed you didn't eat meat," Dane said, "but your dietary preferences have nothing to do with the way I feel."

Making fists, she squeezed out the frustration constricting her heart. "Lust is a heady emotion. I'm sure your family misses you. It's New Year's Eve, after all. They didn't plan to spend their holiday helping me run the motel. Go spend time with them. After the New Year, we'll sort out this thing between us."

"I have a feeling my mother plans more than she lets on, but I can take a hint." His boot squeaked on the floor. "I'll see if they need anything. If not, I'll return to help you."

"I don't need help!" She balled up a handful of meat, squished it between her palms, and hoped it weighed close to half a pound. Slapping it on a tray, she repeated the process and steadied her breathing. "I can do it."

Stepping close, he dropped his head.

He smelled like dusty sunshine, and she wanted to savor his warmth, but she had a bowl of raw meat and a crowd to feed.

"I know you can do it, but I want to help," he said.

She heard his footfall and looked up.

"Don't give up on the idea of us." Kissing her cheek, he turned and walked out of the kitchen.

Releasing a sigh, she debated whether to savor his kiss or rub her cheek against her shoulder and focus on her commitments. "Maybe he'll find a pretty, pink distraction and forget he met me."

Mom walked into the room carrying popcorn strung to hang on the tree. She raised the garland and waved it in the air. "Who added microwaves to the *casitas*? Everyone popped a bag of popcorn and brought the popcorn to the pool. Someone's playing *When Harry Met Sally* over a wireless speaker, and we're all laughing."

"Popcorn"—she swallowed around the pain constricting her throat—"might clog the pool filter."

"Come join us," Mom said. "The pool's always been the heart of this place."

"I will." She made more patties. "I'm almost done with this prep work."

Mom came up behind her and laid a hand on her shoulder. "I said I could work remotely, but your dad and I can also move down full-time."

She shook her head. "It's not your vision. Dad has a few more years left before retirement."

"But your vision matters, too," Mom said.

Leave it to her artistic mother to respect another artist's needs. "I can't ask you to give up your art to run the motel. I know how hard managing both interests can be. Work with me on a schedule. We'll alternate."

"Eccentric characters make good stories, but familiarity runs a business." Mom pulled back her hand. "Lucky for you, in this family, we have both."

"We still need to innovate." Closing her eyes, she bit back more tears and focused on her task. If the patties needed salt, she had plenty to offer. Instead, she pulled down the saltshaker and sprinkled white crystals over the mix. Before his death, Pops said his two remaining taste buds loved sweets and salt. She made sure the patties delivered a savory reward.

Dane walked into the kitchen and leaned a shoulder against the doorjamb. "You two have this covered?"

Mom laughed. "I'm good at concepts and prototypes, but most of my pieces fall apart in the kiln. The ones that survive the furnace?" She raised her fingers to her lips and snapped off a kiss. "Magnificent!"

Dane laughed. "Well, I'm not much good at art, but I can make a hamburger patty."

Mom appraised him. "I bet you can." Waving good-bye, she walked out of the room.

Alone with Dane, Kada closed her eyes, regrouped, and shaped another patty.

He braced his hands on the counter. "Maybe I know what you need. Satisfaction."

She gave him a look and hoped he read her meaning. If he wanted a quick release to cool his ardor, he could jump in the pool. She had twenty items on her task list, and even though she prided herself on remembering details, she couldn't slink into the desert with a handsome man and find her kicks.

"Go paint," he said. "Take a break."

She stared. The cold, clammy meat in her hands reminded her of how little time she had for taking breaks. Why would he suggest something so alluring? She had long-term plans and short-term needs, but painting the *casita* walls was a selfish indulgence. Shaking her head, she made another patty and regretted his suggestion earned a G-rating. "Maybe later."

He washed his hands, picked up a handful of meat, and shaped it into a puck.

The man was stubborn, but she was desperate.

"Flatter."

He nodded.

Their easy camaraderie felt too good. Clearing her throat, she made progress, but the minute she bumped elbows, her heart rate spiked. Dropping a finished patty on a tray, she washed her hands. "Painting is the last thing I have time to do, but we're almost done here. Thanks for the help."

"No problem."

Second-guessing her seasoning choice, she broke off a piece of meat and sniffed the spices. Moving from a college dining hall to a San Francisco design firm left her little time to learn to cook. Truthfully, Mom had limited cooking skills, too, but she made beautifully hand-built coffee mugs. So far, Kada painted pretty pictures. Turning on a gas burner with her clean hand, she dropped the meat in the pan and heated it.

The food's savory, sizzling aroma revved up her hunger and her frustration, but she hadn't eaten a hamburger in a decade.

He made another patty. "I can finish up."

Finding a fork, she pulled the cooked meat from the skillet and blew on it. "I don't need you to make patties. I know you're good at doing what needs to be done, but I don't need you to fix everything."

Crossing his arms over his chest, he stared. "Who said anything about fixing?"

She touched a finger to the meat, blew on it again, and popped it in her mouth. Despite her daily habits, the meat tasted delicious, and the spices augmented its flavor. Dressed on a gourmet bun, the meat would do just fine. She spat it into the sink.

Cupping her hand, she raised a scoop of water to

her mouth and rinsed down the taste.

Dane laughed.

She looked up. "What?"

Walking up, he held up two dirty hands and raised his eyebrows. "Nothing. You do you."

She made room at the sink.

After washing his hands, he tore off a paper towel and turned. "You said I'm good at fixing things, but fixing things suggests something is broken. I want you to paint because you love it, but also because you're good. The minute you finish those murals, motel guests will snap pictures, tag the motel, and increase business one hundred percent." He rubbed his chin. "Maybe I'll organize farm tours."

She tried to imagine him on a rumbling tractor while tourists snapped selfies. The customers would be lucky if he didn't wander into the fields and start hand-picking crops. She shook her head. "That's your call."

He planted his hands on his hips. "If you're leaving us, you might as well leave us in good shape."

"I don't want to leave you." The admission slipped out, and she stepped back.

He reached for her and pulled back his hand. "Then don't."

Spending her days imagining him hard at work sounded like perpetual hell. In the last forty-eight hours, she had grown to expect his presence, and she wanted more time with him, not less. She swallowed and wished he made contact. "But I have to leave. I didn't spend the last ten years honing my craft to limit my skills to a life-size paint-by-number."

Working his jaw, he stared. "Then come back."

She opened her mouth, swallowed her words, and

fortified her resolve. Life wasn't that easy, and she couldn't tie down his affections for a casual relationship. She wet her lips. "I can't."

He stepped forward. "This thing between us needs time to bloom. Make space in your schedule. Unless you're already seeing someone, see me. I would try my hand at romance to convince you, but I don't have time for that choice. Jump in, Kada. The water's fine."

Going back-and-forth was pointless. She wanted to free him and to fulfill her needs. She could no sooner bury her art than ask him to plow under his crops. Enjoying the poolside party would make her happy, but in the morning, she would still have the Starlight Motel blank wall's potential. "You deserve more than a part-time girlfriend."

Someone near the pool plugged in the amplifier. Static clicked, and Bing Crosby's rendition of "Let's Start The New Year Right" played. Guests cheered.

He wrinkled his nose. "I hate this song."

She snorted. "You would."

"But it could be the start of a new beginning." Drawing her close, he swayed and pulled her into a slow dance. "We're the only people who can say what's right."

Resisting against his chest, she closed her eyes, relaxed into his hold, and let the music lead. Amid short days, cooler temperatures, and punishing winds, the holidays reminded her to treasure the people she loved and hold them close, but the holidays wouldn't last. Family would, and she had to put her obligations ahead of her needs.

Mom and Dad traveled from Wyoming to visit, but Dane had family, too. She couldn't tie up his interest while she jetted around the country and pursued her dreams. At thirty-five, his interest in flirty texts would wane long before the temperature spiked to one hundred degrees.

When the song ended, she stepped out of his arms, raised a hand, and stroked his rough, afternoon stubble. "Sometimes, I feel like we meet people in our lives who offer us glimpses of happiness, but the relationships aren't meant to be permanent. I wish we had more time, but if Mariah is right, then I'll be gone sooner than either of us expected. Popping in and out of your life is cruel. Art is life. Life is"—she dropped her hand—"complicated."

He stepped back. "You're not shy about putting a man out of his misery."

"Is it ever easy?"

His gaze softened, and he shook his head.

Released from his spell, she laid a sheet of parchment paper over the meat patties, lifted the tray, and fled from the kitchen. In the fresh air and pastel twilight, she drew a deep breath and squeezed back tears. "He'll find someone kind and beautiful like Dr. Vo." Raising her head, she forced a smile and walked away from the kitchen and Dane Palmer.

Following the palm trail, she focused on the growing pool party. Dad loaded up the pink firepit with firewood, and people stood around the decking, laughing and drinking. Chests of champagne waited beneath a table. Stepping to the edge of the rippling turquoise waters, she watched the party's wavy reflection. Guests mingled, took pictures, and found common ground. What more could she ask for? Smiling, she realized the valley's residents were onto something. Poolside New Year's Eve parties weren't a new fad. The allure of twinkling light and sparkling water always brought together partygoers.

In the desert, water brought together people. Pops taught her love, like water, wells up in the most unexpected places. If the valley's creatures waited for rain showers, they might lose their chances. Instead, they found hidden springs and green shoots. They built upon success, and they moved forward. She offered her guests whatever ease she could provide. Each offering returned dividends. Instead of defining a relationship as a binary choice between love and heartbreak, she could leverage the lessons she learned from her parents. She merely needed time to find a way forward and an ounce of Dane's confidence in her success. She dropped the tray of patties near the smoking grill and appreciated Dad's foresight to place the mobile grill downwind of the pool.

Mack and Sue's kids ran up wearing party clothes.

"The pool looks beautiful! Can we have the horns?" Mary Elizabeth asked. "Please?"

"What horns?" Scanning the celebration, she spied black-and-gold horns hanging from the fence encircling the pool. Someone from the Palmer family must have found an old box of decorations and hooked the treats on the pillars. She had a feeling Dane wasn't that person. His aversion to the holidays worried her as much as his aversion to taking risks, but she understood disappointment. She smiled at the kids. "Sure, but ask your parents."

"Yes!" Mary Elizabeth pivoted and ran back to Mack and Sue.

Her brother trailed.

She watched the girl's animated hand gestures. If the kids avoided an accidental tumble into the pool, then she would count the night a success.

"Make them all medium?" Dad asked.

Turning, she smiled. "Yeah. If someone wants one well-done, we can always throw the patty back on the grill. You're sure you don't mind? When you drove down here, this isn't exactly what you anticipated."

He laughed, picked up a large, metal spatula, and slapped the first patty onto the grill. The meat sizzled and smoked. "The Coachella Valley always surprises me. Sometimes, it changes my life, too. Your mother told me she wants to get more involved in the motel."

"Um, I think she agreed..." Despite the chill in the air, she broke out in a sweat. Had she wasted her chance with Dane and misjudged her ability to complete the grant because of a miscommunication?

"As in, she wants to move her kiln into the back of your *casita*, set up a remote office for me next to the laundry machine, and give you time to pursue your art."

Her heart clenched and released. "Yes."

He slapped her back. "You did good, kid."

The reference to the 1976 boxing film, "Rocky," almost undid her. Dad always fancied himself the underdog. She doubted her ability to speak without crying and nodded.

"She's had a hard time with Hall's death. Taking care of this place and giving her room to grieve made all the difference. Thank you for making that sacrifice. Perspective is a funny thing. With enough time and distance, you see things how they are, and you see them how you want them to be."

With enough time and distance, she would forget

the pleasure of kissing Dane Palmer, solving problems, and dancing in his arms. She didn't want to forget, but she didn't want the selfishness of asking other people to upend their lives for her benefit. How could she espouse community-building in her artistic statement and simultaneously upend people like Dane and her parents from their homes? She blinked away tears. "But your classes?"

Dad squeezed the juice out of the first sizzling patty. "I don't have to be down here full-time. Publish or perish, kiddo. Who said I like to teach?"

"Um, you?"

He laughed and nodded. "Remote learning isn't all bad. I'll take a hybrid approach."

Dad loved the classroom more than any dataset on the planet. If he and Mom could make a dynamic living situation work, then she could, too. Her childhood dreams of a nuclear family leading tidy, manicured lives made so little sense that she viewed the memory like a black-and-white drawing with zero depth. Maybe more of life's problems required a hybrid approach.

A diverse, multigenerational life offered richness and contrast. It highlighted life's beauty. Not everyone could uproot their parents and stake out a claim in the Coachella Valley, but if they could, she recommended the choice one hundred percent. She cleared her throat. "Um, that would be really awesome, Dad. I'll think about it."

He mussed her hair.

She pressed a kiss to his cheek before she broke down in front of the entire valley.

"Where are your black bean burgers?" he asked. "Cicada, did you turn into a carnivore?"

"No!" She made the patties, but pleasing people and pleasing herself were two different things. Scanning the motel, she focused on her *casita* and decided to see if Lucky ate or a hamburger might tempt her into eating. "I'll get them. I'll be right back."

Dad nodded.

She turned to dart into the kitchen and grab her vegetarian burgers from the freezer.

Inés walked up and handed her a cup of hot cocoa.

The veggie burgers had spent six months in a deep freezer. Five more minutes wouldn't make them taste any better. The sauce was the secret. She always added a kick of hot-sauce. Taking the hot cocoa, she felt the warmth of understanding behind the gesture. "Thank you."

"Did you sort out your concerns?"

Sipping the drink, she nodded. "It still hurt."

Pulling her into a side hug, Inés squeezed her shoulders. "Sometimes, life hurts, and we have to focus on the love."

Love felt like such an effusive, indiscriminate privilege. Surrounded by family and friends, she had more love than most people, but she wanted more. Her selfishness worried her as much as her potential heartbreak. Sliding away from the vocalist before she melted into a puddle of tears, she raised the hot cocoa in gratitude. "I'm off to check on Lucky."

"I heard about your rescue dog. Let me know if you need any help."

She nodded. "I will!"

Inés walked away.

Slipping past the palms, she stopped outside the turquoise *casita*, flipped on the floodlights, and examined the half-finished mural. The lights cast her shadow onto the wall, and she shifted her position to reveal the ocotillo plant. It outlasted the heat, cast out its seeds, and propagated a new generation, but it did so beautifully. She would also persevere and flourish.

She chose printmaking because she wanted her art to go out into the world and make a difference. In San Francisco, she glimpsed the power of social change and leveraged her skills to create an egalitarian statement. Her art would honor rising generations. When people saw it, they would focus on the message.

Raising a hand, she traced the unfinished ocotillo plant's dark outline. Did she have to be a muralist? Most artists subscribed to a studio environment. The communal aspect kept the artists happy, engaged, and encouraged. Every time she worked in a studio, she chafed to be outdoors. In front of the ocotillo mural, she felt the wind lift her hair from her shoulders and understood how much she needed wide, open spaces.

Banksy and Swoon propagated printmaking and mural art, but she had no idea where they sought refuge. She found it at the Starlight Motel, and as long as her family owned the motel, she could return. She doubted Dane would be there.

Pulling a hand from the stucco, she stared. She couldn't have everything. For months, she had worked on the grant with Mariah and poured her heart into describing the power of public art. The motel thrived, her hard work made a difference, and motel staff would keep her parents in check. A smile ghosted across her lips. If she was wrong, Randi, Stephanie, and Benito would keep her fully informed.

A man's long shadow slipped up the wall.

Without turning, she knew Dane stood at her side. "You don't give up easily."

"Well, romance didn't work," he said.

She smiled and kept her gaze trained on the mural. " 'Let's Start The New Year Right' is a lovely first dance."

"Sentimental gibberish. It's the worst, most painful song I've ever heard."

Laughing, she turned and found him facing the mural, but his narrowed gaze and firm jaw looked set in stone. Telling him she didn't want a relationship was one thing, but telling him *good-bye* hurt more than she anticipated. She swallowed her laughter and waited.

He faced the mural like a man reviewing a life sentence.

Instead of tormenting him with the life-sized calling card, she could whitewash the wall and leave him with a blank canvas. Why wouldn't he look at her? She searched for a flaw in the design, but even the lizard left her to fend for herself. "If you hate the song, why did you pull me into a dance?"

"Desperation," he said.

She wanted to reach out and touch him. Grazing her fingers against his cheek or stepping into his embrace would feel right, but she'd already secreted away those memories. "So, why are you here?"

A slow smile cracked his set profile, and he made eye contact. "Innovation."

Chapter Twenty-Two

Dane and Kada stared at each other. Too much ease could send a man off the deep end, but too much work could drown him. He had a plan to balance his needs, but he needed the balls to execute it. A shooting star wouldn't hurt.

"This Will Be Our Year" by The Zombies played from the pool. The song's open-hearted positivity and sprightly piano line drove the song, but the positivity meant more because of how the song hinted at darker times without dwelling on them. He questioned his role in the valley at the same time he pursued it. Kada fought for her chance to shine. If the couple at the heart of the song earned their happiness, maybe he and Kada could, too.

The song's melody wove through the palms and surrounded him and Kada. Even though holiday music drove him crazy, the song was a classic, and he could unwind enough to listen to 1960s rock stars sing about hope. When he followed the melody, his heart warmed because he respected the optimism that fueled holiday wishes. Every time he planted a seed, he propagated the same hope for a brighter future.

Backing Kada against the mural, he rested one palm against a blank section of wall, spread his fingers against the stucco, and chose his words.

She turned her head toward the music coming from

the pool and parted her lips.

"I like this song," he said. "It's better than most."

She blew out her lips and smiled. "Great."

So much for eloquence. He wanted to lean in and kiss her, but he knew the next kiss might be his last. He feared squandering it without making his final stand. Her spotlight created a halo and illuminated the mural, but his shoulders cast a comforting shadow. If neither party moved, they could stay cocooned in the soft, jazz-soaked darkness for the rest of their lives.

She raised her eyebrows.

Her challenge spurred him to action, and he wet his lips. He wanted to find a way to be together. The options spun through his mind like the dial on a safe, but he couldn't find the right combination. The probability of solving the problem himself was so slim that he considered laying himself at her feet and hoping for the best.

She touched her lips to his.

Never one to look a gift horse in the mouth, he leaned into the kiss and stopped thinking of equines. Her lips, soft and yielding in the past, claimed his lips with a ferocity that gave him hope. A woman who kissed a man like that wasn't about to knee a man in the crotch and send him packing. Was she?

Closing his eyes, he marveled at how perfect being with her felt. Whether they were head-to-head solving mundane problems, hiking up hillsides, or sitting down to family dinners full of banter and open conversation, being with her felt right.

She pulled back and swallowed.

Kada had something to say. He hoped like hell he would like her next words. Keeping his palm against the wall, he prayed denial could stop time. Lonely didn't begin to describe his current state. How was he supposed to go back to running the farm while the sun shone in Kada's eyes? He might not like her words, but he wanted more of her kisses. "You surprise me."

A slight smile graced her lips. "You rode onto my property like a cowboy."

He tipped up her chin. "And if all I wanted was a roll in the hay and a long good-bye?"

She dropped her chin and kissed his fingers. "You might have to fix the fence, but I'd be on board. Too bad life isn't simple, black or white." She turned away and closed her eyes. "I shouldn't have kissed you again. I already told you good-bye, but you smell so good. It's criminal."

He laughed. "I'm glad you kissed me, but I also thought you might slap me."

Eyes closed, she smiled.

As long as she didn't cry, he could do this. He cleared his throat. "Kada, I don't want work to come between us. If your folks can adjust their lives, we can, too. You want to elope? If you'll have me, then I'm yours."

Jerking to center, she violently shook her head.

He laughed. "Better yet, give me conditions. Tell me what you need to give this relationship a chance. I don't always have to lead."

She tilted her head.

He doubted he would ever feel this way about someone again. Fear and anticipation slowed his heartbeat. If he couldn't meet her conditions, he would sink into his work, but he had to try to make it work.

"Every other weekend," she said. "But I don't have

a car, and Pops' truck won't make the drive to Los Angeles. And what about when I travel? I can't put that burden on you."

Her first condition diffused his worry. He had wrestled more-stubborn problems at the local rodeo. If money could meet her conditions, consider them met. "I'll buy a plane."

She rolled her eyes.

"Pilot's license. Hitchhike."

"Dane Palmer! I thought we were being serious."

Pulling back his arm, he stepped to the side, leaned against the wall at her side, and turned his head to face her. The spotlight was near-blinding, but as long as she held his gaze, he would hold his breath and hear her conditions.

"You live with your parents." She pursed her lips. "Like, really live with them."

"True." Patience had never been his virtue. Stepping off the wall, he turned the light into the palms. The resulting shadows left intimacy, but enough light to read her expressions. "Your parents are about to move to the Starlight Motel, and unless I'm mistaken, we'll have four chaperones."

She worked her jaw. "Fair enough."

Reclaiming his place at her side, he pondered his words. "What's really eating at you, Kada Ritchie? Your beauty and your strength drew me right away, but watching you manage this motel and manage me…"

She bumped her shoulder against his.

He would take any contact he could get. "…made me wish I'd met you a year ago. I wish I'd had the time to woo you, find out what makes you the happiest, and listen to your fears. When I hear you talk about why this thing between us can't work, I hear fear. I don't know how to abate that fear unless you tell me what you need. Every other weekend? Done. What else?"

The silence stretched so long that he wondered if he should take a hint.

"I want you to pick up a hobby that's creative and difficult. How can you understand me if you've never experienced the vulnerability that comes from making art? I don't know if I can plant a field of grapes, but I'll try to learn about your life, too. I want to understand the emotions behind your words. If that means I'm riding shotgun while you troubleshoot slugs, I want to be there."

Slugs? He took a steadying breath. She could tail him through the fields until the sun went down, but painting would be his biggest failure. The plane seemed like a much better deal. "You want me to paint? Like, we're talking grade school art. Stick figures and flat little ponies riding into the two-dimensional sunset."

"It's not a competition."

"Thank goodness. You'll take one look at my art and laugh your butt back to Los Angeles."

She stroked his cheek. "I doubt it."

Turning, he pressed a kiss against her palm. "That's all you want? Time and art? I'll recreate the entire Sistine Chapel. Don't let this kiss be a good-bye kiss."

Dropping her hand, she sighed. "Behind that handsome façade, you're a perfectionist. You might have learned to hide the trait, but I'm guessing that's why your fields thrive, and you never take risks. If you spend hours trying to paint an apple, you'll hate the outcome."

"No wonder nobody invites me to parties," he said.

She toyed with his shirt collar. "If you don't want to paint, pick up a guitar or write a story. I want you to glimpse the vulnerability and the joy that comes from creating art. Isn't that why you like me?" She tilted her head and chewed her bottom lip. "We're worlds apart."

"I like you because you're beautiful, and you don't take anybody's sass."

She smiled. "Close enough."

He cupped her elbows. "If you'll teach me, I'll paint."

"Really?" she asked.

For an instant, he felt hopeful and expectant, like the moment he first tasted her lips, but he didn't know how to express himself without scaring off her interest. When the silence stretched on, he held his breath and feared a second, more definite shutdown.

"And when you're so mad you want to throw the brush because your apple looks like a diseased kumquat?" she asked.

He worked his jaw. He could deal with ineptitude. She wanted to see progress. Playing catch-up was never his style. He would choose an artistic hobby she hadn't mastered. "Maybe I'll pick up the guitar. I already have the calluses."

She smiled. "And serenade me?"

"Any song you like."

Her smile faded. "Except Christmas carols."

Running a hand through his hair, he sighed. "You said I had to try, but you didn't say I had to enjoy the process."

"Dane…"

He held up a hand. "You're right. I am a

perfectionist. I understand the variables for farming. Art?" He exhaled. "It depends on me. My hands shake. My voice sounds like crushed gravel. But for you? I'll try. Should we start with 'Jingle Bells'?"

"Okay," she whispered the commitment. "But you don't have to sing."

Relief rushed through his system, and he dropped his forehead to hers. "Okay? What else?"

"Dane, there's nothing else. I need a little bit of freedom, a little bit of vulnerability, and a lot of your kisses. You're awake in the middle of the night because you think you're stressed, but what if you need more? What if hardcore isn't enough? Maybe you need me."

He pulled her into his arms. Holding her felt so good, he wanted to tighten his grasp and never release her. Dust and her delicate shampoo mingled into a sweet, earthy scent that smelled better than the desert after a rainstorm. "I definitely need you."

"WOOOooooo." A dog howled. The long, lonely sound split the night.

Someone cut the music by the pool.

"Is that Lucky?" he asked.

She pulled away. "I don't know. I haven't known her long enough to learn her sounds. I was on my way to check on her when I got distracted."

"The best distraction," he said.

She laid a hand against the mural.

The sound came again, and the dog's wail held hints of pain and alarm.

He'd heard animals signal cornered game, alarm, and danger, but he'd never heard a dog make the lonely, mourning note splitting the night sky. "It's coming from the other side of the motel."

"Gustavo has Esmeralda. Maybe she tangled herself in something." Looking back and forth between her guests and her *casita*, she stalled in the middle of the path.

"I'll check on Gustavo," he said. "You check on Lucky."

Relief washed over her features. Nodding, she turned toward her *casita*.

He caught her hand. Her final condition might make or break his life. "Kada, what's the final thing?"

Guests filtered away from the pool.

"Maybe it's the *chupacabra*," a guest said.

A second guest laughed. "More likely a javelina."

Their fading chatter interrupted the moment of solitude he shared with Kada.

She looked at their joined hands. "I need…"

He held his breath.

"What's that awful sound?" Missy Robert asked.

He bit his cheeks to stop himself from saying something he might regret. Stepping in front of Kada, he faced the realtor. "What sound? I hear music. Maybe a car backfired on the highway. Is that what you heard?"

She crossed her arms over her chest. "The sound I heard was like a cheap violin."

He cocked his head. "Can you give me a demonstration?"

Missy peered around his shoulder.

He followed her gaze.

Kada had fled.

For an instant, he felt like joining the animal's lonely, mourning song. Instead of making a spectacle, he escorted Missy back to the pool, scanned the party, and wondered where he would find Gustavo and his howling canine. From the grill, alluring smoke wafted between hungry guests. A few kids played tag. Lights swayed overhead, floats drifted across the pool's surface, and two intrepid guests kicked off their shoes and dangled their legs in the water.

The chill, evening air made him think about his leather jacket. His long-sleeve shirt felt warm enough, but he could keep the chill from bothering Kada. She didn't need his help.

Walking to the pool's edge, he looked into the sparkling turquoise waters and wondered if everyone who glimpsed him saw the same man Kada described. He took risks, but they were calculated risks. Four generations of hard-fought success bred economic conservatism into his bones, but he didn't have to be a stick in the mud.

"I hope you're not planning to jump," Gustavo said.

He shifted away from the pool coping and turned. "Jump?"

"It's too late to swim. We'd all stop and watch you flounder about like a disoriented college student wearing floaties."

Snorting, he scanned the assembly. He was hardly the life of the party. "Noted. Where's your yodeling dog?"

"I brought her back to the *casita*. She's sensitive. Her sense of smell is so subtle she notices the slightest changes in a human's scent. She's shown interest in more than one person who went to the doctor and caught a disease before it spread."

"Impressive," he said, "but her nose is a little off.

Kada's dog isn't sick. She's pregnant and probably delivering as we speak."

"Ah, that explains Esmeralda's reaction." He stroked his chin. "She's empathetic, too."

He bet Esmeralda would empathetically chomp a dropped hamburger, but he stopped short of undermining Gustavo's praise. He had heard of dogs that could detect cancer, malaria, and Parkinson's disease. If Gustavo said the dog responded to distress, then he believed him. Stepping back from the pool coping, he kept his arms crossed over his chest. "Well, give her some love and tell her Lucky will be okay."

"Will you be okay?"

He looked up. "Excuse me?"

"For a man who lives up the road, you've been at the motel a lot in the last forty-eight hours." He raised his eyebrows. "Now, I've met your mother and your father. This might be a party, but it isn't a celebration. Kada rejected you, eh?"

"Not exactly." He needed an escape, and he needed one fast. "She told me to consider new experiences''— he watched two kids sit to do paper crafts with Inés — "like art. Like I'm a student."

Gustavo grinned and clapped his back. "First, the art galleries, and then, the chapel. You're toast, man. Come have a drink."

He didn't want to ruin the festivities with his uncertainties. If the kids wanted to festoon the pool fencing with bouncy balloons, dangling streamers, and glittered numbers, their joy cost him nothing. He could retreat and ponder Kada's final request, but he had hope. He followed Gustavo to the poolside bar and picked up a steaming mug. Expecting coffee, he took a deep sip and sputtered on spiced hot chocolate. "I thought this damn holiday ended."

Dropping a sugar cube into his mug, Gustavo slapped his back. "Take a good, long sip. Don't worry, the sugar balances the cinnamon."

He doubted a truckload of irrigation water could balance the cinnamon. Cupping the mug in both hands, he raised it a second time. Gustavo was right. The sweetness went down smoothly and conjured up memories of childhood celebrations.

Mom always went all out. Snow globes, illuminated villages, and tiny, fluffy specs of fake snow had decorated the farmhouse living room. Then, like a Grinch, he packed away her treasures. Before he turned into such an ass, he decorated a cactus, named it Mr. Pokey, and had enhanced the festive scene. Kada made him want life's eccentric pleasures. As a child, he remembered closing his eyes and wishing for snow, Santa Claus, and a pellet gun. Now, he wished for her. "I can't take it. Give me something else."

Gustavo handed him a glass of Ranch Water.

The three-ingredient cocktail required tequila, lime juice, and sparkling mineral water. He let the drink's simplicity wash away the fussy hot chocolate.

As his father's hand and practicalities took hold, he let go of his fantasies and focused on farming, but what harm came from holiday celebrations? He didn't put much stock in religion. People wanted to gather during the darkest part of the year and celebrate with light and sweets. He could buy into their optimism. The other half of the year, they could bite into a sweet, red bell paper and fuel his happiness.

Looking around the pool, he counted more than

twenty people reveling under the stars, sharing a meal, and counting down the hours until midnight. Half the partygoers might make their goal, but their smiles suggested the party fulfilled their needs. Given another twenty minutes of revelry, he would be two glasses into the Ranch Water and forget his regrets.

He told Kada he wasn't opposed to the holidays, but maybe he needed to be open to them. If people behaved badly most of the year, their selfishness and ineptitude had deep root causes, but the guests at the Starlight Motel offered real smiles. He could trip through another decade, shunning life's small moments of joy, but Kada opened his eyes to the beauty surrounding him. No matter how trivial a guest's problem, she believed she could find a solution.

Faced with such optimism, he could double-down on fizzy stubbornness, or he could choke down a peppermint and admit he enjoyed the naïve, sweet indulgence. If he stuck around long enough, then Kada would probably find him a birthday cake. He suspected she had better things to do.

"Life's good, isn't it?" Gustavo asked.

He smiled. "It's good, man."

Gustavo slapped his back.

Greeting his parents, he felt lighter and better able to navigate life's challenges with hope in his heart. Every year, the holidays would return. Whether he met them flush with success or with a humble heart depended entirely on him. Whatever Kada's third condition, he would meet it.

On the way back to the *casita*, he recounted Kada's requirements. He could lean on Walter's expertise and carve out the visits she requested. He could take up art.

As long as he could stomach her feedback on his humble creations, he would lay bare his soul and try his best to make something out of nothing. Given a proper chance, he thought he could spend the rest of his life with her, and he needed her to outline the missing puzzle piece. Opening the garden gate, he listened to the quiet evening, walked up the worn steps, and softly knocked on the door.

"Come in," Kada said.

Stepping inside the brightly lit *casita*, he found her ensconced between two half-height bookshelves.

Lucky lay on an old quilt, licking a newborn, black puppy.

Tears brightened Kada's eyes.

Dropping to a crouch outside the makeshift pen, he smiled. "One down. It's a sweet little thing."

"Isn't it?" Kada clasped her hands to her chest. "I'm trying my hardest to watch, but keeping my hands to myself is nearly impossible."

Dropping to his backside, he stretched out his legs, pulled her against his chest, and wrapped his arms around her middle. "I'll keep you from interfering."

She leaned against him and made a soft, contented hum.

He could spend his life holding her in his arms.

"I'm glad you're here. The pamphlet said having another person around to help keep the puppies warm or provide assistance is a good idea. If things go south, we can call the vet."

He rubbed his jaw against her hair. Having acquainted himself with most veterinarians in the Coachella Valley, he doubted anyone else in the valley would come to the Starlight Motel on New Year's Eve.

For better or for worse, he and Kada were scrubbing in for Lucky's delivery. He adjusted his seat. "She looks like she's handling everything. Your quilt, on the other hand, might never be the same."

"That's fine. What's a quilt against new life?"

Turning her in his arms, he considered his words. "If you hadn't chosen printmaking and murals, what kind of art would you have studied?"

She leaned her head against his shoulder. "Printmaking doesn't receive the same public admiration like painting or sculpting, but it holds a vital place in art history. Printmakers produced some of the most recognizable artistic images in history. The Barack Obama *HOPE* poster. *The Great Wave off Kanagawa.* Andy Warhol's *Marilyn Diptych.* The inspiration library runs deep. When students participate in that process, they see themselves as part of the world."

"And that's what you want? Recognition?"

Closing her eyes, she shook her head. "I want people to know how important they are to their communities. They have a place in their neighborhoods. We all have a place. I think I can be part of that place."

From his earliest memories, he knew where he belonged. Ambiguity would tug at his consciousness like an itch he could never scratch. Her desire to help people celebrate their communities matched the way she ran the motel like a joyful melting pot. He wondered if she felt like an outsider always looking in. He worked his jaw. "And where's your place?"

She wet her lips. "My parents poured so much love into me. Pops loved me. The motel guests trusted me. I feel at home anywhere I go. I have more than any person should have. And yet?" She closed her eyes. "Sometimes, I don't know where I belong."

He tightened his grip.

Drawing a deep breath, she straightened and threaded her fingers through her hair. "Maybe I belong with you."

"Glad we settled that." Standing, he offered her a hand. "Let's enjoy the party."

Sitting on the floor, she looked up and smiled, but her expression stopped short of lightening her gaze.

He bent his knees to help lift her and wished a confident smile could soothe over every rough patch.

Taking his hand, she flexed her muscles and stood. "Maybe I don't belong anywhere."

"You do." Wrapping an arm around her, he held on tight. "Everyone deserves a home."

She jostled his shoulder. "How can you say that and be such a stubborn, practical, hard-headed man?"

The lady had a point, but he couldn't quite see how his character impacted her decisions. Hadn't she kissed him back every time? If he had to break out his glasses to make the pieces of her argument fit, he would do it. Why couldn't he have fallen for a lawyer?

"Do you know who comes to the Starlight Motel? Modest people. Maybe they lost their way, carry a whiff of scandal, or need something quirky the mainstream hotel chains can't provide."

"Like pet-friendly lodging," he said.

She nodded. "Kinda."

Finally, he was getting somewhere. His family had status in the valley, but they weren't political leaders or social organizers. If she needed glitz and media write-ups, then he couldn't provide them. Palmer Farms grew the best produce in the valley, but farming wasn't a high-status occupation. If she wanted to count him as a social misfit, then he would gladly wear the T-shirt.

Lucky moaned. Her abdominal muscles contracted and sent a wave rippling along her belly. Straining and vocalizing, she closed her eyes and delivered a second, tan puppy.

Pulling free, Kada crouched near the bookcases and held a hand to her mouth.

The sight of the stray dog giving birth brought a smile to his lips. If he could close the loop with Kada and give her what she needed, he would be happier than he had ever been.

Vigorously licking the new puppy, Lucky cleaned her offspring, tore off the placental membrane, and severed the umbilical cord.

He exhaled. Farmers couldn't be squeamish about the circle of life. If Hạnh was right, they had two puppies down and four to go.

Kada doused a cotton ball with iodine, held out her clean hand until Lucky sniffed it, and quickly scooped up the second puppy. Swabbing the puppy's stomach with the iodine ball, she held it for a quick inspection, grinned, and settled it back near Lucky's warmth.

Lucky nosed the puppy.

Standing, Kada shimmied in place and grinned.

Watching the good-natured dance, he realized how nervous Kada must be to help Lucky deliver her puppies with nothing for guidance but an Internet connection and a creased pamphlet. His concerns about power and riches had little bearing on her happiness. She wanted to help struggling students, weary travelers, lost dogs, and quarrelsome farmers. He stepped back.

Maybe he didn't deserve her attention.

Turning, she clapped her hands and interlaced her fingers. "What should we name them? Rocket? Sparky?" Eyes bright, she spun in a circle. "This is how people end up keeping the whole litter, isn't it? You fall in love at first sight, and you can't ever talk yourself down from the high. How about Jack?"

Working his jaw, he knew he had fallen but didn't deserve her dedication. What kind of fool thought he could rearrange a schedule and lock up her love? "How much time between the first two puppies?"

"About an hour," she said.

"Let's get dinner. I heard someone made hamburgers. I'm sure Benito keeps veggies burgers stocked. In forty-five minutes, we'll come back and check on Lucky and her pups. She and the two littermates look like they're doing fine."

Nodding, she ran into the bathroom and washed her hands.

The water ran and splashed in the sink, and he dropped to one knee. Watching Lucky lick and nudge the pups, he smiled. "She'll do great things."

Lucky raised her head.

"She'll comfort and inspire people who deserve her attention."

The second puppy yawned.

"She'll probably spoil all of you rotten and immortalize you in paint."

Tilting her head, Lucky stared.

He stood. "You deserve it."

Kada bounded back down the hallway. Full of smiles, she took his arm and pulled him toward the door.

But for the first time since he met her, he faked a smile and wondered how quickly he could excuse himself. If he stayed, he would muck up her life with a deal he didn't deserve.

With a bounce in her step, she pulled him toward the party. "I'm starving. Have you eaten?"

"I had some hot chocolate," he said.

"Oh, was it good?"

He squeezed her hand. "Surprisingly good. Your family puts out a welcoming spread."

She winked. "It runs in our genes."

And bare-bones practicality ran in his genes. Placing a hand at the small of her back, he fell behind her and urged her toward the party.

Skirting the palms, she stepped up to the blazing pink firepit and held out her palms.

Gustavo spotted her and walked, trailing Esmeralda on a leash. "How are the puppies?"

"The puppies?" she asked.

"Dane said they're coming."

She exhaled, turned back to Gustavo, and held up two fingers. "So far, so good."

Gustavo pumped a fist into the air.

Esmeralda yipped her approval.

Turning, Gustavo cupped his hands around his mouth. "Two puppies!"

The crowd processed the news, exchanged information with their neighbors, and cheered. The announcement pulled them from discrete groups and anchored their attention on Kada.

Dropping his head, Dane tried not to let her excitement and satisfaction lull him into a false sense of security. She laid out two conditions, but he doubted the third required tweaking logistics or taking up a new hobby. "You might want to say something."

She turned her head. "About the puppies? The staffing challenges? How I sweated through my shirt because I was so scared Lucky would have a problem, and I would fail her? Don't get too close. I probably reek of smoke and body odor."

"You smell just fine." He fisted his hands at his sides. He wanted to wrap his arms around her and protect her, but she didn't need his protection. She was as fierce and determined as any man or woman he had ever met. "I meant the fireworks. The whole holiday thing. I guess you could ignore it. It's not their first holiday season, right?"

She swatted his chest.

Catching her hand for an instant, he then dropped it. Side lit by the blazing fire, he'd never seen her look so beautiful and untouchable. "Say whatever feels right."

"Okay." Pulling over a chair, she stood on the seat and cleared her throat. "Thank you all for coming outside to celebrate New Year's Eve with me, my family, and my neighbors."

He stepped back into the crowd forming around her.

"When I ordered fireworks, I had no idea how I would get them set up or complete my first holiday season as motel manager. I should have realized I ordered too much."

The crowd laughed.

"Thanks to my family and the Palmer family, we're ready for a show!"

Mack and Sue's kids cheered.

"A few pink glass balls won't make the pool shine, but your hopes for the coming year, key chains, origami, and crafts will do the trick. Whatever you have handy, find a loop of ribbon and add your piece to the pool fencing. Paris might have its love locks, but we have the Starlight Motel." She cleared her throat. "If you want your trinkets back, please, oh, please, write your name and *casita* on the back of your contribution."

Someone laughed.

"Every New Year's Eve, my grandfather and the motel guests stayed up until midnight and ushered in the New Year with a poolside celebration. Depending on the guests, some nights they had a guitar, and some nights they had an old record player. At the stroke of midnight, Pops sang 'Auld Lang Syne,' and the crowd welcomed a new beginning. If you can make it until midnight, know that I'll be here."

"So will I," Chris Nicholson said. "I'll outlast all of you!"

Kada saluted him.

Dane stepped farther back and bumped into his father.

"Time to go?" Dad asked.

Nodding, he stood beside his old man. They had the same posture and the same outlook on life, but Dad found Mom. Dane would have to keep looking for true love and someone to cherish beyond the glow of the holiday season.

"More than you can handle?"

He shook his head. "More than I deserve."

"Well, I find that hard to believe. You heard the lady. She wants hopes and promises. What do you have to contribute?"

"My belt buckle?"

Dad laughed. "It's not that kind of show."

He would find a scrap of paper in the reception area, write out his wishes for a fruitful year, and hope when she found it, the message would brighten her day. No matter what the New Year brought, they would find a way to be friends.

Chapter Twenty-Three

Kada checked on Lucky twice more and found two additional puppies nuzzling against their mother's side. Announcing each birth to the assembled guests brought cheers and smiles from the crowd.

Guests demanded pictures and naming rights.

But she gave Lucky space to labor.

Stephanie walked up to the lounge tables carrying a platter of cookies. Bending her knees, she slowly lowered the rocking platter to a table, stood, and exhaled. "Poor Benito still can't get out of bed." She dusted her hands and smiled. "No matter. I left him well-provisioned. Even I can make sugar cookies."

Kada eyed the irregular sugar cookies with burnt edges. The slice-and-bake packaging said they were foolproof. She hoped Benito appreciated Stephanie's gesture more than he appreciated her finished product. Looking up, she smiled. "Did he finish the cheese balls?"

"Every last one of them!"

"Have you eaten? It's late, but as long as you're not too picky, we have plenty of food."

"Oh, I'm fine." Stephanie wrung her hands. "I needed fresh air, and I didn't have anywhere else to go. You asked me to come back for the dinner rush, didn't you?"

Patting Stephanie's back, she ignored the part

where coming back for the dinner rush meant showing up for work. "You're always welcome here. Do you think Benito wants a puppy?"

Stephanie paled.

"Yeah, I didn't think so, either." She gave Stephanie's back another pat and dropped her hand.

"He wants to open a restaurant." Stephanie leaned in close. "Isn't that complicated and risky? Do you think he'll let me help him?"

"Of course!" She wanted to cheer Benito's ambitions, but he was integral to the Starlight Motel's successful year. She scanned the desert oasis and noticed the small improvements she made. If Pops taught her anything, times could change. Benito could swap his cantina credentials for entrepreneurship, and she could recruit a new talent to helm the kitchen. Gustavo might have a few recommendations.

Despite her resolve, telling Mom about impending staff changes could wait until tomorrow. She patted Stephanie's shoulder and nudged her toward Mom and Dad. "Let's get you a drink and introduce you to my parents. They'll be taking a more active role in the motel. I think you'll like Larissa. She met my dad while waitressing, and they've been happy ever since they met."

Stephanie clasped together her hands. "Oh, I love a good love story."

Tilting her head, she wondered when Stephanie would realize she starred in one. As soon as Benito reclaimed his mobility, he might work up the nerve to make his big move, but people operated on their timeframe. How long had it taken Kada to realize she might not have started as a valley resident, but she could be part of the renaissance? If Benito's move led to a tragic loss for the Starlight Motel, then she hoped it led to a big gain for Stephanie.

A pair of headlights brightened the parking lot.

Squinting, she wondered who else would make a late entrance.

Arms waving and carrying sparklers, Randi rolled toward the pool like a queen. "I'm back, bit—babies! I heard we're having a party!"

The kids mobbed her for access to the sparklers.

She magnanimously handed them out one by one. "Anyone else?"

Kada reached for a sparkler and mimed blowing out the fuse.

Kids laughed.

Randi arched an eyebrow. "Can you handle it?"

"We'll find out," Kada said. "I thought you had a party to attend."

"I thought you'd be long gone by now." Randi flicked a lighter and started a new pack of sparklers.

Her character assassination stung, but Kada accepted the rebuke. "I have a lot on my plate."

"You're tougher than you look." Randi painted sparkling hearts in the air. "The desert brings out the best in people." She stabbed out an exhausted sparkler in a plant bed. "Evolve or perish."

"I think it's publish or perish," Kada said.

Lighting more sparklers, Randi fanned the glowing bouquet. "Not in this neck of the woods." She turned and passed out the fireworks like a magnanimous queen.

Left alone, Kada stared at the burnt-out stub Randi had extinguished and hoped it wasn't a fire hazard.

Given the concrete and rock surrounding the pool, a fire would have limited fuel.

Near the exit, Walter gripped Dane's arm, looked after his niece, and shook his head. "I never could keep tabs on that girl."

"Why did you try?" Dane asked.

"Well, that's the truth!"

Dane laughed.

Walter raised his eyebrows. "You know what she did once?"

Across the patio, Dane met Kada's gaze and arched an eyebrow.

She forced a smile. Tonight was a night worthy of celebration.

The pair settled in by the firepit, told stories, and supervised s'more making.

The glimpse of camaraderie prompted Kada to smile, but alone in its wake, she felt the cool desert wind and rubbed the hairs standing on her arms. Looking for something to occupy her time, she spied Stephanie and made her way toward the server.

Over the next hour, Kada introduced Stephanie to her parents, checked on the quieter guests, and found herself leaning against a palm tree. A pink wreath fell to the ground. She picked up the decoration and dusted off the grass, but instead of rehanging it, she set it aside. Her feet ached, and her future seemed uncertain, but the motel deserved more than a caretaker hiding from the world. She would move on and let Mom pour her soul into the place.

Dane approached and offered a plate. "I found your secret stash of black bean burgers."

Yanking the offering from a hand wouldn't help

the situation, but it would fill her stomach. "Thank you." She lifted the plate from his hand, avoided brushing his fingers, and took a bite of the warm, toasted sandwich. Protein and mayonnaise soothed her anxiety.

"The fence decorations look good," he said.

She chewed.

"The guests seem happy."

Swallowing, she scanned the crowd and nodded.

"Do I have to wait until January to hear your final requirement?"

Turning her head, she made eye contact and swallowed. She thought the conditions she laid down would scare him away, but he stood beside her radiating thoughtful warmth and gorgeous stability.

"I haven't spent much time outside the valley," he said. "Visiting you will give us time to get to know each other. It will also be good for me. I can draw the country and name the state capitals, but I've visited only two."

"Sacramento?" she asked.

"Phoenix and Santa Fe."

"You'd like Cheyenne." Biting her cheek, she wondered why she made that observation. He might hate spring's muddy excess.

"How's that?"

She swallowed another bite. "Plenty of land to conquer."

He worked his jaw.

Mary Elizabeth ran up and grabbed his hand. "Will you help me make decorations?"

He nodded and looked at Kada.

The hesitancy in his gaze triggered a flood of

empathy. She couldn't string him along. As much as she wanted to be with him, she suspected his hardcore exterior would tarnish in a new environment. Immoveable mountains were gorgeous, but she needed someone with the vulnerability to understand why she pursued her art. She pushed off the palm tree. "Go ahead! The night is young."

Nodding, he followed Mary Elizabeth.

After eating the rest of her burger, she played with the other kids, shared jokes with her parents, and exchanged small talk with a dwindling number of guests. No matter where she went, she kept track of Dane and his surefire presence. With a moment to herself, she gazed toward the *casita* and the sweet dog that had also captured her heart and upended her life.

Somehow, she would bring Lucky on her work trips or accept her happiness at the Starlight Motel. Mom loved animals, too.

The temperature dropped, and guests pulled jackets from their rooms and *casitas*. While music played from a set of speakers, dinner gave way to conversations, laughter, and good-natured jokes about getting in shape and giving up vices.

Chris Nicholson read stories, stopped after every page, and scoffed at the logistics. "There's no way the pilot could fly that long without a fuel stop!"

By ten, the fifth puppy had appeared, but Lucky slowly raised her head and tended it.

She grabbed a sweater, hovered in the doorway, and wondered what she could do to help. When another hour passed without a delivery, she eased into the enclosure, lifted Lucky's head into her lap, and looked into the dog's eyes. "Is it time to call the vet? She said you had six puppies to deliver."

Lucky closed her eyes.

Through the *casita* window, she could see the party, and she could hear Inés singing. The party would go on without her presence, and she could pass the night soothing Lucky through the last hours of her labor. "Don't worry, sweetie. I'll figure out what to do next." Closing her eyes, she took a deep breath and flushed out her nerves. "That's what I'm good at doing."

"How's she doing?" Dane asked.

Looking up, she found him leaning a shoulder against the doorjamb in the same spot she had occupied. He wore his jacket over his staff shirt, and the shadow of a beard darkened his jawline, but he looked as familiar and capable as the first evening she met him. "I'm worried about her. Do you think Dr. Vo will do a video call? Maybe she could drive over?"

He shrugged out of his jacket, crouched, and rocked back on his heels. "I'm not sure if she's still awake. Her family lives about an hour's drive from the motel. I don't mind calling and asking, but the odds are slim. How badly do you think we need her? Maybe Walter can help."

She stroked Lucky's head and looked for signs of continuing labor. "I don't know what to do. She looks spent. I feel bad leaving her, alone and laboring, but I'm not sure what else to do but encourage her and offer her water. As soon she delivers the puppies, I can clean up the mess, but I need all six, precious little mutts to appear."

Scanning the room, he located the pamphlet and pulled out his glasses.

"That's a good thought, but I've almost memorized the text," she said.

He ran a finger beneath the words.

"If there's a break of more than two hours, the pamphlet advises calling a veterinarian."

Reading, he nodded.

She could visualize every line. "Trembling, collapsing, and shivering are warning signs of serious complications."

He looked up and quirked an eyebrow. "Kada, darling, will you let me read the pamphlet?"

Biting her lip, she nodded. Feeling pulled in a hundred directions, she still felt drawn to him, and the sound of him calling her darling nearly undid her defenses. If he kissed her wearing those stupid glasses, then she might forget the successful grant and happily sink into desert life.

He adjusted his stance. A brass flamingo sporting a jaunty, faded red Santa hat fell from his pocket.

Reaching forward, she picked up the piece. "Why do you have this?"

Lowering the pamphlet, he looked out the window. "I went to the reception desk to find a piece of paper, but that silly, sweet bird stared back and dared me to come up with a cheerful message. You made it, didn't you? It's whimsical and charming, like your art."

"I glued on a felt hat."

He turned and laughed. "But you made it art. Isn't that what you're pushing me toward? Seeing the beauty in everyday objects? Making something out of nothing?"

Not quite. Setting the flamingo atop the bookcase, she hoped its jaunty optimism prevailed. If all went according to plan, Lucky would deliver her last puppy, the flamingo would reign over the tree, and she and Dane would settle down by the firepit with a blanket and an honest conversation about their burgeoning relationship.

He said he would visit her in the field and wield a paintbrush, but if she couldn't crack his reserve, she feared their two worlds would never intersect. He rose at dawn to greet the day, and she painted deep into the night. Would they meet over dinner?

Taking a deep breath, she hoped time would improve Lucky's labors, and she feared time would pull him from her sights. Abandoning the firepit plan, she cleared her throat. "If we're trying a relationship, let's talk about logistics. Some locations must be easier. Direct flights. Trains. That kind of stuff."

He ran a finger along the pamphlet text.

Was he paying attention? She adopted his language and focused on logistics. Rambling off ideas, she watched him, but he showed more enthusiasm for lunch than for travel schedules. Replaying their kisses, she knew she and the man had something, but she struggled to see past New Year's Eve. "Do you really want to do this long-distance thing?"

Looking up, he stared. "Excuse me?"

"Maybe we're just hormones and convenience."

Lowering the pamphlet, he stared. "Convenience?"

She wanted to tackle him and prove their connection was more than proximity, but she felt as vulnerable as Lucky. "Why me?"

He frowned. "Aren't we talking about the dog?"

She shook her head.

Pulling off his glasses, he blinked and focused.

"You see the beauty in plants, and I see them as products. You see water as a force of nature, and I see it as a commodity. When we're together, I forget life's weight, and I feel like I'm watching the sunrise. You're beautiful and hopeful, and I want to be by your side." He cleared his throat. "Do you need a sonnet?"

Poetry might be nice, but he was a strong, silent man. Asking him for verse would be like asking him to walk a tightrope. He could do it, but sheer stubbornness would motivate him. More than a sonnet, she needed the glimpse of emotional sensitivity he offered. She might have misjudged his capability for vulnerability, and she wished she had recorded his outburst. Rubbing the edges of her shirt between her fingers, she paced herself. "You want to be by my side?"

He nodded.

His rigid shoulders and tense posture made her worry his romantic outburst was a means to an end. Thinking of Nana's legacy, Kada wanted to paint, but she could no sooner sentence Dane to life in her shadow than she could assume a life trailing him. Rubbing her forehead against her palm, she averted her gaze and sorted through her feelings. "Dane, not everyone could do what you do. This single-minded commitment to your family and your task? It scares me." She looked up. "What if stubbornness isn't enough?"

"For you?" He leaned forward and peered.

She shook her head. "What if it's not enough for you?"

He exhaled. Setting down the pamphlet, he planted his backside on the floor and faced her. "I provide the crops families need, but I want a family, too. If that's you and me, I'll be happy. If it's more than you and me,

I'll be blessed. Don't worry too much about what I need. I'm not shy about asking for it and trying until I get what I want."

She opened her mouth and caught herself. He pledged to make the relationship work, but he admitted to being a hard-headed mule. If Smoky were here, the tall, chestnut horse might have shaken its black mane and kicked its owner. She raised her eyebrows. "Come hell or high water, you'll make it work?"

He smiled. "Within reason. I'm a reasonable man."

Hah! Judging by the scale of his family holdings, and his appetite for land, he was as reasonable as a barbed wire fence, but no matter how hard she pushed back, she felt safe in his arms. Wetting her lower lip, she wondered if she could tease out the vulnerability she needed or trust life to humble him and pull it from his core. Rising to her knees, she crawled toward him and wanted another kiss. "I'll tell you when you're being unreasonable."

Lucky moaned.

Jerking her head to the side, she tangled her feet, fell forward, and landed in Dane's lap. His glasses skidded out of his hand, he wrapped his arms around her, and he grinned. "Kada, darling, if you wanted a tumble, you could have asked."

Heat flooded her cheeks. Climbing out of his warm embrace, she stared into his dark-brown eyes and wondered if she would ever look at another man like she did him. Mariah said the desert needed time to sink into a person's skin, but he had saturated her senses with one deep, cleansing breath. "Dane, I want to do life with you."

He cupped her head, shifted his weight, and pulled

her back into his lap. "Good call."

His grip gentled like he no longer feared she would bolt. Resting her head against his shoulder, she rubbed her cheek against his neck and buried her face in his warmth and the heady smell of lime, warm spices, and a hint of honey. With him in her corner, she could do anything.

A knock sounded on the door.

Pulling back, she felt like a teenager caught with the hero of her dreams. Whoever knocked on the door could go hug a firework!

Gustavo peeked in and clasped his hands to his cheeks. "I heard the good news! Five puppies, what a blessing! Xolo will be their *Tia*."

Nodding in recognition of his generosity, she climbed from Dane's lap and forced out the truth of the situation before Gustavo's celebrations eclipsed her fears. "We're waiting on number six."

Mack and Sue peered around him. "Are we in trouble? Should we call the vet?"

Brushing off her pants, she reclaimed her role as manager of the Starlight Motel. Dr. Vo told her to live in the now, but living in the now sounded a lot easier when menu planning, champagne toasting, and firework lighting were her only concerns. She owed Dr. Vo a debt of gratitude for checking on Lucky, but she needed more than a pamphlet and a reassuring smile to turn this evening into a miracle. She linked hands with Dane. "He's trying to contact her."

He held up his phone and squeezed her other hand in return. "For whatever reason, Dr. Vo's unavailable."

Gustavo's face fell.

"The kids will be devastated." Hugging each other,

Mack and Sue leaned into each other's strength. "What can we do?"

Kada pulled free from Dane and rubbed her face. For a moment, her hair shielded her gaze and gave her privacy, but few people solved their problems in a vacuum.

Dane and the guests wanted to help, and she wanted to include them. Brushing the hair out of her eyes and over her shoulder, she raised her chin. "Thanks for the offer, but let's give her more time. Sometimes, life has its own agenda. Lucky delivered five little miracles, and I think she can summon the energy for one more."

Gustavo dropped his head and whispered to himself.

Inés shouldered her way through the crowd filling the door, dropped to her knees by Kada and Dane, and counted the puppies. "What a gift. Animals play wonderful parts in our lives. Families will welcome these sweet gifts into their homes with kindness and love."

Crouching by Lucky, Kada stroked the dog's back. "Come on, beautiful, you can do it." Whispering words of encouragement, she told Lucky what a wonderful family she found in the desert, how much fun she would have lounging by the pool, and how many scraps Benito and the servers would sneak her.

Lucky opened her eyes and moaned.

Her abdomen rippled beneath Kada's hand. "You can do it!"

Leaning back, Inés covered her mouth.

Dane rested a hand on Kada's shoulder.

As Lucky's contractions slowly intensified, the dog

strained and panted.

Guests peered through the doorway and jostled for news, but the bookcases and Dane's broad back gave Lucky the space she needed.

Reluctant to move from the dog's side, Kada cupped her head and offered sweet words of encouragement.

With a final push, Lucky delivered the sixth puppy and went lax.

"We have a puppy!" Inés jumped to her feet and raised her folded hands in the air.

Gustavo, Mack, and Sue cheered.

Kada closed her eyes. The sweet, tiny animal brought nothing but hope to the world. Hope was more than enough to celebrate the puppy's safe arrival. She stroked Lucky's ears. "You did a good job, Mama."

Dane pushed past her.

The *casita's* occupants fell silent.

Startled, she opened her eyes and followed his movements.

Scooping up the puppy, he pulled away its placental membrane and rubbed the puppy against his shirt until the animal cried. Cradling the puppy against his chest, he closed his eyes and drew a deep breath. "It's okay, buddy, I have you." A tear ran down his cheek.

She spread a palm along Lucky's back and felt every tired breath and measured heartbeat. She would recover from her ordeal, but puppies couldn't survive in their gestational sac for more than a few minutes before the supply of oxygen ran out. While Lucky caught her breath, and she and the guests celebrated the puppy's birth, Dane saw the risk and stepped in. That kind of steadfast commitment and his ensuing vulnerability meant more than valley crops or a portfolio of art. Meeting his gaze, she let her tears fall. "Thank you."

Cupping the animal to his chest, he smiled. "I might have to keep this one. Every farmer needs a good dog. Smoky might get lonely from time to time and..."

She smiled. "That one's yours."

Lowering the puppy to Lucky's side, he wiped clean his hands and offered her his shoulder. "Tonight's full of happiness."

She dried her tears on his shirt. "It is."

"Please, take my shirt," Gustavo said. "It's clean."

"I have extra towels in the camper," Sue added. "Do you have enough bedding on hand? We have to keep the puppies warm."

The *casita* suddenly felt too small and yet never large enough. If Dane thought people put on a play for holiday cheer, the motel guests offered sincerity and help. Love, goodwill, and brotherhood were the true meaning of the holidays. Judging by the way Dane kept his gaze glued to the puppies, he felt the season's hope and joy, too. She hoped the feeling carried forward to his birthday celebrations. Given a chance, she would make them special.

Fireworks exploded in the sky.

"Should auld acquaintance be forgot..." a woman sang.

Cocking her head, Kada listened to the verse. The sultry, deep voice sounded familiar, but Inés stood beyond the bookcase and kept guests from storming the *casita*. "Who's singing?"

Turning her head, Sue listened. "I think that's Missy Roberts."

The fussy realtor had a beautiful voice. Following along, Kada picked up the verse and watched Lucky's litter settle to nurse while multicolored lights flashed above the motel.

Dane's rich voice joined her.

Looking up, she met his gaze and smiled. No matter what life threw at them, the last two days proved if they could stick together and support each other, they would find a way.

The Coachella Valley might be an agricultural backwater, but it served the state and produced enough glamour and agriculture to support a robust, diverse population. She told Dane the Starlight Motel attracted quirky travelers, but every person leaning into the *casita* came for the right reason.

Whoever abandoned Lucky in the desert loved her enough to send up a signal. She and Dane answered it, but any number of people would have done the same. That generosity and hope fueled her days, and the minute she saw Dane cuddle a puppy, she knew he had her heart. Admittedly, she might have to pry out the ember, but it persisted. Stubborn man.

Palm Springs might have the glamour and star appeal guests craved, but for those who needed an extra hand and a dose of love, the Starlight Motel would always sit outside the city limits with a glowing *vacancy* sign to welcome life's weary travelers.

As the song ended, she stood and took Dane's hand. "Let's give Missy a round of applause."

Squeezing her hand, he looked over his shoulder at six eagerly nursing pups and followed her out the door.

"Who turned off the heat?" Gustavo asked.

Handing the man his jacket, Dane swung an arm

around her shoulders. "Happy New Year."

Gustavo nodded his thanks and donned the jacket.

Mack, Sue, and their kids ran ahead to spread the news about the sixth puppy.

She and Dane lingered back. The cool, night wind stirred her hair. She wanted to wrap her arms around herself, but she wanted to feel his embrace more. She met his gaze. "I don't want to be presumptuous, but you're right. I might want to spend the rest of my life with you."

Yanking her into his arms, he buried his face in her hair. "Be presumptuous."

Wrapping her arms around his neck, she stared into his handsome eyes. Behind him, stars shone and patio lights glittered, but she anchored herself to a man who saw her and saw what she needed. Even if his painted apples looked like kumquats, or he showed up late to every date, he would move heaven and earth to please her. His devotion counted more than any candlelit dinner.

Somewhere, a corporation had the cash to fund her art, but she hoped the world's leaders experienced a shadow of the love she felt for Dane Palmer. Stretching up, she pressed a soft kiss to his lips and pulled back. "What will you name the puppy?"

"Cholla," he said.

She slapped his chest, but she smiled.

Catching her hand, he raised it to his lips. "Happy New Year, Kada. I can't think of a better gift than having you in my life. We'll make this thing between us work. We'll make each other stronger. You kindle so much love in this world. Until I met you, I didn't know how much I needed hope to fill the void in my life."

"Don't be ridiculous. You would have planted more acres."

Throwing back his head, he laughed and wiped away a tear.

His amusement and his self-awareness both meant something. Old Dane might have agreed with her pronouncement, but the man standing before her could weather an emotional risk. As her cheeks warmed, and she reveled in his praise, she feared his evolution would continue without her. "Any man who plants a seed and expects a bell pepper has hope. I didn't see it at first, but I see it now."

Dropping his head, he smiled. "That's the perspective that keeps me going. You've already brought me a glimmer of love, and I can't thank you enough."

Smiling, she stroked his neck with a thumb and felt his pulse. "One hint of puppy breath, and you're already in love with that dog?"

He dropped his head.

She felt his heartbeat accelerate. Her heart responded in kind.

"No, I'm already in love with you."

Tightening her hold, she pressed her lips against his lips and claimed his mouth. Kissing him felt like quenching her thirst beneath the hot sun. She needed the taste of his lips more than she needed the sweet taste of water. Their mothers and the desert pushed them together, but the sand's soft caress, the palm tree's gentle sway, and the insect stretching its wings would keep them together forever and always. Feeling his response, she gentled her desperation and lowered her hands. They would have time to love each other.

He cupped her cheek. "If I hold you back, tell me. I don't want you to make concessions on my behalf."

"What if I want to spend more time together? Am I enough for you?"

"You're more than enough." He cradled her face. "Marry me."

She beamed and understood that moment of joy and hope that pulled together her parents and cemented their lives. Still, times had changed, and she had to make sure Dane didn't leave his towel on the floor, his cereal bowl on the table, or his boots by the bed. Who was she kidding? She would take him and all his grievous, manly mistakes. Acknowledging the future, but savoring the moment, she turned her head and pressed a kiss to his palm. "Slow down, cowboy."

"Farmer"—he smiled and dropped his hands—"but you can call me whatever you want."

Laughing, she draped her arms over his shoulders. "Mine."

He wrapped his arms around her and squeezed. "Perfect."

Leaning against his strength, she looked toward the distant mountains and thanked Pops and Nana for their guiding influences. The Starlight Motel gave her everything she needed. She could accept the grant *and* cherish her home in the desert. A star twinkled, and she looked away from the beacon and into the gaze of the man she loved. "Happy New Year, Dane."

Cupping her face, he pressed a soft kiss against her lips and lifted his head. "You're my reason for cheer, Kada. You're the best thing the holidays ever brought me. This day marks the beginning of our life, and we have so much joy ahead. We'll work out the logistics, but I love you."

Hope flooded her chest, and she squeezed tight her eyes. Savoring his declaration, she knew he waited for her response. She could say the phrase a thousand times and never convey how much he meant. She opened her eyes and memorized the tender confidence in his chiseled expression. "I love you, too."

Dane breathed out a sigh and grinned.

Staring into his eyes, she had everything she needed and more, but she claimed a satisfying kiss and let the pleasure linger on her lips. She would never think of new beginnings without thinking of Dane. He would move mountains to be by her side, and she would come home to him and the desert they both loved.

A word about the author...

Amy Craig lives in Baton Rouge, Louisiana with her family and a small menagerie of pets. She writes contemporary romances and women's fiction with intelligent and empathetic heroines. She can't always vouch for the men. She has worked as an engineer, project manager, and incompetent waitress. In her spare time, she plays tennis and expands her husband's honey-do list.

https://www.amy-craig.com/

Other Titles by the Author
A Winter Rose
The Crevasse
The Peninsula